Musical Truth
Volume 3

Mark Devlin

Musical Truth Volume 2
Mark Devlin

Paperback Edition First Published in Great Britain in 2021
Hardback Edition First Published in Great Britain in 2021
eBook Edition First Published in Great Britain in 2021

ISBN: 978-1-913438-55-5

aSys Publishing
http://www.asys-publishing.co.uk

ACKNOWLEDGEMENTS

A huge debt of gratitude goes out to Robbie Allen (www.robbieallenart.com) for another cover design masterpiece, to John "Razor Eye" Hamer for the proof-reading, and to Nicola Mackin of Asys Publishing (https://www.asys-publishing.co.uk/) for the typesetting and production.

*

If any reader would like a free pdf e-mailed, containing all the URL links listed in this book for ease of access, please just e-mail a request to: **markdevlinuk@gmail.com**

Also by the author

MUSICAL TRUTH, VOLUMES 1 AND 2

To most people, the music industry represents a source of harmless fun and entertainment. Beneath the glossy veneer, however, lies the devastating truth of who really controls these institutions, and the deeply malevolent agendas for which they're being used.

Mark Devlin is a long-standing DJ and music journalist. The two volumes of *'Musical Truth'* are the culmination of his several years of research into the true nature of the industry and its objectives—from dark occult rituals, to mind-controlled artists, and all points in between. The book shows how these agendas fit into the much wider picture of what's really going on in the world, and—crucially—how the power lies with us to bring it all to an end.

*

THE CAUSE & THE CURE

1990, Oxford, England, and the respectable facade of the City of Dreaming Spires is being shattered by a series of brutal murders.

Police chief Neil Lowe needs a quick result, especially if it allows him more time in the cafe. Rookie constable May Pearce is left disillusioned by what appears to be an orchestrated cover-up at the highest level; this is not why she joined the force.

Radio reporter Verity Hunter has noticed that the choice of victim suggests a far deeper motive than that of a straight psycho-killer—a particular breed of retribution is at play—and she stumbles upon another aspect of Oxford hidden from view—the world of "elite" secret-societies.

Her boyfriend Keith is on the same page, and his consulting of the direct-talking consciousness guru Max Zeall makes him realise that there are spiritual components dictating the way things are playing out. It's these very same forces which provide the opportunity to restore justice and balance.

A crime thriller set during a time of great cultural change, (the last days of Thatcherism, the Poll Tax riots, the fall of Communism, the first Gulf War, Acid House and Rave culture,) gets taken to uncharted territories through allegory and metaphor, and the narrative's interplay with spiritual teachings. As such, *'The Cause & The Cure'* can be read on many different levels, according to the reader's own consciousness.

All books are available via Amazon, Barnes & Noble, or direct from the author. E-mail **markdevlinuk@gmail.com** to order signed copies.

*

THE CAUSE & THE CURE SOUNDTRACK

This may well be the first novel to come with its own movie-style soundtrack!

Compiled by Mark Devlin, this two hour sonic journey brings the TCATC story to life with a selection of the music that was around during the book's timeframe, interspersed with news footage, radio station recordings and other relevant snippets from the times.

The soundtrack audio can be streamed or downloaded for free from the following link:

https://www.mixcloud.com/djmarkdevlin/
the-cause-the-cure-soundtrack/

*

THE SOUND OF FREEDOM

T.S.O.F. is a free showcase of conscious music, old and new, compiled by Mark Devlin. It stands as the inspiring antithesis to the corporate agenda, offering meaningful music by switched-on, awakened artists.

The full archive so far is available at:
https://www.mixcloud.com/TheSoundOfFreedom/

*

GOOD VIBRATIONS

A free, ongoing series of conversation-based podcasts, covering a huge array of topics within the truth/ conspiracy/ consciousness/ spirituality fields.

The entire archive so far is available at:
https://www.spreaker.com/show/good-vibrations-podcast

*

Mark Devlin's main website:

www.djmarkdevlin.com

Please subscribe to The Author's YouTube channel, containing a huge archive of live talks, Q&A sessions, interviews and podcasts:

www.youtube.com/markdevlintv

FOREWORD FROM THE AUTHOR

"A book is a suicide postponed."
Emil Cioran, Philosopher.

"Well," I thought when the war started, trying to hope for the best, "it will be horrible but if it will be so horrible as to frighten and wake up the mind, it will be the salvation of many. Many are going to die, but those who are going to survive will have a real life, with the mind awake . . . "
(Poet Demetrios Capetanakis, 1912 -1944)

Although this volume follows in the spirit of its predecessors in continuing to expose the controlled corporate music industry, by necessity its subject matter has had to stray from strictly music-related business at several points, (even though everything is intrinsically connected when all is said and done.)

Despite having researched the New World Order agenda of those who like to consider themselves this world's "elites," (though I prefer Mark Passio's take on their true status — "they're the elites of the sludge and slime that gathers in the bottom of a garbage can,") and despite having learned about and warned about their devastating plans for humanity, I still never saw the events of early 2020 and beyond coming, and never imagined that the crazy, psychopathic maniacs would have had the audacity to throw everything they had at us all at once.

This is not their regular *modus operandi*; that has always involved them taking slow, gradual, incremental steps towards their desired goal, lest the masses notice what is happening and be alerted to the agenda. Whether through supreme arrogance, or panicked desperation, the fast-tracking to the end game which has been in the controllers' sights for so very, very long, has hit warp-speed, and the risk of its true nature becoming obvious for all to see has, for them, had to be written off as unavoidable "collateral damage."

This book, though it also completes my trilogy of exposés of the devastating nature of the music industry and those who populate it, has been produced in urgent response to recent world events. As such, it delves into subject areas which fall outside of my usual remit.

This being the case, it is my hope that it may serve of great value in "waking up" family members and friends of my regular readers at this crucial and epoch-defining juncture in the timeline of human activity. It has certainly been my experience that the interest of many an otherwise uninterested new recruit can be tactically engaged by drawing them in with revelations about the world of music, then upgrading them to higher-minded Truths.

Readers of the previous two volumes will already be aware of the broad assertion of my work—that the world is a very different place to what we've been societally conditioned our whole lives to think of it as, and that a significant proportion of the mind-control and propaganda necessary to bring that state of affairs about has been achieved through popular music.

It is my wish, therefore, that this book and its predecessors are shared as widely as possible among anyone prepared to give them the time of day, in the hope that the number of awake and aware folk can be reached whereby a tipping point is achieved beyond which there can be no turning back. Where the only possible outcome is for Evil and darkness to stand fully exposed, and for Truth, Freedom, Justice and Love to be restored as the default value systems through which humanity continues to live. If this book can play a significant role in bringing about that process, my time spent incarnated into this realm in this era will not have been for nothing.

Volume 3 then, is very much a product of its time, and spends many of its pages examining the strange and dangerous days of 2020 and beyond—specifically the reactions of many musicians to the circumstances in which we have all found ourselves forced to live. While the vast, overwhelming majority have simply kept their mouths shut for fear of how appearing "politically-incorrect" might harm their careers, a great many have revealed their true nature by shamefully and treacherously reinforcing official narratives. This book calls them out on their treasonous positions. Conversely, a tragically small few have stood up to be counted, and these names are therefore commended as honorary exceptions.

This book sees a new feature in the form of *'Sound Bites.'* These are stories which draw upon the tone of the previous volumes and reinforce many of the points made, but which don't fit the flow of any of the main chapters. Instead, they appear interspersed throughout, and provide a break from the pace of the main narrative, hopefully revealing many a fascinating and captivating fact along the way.

As ever, I have provided full references and resources for all the information conveyed. In an era where disinformation, misinformation, and personal conjecture are rife throughout the internet, being able to back up any claims made with verifiable citations becomes of paramount importance for any professional researcher who wishes to be taken seriously. This is particularly vital when challenging an official narrative as all-pervasive as that of the Co(n)vid "Pandemic" (which never was one.) The sources I have provided for my countering of the scam will prove to anyone with the capacity for independent, critical thought, and without any ulterior motives or pre-existing belief systems to uphold, that what we have been told by official sources all over the world amounts to the biggest criminal conspiracy ever inflicted in human history.

Ultimately, however, this story ends on a note which is the dualistic opposite of that dreadful scenario—with the greatest story ever told, and of how even in spite of all the dark and devastating motives the controlled music industry has so often had, this Truth has been encoded into many a classic rock song through the decades, and has been sitting in plain sight waiting to be decoded ever since.

There's pretty much only one Truth that has been uttered by the criminally compromised governments and mainstream media of the world since early 2020—that the old world is now gone, and won't be coming back any time soon. This is, indeed, 'the New Normal"—but *we,* the people, still have the opportunity to ensure that it's a Normal that *we* actually want, the psychopaths be damned—and which is so much better than all that went before it.

Mark Devlin

Contents

It's not for nothing that the Co(n)vid-19 debacle has been frequently described as "The Greatest Scam Ever Perpetrated Upon Mankind," alternatively as "The Great Cough 'N' Cold Swindle," or in the words of a group of Spanish and German doctors, "the biggest crime of the century."

What to do with information that remains vitally incisive, but doesn't fit the flow?

The "coronavirus" Scamdemic offered a valuable opportunity to assess which musicians were still in the pocket of the controllers, and which ones still had a voice to call their own. Genocide is genocide. Whether pushed by doctors, politicians, news presenters or "celebrities," the crime is still the same.

The controllers of Organised Society - and therefore the Scamdemic - continue to adhere with religious fervour to their tenet of Placing the Truth in Plain Sight. And the amount of slow-drip subliminal program-ming in the years up to 2020 gives a shocking insight into just how far back this was all getting cooked up.

CHAPTER 1

CO(N)VID-19: THE MOTHER OF ALL PSY-OPS

It's not for nothing that the Co(n)vid-19 debacle has been frequently described as "The Greatest Scam Ever Perpetrated Upon Mankind," alternatively as "The Great Cough 'N' Cold Swindle," or in the words of a group of Spanish and German doctors, "the biggest crime of the century."

> *"He is not a good man who, without a protest, allows wrong to be committed in his name, and with the means which he helps to supply, because he will not trouble himself to use his mind on the subject."*
>
> John Stuart Mill, Philosopher, 1867.

> *"Hanging on in quiet desperation is the English way."*
>
> Pink Floyd: "Us And Them."

> *"I'd like to share a revelation that I've had during my time here. It came to me when I tried to classify your species and I realised that you're not actually mammals.*
>
> *Every mammal on this planet instinctively develops a natural equilibrium with the surrounding environment but you humans do not.*
>
> *You move to an area and you multiply and multiply until every natural resource is consumed and the only way you can survive is to spread to another area.*
>
> *There is another organism on this planet that follows the same pattern.*
>
> *Do you know what it is?*
>
> *A virus."*
>
> Agent Smith dialogue from 'The Matrix' (1999)

My research into mind-control and social-engineering introduced me to the world of the psychological operation — or psy-op — many years ago. These are exercises sponsored by various governments of the world — or at least those who control them — with the aim of fulfilling some aspect of the New World Order masterplan of what the late researcher Ian R. Crane was fond of describing as "those who consider themselves the rightful rulers of a planetary fiefdom," and what singer Mel Bell-Grey on his track *'You're Not invited'* described as "those designers of the terrible lie."

The key to making sense of this world into which we have all found ourselves plunged, is to take anything told to us by "Establishment" sources like governments or mainstream media outlets, and turn it completely on its head. Somewhere in the vicinity of the 180-degree polar opposite is then where the real Truth is likely to lie. These psy-ops are carried out with the full complicity of the military-intelligence services which — in this Satanically-inverted reality which has been constructed over aeons — exist *not* to keep us safe, as we are entrained to think through the likes of the James Bond movies, but to actually *do us harm*. The population of the nations in which they operate are the *real* targets of the likes of MI5, MI6 and the CIA.

Also involved are social-engineers, psychologists and behavioural scientists, whose full-time jobs involve working out how best to manipulate the collective human psyche and entrain the masses in certain desired belief systems, perceptions, and behaviours. Some classic 'psy-ops" of recent years have involved countless so-called "terror events," with the blame invariably placed at the doorstep of various "terrorist" groups, (usually Islamic/ "jihadist" in nature, according to the narrative,) and often attributed to a single "lone nutter" to avoid any suggestion of a "conspiracy." Some vigilant research of the nature that is possible for anyone with a computer, a brain to think with, an internet connection and the time and will do it, always reveals that such events actually took place at the hands of the Establishment control system itself.

Never a "pandemic" by any definition of the word, (as a friend of mine has been fond of saying, "if you think this is a real pandemic ask yourself how many days Tesco has been closed this year,") Co(n)vid-19 has only ever been a Scamdemic. Indeed, it's accurate to say that *every single aspect* of the official narrative beaten into the consciousness of the public has been laden with fraud.

Fear is the key

"The masses have never thirsted after truth. They turn aside from evidence that is not to their taste, preferring to deify error, if error seduces them. Whoever can supply them with illusions is easily their master, whoever attempts to destroy their illusions is always their victim."

Gustave Le Bon, 'The Crowd: A Study of the Popular Mind,' 1895.

Co(n)vid-19 has been the psy-op to end all psy-ops, affecting, as it has, virtually every man woman and child on Earth. From the point of view of the "elite" control system that presides over all aspects of Organised Society, It came as the product either of staggering levels of arrogance and hubris, or of sheer desperation. Or possibly a combination of the two. Either way, it stands as the culmination of many, many decades of slow and methodical planning with the aim of completely enslaving and subjugating humanity into a technocratic control grid.

In 1967, the American writer turned "conspiracy theorist" (that's what Wikipedia says, anyway) Myron Fagan, delivered a now fabled speech, (available from Amazon as a three-record vinyl set, incredibly!) warning the audience of the plans for a "One World Government" and a monumental conspiracy to enslave, control, and genocide the general public at the hands of what he referred to even back then as "the Illuminati." Truly a man ahead of his time. Though Fagan focussed on the United States, we can be sure that the same plan is in place for the rest of the world also. Amidst this vital lecture he observed:

> *"At this point, bear in mind that the Illuminati was not set up to operate on a short-range basis. Normally a conspirator of any type enters into a conspiracy with the expectation of achieving his objective during his own lifetime. But that was not the case with the Illuminati. True, they <u>hope</u> to accomplish their objectives during their lifetime. But paraphrasing, "the show must go on." The Illuminati operates on a very long-range basis. Whether it will take scores of years*

or even centuries, they have dedicated their descendants to keep the pot boiling until they hope the conspiracy is achieved."

Though his words were delivered in 1967, they could have been spoken yesterday. The show does indeed go on.

Chapter 5 will examine the evidence for this pre-planning by citing the numerous depictions of the narrative that was known to be coming in music, movies, TV shows and other popular culture vehicles. Before that, however, let's just lay any lingering doubt that may persist as to the Co(n)vid Scamdemic *not* being the biggest psy-op ever played on humanity, well and truly to rest.

The official story of how the whole sorry Shit Show got started stands as yet another exercise in the Satanic, morbid mockery of the profane masses, (as they see us) at the hands of the so-called "elite" ruling class. In all seriousness, mainstream news channels were asking us to believe that the "virus" had mutated from a bat, supposedly consumed by some unknown individual in a "wet" market in Wuhan, China. Despite causing pretty much the entire world to grind to a halt, sending the death count plummeting, (though more from suicides and untreated cancers than from any "virus,") devastating the worldwide economy, psychologically damaging an entire generation of children, splitting apart families, and causing untold levels of shock, trauma, stress and long-term mental health damage, no-one has seemingly thought it important to try and track down the individual concerned. The whole plot is, of course, a farce.

Throughout the early months of the Scamdemic, opinion remained divided among medical professionals as to whether a "virus" even exists in the form that we've been entrained through our doctors and mainstream medicine to think it does. In Spring 2020 I interviewed Dawn Lester and David Parker, joint British authors of the book *'What Really Makes You Ill,'* whose extensive research convinced them that a "virus" is merely the body's way of purging itself of disease or toxicity through shedding biological material known as "exosomes."

Their findings very much echoed those of the American Dr. Andrew Kaufman, who courted controversy by challenging the official "Germ theory" narrative through instead proposing "terrain theory" as the more viable alternative. The renowned German virologist Stefan Lanka in a 2020 interview, meanwhile, observed that viruses are neither microbes nor do they have infectious capacity so Co(n)vid-19 cannot have been caused by the alleged SARS-CoV-2, whose existence, moreover, has not been demonstrated. Furthermore, he disputed that there was a pandemic, that there were millions of people infected and killed by this "coronavirus," and that vaccines are justified since they are neither effective nor innocuous but actually very dangerous.

In turn, this overall take has been shared by natural health practitioner and writer Eve Gilmore, who has commented:

> *"As no virus has ever been identified as a living entity so cannot exist independently, it cannot be passed on from one person to another in the same way as bacteria. What is purported to be a virus is a collection of discarded cell fragments. Viral diseases are detox processes and share characteristics and energetic patterns unique to the disease. They are transmitted energetically. In other words, a body undergoing the detox of a particular substance, emits the frequency of that process. Like a tuning fork, it can cause another person's energy field to synchronise with that frequency which would have the effect of stimulating the "virus" or viral process in them.*
>
> *"With Covid, Graphene Oxide is responsible for the symptoms and acts as an antenna for Electromagnetic Frequencies (EMFs) which can act as the trigger. Since many are affected, the misconceptions (lies) about viruses that have been implanted over the last hundred years when, I believe, this very scenario was planned, they were primed to accept the idea that viruses are an infectious organism."*

And this stance was echoed by David Icke in the series of interviews he gave to Brian Rose of the *'London Real'* internet TV platform in 2020. This was the year in which Icke became vindicated for so much of what, over the previous three decades, he had been claiming about who really runs the world; indeed, every "conspiracy theorist" who had previously been derided by friends and family received some validation through these times. It has been entertaining to note that those who previously called out critically-minded truth-seekers as 'tinfoil hat-wearers" have been quick to don a facemask or visor, and obsessively wash their hands and wipe down the handles of their supermarket trolley right on instruction from the lying criminals in the mainstream media.

Completely pointlessly, too, since numerous medical professionals have pointed out that, far from offering any kind of protection, the frequent wearing of face coverings actually *causes* disease through harbouring germs that would ordinarily be expelled through normal breathing, and limiting the amount of oxygen necessary for optimum health to the brain. Sure enough, medical "advisors" (compromised traitors) like Dr. Anthony Fauci and Professor Chris Whitty publicly proclaimed the uselessness of masks in the early days of the Scam — before backtracking completely and advocating for their usage some weeks down the line. (Satanic inversion — remember?) David Adelman, known in the UK as The People's Lawyer, had a very sound take on the subject when he commented at a conference, "I already have a face covering. It's called my skin."

Cathy O'Brien, a survivor of Satanic Ritual Abuse, weighed in on the issue of masks, and connecting into the music business, when she commented in late 2021:

> *"In MK-Ultra project mind-control, Michael Jackson had to wear a mask to silence his voice so he could not reach out for help. Remember how he developed that whisper voice when he wasn't singing? Masks control the mind from the outside in, like the redefining of words is doing."*

Whether a "virus" is what we think it is or not, to date, "Co(n)vid-19" has still not been proven to exist, as it has never been isolated or purified in the way any disease to be labelled a "virus" must be according to international medical standards, and has not fulfilled the criteria of Koch's Postulates — the four conditions that must be met before a micro-organism can be deemed a human pathogen. A favoured alternative narrative to the mainstream "bat" one is that the "virus" was deliberately created in a laboratory in Wuhan, and connections back to Barack Obama and Dr. Anthony Fauci have been alleged in this regard, suggesting that they funded the covert research and development.

Either way, the claim that this pathogen was created in a lab and deliberately or accidentally released, after which it spread like wildfire across the world, helps keeps the "super killer virus" myth alive. And then we're back to the same problem: no novel pathogen has ever been identified according to *official*, tried and tested, long-standing, *universally-accepted* criteria. And even if a "virus" did appear in late 2019, the same "virus" cannot be with us now. As mainstream virologists will confirm—if we assume for a moment that they exist in the accepted sense—viruses constantly mutate and die out to be replaced by new strains, most of which are harmless. So if there has never been any original "virus," how is it possible that there can be any kind of "variant" randomly mutating?

And so, because there is no identified pathogen, (former vice-president of pharmaceutical giant Pfizer turned whistleblower Dr. Mike Yeadon has said that that "no-one has any of this stuff,") it is therefore impossible to create a "vaccine!" You need the pathogen to do it. The "vaccines" that have been offered in the wake of "Co(n)vid" are not "vaccines" in the traditional and accepted sense at all.

And even if they were, vaccines are never as "safe" and "effective" as the medical establishment—funded by the Big Pharma giants who produce these products in an industry worth multiple *billions*—likes to blindly claim they are. According to a report titled '*Covid-19 RNA Based Vaccines and the Risk of Prion Disease*' by J. Bart Classen, MD published in December 2020:

> *"Vaccines have been found to cause a host of chronic, late developing adverse events. Some adverse events like Type 1 Diabetes may not occur until 3-4 years after a vaccine is administered. In the example of Type 1 Diabetes the frequency of cases of adverse events may surpass the frequency of cases of severe infectious disease the vaccine was designed to prevent."*

And according to an article on the mercola.com natural health website:

> *"mRNA "vaccines" created by Moderna and Pfizer are gene therapies. They fulfil all the definitions of gene therapy and none of the definitions for a vaccine."*

Yeadon is far from alone in coming forward as a whistleblower. Medical professionals all over the world have warned of how dangerous these "vaccines" are, (as any product which lists death as a possible side-effect would be.) Here, doctors worldwide break down the risks:

https://rumble.com/viqn29-worldwide-doctors-warn-for-the-vaccines-must-see.html

Furthermore, microscopic analyses of the ingredients of some of the Co(n)vid vaccines have shown them to contain spider-like living organisms, as well as Graphene Oxide, a compound suspected to interact with the 5G technology now being rolled out, turning the carrier into a walking Transhumanist receiver/ transmitter. Not great news for anyone who has been coerced into taking "the jab"—especially since no-one really knows whether theirs contained any of these horrors, or was one of the more benign ones. But it's never too late to stop, and resist all the calls to continually go out and get "booster" shots.

There is a reason why "anti-vaxxer" has become a term of derision for those who exercise their right and duty to independently research topics for themselves, rather than being coerced and swayed by engineered popular opinion. It comes from the same people who brought you "conspiracy theorist," "homophobe," "anti-Semite," "holocaust-denier" and now "Co(n)vid-denier." These are terms designed to shut down any argument and avoid any kind of considered debate, by instantly demonising an individual, and deeming them therefore unworthy of any further discussion on a subject, (lest they might actually reveal the truth of the matter.) There's a reason why Dr. Andrew Wakefield was struck off the register as a practicing doctor and viciously set upon by the media when he suggested the link between childhood autism and the MMR vaccine back in the 1990s.

There's a reason why vaccines are being presented as *the only possible* solution to the "pandemic," and natural cures or alternatives such as Ivermectin and Hydroxychloroquine are being either ignored or systematically oppressed.

There's a reason why celebrities-for-hire are being wheeled out at every possible opportunity and, as a condition of their continued careers, being instructed to enforce the vaccination agenda to their fan-bases of millions, (see the following chapter for more on this.)

There's a reason why the public has had to be blackmailed and gaslit into accepting that vaccination is *the only way* society can ever get 'back to normal," and that "vaccine passports" will have to be necessary to continue simple lifestyle choices like going to a pub, restaurant or nightclub or getting on a plane as a way of discriminating against those who exercise their free will choice *not* to have an unknown, untested substance injected by a stranger into their bloodstream.

And there's a reason why, for decades, the general public has been subliminally entrained through mind-control in entertainment to accept vaccinations as *the only possible* cure for a "deadly virus." Again, see the upcoming chapters for much more on this phenomenon.

We're left, therefore, with the quandary of whether there has been any kind of disease—whether a "virus" or not—that has been sweeping the world and striking down victims, or whether in fact we have simply been witnessing bad strains of the flu or common cold that have been present within human society since time immemorial and which, in any year prior to 2020 when Common Sense took leave, society would have routinely coped with. Certainly the death figures for most nations around the world—even taking into account the suicides and deaths from medical conditions that went untreated as "Co(n)vid" took priority over all else—were no greater in 2020 or 2021 than in previous years, and in many cases, according to official Government figures, have actually *decreased*.

The very definition of a "pandemic" according to Wikipedia is: is "an epidemic of an infectious disease that has spread across a large region, for instance multiple continents or worldwide, affecting a substantial number of people." Yet this is *not* what we saw in 2020 and 2021. Had Co(n)vid been a *real* "pandemic," we could have expected to see people literally dropping dead in the street daily. This has not been anyone's experience, nor will most know anyone in their circle of family and friends who contracted the "virus." It would seem that, in the same way that Marathon and Opal Fruits became rebranded as Snickers and Starburst, the flu and the common cold got a rebranding as "Co(n)vid-19."

A Constable speaks

"When a well-packaged web of lies has been sold gradually to the masses over generations, the truth will seem utterly preposterous, and its speaker a raving lunatic."

> *Dresden James.*

On Monday 19th July 2021, Mark Sexton, a retired Police Constable, staged a call to action outside Parliament in London. His address to the assembled crowd constituted a very thorough and accurate assessment of the overall Co(n)vid scam and associated agendas, and bears some relating here:

> *"The whole "pandemic" has been based around the number of "cases," and the testing system, namely PCR. There is irrefutable, undeniable, factual evidence to show the PCR tests are 100 per cent false, fraudulent, or not fit for purpose. Not gold standard . . . There is irrefutable evidence to show the SARS-COV 2 virus has never been isolated or purified. Using a false testing mechanism to find a virus that is yet to be proven to exist!*

> *Many thousands of top scientists, professors, doctors, immunologists and biologists are speaking out about the "pandemic" and the restrictions imposed by every Government around the world. The same experts are being deliberately silenced and removed from all social media platforms for going against the scripted narrative.*

> *"The people of Britain have been subject to lockdowns in their homes, wearing of face masks, "social" distancing, not being allowed to see their loved ones—especially the elderly, who have been left to die alone en masse in care homes and hospitals.*

> *"There have always been reliable, proven, cheap and safe medications for the treatment of Coronavirus—Ivermectin, Hydroxychloroquine, Zinc. These are proven to have almost 100 per cent success in reducing symptoms within 48 hours. This irrefutable evidence has been suppressed on nefariously demonised. A newly-released report also proves that intravenous vitamin C has a 100-per-cent success rate in*

treating Coronavirus. We all need to know that this treatment was deliberately hidden away by all Western governments.

"All they wanted to do was force a vaccine on the world's population and we know that at no point has any Government advertised: stop smoking, stop drinking, eat healthy, get regular exercise and sunshine. Instead all we hear is 'vaccine, vaccine, vaccine.'

"It is now clear the vaccine is causing a significant number of deaths, serious harm and injury to over a million people in the UK alone. The Government's own Yellow Card scheme of reporting these events shows this irrefutable and damning evidence. All of this considering there's a 99.96 per cent chance of recovery, and the Government admits very few people will actually die. The total vaccinated are now filling up the hospitals and "testing positive" for "Covid." The vaccine does not work and is more deadly than the virus itself.

"... The constant terror we have been exposed to, and the fear-driven propaganda since March 2020, has destroyed our economy, killed our elderly, destroyed many home lives, created a significant increase in suicide, but the worst and most significant and devastating effect has been on our children ... Our children have been told if they hold Grandma, they will kill Grandma.

"This is mental torture, mental abuse. And this is all at the hands of the Government and the mainstream media."

Hypochondria as a fashion statement

"You lying whores in the mainstream media are just lying to people for a paycheck. And dumb people believe you. And that's all this whole thing really is ... Get as offended as you like."
Mark Passio, 'What On Earth Is Happening' podcast, 2020.

Sexton was absolutely correct. The Scamdemic narrative could *never* have taken hold without the full complicity of the world's mainstream media who, throughout the entire debacle, merely parroted official

Government policy at every turn, never *once* applying any critical investigative journalism to establish, independently, whether the official accounts would stand up to scrutiny. Had they done so they would have discovered what the *real* investigative journalists in the alternative media did—that *every single* aspect of the Scamdemic was fraudulent and genocidal. It's no surprise that they didn't, of course, given that all mainstream newspapers, radio and TV stations and internet sites are ultimately controlled by the very same forces which cooked up the narrative in the first place. Mainstream "journalists" are merely mouthpieces for the Establishment, obediently reciting what they have been told to in exchange for a paycheque. In the case of Co(n)vid, their job was to generate public compliance through fear, generated by their carefully-drafted propaganda.

Covid social distancing:

The Land That Common-Sense Forgot. Only two slight discrepancies: 1. "Covid" has never been proven to exist, and 2. "Distancing," by its very definition, cannot be "social." Apart from that, it's spot on.

https://commons.wikimedia.org/wiki/File:COVID-19_Social_Distancing_Sign.jpg

And that factor could not have fulfilled its role without the fraud of the PCR viral load test—the gold standard for creating "cases," and therefore ramping up casualty figures to give the impression that the "virus" was rampaging wildly through populations.

The test, however, was completely unsuitable for detecting any kind of disease, let alone a specific breed of "virus." Its creator, the Nobel prize-winning American biochemist Kary B. Mullis, said as much when he developed it, stating that it merely detected the presence of biological material, and *should not be used* for diagnosing disease.

Mullis died in August 2019, reportedly of pneumonia, two months before Co(n)vid first hit the headlines, so any objection from him when his test became adopted by the World Health Organisation was conveniently silenced. Official Co(n)vid testing relied on ramping up the cycles of amplification on the test to 45 cycles, way beyond what was recommended by its founder. The PCR is said to be 100 per cent faulty at anything beyond 35 cycles. The CDC itself has admitted that any tests over 28 cycles are not admissible for a positive reliable result. This alone invalidates over 90 per cent of the alleged cases/ "infections" tracked by the use of this faulty test.

By any standards, a "case" only means that somebody has tested positive through a process which, acknowledged even in the mainstream headlines, has been creating many "false positives." The public was then given the absolutely absurd premise that people could be "asymptomatic" with its own catchy new slogan to match—"act like you've got it." There's another term for not having any symptoms of a disease. It's called being healthy. As a popular meme sticker from the brilliant White Rose activist group that was doing the rounds at the time stated: "Imagine a disease so deadly that you have to take a test to see whether you've got it."

Prior to 2020 anyone visiting their GP and stating that they thought they might be ill even though they were exhibiting no symptoms would have been told to go home and stop wasting the doctor's time. But all common sense went out of the window with Co(n)vid. Instead the lie was spread that people could be carrying and therefore spreading "the virus" without knowing it, ratcheting up the fear factor yet further through the recognition that a population consumed by fear does not think rationally, and is therefore so much easier to control and manipulate than if they were able to apply critical thought to a situation. This notion is an insult to human intelligence, and another example of the disdain and contempt that the "elites" have for the hordes of "useless eaters."

Two of the most sober and sensible comments I heard during the entire first year of the Scamdemic were: "A sane and compassionate society would seek to quarantine only the most vulnerable, rather than forcing everyone into lockdown and destroying the entire economy." And: "If masks and lockdowns work—why are we still doing them? If masks and lockdowns <u>don't</u> work—why are we still doing them?" Sadly, common sense became an endangered species in 2020. Along with, it seems, integrity, dignity and courage.

The fraudulent nature of the PCR tests formed the main basis of the legal case launched in 2020 by German/ American Doctor Reiner Fuellmich and the team of international lawyers he had assembled to form the Coronavirus Investigative Committee. Fuellmich had the World Economic Forum in his sights, accusing its executives and collaborators of crimes against humanity for their perpetration of Co(n)vid response policies. His trial has been informally dubbed "Nuremberg 2:0" due to its similarity to the military tribunals of thousands of Nazis and collaborators at the end of World War 2.

More fraud came from the phenomenon of doctors being financially incentivised to place Co(n)vid as the cause of death on countless certificates in the early days of the Scamdemic. Anyone testing positive (in many cases falsely due to the unreliable tests,) within 28 days prior to death automatically had Co(n)vid attributed as the cause, no matter what other conditions they may have had. Terminal cancer patients were being said to have died of 'the virus" rather than the rather more obvious cause.

You've had a little too much to think, sir

"The opposite of courage is not cowardice, it's conformity."
    Dave Murphy

That propaganda is utilised to affect and change public thought and behaviour is not under dispute. There are agencies which exist purely for this purpose, and many of them were put to use by the UK Government during the Scamdemic. Foremost among these was S.A.G.E., the Scientific Advisory Group for Emergencies. We got an insight into how the "behavioural scientists" working for this agency think when one of its key figures, Susan Michie, appeared on a Channel 5 news report in June 2021, revealing her psychopathy as the interviewer asked how long she felt the public should continue "distancing" and wearing masks, and she laughingly replied, "for ever!" (She's also an avowed Communist—what could possibly go wrong?)

S.A.G.E.'s minutes of 22nd March 2020 stated:

> *"The perceived level of personal threat needs to be increased among those who are complacent," by "using hard hitting emotional messaging."*

These are the people from whom the Government was (officially, at least) taking its directions regarding lockdown policies. How these "people" can bear to look at themselves in the mirror, get up for work every morning and take a paycheque in exchange for scientifically working out how best to psychologically torture the people of their nation and beyond and ruin their lives, is beyond my comprehension. I can only console myself with the sure knowledge that actions have reactions, chosen behaviours have consequences, and that they *will* pay the price for their Treason and Genocide-by-proxy. If not in this life then in what lies beyond. *That's* the Natural Law of the Universe, and no amount of trickery or sneakiness can avoid the consequences it brings.

One of my podcast listeners was on the same page as me regarding these abominations when he messaged to say:

> *"As a psychotherapist of 20 years I detest the Tavistock and S.A.G.E. traitors who have hijacked the name of psychology for their evil purposes. The masses have had their minds abused and manipulated through a form of psychotic-inducing hypnosis by these sub-human bastards. Protesting outside their offices on a weekday would be excellent. It would be getting to the core of the rotten apple!"*

Another unit is B.I.T., the Behavioural Insights Team attached to the UK Government's Cabinet Office, whose nickname of "the Nudge Unit" tells you all you need to know about this being a covert mind-control agency. Even Wikipedia doesn't attempt to hide its true nature, stating:

> *"Using social engineering, as well as techniques in psychology and marketing, the purpose of the organisation is to influence public thinking and decision-making in order to improve compliance with Government policy . . . "*

Elsewhere from the Cabinet Office came a 2021 document titled *'Mindspace: Influencing Behaviour Through Public Policy.'* As the document brazenly admits:

> *"Influencing people's behaviour is nothing new to Government, which has often used tools such as legislation, regulation or taxation to achieve desired policy outcomes. But many of the biggest policy challenges we are now facing—such as the increase in people with chronic health conditions—will only be resolved if we are successful in persuading people to change their behaviour, their lifestyles or their existing habits."*

When Boris Johnson stood at the podium and announced what UK Government measures would be introduced in the midst of Co(n)vid, he was merely reciting what he had been told to say by these agencies, who were the *real* guiding force behind the Scamdemic narrative. It would have been an equivalent scenario in most other nations. Besides the influence of S.A.G.E., so much of the UK's early lockdown frenzy was "justified" by the famously inaccurate "computer-modelling" of Imperial College London Professor Neil Ferguson. The only thing that's really been justified here is Ferguson sharing a traitor's fate alongside his treasonous peers. Imperial College houses The Abdul Latif Jameel Institute for Disease and Emergency Analytics, whose Hassan Mohammed Abdul Latif Jameel turns out to have been in a romantic relationship with Rihanna from 2017 to 2020. Nothing unusual about an international oligarch being paired with a pop singer, of course. No, really—there isn't.

The sick ones have also been betraying their true nature as dark occultists through gleefully announcing so much of the tyranny on dates that carry occult or historical significance. This constitutes, in part, more morbid mockery of the profane masses, (as they see us) as one of the central tenets of their Satanic ideology. Johnson, for instance, announced on the Pagan festival of Samhain/ Hallowe'en that more harsh lockdowns had to be introduced in England. Rather than apply them straight away, however, he further announced that these would come in the following Thursday, which *just happened* to be 5th November/ Bonfire Night, a date loaded with history and symbolism concerning the attempted overthrow of a tyrannical Parliament. If the "virus" was as "out of control" as Johnson, (S.A.G.E.) claimed, what sense did it make to wait five days rather than shutting everything down immediately? And since when has the Government made an announcement at 7pm on a Saturday rather than waiting until Monday morning?

None of this was random. All was meticulously planned for optimum psychological effect. We are in a psychological war plotted not by military generals, but by social and behavioural scientists and anthropologists. Which is why another historically important date did not go to waste. The date on which the wearing of face coverings on public transport was first mandated was 15th June—another one imbued with historic significance given that this is the date in 1215 on which the Magna Carta was signed, giving England the Constitution which, according to countless legal experts, has stood ever since. By arrogantly hijacking the date to unload yet more impositions on us, the controllers were mocking the people of the nation and showing their scathing contempt for our rights.

The general public of most of the world's nations could *never* have been entrained to adopt bizarre, ritualistic new behaviours that go against their own self-interest and those of their loved ones, without the intervention of social-engineering units and clever psychological techniques such as these. Like a scene straight out of the cult favourite movie *'They Live,'* the process relies heavily on slogans which act as mind-control triggers, hence the use of "Hands, Face, Space," "Stay Alert, Control The Virus, Save Lives" and "Stay Home, Save Lives, Protect The NHS." This is the science of Neuro-Linguistic Programming (N.L.P.) which seeks to generate a specific behavioural response in a subject through the clever and considered use of "trigger" language and speech delivery.

The ultimate in N.L.P. and emotional manipulation came from the tacit suggestion that by leaving your home and moving freely around, you could be killing other people's grannies. All logic and discernment goes out of the window when appeals to emotion are skilfully triggered. One technique relied upon is what's known in the advertising industry as "consumer confusion" or "confusion marketing." This is the art of deliberately sending out baffling and contradictory messages so that the target becomes so befuddled they are no longer capable of making a decision for themselves based on rational thought. It's been suggested that this is what black magician and Establishment insider Jimmy Savile was employing with his famous "now then, now then" catchphrase, these words holding conflicting meanings and having a kind of hypnotic effect on the listener.

"Confusion Marketing" is merely a variation on a mind-control method dubbed "The Alice In Wonderland Technique," (that movie itself having long been identified as being laden with triggers for mind-control programmed subjects.) A C.I.A. document from 1963 detailing this technique as a method of interrogation, was declassified in 1997. It states that the aim is to confound the expectations and conditioned reactions of an individual being interrogated. The interrogators, often working in threes, would bombard the subject with unrelated questions, double-speak, and questions that conflicted with one another. As soon as the subject tried to answer a question, another interrogator would interrupt with something completely unrelated. The questions or queries would be altered in pitch and in tone—sometimes they may be shouted, and sometimes they may be whispered. This bombardment would continue until the subject is totally disorientated, confused and bewildered. Director William Friedkin slipped an homage to this technique into his movie 'The French Connection.' Gene Hackman and Roy Scheider's cop characters have cornered a suspect, and while Scheider asks valid questions about his contacts, Hackman confuses and confounds him with irrelevant questions like "when's the last time you picked your feet, Willie?"

Of the phenomenon of millions around the world allowing their thoughts and behaviours to become unwittingly dictated by agencies of which they have no knowledge, the rawjuiceguru.com website nailed it when it observed:

> *"Our enemies use documented behaviour modification psychology to make the public do themselves, what our enemies could never do by force. If people researched behaviour modification psychology, they would realise that they're being mentally manipulated into destroying themselves and their own children."*

Though many will reject the very suggestion out of hand, Covid has actually been made into a cult, ticking many of the boxes in terms of how such a dynamic operates. Cult members are brainwashed and gaslit into compliance with the cult's edicts, and those brought on board are encouraged only to fraternise with other cult members, and to leave behind former friends and family members if they themselves don't join the cult.

In 2021 I recorded a *'Good Vibrations'* episode with a British lady, Jade Bidwell, who is a survivor of Satanic Ritual Abuse, (more on this phenomenon in the upcoming chapters.) Through having been raised in a mind control cult, Jade was able to recognise some very distinct aspects of Satanic ritual in the way the public was being coerced to behave through Covid. The standing six feet apart, the wearing of masks and the incessant hand-washing are all straight out of these traditions. The masses have been deceived into participating in a mass-scale ritual of which they could have had no comprehension, devised by parties of whom they could have had no knowledge.

Even more disturbingly, Jade told me of how, as part of her early trauma-based programming, another child in the cult would be killed, and she would then be told that it was her fault to cripple her with guilt.

Sound familiar? Remember when we were told that if we went round to see our elderly grandparents or had them round the house, that we could be killing them simply by that very act?

No virtue in compliance

"Fascism is never imposed by fascists. There's never enough of them. Fascism is imposed by the population <u>acquiescing</u> to Fascism."
David Icke, Trafalgar Square, London, 24th July 2021.

So often I've heard phrases like, "none of what the Government says makes sense. They just can't make their minds up," as if it's all merely down to Boris Johnson, (just as with his equivalents in all other nations) being an inept, bumbling oaf and inept ministers not knowing their arse from their elbow. No, none of it makes any sense because it's not *supposed* to make any sense. That's the whole point. The public of our nations have had a military-grade interrogation technique weaponised against them, and yet still the masses walk around in a deluded daze thinking their Government has their best interests at heart and wants to "keep them safe" when the opposite has *always* been the case.

In 2021, the public got one of many free trial samples of these methods when the "virus" became referred to by governments and the media sometimes as "Co(n)vid-19," sometimes as "SARS-COV 2," sometimes as "long Co(n)vid," sometimes simply by the ludicrous phrase "coronavirus," and sometimes "the novel coronavirus," (because it's all fiction.)

Similarly, the "Indian variant" of "the virus" miraculously changed when the Indian Government threatened to sue the W.H.O. and the governments of the world with its insistence that no such thing existed, and so it became the "Delta variant" instead. (Delta is the lowest and slowest form of human brainwaves, indicating that you'd have to be asleep to believe it.) This all creates deliberate confusion in the public mindset, along with the unspoken assumption that this is a highly complex subject area that is best left to the scientists and the "experts" in white coats since the average Joe can't make head or tail of all these phrases, or what the difference is between them. If this didn't come out of S.A.G.E. or B.I.T., it was most likely a creation of the Tavistock Institute which I covered at great length in *'Musical Truth 1'* and which has specialised in finely-honed methods of mind-control, behaviour-modification and thought-entrainment now for over a century.

We got exactly the same dynamic when the "Jihadi" (yawwwwn) "terror" group I.S.I.S. was reportedly rampaging through nations in the pre-Co(n)vid years, sometimes alternatively referred to as "Islamic State," sometimes as "I.S." and sometimes as "Daesh." (Incidentally, have you noticed how these crazed, wild-eyed "terrorists" who would previously stop at nothing for their cause, have all just gone away since the outbreak of "the virus"? Do you think they're all self-isolating to protect their grans? Or could it be that they were the creation of the very military-intelligence units and state-sponsored social-engineering think-tanks behind Co(n)vid, and that, the "terror" tactic having achieved its goals, the narrative has now moved on to the next chapter. Yes, on reflection, that does seem a little more likely, doesn't it?)

Another favoured tactic from the Tavistock school of thought-entrainment, involves systematically building up the public's hope and optimism—often to levels of euphoria—then cruelly sending them crashing back down again. The UK got a taste of this back in July 2005 when within a few days of each-other it experienced the entertaining spectacle of the Live 8 concert at Wembley, followed by the jubilation of learning that London had won its bid to host the 2012 Olympics . . . followed immediately by the shock, trauma and horror of the 7/7 "terror attacks" in the capital.

How many times did the British public see the same strategy being employed when the Government announced a relaxing of the fascistic "virus" regulations . . . only to dash all hope and optimism by then reneging on its promises? We were told we could have five days over Christmas 2020 where we could freely mix households and have family members in our homes . . . only to be subsequently told that, actually, we could only have one day, and that we would have to pay for it by spending the next five months in lockdown.

We were told that 21st June 2021, (the Summer Solstice—more occult significance) would be "Freedom Day" where the Government "promised" that "all" remaining "Co(n)vid" restrictions would be lifted. Businesses made staffing and promotional arrangements ready for this date while families made holiday plans . . . only for us all to be told that "Freedom Day" couldn't actually occur after all.

And on and on it goes. And will continue to until enough people wake up to the obvious nature of what's being done to our lives. To state that the individuals behind such manipulations are evil and psychopathic isn't going nearly far enough. There aren't enough words in the English language to describe how sick and diseased a mind must be to be *capable* of dreaming up, let alone applying, such tactics, and the idea that anyone could possibly be OK with turning up to work each day to systematically ruin the lives of multiple millions who have done them no harm, truly beggars belief. At the very least it stands as proof that these individuals, in the broadest sense, cannot accurately be described as fully "human" since they lack the compassion, empathy, and so many other aspects of the full range of emotions and characteristics that it would take to qualify them as such.

The Castration of Care

"But if you close your eyes,
Does it almost feel like nothing changed at all?
And if you close your eyes,
Does it almost feel like you've been here before?"
    Bastille: 'Pompeii'

The jaw-dropping audacity, arrogance and hubris that the Co(n)vid Scamdemic reveals in its originators is truly astounding, particularly when considering what the implications would have been for them had they misjudged the situation and *not* got the collective public mindset exactly where they wanted it to be. A world population of sovereign men and women standing in their true, God-given rights and powers, able to think clearly for themselves, and able to see through the same propaganda and mind-control tricks which have been employed by proven liars, frauds and eugenicists countless times before, would have stopped the insidious agenda right in its tracks.

So too would organised militias of real men, standing on the side of Right Action, rising up to defend their families and communities, and prepared to do whatever might be necessary to put down the tyranny and negate the threat.

While successive generations of programming through media and entertainment, plus the systematic dumbing-down of intelligence levels through food and drink additives, fluoride in the water, brain-destroying nano-particles being ingested from Chemtrails, and other methods of calcifying the pineal gland, the mind's portal to advanced levels of consciousness and higher thinking, have seen to it that the first scenario would not prove to be a problem, so too have careful methods been put in place to prevent the latter.

I have made the observation in a handful of interviews recently that, had the architects of the Scamdemic tried to pull their audacious stunt back in the 1970s or 1980s, they would quite likely have been met with considerable public resistance and, quite possibly, armies of real men rising up to take physical, preventative action. No such concerns were evidently in place in 2019, however, because the psychopaths knew that they had done a successful job over the past generation or two, of both physically and psychologically emasculating men. Again, this would have been achieved biologically, with hormone-altering chemicals present in food, drink and the water supply, (having the additional gender-blurring effect of masculinising females as well as softening-up their counterparts.)

Media and popular culture would have played its part also, however. The promotion of homosexuality through the over-abundance of gay television hosts and movie and TV show characters has formed part of this, as has the otherwise inexplicable obsession in the media of promoting Transgenderism and the LGBTQ community. (Before any reader jumps to an accusatory knee-jerk reaction, observing these factors does not make me "homophobic" in any way. On the contrary, I am demonstrating how the LGBTQ community has been systematically exploited — as so many other groups have been through the years — in order to push the society-altering goals of the "elite" social engineers who care *nothing* for the genuine concerns of such communities and will discard them in a heartbeat as soon as it considers them to have outlived their usefulness.)

Fashion has also played a part. The gradual entrainment of young males to wear skinny jeans and other tight-fitting clothing, along with the promotion of the colour pink, has all been part of turning traditional perceptions of manliness on their head. What else could explain the concepts of "toxic masculinity" and "man-spreading" so enthusiastically pushed by the media in recent years? The unspoken implication is that traditional masculinity and the concept of a "real man," (which includes standing in self-defence in the face of threats to personal safety and wellbeing,) is outdated and irrelevant in these times. "Woke" culture to give it its fashionable name. (There's another Satanic inversion. There's nothing "woke" about such an artificially-induced mindset!)

I personally feel the Ice Bucket Challenge of a few years ago was a social-engineering test run to see how willing gullible fools would be to douse themselves with ice cold water purely on the say-so of some "celeb" hero or other. If they would be willing to do that in their millions, (and they were,) it would tend to suggest that they'd be equally willing to inject an unknown, untested chemical compound into their veins similarly on the say-so of some pointless celeb.

The social-engineers must have been clinking their champagne glasses at their private members' clubs and congratulating themselves on a job well done as they observed the Co(n)vid Scamdemic going down *exactly* as their meticulously-applied social science told them it would do, without—generally speaking- so much as a whisper of dissent or revolt from the collective men of the world.

Now, *that's* social-engineering.

A jab in the dark

"If freedom comes with a caveat . . . it ain't freedom!"
Gareth Icke, Trafalgar Square, London, 24th July 2021.

All roads in the Scamdemic were only ever designed to lead to one place—the mass vaccination of the vast majority of the world's general public. Bill Gates, who comes with zero medical qualifications, yet somehow gets to decide the way people are and aren't allowed to lead their lives, stated in a TV interview in March 2020 that society would not go "back to normal" until everyone had been vaccinated. (See the next chapter for more on Gates' family links and affiliations.) The Co(n)vid "vaccines" produced by the likes of Moderna, AstraZeneca and Pfizer were somehow rushed through in record time, the first being made available in December 2020, the truth being that they had all been developed well ahead of time just waiting for the green light.

Vicious psychopathic eugenicist disguised as socially inadequate nerd. Bill Gates, indirectly responsible for the suffering and deaths of untold millions. Not a "man" you'd want to be on karmic payback day.
Good luck there, Bill.

*https://commons.wikimedia.org/wiki/File:Bill_Gates_speaking_at_DFID_*
(5093072151).jpg

These products did not undergo the usual years of rigorous testing that vaccines are required to pass, the truth being that the general public have been used as the experimental lab-rats, and that these products cannot accurately be described as "vaccines" in the traditional sense, but rather represent what even one of their manufacturers has described as "experimental gene therapy." Little wonder that so many of the hordes who obediently queued and rolled up their sleeve to take the "shot" (none of these words are by accident,) either died, or underwent horrific health defects, very few of which, predictably, went reported by the mainstream media which merely continued to push the "cases" fraud.

In fact, the experimental "vaccines" are in violation of Article 32 of the 1949 Geneva Convention IV which holds that "mutilation and medical or scientific experiments not necessitated by the medical treatment of a protected person" are prohibited. According to Article

147, conducting biological experiments on protected persons is a grave breach of the Convention. The "vaccine" is in violation of all ten of the Nuremberg Codes, which carry the death penalty for those who seek to violate these International Laws. Another one you won't have heard about on the BBC Evening News.

Many whose instinct might have guided them otherwise, were coerced into taking the jab (another carefully-chosen word) purely in order to be able to go on their Summer holidays, it having been suggested that "vaccine passports" were on the way, and only those who had taken their shot would be allowed to fly. There was an ironic reversal of fortunes when the vaccinated were said to have been "shedding" the "virus," and therefore deemed unfit to fly after all. The story also emerged in Spring 2021 that several of British Airways' pilots had either died or fallen ill shortly after taking their "vaccines," leading to chaos and deep fear about the safety of travelling with that particular airline. There was also delicious irony from restaurants being forced to only cater and serve those who advocated for businesses to be closed for the previous 18 months, (brainwashed "normies") while banning those who fought for them to stay open, (critical thinkers.) You couldn't make it up. And you don't have to.

With so much effort having been employed to get vaccination levels as high as possible throughout the world, any free-thinker's ultimate question must surely be, therefore—what could possibly be the ultimate aim of this phenomenon?

Co(n)vid–the gift that keeps on giving

"Ordinary people are likely to follow orders given by an authority figure, even to the extent of killing an innocent human being. Obedience to authority is ingrained in us all from the way we are brought up. People tend to obey orders from other people if they recognise their authority as morally right and/ or legally based."

Conclusion from The Millgram Experiment, 1963.

The multitude of Common Sense-defying measures that were introduced in the wake of the "pandemic" make far more sense when you have a handle on what the long-term schemes of the world's "elites" are in line with their New World Order masterplan. This works hand-in-hand with the Agenda 2030 project coming out of the United Nations and The Great Reset project coming out of the World Economic Forum, (both nothing more than "Illuminati" think-tank organisations, and like all others, dedicated to the same ultimate goals.) The "pandemic" has ticked so many boxes on the "elites" long-standing wish-list that it's very hard not to take on some grudging admiration of the sheer evil genius of the entire scheme.

No-one should be surprised to find that the Co(n)vid scam has been used as a warm-up for the next item on the NWO agenda, either, which is the equally fraudulent con that is "Climate Change." Notice how talk of this has been ramped up majorly in recent months, getting addressed in everything from TV chat shows and soap operas to "newspapers" and magazines? If Co(n)vid was the *hors d'ouevre*, then Climate Change will prove itself to be the main course. The reality is that the world's climate has gone through patterns of change since time immemorial, that this is all part of the natural and regular rhythms of the earth, and that the deadly and hazardous events that get blamed on "Climate Change" are actually engineered by weather modification technology such as HAARP that lies in the hands of the sick ones.

Now that the public has been acclimatised to the idea of lockdowns and previously unacceptable restrictions on personal rights and freedoms all in the name of "keeping us safe," expect to see more of the same all in the name of "protecting the environment" *unless* these psychopathic maniacs are stopped in their tracks—a process that can *only* occur at the hands of we, the people, and no-one else.

Author Alistair MacLean observed in one of his book titles that *'Fear Is The Key.'* And it absolutely is. A population kept in a perpetual state of fear is one that is far less likely to employ critical thought to a situation, and is thus far easier to control. With fear constantly pumped out of every television set in the world, combined with never-ending reminders of a "deadly virus" on the rampage, even through something as routine as a trip to the local supermarket, there has been zero chance of anyone avoiding the fear-based propaganda surrounding Co(n)vid. Tick.

Fear leads to conditions such as stress and anxiety, which themselves deplete the body's immune system, and can trigger all kinds of other debilitating symptoms. The irony, considering those pushing the fear factor constantly proclaim, (with the usual Satanic inversion,) that they're doing it only because they wish to "keep us safe." And yet these proclamations never come with any advice to get out in sunlight to absorb as much health-boosting Vitamin D as possible, to exercise, to drink only filtered or natural water, to take natural health cures, or to eat as much fresh fruit and veg as possible. Instead we're told that only Big Pharma-mandated "medicine" can help us, ensuring that the billions these industries make continues to pour in, maintaining the billionaire lifestyles of their CEOs, and ensuring a lifelong customer base dependent on their products in the process. Tick.

The lockdown agenda has kept individuals from having social contact with each-other—an essential, therapeutic, and entirely natural requirement of the human condition. Instead, the public has been entrained to accept that doing everything from gym classes to preparing Sunday lunch by Zoom or some similar on-line tool, is every bit as good as being there. Why bother driving to your mum's, hugging her and looking into the whites of her eyes when you can simply wave at her on your phone screen? Far less hassle. And think of the fuel savings. Tick.

The enforced isolation has impeded the ability for people to organise themselves into groups to discuss and scrutinise the accuracy of the information they have been told by the Government and the media. The forcible closures of common meeting places such as pubs and cafés, enforced by obedient and unquestioning police, has prevented any public meetings of this nature. Tick.

Enforced confinement has also led to untold numbers of suicides through the trauma and desolation of enforced isolation, leading to further population reduction. Tick.

Constant Big Brother-style suppression of information that goes against the official narrative has been employed by the Big Tech giants such as Google/ YouTube, Facebook, Twitter and others, with de-platforming and channel bans rendering it extremely difficult for alternative voices to be widely heard. Tick.

The lockdowns have also caused untold numbers of small, independent businesses to go bankrupt, with many more still to come, ensuring that only large, multinational "globalist" corporations will have been able to weather the financial storm. Tick. Meanwhile, the former proprietors of those, now-ruined small businesses, are forced to rely on Government handouts such the Universal Credit Scheme as their only remaining way of feeding their families, this rendering them dependent on the state and whatever future dictates it may choose to impose a condition of receiving such payments, (such as, oh, I don't know—taking a vaccine perhaps?) Tick.

The bad science cultivated by Government and scientific community traitors, has led many to believe that "the virus" can live on anything from supermarket trolley handles to a £10 note in your pocket, and the germs can leap off these items with no notice, jump straight into your mouth and nostrils, and infect you on the spot. This has led to many businesses becoming 'cashless" on the grounds that cash is "dirty." A cashless society has long been in the plans of the sick ones, where digital currency co-exists alongside a Social Credit System of the type already active in Communist China, operating within Smart Grids powered by Artificial Intelligence and toxic 5G technology. There are more ticks with this one than in an Afro full of head lice.

Incidentally, the constant use of sanitiser, as enforced by supermarkets and all kinds of other public buildings, leads cumulatively to a weakening of the body's immune system and its natural ability to combat germs on its own, with no artificial assistance, thus rendering millions far more susceptible to infections in the future, and therefore a reliance on the pharmaceutical industry for treatment. Tick.

Curtailment of travel—particularly internationally—all on the grounds of "keeping us safe" and "preventing the spread of the virus" have infringed on the natural, God-given right that every man and woman has to Freedom of Movement. The experience of flying has now been made so inconvenient, (through enforced quarantine,) traumatising (through enforced mask-wearing and never-ending "safety" announcements,) invasive (through enforced track-and tracing) and expensive, (through enforced testing at the customer's expense,) that few will want to put themselves though the burden of it all any longer.

Preventing the public from travelling freely, instead keeping them in one place where they can be routinely monitored and surveilled, has long been a tenet of the New World Order masterplan. Tick.

And how long before the apparent (though orchestrated) ineptitude of governments towards effectively handling the "pandemic" in their respective nations leads to calls for a centralised One World Government, with a One World Currency, and a One World Army to enforce its will, as "the only way to ensure this type of problem can never occur again."

Tick.

Resources:

COVID-19: The Spartacus Letter: The ultimate goldmine of proofs exposing the entire COVID scam:

- https://www.docdroid.net/mQZHyT7/ covid-19-the-spartacus-letter-pdf

Awesome resource—Off-Guardian.org: 30 facts you NEED to know: Your Covid Crib sheet:

- https://off-guardian.org/2021/09/22/30-facts-you-need-to-know-your-covid-cribsheet/

The biggest hoax ever to be carried out on the masses in history. Godfrey Bloom On-line:

- http://godfreybloom.uk/your-health/?fbclid=IwAR1n_Qyc-QqqLMAi-wyL_nO5RDKNR4baHltvvu4591zr3VeUQfHkz-v3Q-orE

Andrew Johnson's CV "Pandemic" Investigation:

- https://cvpandemicinvestigation.com/

Co(n)vid-19 SCAM IS THE BIGGEST CRIME OF THE CENTURY AND IT IS THE FOURTH TIME IN HISTORY:

- https://www.bitchute.com/video/qiFQHOW4AcbD/

Political Moonshine: COVID-19 Enterprise Fraud Construct Timeline: Major Dates, Events, Entities & Legislation:

- https://politicalmoonshine.com/2021/09/29/covid-19-enterprise-fraud-construct-timeline-major-dates-events-entities-legislation/

2030 UnMasked Documentary Connecting COVID19, Masks, Vaccines, The Banking System & the Great Reset via Shane St. Pierre:

- https://www.brighteon.com/3159e393-d871-4c66-ae1a-6f4c-8dcfdb2a

Interview with German virologist Dr. Stefan Lanka: "Viruses are neither microbes, nor do they have infectious capacity:

- https://ia804509.us.archive.org/31/items/stefan-lanka-viruses-are-not-microbes-and-have-no-infectious-capacity-iii-of-iii-dsalud/Stefan%20Lanka%20%22Viruses%20are%20not%20microbes%20and%20have%20no%20infectious%20capacity%22%20%28III%20of%20III%29%20DSalud.pdf

Newstarget: Patent document shows that DARPA built Co(n)vid with the help of Bill Gates, who:

- https://newstarget.com/2021-06-29-darpa-built-covid-help-bill-gates-who.html

Pfizer whistleblower says vaccine 'glows,' contains 'toxic' luciferase, graphene oxide compounds:

- https://www.lifesitenews.com/video/bombshell-pfizer-whistleblower-says-vaccine-glows-contains-toxic-luciferase-graphene-oxide-compounds/?utm_source=gab

Worldwide Doctors Warn For The Vaccines :

- https://rumble.com/viqn29-worldwide-doctors-warn-for-the-vaccines-must-see.html

The Global 2000 Report:

- https://files.eric.ed.gov/fulltext/ED212523.pdf

According to many medical professionals, the Co(n)vid "vaccines" constitute experimental gene therapy, with the public being used as unwitting test subjects:

- https://articles.mercola.com/sites/articles/archive/2021/03/16/mrna-vaccine-gene-therapy.aspx

- https://scivisionpub.com/pdfs/Co(n)vid19-rna-based-vaccines-and-the-risk-of-prion-disease-1503.pdf

- http://stateofthenation.co/?p=51461

The Guardian: India orders removal of content referring to 'Indian variant':

- https://www.theguardian.com/world/2021/may/22/india-orders-removal-of-content-referring-to-indian-variant

HYPNOTIST REVEALS Government BRAINWASHING TACTICS / HUGO TALKS #LOCKDOWN:

- https://hugotalks.com/2021/07/17/hypnotist-reveals-Government-brainwashing-tactics-hugo-talks-lockdown/

Mob Mania: Why Did So Many Fall For The Covid Narrative?:

- https://gemmaodoherty.com/mob-mania-why-did-so-many-fall-for-the-covid-narrative/

BOMBSHELL" Viruses Are Nothing More Than Dead Cell Debris — Virus Particles Are Neither Airborne Or Contagious — Nor Do They Cause Any Disease Or Illness! All Germ Theory Has Been Completely Debunked! THE Government CLAIM THAT VIRUSES CAUSE PANDEMICS IS A GIANT HOAX!!:

- https://darrellhines.net/2021/07/14/bombshell-viruses-are-nothing-more-than-dead-cell-debris-virus-particles-are-neither-airborne-or-contagious-nor-do-they-cause-any-disease-or-illness-all-germ-theory-has-been-completely/

Sheep Farm Studios: Dom & Chris' brilliantly researched and witty exposés of the psychopathic "behavioural scientists" behind London's S.A.G.E. Group:

Part 1:

- https://www.sheepfarm.co.uk/videos/
  sheep-farm-23-meet-the-flockers-S.A.G.E.-unmasked-pt1/

Part 2:

- https://www.sheepfarm.co.uk/videos/sheep-farm-24-meet-the-
  flockers-S.A.G.E.-unmaksed-2-astrazeneca-van-tam-michie/

- Part 3: https://www.sheepfarm.co.uk/videos/
  sheep-farm-26-S.A.G.E.-unmasked-pt3-nutty-professors/

The "Alice In Wonderland" technique in "The French Connection" movie:

- https://www.youtube.com/watch?v=ZvvlFocf6LU

Hugo Talks Lockdown — the Alice In Wonderland Technique:

- https://www.youtube.com/watch?v=7a1eTlLRs5M

Anti-Lockdown: A huge depository of articles highlighting the nonsense of official COVID-19 responses and measures:

- https://antilockdown.org/posts-output/2021-07-22-welcome-
  to-anti-lock-down/#covid-19-vaccine

CHAPTER 2

SOUND BITES, PART 1

What to do with information that remains vitally incisive, but doesn't fit the flow?

While it would have been great to have woven all of the following information into logically-flowing chapters, the disparate and eclectic nature of the data would have made keeping any kind of order to it all an exercise in futility. These are titbits that have either caught my eye, or have been sent to me by vigilant readers. Consider these as add-ons to the main chapters in question, therefore.

Most, if not all of the following snippets do correspond to subjects covered in one of the three books. One thing they do all have in common is that this information rarely features in official biographies, and all go some way to confirming *Musical Truth's* overall stance — that nothing about the corporate-controlled music business is the way it's been presented to us all our lives. Many stories simply serve as yet further evidence that the corporate-controlled music industry is a den of Satanism, dark occult ritual, paedophilia and trauma-based mind-control, is populated by Lifetime Actors from important bloodline families, and affiliated with Freemasonry, the military intelligence services, and social-engineering agencies such as the Tavistock institute.

That said, welcome to a new feature exclusive to *'Musical Truth Volume 3.'* These are the *'Sound Bites.'*

> *"It's the terror of knowing what the world is about,*
> *Watching some good friends screaming, let me out!"*
>
> *Queen & David Bowie: 'Under Pressure'*

> *"Are we living in a land, where sex and horror, are the new gods?"*
>
> *Frankie Goes To Hollywood: 'Two Tribes'*

35

*

Fleetwood Mac remains one of the longest-serving and most multi-membered bands in the industry, still around in some shape or form after more than 50 years and 15 line-ups. The group's history is littered with misfortune and death, however, leading some to question whether dark energetic influences or "witchcraft" might have played a part. Insiders have reported that drummer **Mick Fleetwood** regularly held seances in hotel rooms where the band were staying, and that he had picked up the habit from **Brian Jones** of the **Rolling Stones**, (who died in mysterious circumstances at the age of 27 in 1969.) Even a '*Daily Mail*' article on the group's history made reference to the group succumbing to "what many people regard as something of a hoodoo."

Peter Green, (real name Peter Greenbaum,) the founding member of Fleetwood Mac, and generally revered as one of Britain's all-time guitar greats, passed away on 25th July 2020, aged 73. No cause of death was publicly released. Rather like **Syd Barrett** and **Pink Floyd**, Green spent only a short period in Fleetwood Mac, eventually leaving due to his failing mental health, attributed to his taking of LSD. He was eventually diagnosed with schizophrenia and spent long periods in psychiatric hospitals undergoing electroconvulsive therapy, (reported to be used in MK-Ultra-style trauma-based mind-control experimentation,) during the mid-1970s. Friends reported that he seemed to be in an almost continual trance.

Earlier in the year, Mick Fleetwood had curated a tribute concert to the work of Green and the early years of the group which took place at the London Palladium on 25th February, only weeks before all music venues got plunged into the UK's Draconian lockdown. Green himself did not attend his own tribute, choosing to stay at home. The array of musicians performing included **Dave Gilmour, Noel Gallagher, John Mayall, Pete Townshend, Christine McVie, Bill Wyman** and **Steven Tyler**. The gig was of the type that normally gets staged after a music legend has died. In Green's case, he still had five months to live. In November, it was announced that the concert would be made into a movie, to be released in cinemas in Spring 2021.

*The Fleetwood Mac guitar legend who died in 2020 and whose story
bears many parallels with that of Pink Floyd's Syd Barrett.*

https://www.flickr.com/photos/kitmasterbloke/4434482957

Credit: Steve Knight

Green's tragic life aside, some further deep-diving into Fleetwood Mac
history reveals some rather disturbing stuff. The theme of witchcraft
emerged early through the Peter Green-penned concert favourite, (later
made a hit by **Santana**,) *'Black Magic Woman.'* When **Stevie Nicks**
joined the group she took to ending live versions of the song with the
line "and you'll never get the devil out of me."

In late 2018, Nicks' former partner and fellow band member **Lind-
sey Buckingham** was axed from the group amid various professional
and legal disputes, and a falling-out with Nicks. Buckingham filed a
lawsuit against the band. Within a few weeks, he was complaining of
severe chest pains and was taken to hospital where he underwent open
heart surgery. Although the operation was successful it left him with
damage to his vocal cords, calling into question whether he would ever
be able to sing professionally again.

Three former members of Fleetwood Mac, all named Bob, (**Welch,
Weston, Brunning**,) died within eight months of each-other in 2011/
2012. All are reported to have upset the hierarchy of the band in some

way. Welch is said to have shot himself after undergoing spinal surgery and learning from his doctor that he would never recover the use of his legs. Weston was found dead in bed in his flat after seemingly suffering a haemorrhage. He had been sacked following rumours of his having an affair with Jenny Boyd, the wife of Mick Fleetwood, (and the sister of Patti Boyd who had been wife to both **George Harrison** and **Eric Clapton**.) Brunning suffered a massive heart attack at his London home.

Guitarist **Danny Kirwan** (real name Daniel Langran) died in 2018 following long periods of being homeless and destitute. Like Green, he had suffered mental health decline during a long period of alcohol and drug use. In a 2009 BBC documentary the band's manager, Clifford Davis, cited an incident in March 1970 at a hippie commune in Munich as having been responsible for both Kirwan and Green's mental health decline when both had taken LSD there. Other sources, however, disputed the claim that Kirwan was present.

Another original member, **Jeremy Spencer**, exhibited something of a schizophrenic personality during his time with the band. Off-stage he was a quiet, studious Christian, frequently found reading the Bible, yet in performances seemed to take on an entirely different persona as a wild and flamboyant entertainer. Spencer walked out after an earthquake hit Los Angeles, predicting something bad would happen to the group. He was next heard of as a member of a sex cult called Children of God. This is the same group once headed by disgraced former 'Truth movement' personality Zen Gardner. The organisation, plagued with claims of paedophilia, later renamed itself The Family International, and Spencer reportedly is still associated, writing and illustrating stories.

Liam Firlej, the son of Peter Green, has begun making videos addressing many of the above subjects. You can find them here—https://www.youtube.com/channel/UC2aTlYcp88f6jv99pWsYuHA

*

Sting (CBE—real name Gordon Sumner) has had no problem expressing his political leanings in his years since leaving **The Police**—even if his affiliations have been with the usual predictable array of Globalist/ New World Order agenda-pushers. Reportedly, he has maintained strong views on political and social issues right from the early days of the band, and had wished to include more of this material in its output, but was stifled from doing so.

The claim came from **Dave Wakeling**, former singer with English New Wave/ Ska group **The Beat**, who were contemporaries of The Police. The two groups toured together in the early 1980s. According to comments given by Wakeling to David Weiner of '*The Insider*' website, a sister project to '*Entertainment Tonight*,' Sting and his fellow band members were "kept on an incredibly short leash" by Miles Copeland III, the elder brother of Police drummer **Stewart Copeland**, who acted as the band's manager. As Wakeling recalled:

> *"Touring with The Police was an odd situation. They were ruled by fear by Miles Copeland. They were not allowed to speak their minds. They were heavily contained, and we felt very sad for them, really, because they did have ideas and opinions that they were banned from being able to say.*
>
> *"It was really The Monkees of Punk, you know? It was the Punkees: we're too busy singing to sing about anything that's really going on. And that was awful sad, because they were decent folks, especially Gordon ... They sort of eviscerated the end of Punk, didn't they, to make it like it was pure pop entertainment, which was a bloody shame. And they got away with it, which is even worse."*

Interestingly, Wakeling also mentioned that Miles Copeland III had "wanted to be Secretary of State." As reported at some length in '*Musical Truth 2*,' Copeland was the son of Mlles Axe Copeland Junior, a career CIA officer, serving in various international roles right from the agency's inception in the 1940s. Copeland had three sons—Miles, Stewart and Ian—and all were put to work in the music industry. The Copelands were instrumental in both the establishment and the ongoing control of many acts falling into the Punk/ New Wave categories in the late 1970s and early 1980s. They operated various companies among which were Copeland International Artists (CIA,) Frontier Booking International (FBI,) and International Records Syndicate, (IRS.)

As has now been reported by multiple sources, the CIA has divisions which seek to influence societal attitudes through popular culture, working closely with Hollywood and the television and corporate-controlled music industries. It seems that, either as a form of bragging mockery or their dutiful adherence to placing the truth in plain sight, these organisations like to give subtle clues as to their influence every now and again, such as through the naming of the Copelands' organisations. "The Police" could be taken as a further example of this dynamic, suggesting perhaps that the group's real role was to "police" others in the game.

Then we have the double-meaning of Sting's moniker. The official, and wholly unconvincing story of its origin is that Sumner used to wear a yellow-and-black-striped jumper, making him look like a bee! Perhaps the truth lies in the alternative meaning of the word "sting," as in a police sting operation?

Curiously, the three members of the Police were previously in a short-lived band named **Strontium 90** alongside vocalist Mike Howlett. Given that Strontium has been identified as one of the nano-particle constituents present in chemtrails, an agenda that would begin some 20 years later, you have to wonder whether this was an innocently-named band, or whether there was some inside knowledge at play here?

*

The claim has long been made that entertainers are secretly employed as spies for the military intelligence agencies. Any sceptics and naysayers got it straight from the horse's mouth when **Eugene Robinson**, vocalist with the experimental rock band **Oxbow,** was interviewed by The Quietus site (www.thequietus.com) for an article in January 2019. Speaking of his first introduction to the records of Nina Simone, Robinson recalled:

> *"My first introduction to Nina Simone was via my father who had been a jazz bassist who was working for US Air Force intelligence. He was a bass-playing spy, essentially. He spoke four languages and the Air Force made him form a Jazz trio so they could tour Eastern*

Bloc countries at a time when nobody would expect three black guys to be speaking any other languages than English."

Similar accounts persist of other Jazz musicians, including Louis Armstrong and Dizzy Gillespie, being employed by American intel as "ambassadors" and sent to tour the USSR during the Cold War years.

*

Boleskine House, the notorious former abode of the mythical dark occultist **Aleister Crowley**, whose influence upon a multitude of famous musicians was covered in Volume 1, was the subject of a planning application made in 2020 to The Highland Council of Scotland.

Since August 2019 the category-B listed building on the shores of Loch Ness, only part of which remains standing following a mysterious fire just prior to Christmas 2015, has been under the stewardship of the Boleskine House Foundation. This was established by a couple, Keith and Kyra Readdy, and is described as a non-profit charity concerned with maintaining the estate. The Foundation's stated aims are to restore the house and its gardens, reflecting its history as a Jacobean and Georgian hunting lodge, and to offer access to the public once completed.

The council objected to the application on the grounds that the current owners put the historic building at risk by selling pieces of its rubble on Ebay, and that, "the proposal essentially involves making the site a place of pilgrimage for Satanists and other followers of Aleister Crowley, constituting a serious nuisance to the local community and a blight on the district."

The battle appears to be ongoing, however, with the Ordo Templi Orientis (OTO,) one of the occult secret-societies which Crowley once helmed, now reportedly owning some 4 hectares of the site and having earmarked £1.4 million to restore it through their Boleskine House Foundation, as the leading Satanic temple in Britain. This, if achieved, would make it a place of pilgrimage for Satanists and dark occultists from all over the world and—given these groups' enthusiasm for human child sacrifices—would pose a potential deadly threat for children everywhere.

Boleskine House was bought by **Jimmy Page** of **Led Zeppelin**, a devoted follower of Crowley and his Thelema religion. He sold it 20 years later after having reportedly only spent a handful of nights there in that whole period. Boleskine was referenced in the lyrics to the Police's Sting-penned song '*Synchronicity II*' in 1983, in the line: "Many miles away there's a shadow on the door, of a cottage on the shore, of a dark Scottish lake."

In other Crowley-related property findings, according to reports The Great Beast resided at 2 All Souls Place in Fitzrovia, London, in around 1930. The interesting thing about this address is that it just happens to be directly opposite the BBC's iconic Broadcasting House, which began transmitting radio programmes in 1932. The building has gained notoriety from the statue above its main entrance. Created by convicted paedophile Eric Gill, and named Ariel & Prospero after a Shakespeare play, it depicts a naked child writhing against the crotch of a naked male adult, who seems to be enjoying the experience. Given that Crowley was into sex magick and once advocated the slaying of a pre-pubescent male child as the purest sacrifice in an occult ritual, he surely would have approved. The prolific paedophile and necrophiliac Jimmy Savile, who was employed at BBC Broadcasting House for many years, is said to have been a follower of Crowley's work.

*

On the subject of interesting locations in London, another intriguing one with music industry connections is the tellingly-named Mason's Yard, in the area of St. James.' Reminders of its Freemasonic heritage come from The Director's Lodge, with the address of 13a, and the pub on the corner named the Chequers Tavern, evoking the black-and-white checkerboard floors found in FreeMasonic temples. Chequers is also the name of the official residence of the sitting British Prime Minister, incidentally.

The Yard became a popular hang-out spot for the high-profile musicians of the 1960s counter-culture era, where London had its own "scene" based largely around the avant-garde art movement of the time, running concurrently with the Hippie/ Flower Power scene over in

America. While Carnaby Street, Mary Quant, Twiggy and David Bailey were the accessible icons of "Swinging London," the avant-garde movement was more a "best-kept secret" reserved for a highly select crowd. The key location in this regard was to be found at 6 Mason's Yard.

This was the Indica, a small art gallery and rare book store curated by partners Barry Miles and John Dunbar, (who for a brief period was married to **Marianne Faithfull**, the one-time girlfriend of both **Mick Jagger** and **Brian Jones** of the **Rolling Stones** and who, research has shown, descends on her mother's side from the Austrian Sacher-Masoch bloodline from which we get the term 'Sado-Masochism.) It's a small world.) The other partners in the business—named after the Indica cannabis plant—were **Peter Asher**, known as one half of the 60s group Peter and Gordon and brother of the child star-turned actress Jane Asher, who for a period in the 60s was the girlfriend of **Paul McCartney**. McCartney himself lived with the Ashers at their family home in Wimpole Mews, from which Jane and Peter's father Dr. Richard Day had his medical practice, and completed the quartet of Indica partners.

It is at the Indica where **John Lennon** is first said to have met **Yoko Ono** at a display of her conceptual art. By that point, the Indica had become one of the key spots in London's avant-garde movement. The date that has gone down in lore for this meeting is 9th November 1966, (9/11/66,) though this is often disputed. The Indica was one of the sites that featured in my whistle-stop tour of key Beatles locations in the capital that can be watched here—https://www.youtube.com/watch?v=9fOPV55eZP0&t=37s

Another notable building is just a stone's throw from the yard, and this may raise an eyebrow among those who have studied accounts of the Beatles being a social-engineering project, designed to play their influential role in shaping and moulding the changing social attitudes of the 1960s. This is Chatham House, home of the Royal Institute of International Affairs. Though the official line is that Chatham "aims to promote debate on significant developments in international affairs and policy responses," its activities are actually similar to those of the Tavistock Institute of Human Relations, in steering culture and social attitudes off in pre-agreed desired directions. This institution is the origin of the phrase the 'Chatham House Rule' which advocates that members must not divulge the identity of other attendee meetings, or what a specific individual said. A variation on the Freemasonic oath of secrecy.

It's reported that, when **Jimi Hendrix** first came to London in 1966, his first performance was in the Scotch of St. James Club, located at 13 Mason's Yard. The Beatles were reportedly seated at one of the club's tables, with the Rolling Stones at another. Hendrix met his girlfriend of the next two years, Kathy Etchingham, at this gig. **Chas Chandler**, a former member of the Newcastle group the **Animals**, is credited with having arranged for Hendrix to come to London, and with setting him up in a management deal with Michael Jeffery, who had also managed The Animals. Chandler himself went on to manage **Slade**. As reported in Volume 1, Jeffery had connections into military intelligence, and the general consensus among alternative researchers is that he arranged for Hendrix's death, in September 1970, which was passed off as "accidental asphyxiation."

The one-time road manager of the Animals, James 'Tappy' Wright, in his book '*Rock Roadie: Backstage and Confidential with Hendrix, Elvis, The Animals, Tina Turner, and an all-star cast*', declared that Hendrix was murdered by orders from on-high, reinforcing the persistent rumours that he, like so many other rock acts of that pivotal era, was a military intelligence operative. Reportedly, some heavies from the Newcastle underworld were sent down to London to do the job, in a kind of reversal of the plot from the classic 1971 film '*Get Carter.*' A couple of plaques still document Hendrix's presence in Newcastle. I was taken to see one outside a chip shop in Tynemouth Village, which proclaims that Jimi ate fish and chips from there on a bench overlooking the sea after playing at the Club A Go Go nightclub on 10th March 1967.

*

Given that '*The Wizard of Oz*' is, (alongside '*Alice In Wonderland*' and '*Catcher In The Rye*,') one of the stories that crops up the most as a known trigger in mind-control programming, (going "somewhere over the rainbow" is said to refer to the dissociation from reality that subjects experience when traumatised,) this surely justifies some closer consideration of 'Goodbye Yellow Brick Road,' one of the earliest hits for a young **Elton John**.

Much metaphysical interpretation has been put on the 'Oz' movie as representing the duality between the 3D physical world and the spiritual realm, and the characters "following the yellow brick road" is said to represent them on the path to enlightenment. Though the song, written by Elton and **Bernie Taupin**, is clearly loaded with allegory, certain lyrics could be seen as Elton hinting at his ownership by the industry machine, including "you know you can't hold me forever, I didn't sign up with you," and "maybe you'll get a replacement, there's plenty like me to be found." Or possibly, his being handed around those who frequent the industry against his consent.

Many of the contributors to a thread on Reddit, accessible from the Resources listed at the end of the chapter, felt that the song referenced Monarch Programming. As the original poster commented: "OK then, this song seems be about the loss of consent and autonomy. Going 'beyond the yellow brick road' is slang for disassociating during times of extreme trauma." (The post also acknowledges that Bernie Taupin, Elton John's lyric-writer, also co-penned 'These Dreams' by the American group **Heart**, which includes the line "I need to hide away from the pain," and a video so loaded with occult, Masonic and Monarch symbolism, that it stands as an A-Z guide of how to do it.

As the biopic 'Rocket Man' starring Taron Egerton as Elton acknowledged, his breakthrough to industry success was largely fuelled by his 1970 performance at the Troubador Club in West Hollywood, just a stone's throw away from the fabled Laurel Canyon, where he was introduced by **Neil Diamond**. Some researchers wonder whether this performance represented a rite of passage, given that the venue is said to have springboarded the successful careers of many other musicians who had debuted there.

There's nothing obvious in Elton's family background, from his days as Reginald Dwight of Pinner, Middlesex, to suggest important bloodline links, but we're into familiar territory when we discover that his father served as a Flight Lieutenant in the Royal Air Force. Either way, something has to account for his becoming such a darling of the Establishment, earning himself a "Sir"-hood and the status of "National

Treasure" and being selected to sing at Princess Diana's funeral, causing his '*Candle in The Wind*' to become one of the biggest-selling singles of all time. The original song was all about Marilyn Monroe, a mind-control victim and original archetype of the Beta Sex Kitten Programming derivative.

Elton is a known collector of Satanic and paedophilic art, but this proved no barrier whatsoever to his being permitted to adopt two baby boys, alongside his husband David Furnish. Phrases like "it's who you know" never come about by accident.

As this book was being finished, news arrived of the so-called "Pandora Papers"—a document dump detailing the offshore tax avoidance schemes being exploited by various celebrities. Among those music artists named as involved were **Ringo Starr, Shakira** and . . . **Elton John**.

*

In '*Musical Truth Volume 2*', I spent two of the chapters investigating the parallels between the counter-culture/ Hippie scene of the 1960s, and the Acid House/ Rave scene which emerged out of the UK in the late 1980s and paved the way for the worldwide phenomenon of Electronic Dance Music, the Superclubs, and the large-scale dance festivals that followed.

My contention was that both scenes were complex exercises in social-engineering, occurring at the hands of organisations which specialise in shaping culture by skilful and covert means. The latter scene was something of a reboot of the first, and both constituted massive social experiments which were carefully monitored and recorded. Both scenes involved new, renegade styles of music appearing to challenge the popular music styles that had gone before. Both involved the emergence of a drug of choice—LSD and MDMA/ Ecstasy respectively—to go hand in hand with the music and parties. And both involved tapping into the dynamic of young people expressing themselves through social communion and dancing just as their ancestors had done in the ritual and ceremony of ages past. The problem though, was that these factors were on the terms of unseen parties of which the participants had no knowledge, rather than being mutually understood and agreed to by the entire community involved.

According to "official" lore, Ibiza is the spiritual home of modern-day dance music. It went from being a hang-out of choice for the Hippies and Bohemians of the 1960s, to being the breeding ground for the Balearic Beat style of dance music that—again, according to oft-repeated legend—was brought back to the UK by four young adventure-seeking DJs in 1987. There is another location just as finely-tuned to the ceremonial aspect of music and dance, however, and this is the location in which I chose to set the final scene of my novel '*The Cause & The Cure.*' It is the former Portuguese colony of Goa in Southern India. With miles of beaches lined with palm trees, and a tropical climate, Goa had been a stopping point on the same Hippie trail that had included Ibiza. A friend from Australia who had participated in many Goa Full Moon beach parties got in touch to add some detail to my chapters on Acid culture. In his view, the concept of open-air dancing under the stars under altered states of consciousness, was birthed in Goa, before moving on to Ibiza, then London, then the rest of the world.

> *"This, I believe harks right back to our collective ancestral memory. There were certainly Hippies making the scene way before '88. By that time there were full-on, massive, out-of-control Acid Trance parties in full swing—thousands of people from all over the world. To those that went it was known as 'The Season.' The Osho Rajneesh temple in Pune, (just down the road from Goa,) was rumoured to be making MDMA and flooding that Goa scene with it, and Acid was everywhere."*

In the 1990s, a particular style of music specifically geared towards the beach parties had been created. This was known, appropriately enough, as Goa Trance, (what's in a name?,) the best-known purveyor of which was British DJ/ producer **Paul Oakenfold**. His '*Goa Mix*' that aired on BBC Radio 1's '*Essential Mix*' show is considered a landmark showcase of the sound, and his Perfecto record label was responsible for popularising many tracks created in the style during the 90s. Goa Trance proved the inspiration for the newer style now known as Psychedelic, or 'Psy' Trance, popular throughout the world. There's little of any suspect detail to be found in Oakenfold's background, except for his biography stating that during his early years working as a chef he spent a stint at the Army & Navy Club, a private members' club in London's Pall Mall for those in military service.

(Incidentally, I was interested to learn of several of Oakenfold's contemporaries, including the DJ/ producers **Sasha, Jon Digweed** and **BT,** being managed for a time by an agency named 7PM operated by the mogul Seven Webster, one of the funders of which was one Anthony de Rothschild, eldest son of Sir Evelyn of *that* family!)

On the face of it then, thousands dancing open-air under the stars, expressing themselves through dance, and having their states of consciousness elevated, would appear to be something that a Satanic control system would want to stop, rather than encourage. Hordes of young people embracing their primal instincts, rediscovering their divine aspects, and opening themselves up to eternal Truth is a power-hungry psychopathic dominator's worst nightmare. (I was impressed to hear this very concept conveyed so engagingly in the lyrics to producer Cevin Fisher's excellent 'The Message' in early 2020. I recommend a listen to it via the YouTube link listed in the Resources section at the end.) And yet no attempts were made to shut down either the Goa beach parties, or the Ibiza and London scenes they spawned.

That's not, however, the full story of what was really going on with these parties, as my friend pointed out.

> *"It's a perversion of the old original psychedelic ceremony. Yes, the DJ is the Shaman of the current day that guides the dancers through the night. But in reality, a DJ is not a Shaman. I've met and participated in a ceremony with a real Native American Indian Shaman, and the Peyote. It's a totally different ball game.*
>
> *"... After that I knew what psychedelics were really for, and it wasn't what we were doing with them in London, Ibiza or Goa. In fact, we had no elders, no-one to guide us. The first people I tripped with were dodgy gangster types, not highly spiritually advanced Shamans that understood the mysteries of life.*

> *"I think the Powers That Should Not Be know that deep down there is an in-built human need and desire to dance ecstatically and trip under the moon and stars. They know this is a true connection to Nature. But, unless it is done correctly in a ritualised manner, with a guide that actually knows and understands how to guide people through what is a massive psycho-analytical experience, then it can go seriously wrong for a lot of people. Teenagers sniffing so much Ketamine that their bladders have to be removed is not what the psychedelic experience is about. Nor is tripping on mushrooms with your mates in a field. Yes, it's fun, but it's not even 1% close to what they are really all about."*

Where ancient ceremonies would have used plant medicines inherent to Nature to induce the participants' mystical experiences, with the Goa parties, the stimulants were more likely to have been cooked up in a laboratory, the participants having no clue as to their origins. There's also the question of their supply lines. The beach party setting in my novel paints the following picture:

> *"Dancing unconvincingly and doing their best to blend in with the rest, were a small handful of middle-aged CIA and British Military Intelligence agents, in home-made tie-dye T-shirts and combat pants, quietly observing the proceedings from beneath their tinted sunglasses. The other dancers were giving them a wide berth."*

Though this was a work of fiction, given what I've researched about the CIA's involvement in putting LSD into the Flower Power scene, and British Military Intelligence seeding the Acid House and Rave game with Ecstasy, it wouldn't surprise me to learn that this scenario is closer to the truth of the matter than we might have guessed.

(Incidentally, isn't it intriguing that one of the premier brands for dance music parties in the UK during the 1990s was UltraVegas, which held regular events in Milton Keynes... as in MK... as in MK-Ultra? A subtle clue as to the original true nature of corporate-organised dance events for those who know, possibly?)

All social experiments at the hands of society's psychopathic controllers have a cut-off point, it seems—a place where it's considered that all that needed to be studied, observed and learned, has been, and the resources expended in keeping the experiment going indefinitely can no longer be justified. It seems that point may have been crossed when, in early 2020, "justified" by the Co(n)vid "pandemic," nightclubs and dance festivals in many parts of the world were shut down indefinitely, and any creators of new music from that point forward would not have been able to gauge how a crowd would respond to it in a communal experience. Dance music loses all its meaning when dancing has been outlawed by the State.

*

It may not only be the dance music scene that the social controllers are now prepared to trash, after decades of it serving them very well as a vehicle for mind-control. The same might be said for pop music generally in the post-Co(n)vid era. Fewer records were made in 2020 than in any other year since the 1960s, and, post-March, no large-scale gigs, festivals or award shows were available to showcase any new 'stars' — had any emerged in the first place.

*

Three names from the music world were among the pardons and commutations that US President **Donald Trump** granted during the last days of his first term in office. New Orleans-raised rapper and Young Money Entertainment executive **Lil Wayne** received a full pardon. Wayne, real name Dwayne Carter Jr., was facing a federal weapons charge relating to an incident at Miami-Opa Locka Executive Airport in December 2019. The *'Miami Herald'* had reported that a private plane transporting Wayne from California to Florida was also carrying weapons and marijuana, and that federal authorities had been tipped off by Miami-Dade police. Wayne was subsequently charged with possession of a firearm and ammunition by a convicted felon, and faced up to ten years in jail after pleading guilty in December. He had previously been arrested multiple times on drugs and weapons charges. A statement released from the White House following Wayne's pardon quoted support from Deion Sanders, who referred to him as "a provider for his family, a friend to many, a man of faith, a natural giver to the less fortunate, a waymaker, (and) a game changer."

Florida rapper **Kodak Black**, real name Dieuson Octave, was granted a commutation on a prison sentence relating to a 2020 conviction with illegal gun possession. His term was to run concurrently with a further 46-month sentence for falsifying paperwork to buy firearms in Florida on two separate occasions. Trump's intervention saw the rapper released from jail on 20th January 2021. To mark the occasion, he quickly recorded and released a track named *'Last Day In,'* which includes the line "Trump just freed me, but my favourite president is on the money."

The third name from the rap world to receive Trump's clemency was Michael 'Harry-O' Harris, co-founder of Los Angeles' Death Row Records alongside the incarcerated Marion 'Suge' Knight. Harris was released early from a prison spell on attempted murder and drug distribution charges. His original release date was set for 2028, 32 years after the initial conviction. Following the release, rapper **Snoop Dogg**, who was formerly signed to Death Row, Tweeted "Thank u @realdonaldtrump" as he posted a picture of himself alongside Harris, (though by this point Trump had already been deleted from Twitter as well as several other big-tech media platforms.)

Trump was derided several times in lyrics from **Public Enemy**'s *'What You Gonna Do When The Grid Goes Down,'* including the lines: "Whatever it takes, rid this dictator, POTUS my tail, ass debater," and: "White House killer, dead in lifelines, vote this joke out, or die tryin,' unprecedented, demented, many president'd, Nazi Gestapo dictator defended" on *'State of the Union,'* while **Busta Rhymes** rapped: "while Trump is present with a mouth screaming louder than trumpets, while you bow to the puppets, I'm a stand and stick around for the judgement" on the introductory track to his comeback *'Extinction Level Event 2: The Wrath of God'* album.

Despite these rebukes, however, Trump divided opinion within the hip-hop community as much as he did in society in general, and earned supporters as well as detractors from the field. Prior to his pardon, Lil Wayne had already voiced his support for Trump in the 2020 election, causing fellow rapper **50 Cent** to accuse him of getting paid for his endorsement, and claiming that he himself had been offered $500,000 for performing at Trump's inauguration event should he win a second term. More positive support for Trump had come on multiple occasions from **Kanye West**, however. The two met in December 2016 shortly before Trump took office, Trump re-Tweeted many of Kanye's messages, and Kanye hinted that he himself planned to run for President in 2024, inspired by Trump's 2016 win. Trump's connections to the hip-hop world helped diffuse the constant accusations by the mainstream media of his being a racist, though others decried them as a cynical attempt to win black votes.

One more factor links Trump with the rap music world. His property magnate father Fred, (who went by the intriguing middle name of Christ, taken from the maiden name of his wife Elizabeth,) headed up the building of many of the social housing apartment blocks in New York City known as 'the Projects.' These were immortalised on the cover of Nas' classic *'Illmatic'* album and were home to countless rappers who went on to become prominent artists and rhymed about their experiences on track, such as Diamond D's line "niggas gettin shot for a lack of respect, no wonder where we live is called the Projects" on *'No Wundah'*, and "Projects, try to escape the flyin' shells dodgin'" on Wu Tang Clan's *'The Projects.'*

*

In Volume 2 I wrote of the "extra-curricular activities" of many artists who turn out to be "Lifetime Actors." The familiar pattern is that these people are made familiar to the public through an engineered career as a singer, rapper, musician, DJ, record company mogul, or whatever the case may be. Then, at a key point when their household name status has been established, they are seen to support and endorse various 'Globalist" and social-engineering agendas. I've cited Bono as an example of this dynamic on multiple occasions.

A further candidate is Black Eyed Peas frontman and BBC TV's *'The Voice'* judge William Adams, better known by his artist name of **Will.i.am.** When not pushing Transhumanist and Artificial Intelligence themes through his solo and group music, Adams now seems to spend much of his time endorsing the policies of the World Economic Forum. It was the WEF, with major funding from the eugenics-supporting Bill & Melinda Gates Foundation, which proposed its financial 'Great Reset' in the wake of the 2020 "Pandemic."

The WEF hosts a five-day conference each January in the Swiss Alps region of Davos. Like the meetings of similar think-tanks such as the Bilderberg Group, the Council on Foreign Relations and the Trilateral Commission, this sees bankers, business leaders and similar "elite" influencers of society meeting to discuss what society-changing measures they wish to introduce to benefit their own interests and the furtherance of their New World Order agendas.

Will.I.Am, shilling for his masters at the World Economic Forum.

https://www.flickr.com/photos/worldeconomicforum/36501683204

Credit: Ben Hider

Which brings us back to Will.i.am. Among the many roles listed in his official biography is that of "World Economic Forum Fourth Industrial Revolution Advisory Committee and Global Artificial Intelligence Council." He was the winner of the WEF'S Crystal Award for his work in "education and philanthropy" in 2016. Given that the Rothschilds, the Rockefellers and the Clintons all describe themselves as "philanthropists," the true value of identifying with such a term might be called into question. "Foundations" and "Institutes" are something to be wary of also, since it is through organisations billed this way that so many of the elite's malevolent plans are put into action.

Adams has attended WEF meetings at Davos and has been pictured alongside head honcho Klaus Schwab and other WEF high rollers. In a 2017 interview with CNBC about his WEF involvement, in which he commented that "my kids need me to do this," Adams observed of the Davos meetings: "it just so happens that the people who are in the mountain are the 1 per cent. But then there's a lot of folks that are in the mountain that do their part. Bill Gates does his part."

Adams' biography states that he never met his father, about whom little is known, and was raised by his mother, who had two other biological children and adopted four more. They lived in social housing projects in Boyle Heights, described as one of the poorest districts of Los Angeles, so presumably lived on welfare payments. Yet despite this, he was somehow able to attend public schools in affluent West Los Angeles. After meeting future BEP collaborator Allan Pineda (later known as **apl.de.ap**) at John Marshall High School, their rap group Atban Klann was discovered by NWA rapper and businessman Eazy E, who signed them to his Ruthless Records label.

Something has to account for Adams' transformation from fledgling rapper to participant in society-shaping 'Globalist' agendas at a level that only a select few ever reach. (Others to have attended Davos in recent years include **Pharrell Williams, Peter Gabriel** and — try to contain your shock — **Bono**, as well as a host of Hollywood actors.) In Volume 2 I related the many tell-tale, truth-in-plain-sight indicators that .i.am has been heavily mind-controlled. At least part of the key surely lies here.

If there were ever any doubt as to Adams' qualification to be called Shill.i.am due to his agenda-pushing for the cabal, this was cemented fully at the point he became the poster child for a new 'Smart mask.' This featured dual three-speed fans, a mechanical air filter, Bluetooth connectivity, LED day glow lights, noise-cancelling audio and microphone connectivity, and a magnetic earbud docking system. With much of this controlled by radiation-emitting 'Smart' technology in extreme proximity to the brain . . . what could possibly go wrong?

*

In 2011 the '*New York Times*' declared that "no punk band of the 1990s has been more influential than **Blink-182**" in reference to the Poway, California-formed collective so beloved of skater and surfer crowds. Such statements now raise the natural question within me of, "so just what is it about them that allowed them to gain that status?"

In this band's case we don't have to look too far for some clues. It has been noted that founding member **Tom DeLonge** often plays guitars adorned with the square and compass of Freemasonry; the same motif appears on the range of jackets promoting his subsequent band **Angels & Airways**. This has not escaped the attention of the group's fans, and it cropped up during an interview when DeLonge was asked directly if he was a Freemason, to which he laughed nervously before replying, "possibly," then adding, "we just don't talk about that stuff." In the same interview, DeLonge did make reference to his use of arcane symbolism, stating:

> "*Our band's very esoteric. We don't get into a lot of the descriptions and meanings of a lot of the symbology that we use. We let people kind of find out those meanings through the music and through the ethos of the band . . . It's something that we don't really talk about, specifically because the treasure hunt is there for people to find as they get into the band and look into what it is we're trying to do with the music and the films.*

> "*. . . I think the Masonic themes would centre around consciousness and the free-thinking man.*"

In a separate interview in which he attempts to answer 22 questions about himself in two minutes, DeLonge was asked, "who is the most interesting person that you've met recently?" to which, after some thought, he replies, "someone in the government, that I can't say."

Besides Masonic themes, DeLonge's output has long pushed alien and UFO icons and motifs. Virtually the entire output of his second band Angels & Airwaves has artwork depicting Deep Space, astronauts and the NASA-promoted globe earth.

DeLonge took his interest in such themes to extreme lengths when he launched his To The Stars Academy of Arts and Science organisation, described as a "public benefit corporation." In 2017, Luis Elizondo, who had been one of the main executives at the Pentagon's The Advanced Aerospace Threat Identification Program, ostensibly set up to explore the possibility of alien life, was reported to have come to work for DeLonge on his new project. By this point, he was already employing a former CIA contractor named Harold E. Puthoff, and another Defence Department official, Christopher Mellon. It was through the To The Stars project that DeLonge co-authored a 2016 book titled 'Chasing Shadows,' as the first in a series known as 'Sekret Machines.' This purported to be a science-fiction thriller novel that was based on actual events. Of these, DeLonge commented:

> *"After taking over a year to meet, prove myself and acquire eight elite advisors—each of whom has held the highest positions within the military, scientific and executive branch offices—this story contains true information from a secret historical record, some of which has never been heard until now."*

For the 2017 paperback's second edition he called on Jim Semivan, a former member of the CIA's National Clandestine Service, to write the foreword. You know, like you do. Though I know I'll draw the derision of many for saying so, I personally suspect the whole UFO phenomenon to have been a by-product of the CIA's MK-Ultra programme, and for many accounts of sightings and abductions to be one of the mind-control programming templates that is used on subjects.

Perhaps surprisingly, a delve into DeLonge's family background offers no obvious answer as to how he came to be involved in such activities, given that his father worked as an oil industry executive while his mother was a mortgage broker.

Fellow Blink-182 bandmate **Mark Hoppus'** family background does take us into familiar territory, however. Hoppus was born in

Ridgecrest, a city in the Californian desert adjacent to the Naval Air Weapons Station China Lake. His father, like many living in the town, worked for the US Department of Defense, in his case designing missiles and bombs for the Navy testing centre. His grandfather served in the US Marines.

In 2018, The '*NME*' music paper carried the story of a fan asking Hoppus what was the least plausible story about himself that was nonetheless true, and he replied that he had once offered a Navy Admiral advice on how to capture the Iraqi dictator Saddam Hussein. "On an aircraft carrier in the Persian Gulf, I told a Navy Admiral on his way to meet with the Joint Chiefs of Staff my ideas on how to capture Saddam Hussein," Hoppus revealed. Nothing unusual about that, I suppose. I mean, when conducting highly sensitive military missions involving the national security of your country, who else are you going to turn to other than the guitarist in a Pop Punk skater band, right? Sadly the Tweet in which Hoppus revealed the fine detail of his plan has since been removed.

In June 2021, Hoppus revealed that he had been suffering from cancer and undergoing chemotherapy. Someone in his position would surely know about the natural cures that are available for cancer, which avoid the death sentence of Big Pharma treatment.

Perhaps we're now someway closer to understanding why and how it was Blink-182, above and beyond all other contenders, who achieved the level of societal influence that they did.

*

I touched slightly on aspects of **Kate Bush**'s background in the last book when examining the videos to '*Babooshka,*' '*The Man With The Child In His Eyes*' and '*Cloudbusting.*' Given that some further curious delving into her story ticks *so* many of the usual boxes, however, this really does warrant some further scrutiny as to just why Kate became so prominent and influential, and this book would appear to be the appropriate platform through which to do it. As Magnus Magnusson used to say on '*Mastermind,*' "I've started so I'll finish." (And many thanks to my friend Liz in Australia for the extremely thorough research on this subject.)

Although Kate's upbringing and start in the industry are well covered in her biogs, of her father, Robert Bush, we only ever learn that he was a doctor, or a GP—never of the type of work in which he specialised. Given that many of her videos and promotional imagery contain symbolism pertaining to Monarch programming and trauma-based mind-control, however, it's not too much of a stretch to consider that he may have been involved in MK-Ultra-style research. Kate's behaviour in her early videos and stage shows certainly allude to the dissociation and multiple personalities displayed by subjects of such activity.

Kate's mother Hannah, *née* Daly, is listed as a nurse of Irish descent, so both parents have links to the world of medicine. With both of her brothers involved in the field of Folk music, Kate herself is said to have taught herself piano at the age of 11. Some musicologists, however, have noted that her early compositions incorporated elements that go beyond the basic chord progressions of standard rock and pop music. Official lore has it that, at the age of 16, one of her demos serendipitously fell into the hands of **Pink Floyd**'s **David Gilmour**, who was so impressed that he introduced her to EMI and bankrolled studio time for her to record, recruiting assistance from former Beatles producer Geoff Emerick.

By the age of 13 we are told that Kate had already written '*The Man With A Child In His Eyes*,' whose lyrics allude to her being visited by an apparently older man at night as she's about to go to sleep, (she's 13, remember.) It is generally accepted that the song refers to **Steve Blacknell**, said to be Kate's first boyfriend, and he has certainly traded well off this reputation. Interestingly, one of Blacknell's early jobs was working in a mental hospital, and according to biogs this would have been at around the time he is said to have been in a relationship with a pre-pubescent Kate, so here's a potential link back to MK-Ultra. Blacknell went on to become famous himself, first as a record company exec credited with signing **A Flock Of Seagulls**, then as a radio and television presenter including as one of the hosts of the Bob Geldof-helmed '*Live Aid*,' before landing as an MTV presenter in Europe. Upon returning to the UK he founded two of London's most successful media networking ventures, The Network Experience and The Waffle Club. More recently, Blacknell appears to have been pushing Transhumanism through his AutoSpeak concept.

Kate Bush—pure artistic genius . . . or something more sinister?

Attribution 2.0 Generic (CC BY 2.0)

https://commons.wikimedia.org/wiki/File:Kate_Bush_(15312486456).jpg

Credit: Stephen Luff

After reportedly writing around 120 songs between 1973 and 1978, Kate rocketed to prominence upon the release of her debut album *'The Kick Inside,'* (the sleeve to which features half an eye and Kate in a possible mock crucifixion, so we were off to a good start!) and the single *'Wuthering Heights,'* (in which she assumes the identity of a ghost; it's not as if we haven't been given subtle clues as to her fascination with the supernatural and the occult,) which came with two promotional videos. While the interior version featuring her performing in a white ballerina's dress is the best-known, the second version, showing her dancing in a red dress in an outdoor location, has become iconic among fans.

In 2018, Kate's website revealed the exact location to have been an area of land known as Baden's Clump, close to Salisbury Plain. ("To Salisbury" is a lyric that crops up in the song *'Sat In Your Lap.')* This is notable for being close to the mystical site of Stonehenge, as well as

Larkhill military camp, and sure enough, the spot has been revealed to lie on Ministry of Defence-owned land. Military bases often get sited close to areas of mystical significance—a further reminder of the connections between military-intelligence and the world of the occult. (Mind control and paedophilia are often in close proximity too, it turns out.)

Occult themes have permeated Kate's output through the years, and some discernible patterns have emerged. 1980's *'Never for Ever'* had a sleeve design replete with Pagan, Wiccan and Druidic imagery in a collage very reminiscent of what would come later with **Michael Jackson**'s *'Dangerous'* album.

There is much to be seen from her 1993 album *'The Red Shoes,'* the last before she retreated from the public eye for several years. The title itself is an eyebrow-raiser, not only due to its obvious connections to *'The Wizard of Oz,'* consistently cited as a trigger vehicle for mind-controlled subjects, but also given the notion of the ominous 'Red Shoe Club,' (see this book's chapter on Adrenochrome.)

The album's songs include *'Lily.'* As well as possibly referencing Lilith, (the Jewish Kabbalah teaches that the demon Lilith preceded Eve as the first woman and as Adam's first wife, but Lilith managed to disappear from the Garden of Eden,) Lily is also a nickname for Elizabeth, (the Queen being privately nicknamed Lilybet,) and is a known incantation/ritual in witchcraft and Satanic practices. (The official story is that the song was inspired by the late Lily Cornford, Kate's friend and personal healer who, Kate said, "believed in the powers of angels and taught me to see them in a different light".)

The lyrics contain a large part of an incantation known as *'The Lesser Banishing Ritual Of The Pentagram,'* described on Wikipedia as: "A ceremonial magic ritual devised and used by the original Order of the Golden Dawn." The three founders, William Robert Woodman, William Wynn Westcott and Samuel Liddell Mathers, were Freemasons. Aleister Crowley was also a prominent member. The principal components of the Qabalistic Cross and the LBRP are drawn from the works of French occultist Eliphas Levi, the creator of the Hermaphroditic Baphomet archetype.

(Speaking of the Hermetic Order of the Golden Dawn, could Kate have been evoking this fraternity, and the personal evolution that comes through studying its teachings, in her song *'The Dreaming'*, with its line:

> *"Coming in with the golden light,*
> *In the morning.*
> *Coming in with the golden light,*
> *Is the new man."*

A sequence for *'Lily'* is featured in Kate's short film *'The Line, The Cross and The Curve,'* and is laden with dark imagery which many would find unsettling. The imagery hints very strongly at Satanic Ritual Abuse, with mime artist Lindsay Kemp, (an early mentor of David Bowie,) appearing to play the part of Kate's cruel and psychotic handler, with tried-and-trusted mind-control motifs ever-present. The video also features a witch-like woman played by Miranda Richardson — see the story elsewhere within *'Sound Bites'* concerning Gary Numan!

Kate's aforementioned song *'Sat In Your Lap'* hints at an initiate to an occult mystery school seeking to obtain advanced knowledge, but finding that the process is a struggle and is the preserve of only a select few. We appear to be getting an insight into the concepts of Satanic inversion and Orwellian doublespeak, too, with the line:

> *"Some say that Heaven is Hell,*
> *Some say that Hell is Heaven."*

Then, the following line appears to represent a mockery of those who think they can achieve high status and top- level employment without having first obtained secret-societal knowledge through association. Could we be getting clues as to some of Kate's own fraternal connections, truth-in-plain-sight style, as a result of her family background?

> *"I want to be a lawyer, I want to be a scholar.*
> *But I really can't be bothered.*
> *Ooh, just gimme it quick, gimme it, gimme, gimme, gimme, gimme!"*

The song ends with talk of her coming "up the ladder." (See this book's final chapter about the Internal Alchemical Process, and how this appears to have been encoded into the lyrics of many rock songs through the decades.)

Similar themes appeared to be conveyed in the song '*Them Heavy People*' from Kate's debut album '*The Kick Inside*,' with several lines speaking of the process of humans reconnecting with their divine nature while in bodily form, like:

"Every one of us has a heaven inside."
"They open doorways that I thought were shut for good."
"We humans got it all, we perform the miracles."

We also appear to be back to the dissociation caused by lifelong trauma-based mind-control, however, and the thin line between torture and ecstasy, with lines like:

"I was hiding in a room in my mind."
"They build up my body, break me emotionally.
It's nearly killing me, but what a lovely feeling."

Shall we go stranger? In the video for '*Suspended In Gaffa*,' Kate is dressed in what appears to be medieval fencing attire and is in a barn, with chains prominently shown. (SRA victim Jeanette Archer has spoken of being suspended in a barn in Surrey, England.) Not for the first time Kate is caught doing the 666 symbolism and hiding one eye. As the video proceeds, she assumes a vaguely foetal position, sucking her thumb. The lyrics go: "I caught a glimpse of a God, all shining and bright." (SRA victims including Fiona Barnett in Australia have spoken of Jesus appearing in their dissociative state in moments of abuse.) Having evoked her childhood, Kate ends up being comforted by her real mother, Hannah, who makes a rare cameo appearance.

Whatever else the themes in Kate's songs are, they're never boring, and she certainly pushes the envelope. As is the case with '*Experiment IV*,' which hints at inside knowledge of military-grade sonic weaponry as she sings of a secret government experiment to use sound and music to cause great harm:

"We were working secretly for the military.
Our experiment in sound was nearly ready to begin.
We only know in theory what we are doing.
Music made for pleasure, music made to thrill."

The video, directed by Kate, was filmed in a former military hospital near Blackheath reportedly designed by Florence Nightingale, and was banned from *'Top of the Pops'* on its 1986 release due to its being considered too intense for a mainstream peak-time audience.

We also have *'Breathing,'* a song written from the point of view of a reincarnated embryo singing from the womb about its fear of entering an outside world ravaged by nuclear war.

'Agadoo' it is not.

As mentioned in the previous book, the short film for *'Cloudbusting,'* devised partly by Monty Python's Terry Gilliam, charts the work of Wilhelm Reich, the use of the orgone technology he developed for cloud-seeding and weather manipulation, and the theft of his work by shady government agents.

'Deeper Understanding' appears to be a prophetic exposé of the perils of technology advancement and the isolation and interference to normal humanity that it can cause when overused. Some key lyrics include:

"As the people here grow colder,
I turn to my computer,
And spend my evenings with it.
Like a friend.
Well, I've never felt such pleasure.
Nothing else seemed to matter.
I neglected my bodily needs.
I did not eat, I did not sleep."

Sounds like me daughters with their phones.

Kate is known for being technically competent, having overseen the production of much of her music. This appears to have entertained her penchant for backmasking. When once asked her favourite song, she replied it was **John Lennon**'s *'Number 9 Dream'* and that she particularly liked the backwards vocals in it. She once remarked: "By the time I do the videos I know the songs so well, I know them inside out and even backwards sometimes."

This cannot fail to bring to mind, (for me, at least!) the arcane teachings of Aleister Crowley and what he referred to as "the Law of Reversal." In his book *'Magick'* he wrote:

> *"Let the adept . . . train himself to think backwards by external means, as set forth here following.*
>
> *a. Let him learn to write backwards . . .*
> *b. Let him learn to walk backwards . . .*
> *c. Let him . . . listen to phonograph records reversed . . .*
> *d. Let him practise speaking backwards . . .*
> *e. Let him learn to read backwards . . ."*

One very dedicated member on the fan site gaffa.org has observed:

> *"On 'The Dreaming' there is a two-way message that is sung at the end of 'Leave It Open.' When you play it forwards it sings, 'We let the weirdness in,' and when you play it backwards it sings 'and they said they would not let me in'."*

In 2014, two years after she had been made Commander of The British Empire (CBE) by the Queen for services rendered, (well, we've all been there,) Kate performed a much-lauded series of comeback concerts at Hammersmith Apollo, her first live shows since 1979. Among the interesting symbolism at this one were guitarists kitted out in bird masks of the type worn by doctors during the Bubonic Plague. As in a "pandemic." Hmmmm . . . .

Some of Kate's close affiliations become interesting to consider too. She appears to have been close to many of the 'alternative' comedians who emerged in the early 1980s, with Dawn French, Tim McInnerny, Hugh Lawrie and Robbie Coltrane having featured in her videos, and a stage performance alongside Rowan Atkinson in 1986's Comic Relief concert. She was rumoured to be romantically linked to **Peter Gabriel**, with whom she duetted on 1986's *'Don't Give Up.'* Gabriel emanates from an important bloodline with links to the *Ordo Tempi Orientis* (OTO) secret-society.

As was **Rolf Harris,** with whom Kate associated on two of her albums. Harris played didgeridoo on the title track of 1982's *'The Dreaming,'* and was invited back to add vocals to the conceptual side of Kate's 2005 album *'Aeriel.'* Harris was commissioned to paint a portrait of the same Queen who knighted both he and Bush, (all pals together?) before going on to be convicted and jailed on paedophilia charges. By the time of *'Aeriel's* 2018 digital re-mastering, Harris' vocals had been removed from the new recording.

The subject of paedophilia has also crept into Kate's lyrics—albeit with plausible deniability attached. Her song *'The Infant Kiss'* is said to have been inspired by the Gothic horror movie *'The Innocents,'* itself adapted from the Henry James novel *'The Turn of the Screw.'* The story concerns a governess who believes the spirit of her dead lover is trying to reach her through the children she looks after. Hence the lyrics:

"I say good night-night.
I tuck him in tight.
But things are not right.
What is this? An infant kiss,
That sends my body tingling?
I've never fallen for,
A little boy before.
No control."

Throughout her long career Kate has been consistently referred to as "an original one-off," her bizarre, other-worldly, and often unsettling mannerisms during her performances being put down to her merely being "eccentric." But should there be cause for concern here, and should it be considered a conflict of interests that an artist having been awarded a very high-ranking honour by the British Establishment has also made songs demonstrating apparent inside knowledge of that very same Establishment developing secret technology to do harm to its own people?

Is there enough here to be able to reasonably conclude that Kate emanates from a family background with inside knowledge of hidden "elite" technology, including trauma-based mind-control, that she has revealed many of these secrets through her music in line with the concept of Revelation of the Method? And that—notwithstanding her obvious extreme talent—her entire career was facilitated for this purpose?

*

In light of his connections into the CIA via his father, the career Agency operative Miles Copeland, I found it interesting to learn that **Stewart Copeland** of **The Police** used to entertain an alter-ego named **Klark Kent**, under which he would perform solo material. Copeland himself posted a video to his Instagram, the opening text to which read:

> *"In 1978, Stewart Copeland recorded his song 'Don't Care' under the pseudonym Klark Kent in order to not detract from the burgeoning career of his band The Police. Three singles and an album followed."*

Given the CIA's track record in mind-control programming through its now well-documented MK-Ultra project, and the fact that the off-spring of many intel personnel are often inducted into such experiments, I found the following text from the video intriguing:

> *"In some interviews, Copeland's responses to questions about Kent described him as a friend whom he had assisted. In others, Copeland spoke entirely in character, inventing numerous provocatively fanciful back stories."*

Copeland also said the following about the process of getting into the Klark Kent alter:

> *"The kinetic ritual involved in putting myself in a condition whereby I can perform, it takes several days of incantations and rituals and sex to build up the right emotional steam ... "*

A tenet of Monarch programming, a sub-project of MK-Ultra, involves the creation of 'alters' or alternative personalities within the subject's mind. Given that other prominent artists such as **Mariah Carey, Britney Spears** and **Nicki Minaj** have gone "into character" during interviews, could 'Klark Kent', (the '*Superman*' movie featuring the hero's own alter-ego of Clark Kent was doing the rounds in 1978) be an invention of Stewart Copeland's mind as a result of his own programming?

*

On the face of it, there ought to be no connection whatsoever between an Aristocrat with family connections into the British Royals and the Russian Czars, and rumoured to be one of the most powerful people within the whole "Illuminati" power structure, and the corporate music industry. Oughtn't there?? And yet, a deep dive into the background of one deeply mysterious and notorious figure reveals links to two of the most prominent bands of the early 1970s.

Perhaps surprisingly for someone of such alleged influence, Elizabeth Somerset Feodorovna Bowes-Lyon Belenoff—otherwise known as the Countess of Banbury and Arran, or more simply, Somerset Belenoff—does not have a Wikipedia profile, and has maintained such mythical status, rather similar to that of the Keyser Sozay character in the movie '*The Usual Suspects*,' that it has caused some to question whether she actually exists.

According to what information is available on her she was born in 1953—on the significant Beltane date of 1st May—at Glamis Castle in Scotland, the ancestral home of the Queen Mother. She is said to be a great, great, great grand-daughter of Queen Victoria through Victoria's grand-daughter, Princess Elizabeth of Hesse, Grand Duchess of Russia. This makes her a third cousin of Queen Elizabeth II. Some historians believe the Grand Duchess had an affair with Grigori Rasputin, known as the "Mad Monk" (and subject of **Boney M**'s 1978 hit '*Rasputin,*') the mystic who became part of the inner circle of Russia's Czar Nicholas. Synchro-mystically, Boney M's charismatic dancer, **Bobby Farrell**, died in St. Petersburg in 2010, as had Rasputin, whom Farrell portrayed in performances, almost 100 years earlier.)

Belenoff's reputation for dark occultism earned her the nickname "The Witch of Glamis Castle." Singer and Rolling Stones mistress **Marianne Faithfull** once commented that Belenoff was the most beautiful woman she had ever seen, but that she possessed a most terrifying beauty.

According to the website whoissomersetbelenoff.com, the so-called Illuminati Queen:

> "...*chairs the World Governing Council and is the Chief Executive Officer of the World Security Office, which is the prosecutorial and enforcement arm of the House of Wettin's Upper Chamber. This is the powerful cabal which controls all of the elite Illuminati groups familiar to researchers.*"

She is said to out-rank the British Royal Family and is the only person able to turn up at Buckingham Palace unannounced and be granted an immediate audience. The site maintains that Russian leader Vladimir Putin once described her as both the most beautiful woman and the most terrifying person he had ever met.

As well as reportedly owning half of the nation of Suriname, Belenoff was also reported to be the owner of Bohemian Grove, the redwood forest in Northern California which acts as the annual meeting ground for the rich and powerful "elites" of the world, and which hosts a ritual known as The Cremation of Care. In January 2021, the glamiscalling.org website claimed to have disposed of its interests in the site under the headline "Bohemian Grove Divestiture," stating: "As of January 20, 2021, Belenoff-Glamis Group, International and Rosebel Industries have sold all interest in the Monte Rio property."

Somerset Belenoff's connections to the music industry begin with the claims of the late Peter Grant, once the manager of **Led Zeppelin**, that the group's most famous song, 'Stairway to Heaven', was in part inspired by her. Within London's music and art crowd of the 1960s with whom she fraternised, she became known as "The May Queen." She is said to be "the lady who's sure all that glitters is gold and she's buying a stairway to heaven" of the ambiguous song. She also maintains an apparent fascination with the Pied Piper of Hamelin, the 700-year-old German fable of a mysterious figure who lured all the children of a town away from their parents with his enchanting music. In the blog that she seemingly maintains on the site www.glamiscalling.com, Belenoff pays tribute to the story each 26th June, leading many to question the nature of her interest in it. Either way, the Led Zeppelin lyrics "and it's whispered that soon if we all call the tune then the piper will lead us to reason," and "the piper's calling you to join him" are thought to be a reference to the legend.

Belenoff reportedly struck up a friendship with Led Zeppelin guitarist **Jimmy Page**, and the two shared common ground through their fascination with the occult. Belenoff was none too impressed with Page's admiration for Aleister Crowley, however, describing Crowley's Order of the Golden Dawn as "the pathetic order of the golden yawn," and "the order of the golden shower," and considering Crowley himself to have been an incompetent amateur. According to comments given to the '*Melody Maker*' music paper by Peter Grant, the pair would often try to "out-occult" each-other with their adeptness. Grant recounted the following story of an event in 1969:

> "*Well, I knew the Countess when she was 16 years old, before she was a Countess and before the whole Wettin, World Governing Council stuff. She was one of the beautiful young people who orbited the rock and roll scene back in the '60s, and we were a pretty rough lot . . .*

> "*One day we all went up to Hampstead where some of Jimmy's Golden Dawn associates had a big old spooky house . . . Well, we get there and there's this intense feeling of dread and darkness, like pure evil in the house, and it didn't seem right to bring a young girl to such a place . . . Now, these old guys were like real old-school evil sorcerers and straight away they start moving their hands around in the air and you can see Lilibet's (Grant's name for Belenoff) chair start to shake . . . Then one of the guys starts making gestures with his right hand like in a choking motion and pointing it toward Lilibet's throat, and you can see it's having an effect on her.*

> "*So Jimmy and I both decide to get up from our chairs and end this, but we can't move! We can't stand up and we can't even move our*

hands! At first when they did this, you can see Lilibet's face and she has a shocked look, but then she relaxes and she gets a smile on her face, like, 'ah, she's regained control' and at the same time the old sorcerer geezers are getting more agitated and gesturing more intensely.

". . . The other thing everyone notices is it's starting to feel really fucking cold in the house. Now you have to remember, it's the middle of July and it's one of those hot muggy London nights, but now all of a sudden it's getting really, really cold . . . Then Lilibet gets a look of complete satisfaction on her face and she stands up and throws her arms into the air and at that very moment, everything made of glass explodes . . . Then two other things happened at the same time. The room became warm again immediately after everything shattered or exploded, and at the same moment, the radio in the corner of the room came on and started playing that song by The Lovin' Spoonful, 'Do you believe in magic, in a young girl's heart . . . ' Then Lilibet does a little spin and a bow with this innocent smile and as she leans down over the old sorcerer with the shattered hand and the one with the shattered glass eye she says, "That, gentlemen, is the way we do it up at Glamis!"

Belenoff's connections with the music world didn't end with Zeppelin, however. She is also reported to have had an on-off relationship with **T-Rex** frontman **Marc Bolan,** and is said to have inspired his song '*Children of the Revolution*' as she once headed an organisation of that name. It may or may not be coincidental that Bolan's March 1971 '*Top of the Pops*' appearance is often cited as the beginning of the Glam Rock movement, and that it bears some similarity in name to Belenoff's Glamis Castle.

These were far from the only times that members of the Aristocracy had links to prominent musicians, either. As I detailed in Volume 1, jazz artist **Thelonious Monk** was in a relationship with an heiress of the Rothschild banking dynasty, Pannonica Rothschild, known socially as "Nica." There was also the unlikely romance between the enigmatic New Orleans rapper **Jay Electronica** and another banking Rothschild heiress, Kate Rothschild.

Resources:

Peter Green: The Munich LSD Party Incident:

- https://www.channelnonfiction.com/
  peter-green-the-munich-lsd-party-incident-7-minutes-2009/

Daily Mail: Psychosis, sex cults, suicide and the curse of Fleetwood Mac guitarists:

- https://www.dailymail.co.uk/news/article-2157409/Psychosis-
  sex-cults-suicide-curse-Fleetwood-Mac-guitarists.html

Kate Bush Encyclopaedia; 'Experiment IV' video:

- https://www.katebushencyclopedia.com/experiment-iv

Kate Bush and her family:

- https://www.youtube.com/watch?v=wZAVsH8Hkag

Kate Bush News: Exact location of 1978 "red dress" Wuthering Heights video revealed!:

- https://www.katebushnews.com/2018/09/06/exact-location-of-
  1978-red-dress-wuthering-heights-video-revealed/

Stewart Copeland: An attempt to explain Klark Kent:

- https://www.instagram.com/tv/B_5HJrFHb_u/?igshid=wpux6g-
  wrknh7&fbclid=IwAR3gpEvDl3awZi700c156VTYVLf3mPVP-
  CPhsTUC1O3xRmncrMNGQREKAzZQ

The Police: Censored in Their Prime?:

- https://itcamefromblog.com/2017/07/06/
  the-police-censored-in-their-prime/

Strontium 90:

- https://en.wikipedia.org/wiki/Strontium_90_(band)

The Quietus: No Borders, No Boundaries: Eugene Robinson On His Favourite Albums:

- https://thequietus.com/articles/25871-eugene-robinson-interview-bakers-dozen-favourite-albums-oxbow-ozy-confidential?page=5

Beatles London Footage Sites, with Commentary:

- https://www.youtube.com/watch?v=9fOPV55eZP0&t=37s

Reddit: Could Elton John's hit "Goodbye Yellow Brick Road" be about Monarch mind control?:

- https://www.reddit.com/r/C_S_T/comments/6bagtu/could_elton_johns_hit_goodbye_yellow_brick_road/

Rolling Stone: Elton John, Ringo Starr, Shakira Named in Pandora Papers Leak Exposing Offshore Financial Dealings:

- https://www.rollingstone.com/music/music-news/elton-john-ringo-starr-shakira-pandora-papers-tax-haven-allegations-leak-1236421/?fbclid=IwAR2qTm9KJpJIsC6wsr1YzEOCqoqMvhCFOIT1dt5nurSsQz5M4GAfWmVxetc

Cevin Fisher: 'The Message' (Dirty Secretz Mix):

- https://www.youtube.com/watch?v=Blh8QW3Ailo

50 Cent says he's "sure" that Lil Wayne was paid to support Donald Trump before election:

- https://www.nme.com/news/music/50-cent-says-hes-sure-that-lil-wayne-was-paid-to-support-donald-trump-before-election-2819447

Will.i.am at the World Economic Forum:

- https://www.weforum.org/people/william-adams

Rolling Stone magazine: Blink-182: The Half-Naked Truth:

- https://www.rollingstone.com/music/music-news/
  blink-182-the-half-naked-truth-87106/

Tom DeLonge reveals he is a Freemason:

- https://www.youtube.com/watch?v=hF1UHDPh4Io&fea-
  ture=youtu.be

Hoppus On Music: Tom Delonge Is A Conspiracy Theorist:

- https://www.youtube.com/watch?v=ldStlifP-Ug

NME: Blink 182's Mark Hoppus once advised the US military of an ingenious plan he had to capture Saddam Hussein:

- https://www.nme.com/news/music/mark-hoppus-ad-
  vised-us-military-ingenious-plan-capture-saddam-hus-
  sein-2347322#:~:text=Blink%20182's%20Marrk%20
  Hoppus,and%20remove%20him%20from%20power.

Former head of the Pentagon's secret UFO program now works for Tom DeLonge:

- https://consequenceofsound.net/2017/12/former-head-of-the-
  pentagons-secret-ufo-program-now-works-for-tom-delonge/

Somerset Belenoff. "the Illuminati Queen":

- whoissomersetbelenoff.com

CHAPTER 3

ALL ASSETS DEPLOYED

The "coronavirus" Scamdemic offered a valuable opportunity to assess which musicians were still in the pocket of the controllers, and which ones still had a voice to call their own. Genocide is genocide. Whether pushed by doctors, politicians, news presenters or "celebrities," the crime is still the same.

> "*Those who are conscientious objectors to vaccination should, of course, have the courage to face all penalties or persecutions to which they may be subjected by law, and stand alone, if need be, against the whole world, in defence of their conviction.*"
>
> Mahatma Gandhi, Chapter IV, 'A Guide To Health by Mahatma Gandhi,' 1921.

> "*World events do not occur by accident. They are made to happen, whether it is to do with national issues or commerce; and most of them are staged and managed by those who hold the purse strings.*"
>
> Denis Healey, British MP, Fabian Society member, and co-founder of the Bilderberg Group.

> "*It is difficult to get a man to understand something, when his salary depends on his not understanding it.*"
>
> Novelist/ journalist Upton Sinclair.

> "*You brought me fame and fortune and everything that goes with it,*
>
> *I thank you all.*"
>
> Queen: 'We Are The Champions.'

In desperate times such as those of 2021/ 21, the true value of any artist lies not in their regular creative output, but in how responsibly they use the public platform that they are privileged enough to have. Using their vast reach and influence to communicate Truth becomes more important than anything else, and infinitely more important than staying silent for fear of what career repercussions might be brought by them going against the grain.

Natural Rights and Freedoms trump all else in the realm of human activity. Career paths can be worried about further down the road once freedom is won back—not before. And in an era where the imposition of Chinese-style Communism has outlawed all joy, fun, leisure, social opportunities and artistic creativity, there's little else left to lose. As **M1**, frontman of the conscious hip-hop act **Dead Prez** commented to me when I interviewed him back in 2011: "If, as an artist, you are not able to talk about (important things,) I'd like to pose this question: are you *really* an artist?"

Shills, shits and charlatans

> THE CELEBRITIES THAT HAVE PUSHED THIS NARRATIVE, OR HAVE STOOD SILENT ON THE SIDE LINES, WILL NEVER BE FORGIVEN BY THE PEOPLE WHEN ALL THE TRUTH COMES OUT.

Genocide is genocide. Whether pushed by doctors, politicians, news present-ers or "celebrities," the crime is still the same.

Society is entrained to think of musicians as, at the very least, creative, impulsive types who shun convention and pursue a path through life more thrilling than most. According to the genre in which they operate, many are also considered free-thinking mavericks who are distinctly anti-Establishment, and who actively go against the grain of Organised Society. It has long been this way with "artists" of all types, whether writers, poets, painters, actors. Indeed, the ostensibly subversive output of the "Beat Poets" of the 1950s was consistently cited as a major influence on the key purveyors of the counter-culture scene of the 1960s, and later on the Punk and New Wave explosion of the late 1970s.

As the research of recent years has shown, however, so many of those presented to us in this way turn out to be wholly owned assets of the very control system they are claimed to oppose. A standard social-engineering tactic employed endlessly through the decades, has been to create household names and A-list "celebrities" and then serve them up as ready-made influencers and role models to the public. Many are what author and researcher Joseph Atwill has branded "Lifetime Actors," a concept that was discussed at length in '*Musical Truth 2.*' In many cases, these are individuals born into what are deemed to be important bloodline families. (A revealing nod to the contempt with which bloodline "elites" view their "lessers" came from the Harry Potter film series, in which those in the wizard school who don't hail from long-running occult families are referred to, disparagingly, as "mud-bloods.")

Successive generations of these families are put to use in various prominent roles in society. The professions often differ from generation to generation, but what the roles employed all have in common is that they have a strong influence on large numbers of people—particularly in conditioning them in their thoughts, perceptions and behaviours. The one-time nanny of Boris Johnson's family, for instance, has said that when he was young his parents would repeatedly tell him that he would one day be British Prime Minister. It was announced as fact, as if there was never any doubt it would happen. (The Johnson family name is actually El Kemal, as Boris' grandfather hailed from the Ottoman Empire in Turkey. The family name was changed to Johnson to sound less Turkish and more British, though Boris was still saddled with De Pfeffel as one of his middle names due to his genealogical links through his great-grandmother to an Aristocratic bloodline coming from Bavaria, the same region of Germany that spawned Adam Weishaupt's original Bavarian Illuminati, and the family of "Globalist" kingpin Henry Kissinger.)

Just as I was writing this chapter an e-mail arrived revealing that the actress Scarlett Johansson is a bloodline descendant of Nadezhda Krupskaya, the wife of Russian leader Vladimir Lenin. This put me in mind of the revelation that John Wilkes Booth, the man said to have assassinated US President Abraham Lincoln, *just happened* an ancestor of Cherie Booth, the wife ("beard") of UK Prime Minister (and so much more) Tony Blair.

The connections never end. Ghislaine Maxwell, for instance, daughter of murdered Mossad spy Robert Maxwell and mistress to prolific child sex trafficker Jeffrey Epstein, turns out to be a cousin of psychopathic-eugenicist-masquerading-as-nerdy-computer-boffin Bill Gates through his mother's line. (Gates was a visitor to Epstein's private Caribbean island, where the rape of many children is known to have taken place, on several occasions *after* Epstein's affairs had been publicly exposed. Why has he not been investigated by police?)

British Prime Ministers David Cameron and Boris Johnson are not only distant cousins of each other, but in turn are also distant cousins of Queen Elizabeth II. (Thank God we live in a "democracy" and a "free country" where we get to "choose" our leaders, eh? Imagine if we lived in a dictatorship where we had no choice in the matter and they were just merely served up to us? Nightmare!) And should we really have been too surprised to learn that Marc Randolph, the co-founder and first CEO of Netflix, *just happens* to be a great-nephew of Edward Bernays? So one generation of an important bloodline is credited with having invented the subtle art of mind-control through public relations, while another sows further societal mind-control through movies and television.

Tom Hanks, whose name cropped up endlessly within the realms of "alternative" research in 2020 and beyond — and in some very unsavoury contexts — has been identified by genealogists as having a dumbfounding array of famous connections in his extended family tree. One way or another he is said to be related to US Presidents George Washington, Abraham Lincoln and both George Bushes, as well as actors Steve McQueen, George Clooney, (also a prominent member of the Council on Foreign Relations,) and Benedict Cumberbatch, (who is related to mathematician Alan Turing whom he himself portrayed in the film '*Enigma,*) William the Conqueror, both Queen Elizabeths and General Patton. And not only did Hanks portray Walt Disney in '*Saving Mr. Banks*', but he's also a distant cousin of Walt himself. Can anyone *really* still believe that actors achieve success and prominence purely through skill and talent?

And somehow, those of us who followed the "Q Plan" with its implications that Donald Trump was all set to bring down the Deep State cabal from the inside during his single term as US President, have some cognitive dissonance to grapple with from the news, as reported by MyHertage.com that, although pitted as her "rival" and bitter enemy, Trump is actually related to Hillary Rodham Clinton. Both are direct descendants of the 14th century first Duke of Lancaster John of Gaunt, and his wife Katherine Swynford. (Unexpectedly, Trump is also second cousin twice removed of Henry John Heinz of Heinz baked beans fame.) Is nothing sacred and is no-one to be trusted? It seems so. As David Icke is fond of saying; "it's all bollocks . . . yes, *all* of it!" But as the researcher Jan Irvin has also said: "it's much easier to spend a few hours or days or weeks researching facts, than it is to spend a lifetime believing lies."

Steering back around to music, another good example of the bloodline dynamic would be the Hewson family. Researcher Johnny Vedmore, writing in an article for the Swamp website, has traced this bloodline back to one Johannes Hewetson, or John Hewson, a merchant and landowner in Yorkshire, England in 1498, during the reign of King Henry VII. His successor, Thomas Hewson, decided to relocate the family to Ireland in the 1570s, and so began a long succession of generations that worked their way into Irish nobility and high society. A present-day descendent of this particular bloodline is one **Paul David Hewson KBE OL**, born in 1960 and better known to the world as **Bono**, the singer with **U2**, (though he seems to have spent far more of his time hobnobbing with various world leaders and prominent "elite" figures and propping up various social-engineering ventures in recent years than doing any gigging. Little wonder, what with his One Foundation having close ties to psychopathic Globalists Bill Gates and George Soros.

I can't stop thinking of a pet dog whenever I hear the name Bono, and I wonder if that's how his higher-ups see him as they send him out on various missions of their choosing?

Was it really down to chance and good luck that Bono became an internationally-recognised rock star turned friend to the world's political elite? Or is it ENTIRELY down to the family that he comes from?

https://commons.wikimedia.org/wiki/File:Bono_-_World_Economic_Forum_Annual_Meeting_2011.jpg

Flickr: Bono — World Economic Forum Annual Meeting 2011

Author: World Economic Forum

It was never a question of chance as to whether Bono would become successful and well-known. It was seen to by those parties who can make such things happen that his career would be extremely high-profile. Once he had established a strong degree of familiarity with the public — and more important, an adoring fanbase who had come to revere and trust him — then his *real* work could begin. We have seen this dynamic play out so many times over the decades, and it becomes easy to spot a key player, or Lifetime Actor, simply by keeping an eye on their extra-curricular activities. Sometimes it can take years, or even decades of cover, before a candidate's true role becomes apparent. (It can be this way in regular life too, as I've discovered for myself. I now realise that the reason I incarnated into this reality at the point in the timeline when I did, was so that I could be participating in these times, doing the type of work I'm doing right now. But it took me until the age of 40, following two decades of DJing and being convinced that music and parties held the key to life's meaning, before the penny dropped.)

These extra-curricular activities tell us so much about just why they were made to become famous over all other candidates who, in many cases, may have demonstrated much more skill and natural talent for the job in hand. Somehow, despite being an Irishman, Bono earned himself a KBE—a Most Excellent Order of the British Empire. His fellow countryman **Bob Geldof** achieved the same feat.

In an entirely different sphere of activity, meanwhile, we find Barbara Hewson, another 21st century representative of the same bloodline but who, in her case, was put to use as a barrister and "human rights campaigner" with a practice in public law. She turns out to be a cousin of Bono and has been no less influential in her own area of activity. She has courted controversy through her outspoken views supporting abortion, the removal of anonymity on sexual abuse cases, and has campaigned for the age of consent for sexual activity to be lowered to 13. In a 2013 blog post, she called the Operation Yewtree investigation into historic sex offences "a far graver threat to society than anything Jimmy Savile ever did." She was suspended from the Bar for two years in December 2019 after posting a series of what were deemed "obscene" and "abusive" comments towards a fellow barrister on social media.

Through these two roles, the Hewson bloodline has ensured it influences the narrative in many aspects of society. In each case, it is the "elite" control system's bidding that gets done.

In 1998, the Irish 'Independent' newspaper carried the story that Maurice and Pamela Hewson—Barbara's grandparents—had died in a house fire at their home in County Limerick, thought to have originated from an oven. It was reported that Maurice had been a magistrate in West Africa, while Pamela had been the daughter of a former Lord Lieutenant for Warwickshire, England. The newspaper headline read "Garda probe after Bono relatives die in house fire."

Barbara Hewson herself died on 9th January 2021 aged 59, of cancer. Her dying wish is said to have been her reinstatement to her former profession, which was granted by the Irish High Court by halving her suspension term. Oddly, none of the published obituaries made mention of her relationship to Bono, which might have been considered of public interest.

The more I research the industry for these books, the more I feel confident in making the statement that *anyone* who has achieved a level of fame and influence to the point that they've become a household name, is controlled and has had their career facilitated for them. I do feel that in some cases, artists may be left relatively free to express themselves as they wish, (so long as they don't cross certain boundaries,) but they're always there to be called upon if their services are needed to help prop up some social engineering agenda or other, (such as, oh, I don't know, peddling the lie that there's a deadly "virus" running rampant and decimating the entire world after a bloke ate a bat in a wet market in China, that kind of thing.)

Where are all the rebels?

When it comes to certain high-profile musicians, we can often glean much from what they *don't* say in a particular instance, rather than what they do. A handful of names come to mind for me when it comes to those generally thought of as being "political activists" or at least, very outspoken in their views.

One would be **Paul Weller**, whose songs have included **The Style Council**'s critique of class inequality on '*The Whole Point of No Return*,' and the devastating indictment of military order-followers on '*Savages*.' While he did comment to the '*NME*' on the "Pandemic" in Summer 2020, he clearly accepted that it was real, and merely reinforced the narrative by putting a positive slant on its effects on society. "We've seen new working methods," he told the paper, "spent more time with our families, seen how nature can repair itself without us being around. I kind of hope we *don't* go back to normal."

As an e-mail correspondent commented to me at the time:

> "*Paul Weller is, for people of my age, an absolute hero. He taught me more than any bullshit system indoctrination was ever going to during my school years. But when we need him to speak up at the*

81

most vital time in the history of mankind he is silent. He could sway so many of the brain-fogged masses it would be a revolution."

Rather than expose the agenda, Weller opted instead to guest on Jonathan Ross' TV chat show, reinforcing the nonsense of elbow-bumping and (anti) social-distancing, but not having a problem with leaving the house to promote his latest "lockdown" album.

That's entertainment!

Weller was a founder member of the musical collective known as **Red Wedge** in the mid-1980s, taking its name from a poster titled '*Beat the Whites With the Red Wedge*' by Russian artist El Lissitzky, dating to the time of that country's Revolution. The main figurehead for the outfit was **Billy Bragg**, a proud Leftist, and always portrayed as something of a Working Class Hero who was particularly critical of Margaret Thatcher's Conservative regime. Like Weller, Bragg indicated his acceptance that the "virus" narrative was real when he opined to the '*NME*' that the cancellation of the Glastonbury Festival for the second year in 2021 was "a bit of a shock," and expressed his hope that music festivals could return "once this ends."

All hope for Bragg had been lost by the following Summer when he revealed himself to be less of a "rebel" and more of a cowardly virtue-signalling Statist, either shilling for the government, or woefully naïve for a man of his supposed values. Posting on his Facebook page he commented:

> *"As someone who has been double-jabbed with the AZ vaccine, I'm aware that I may not be as vulnerable to the virus as I was last year. However, I'm still able to catch Covid and infect others. I really don't want to take that risk, so I'll continue to wear my mask in shops and other enclosed spaces, to protect myself and those around me."*

I have to hand it to the replier on Facebook who came with the wonderful retort:

> *"Yuck. What a virtue-signalling creep and faux man of the people. Every one of you sell-outs will pay a great price spiritually for acting as pied-pipers to humanity's demise."*

I couldn't agree more.

What of **John Lydon**, aka **Johnny Rotten**? Surely that snarling contempt for authority that he displayed during the **Sex Pistols** years would have been channelled into a critical stance against the tyranny of government lockdowns? Apparently not. A few years on from making TV commercials for *'Country Life'* butter, the only controversial thing Lydon appeared to do during 2020 was to publicly endorse Donald Trump.

And not forgetting the poster boy for the civil rights movement and the most high-profile purveyor of the political protest song in the 1960s, **Bob Dylan**. Dylan remains musically active all these decades on, and demonstrated his propensity for controversial subject matter as recently as 2020 with the 17-minute epic *'Murder Most Foul'* from his album *'Rough and Rowdy Ways.'* This revisited the John F. Kennedy assassination of 1963, and implied the complicity of George H.W. Bush through his inclusion of the line, 'Wolfman, oh Wolfman, oh Wolfman howl.' (Bush's codename within the CIA had reportedly been "Timberwolf." Kennedy's grandchildren recorded a song named *'Timber'* on Instagram in 2020 in what is thought to be a veiled acknowledgement of Bush's involvement in their grandfather's murder, some months after Bush's own death.)

Any credibility Dylan may have had left as a champion of civil rights and freedoms was put fully to bed in August 2021, when he was accused of plying a 12-year-old girl with drugs and alcohol and sexually abusing her over a six-week period way back in 1965 at the height of his popularity. According to a lawsuit filed, many of the offences in question took place at the infamous Chelsea Hotel in Manhattan, a venue whose dark and dubious history was covered at length in this book's previous volume.

Despite apparently having no problem speaking out about injustice, inequality and deception wherever they find it, however, none of these four had anything to say publicly about the Co(n)vid-19 Scam. It's not as if there has been any lack of information publicly available to destroy the official narrative about the scale of the "virus" and the measures needed to "counter the spread." Just an hour's research on-line is all anyone would need to *prove* that mis- and disinformation, along with bad science and political ulterior motives, have been consistently touted by the corrupt governments of the world. That and the capacity for independent free-thought—or the ability to openly express it publicly.

It seems that it's in this area that the real shortcomings lie. When considering artists whose public images have been built around their propensity towards challenging injustice, and holding the political class to account for their oppression of the people, is it really so unreasonable to assume that they might have been unconvinced by the rhetoric given about the "Pandemic," and untrusting of those seeking to remove the natural-born rights and freedoms of billions around the world? If they *had* been genuine and sincere in all that they had said and done up to that point, would it not be more reasonable to imagine that they might have sought to use their familiarity with the public to express their concerns, and to encourage others to look beyond the surface narrative at what other motives might be driving the agenda—one which has affected not only the lives of their fans, but of *they themselves* and *their own* families too?

Other names spring to mind. Former **Smiths** frontman **Morrissey** has been no stranger to controversy, having been an outspoken vegetarian, animal rights activist and anti-Royalist. These qualities suggest an individual with a conscience, a propensity towards compassion, and an aversion to authority. Morrissey *just about* redeemed himself in a June 2021 Q&A session for his own website conducted by his nephew Sam Esty Rayner. While stopping short of pointing out Co(n)vid's larger agendas such as The Great Reset and Agenda 2030, he did make a refreshing reference to Con-vid, adding:

> *"More people are now forced into poverty which is another form of slavery, as is tax and Council Tax and all the other ways in which we are pinned down and tracked. Our present freedom is restricted to visiting supermarkets and buying sofas. The government act like Chinese emperors... 'We will allow you to live as we do if you behave yourself'."*

The previous year, Morrissey had drawn the scorn of the mainstream press for going ahead with a gig in London on 14th March when several other music events had been cancelled, but this was a week before the

UK government announced that the nation was officially going into Lockdown. The gig, at the SSE Arena, featured a backdrop image of Morrissey's *'You Are The Quarry'* which had been changed to *'You Are Quarantined,'* and with a mask added to the image of his face on the picture.

Those artists of a religious persuasion—a least as far as their carefully cultivated public images are concerned—have also been conspicuous by their lack of outspoken-ness. The last time I checked there was nothing virtuous or righteous in the eyes of the Gods of any of the organised religions, about New World Order Communism, which is what the Co(n)vid scam has really been all about. One might have expected a man or woman of faith to have spoken up freely in support of personal liberty, and to denounce human slavery. Yet not a peep from **Cliff Richard**, **Cat Stevens**, **Amy Grant**, **Akon**, **TobyMac**, Beyonce (!) (if she's a Christian then I'm Brad Pitt) or the many others of their ilk.

Just a couple of sentences from any one of these familiar names, given the large number of people who have come to hang on their every word, could have changed public attitude overnight. And they would have known this. Yet still—silence.

And anyone searching for that spirit of anti-Establishment rebellion within Heavy Metal would have been left sorely disappointed by the proclamation of **Judas Priest** bassist **Ian Hill**. In an appearance on the Jeremy White podcast, he stated:

> *"We're all double-jabbed, so we're about as protected as we ever will be, unless something else comes out in the meantime. I don't know. And it's just that. We'll be careful, and we're just gonna keep our distance away from people. If we go out in the evenings, we'll try and keep our bubble together. We're gonna try to limit the amount of third parties you get to see."*

As mentioned in the first book, Judas Priest were heavily embroiled in the so-called "Satanic panic" surrounding Heavy Metal music in the 1980s, and were subject of a legal case arising from two youths killing themselves allegedly as a result of hearing subliminal messages hidden in a JP track. The take-away from all this? Pushing

Satanism—good! Challenging official narratives full of contradictions and disinformation—bad!

Iron Maiden's **Bruce Dickinson** would agree. The *'NME'* carried the story of Dickinson having "contracted COVID-19"... despite being double-vaccinated!! (Gee, I wonder what could have caused him to become so ill? Durrrrr!) He then urged all his fans to go out and get vaccinated themselves, presumably so they could all get ill just like him. Seemingly in all sincerity, and unable to recognise the insanity of his statement, Dickinson said:

> *"I've pretty much got no doubt that had I not had the vaccine, I could be in serious trouble."*

And no need to worry about any rousing rebellion from **Jon Bon Jovi**. In his 2020 song *'Do What You Can'* with **Jennifer Nettles**, the pair earn themselves a dog biscuit from their owners by advocating everything the mainstream media says without question with lines like:

> *"Moms and babies blowing kisses,*
> *May be saving someone's life."*
> *And:*
> *"Although I'll keep my social distance,*
> *What this world needs is a hug.*
> *Until we find the vaccination,*
> *There's no substitute for love."*

It is of course possible that many artists have genuinely bought the official line on things. Living in an artificial bubble created by wealth, fame and all the lifestyle trappings they bring—including perception and consciousness-altering drugs—can cause a detachedness from the regular, everyday life experienced by most. And the members of many of the acts mentioned are of above pension age, and doubtless far more aware of their mortality that in their wilder younger years. But it remains equally possible—and far more likely given the evidence—that they're remaining silent for other reasons.

Still Waters run deep

But what of **Pink Floyd**'s **Roger Waters**, a reader may ask? Surely he of all people could be expected to have something critical to say about the Scamdemic lie? After all, he's no stranger to controversy and has had no problem speaking out about the Establishment's incursions into foreign nations, particularly the Zionist state of Israel's illegal attacks on neighbouring Palestine. This topic is the one that few in the public eye dare to talk about, and would surely have sabotaged Roger's career had he started speaking about it during the Floyd's heyday?

Crushing disappointment alert: Sadly, no such stance has been taken by Roger. Instead, he has lent legitimacy to the "Pandemic" by reinforcing the official line on its threat level. Upon announcing the postponement of the tour he had planned a the start of the Scamdemic, (interestingly titled '*This Is Not A Drill*',) he stated: "If it saves one life, it's worth it." In the very same announcement, he revealed his glee at the news of Donald Trump's Dakota Access Pipeline Executive Order being deemed illegal by a federal judge, marking a victory for the Sioux tribes of the Standing Rock site. Mixed messages then, where Roger takes a conscious and moral stance on a humanitarian issue in one breath, yet helps reinforce the lies that have led to the unlawful subjugation of millions of people in another. This seems to be a trend, as in an on-line interview in Spring 2020, he said:

> "*I am isolated. I've been taking this seriously for a couple of weeks now . . . | speak to people in New York obviously, and obviously I watch the figures a little bit. Equally obviously I never watch TV, because there's no point in watching TV in the United States because it's all absolute drivel and complete lies. There is no news.*"

So Roger doesn't seem to see the contradiction between decrying the lies and propaganda told by the TV news, but then reinforcing one of those very lies by referencing (falsified) Co(n)vid figures which he would have got from the very mainstream media that he denounces.

It gets worse. In the same interview, Roger went on to praise Dr. Anthony Fauci, the treacherous public health advisor responsible for perpetuating the "virus" lie in the US in league with the W.H.O. and

C.D.C., and who had played a similar role way back in the 1980s during the A.I.D.S. crisis, (about which serious questions remain concerning the true origins of that particular "virus.") Though he feels to mention him in the interview, Roger can't quite remember his name or job title. Was he "instructed" to bring him up in his comments? He says:

> *"Thank God for Anthony Fauci. Is that his name? The ep...e...epid...whatever it is. He's obviously an extremely, highly educated, brilliant man. How he has stayed in a position of any power, nobody will ever know."*

(Well, I wouldn't bank on that, Rog, but I know what you're getting at.)

Roger didn't miss an opportunity to mention Bill Gates in the same chat, loosely referring to him as a "good" person:

> *"The other thing, since you've given me this airtime, that interests me, is that all the good people out there—I saw Bill Gates had written a long thing recently...they never mention American foreign policy. They never mention the Empire. Ever. None of them. Not one of them says, of course the reason that we're so fucked up is because we spend all our money killing brown people, because for some reason we want to. So disgusting in every possible way."*

He went on to suggest that medical assistance to the rest of the world is coming from China...without appearing to realise that one of the main aims of the manufactured "Pandemic" was to impose Communism on the majority of the world's population and to take away individual rights, freedoms and personal ownership, based on a model perfected in China by its ruling Communist Party!

Roger's reluctance to engage with this subject may stem from his background; his father Eric was a coal miner and Labour Party activist, and himself a member of the Communist party. Waters is the only member of Floyd to come from a working class background. His bandmates emerged from extremely wealthy and privileged families, taking up positions in a rock band rather than entering the kind of professions that might be expected for offspring of Aristocratic families. In Waters' father we find the military involvement that's present with so many rock stars' dads, but here there is a difference; from having initially been a conscientious objector, Eric seemingly changed his stance on war and was commissioned as a second Lieutenant in the Royal Fusliers on 11th September (interesting date,) 1943. He was killed in action in Italy five months later when Roger was just five months old.

In most of his interviews, Roger demonstrates that he still buys into the Left/ Right paradigm of politics, suggesting that a man of his advanced years still hasn't twigged that the entire system is a construct—a dialectic which gives the illusion of "choice," but in which both sides are ultimately controlled by the same force. How is it possible for someone who has been around for so long to still be buying these lies? Unless, of course, he knows this truth only too well, and is doing the bidding of unseen controllers by deliberately putting out mixed messages.

If the research involved in my books has taught me one lesson above all others, it's that anyone in the public eye—anyone who has achieved celebrity status to the point that the average person you might stop and ask in the street would have heard of them—has had their fame and fortune facilitated for them. What Rastafarians would refer to as the "Babylon" system is set up so that only those "approved" by the industry gatekeepers get to these levels. Everything is done on the industry's terms, and the idea that anyone could slip through the net and somehow achieve fame and success on their own terms without becoming owned or controlled by the system, is laughable. I wish it were some other way but I can confidently make the statement that there are no exceptions—and especially not for someone of Roger Waters' status, as part of one of the most celebrated and influential bands of all time, and with a career lasting multiple decades.

Indeed, the very start of Pink Floyd's career gives any vigilant researcher an insight into their role, as they very quickly became the darlings of the counter-culture scene in London in the mid 1960s, performing as house band at the iconic UFO club and pushing L.S.D.-laden and societal attitude-changing psychedelic music and culture. As those trends fizzled out at the close of the 1960s, (by design having achieved their main aims, I would suggest,)—and following the removal of frontman **Syd Barrett** who had, according to official reports, become impossible to work with through having fried his brains with too much L.S.D., (though I suspect the truth lies in him having been a tragic casualty of mind-control programming,)—Floyd's music morphed into the intellectual-friendly progressive rock style for which the group is best known.

Although a very public feud between Roger Waters and **Dave Gilmour CBE** (Barrett's replacement as frontman) ensued, with Roger having always been viewed as a kind of anti-Establishment rebel, it remains my stance—again, through years of painstaking research rather than simply being a matter of personal opinion—that Roger simply would not have been permitted to remain in the public eye for so long if he wasn't pushing some agenda or other on behalf of the music industry's real controllers. Admittedly, at times he can come across as confused and naïve, but at others, his reinforcement of agendas pushed by the very mainstream news he claims to despise, and his refusal to address certain Elephants in the Room which really could do with being exposed by someone of his ilk—give away his true nature as just another Lifetime Actor.

For much more of a deep dive into Waters and the whole history of Pink Floyd, I highly recommend a listen to the *'Good Vibrations'* podcast I recorded with British researcher Martin Brown in May 2020, which we titled *'The Dark Side of the Floyd'* (see what we did there?) Martin is putting together what promises to be a vast and comprehensive book on the group, which will be the first of its kind in straying from the usual mainstream sources, and highlighting aspects of the band that have never been mentioned in any "official" biographies. The link to that *'Good Vibrations'* episode is in the Resources list at the end of the chapter.

On the subject of Waters' seemingly contradictory stances on political issues, Martin observed:

> *"Roger has always had that ambivalent thing about him—multi-millionaire rock star who had a "socialist/ communist" upbringing and background (which means nothing when you realise what politics actually is, and what his background actually is). He's an "outspoken" activist, but what does that really mean? Many of the counter-cultural stars and gurus of the 1960s mention such credentials in their background—nothing about the posh stuff and military intelligence links, though—it gives them an image of being "one of us"—trying to get us to relate to them as our champions. Of course, none of that mythology makes any sense. I love his music, and a lot of the things Waters says*

are righteous—but of course none of it makes any difference in the long run, which is the important thing for the Cabal."

What of Waters' sometime apparent adversary within Pink Floyd, lest anyone ask? Well, no need for panic within Establishment circles when it comes to David Gilmour who, in a June 2021 interview with guitar-player.com after blaming this "lockdown thing" for the delay involved in producing his new album, went on to allay any fears of rebellion by reassuring readers that he and his wife Polly Samson were "both dou-ble-vaccinated, so things are looking a little brighter." Phew! I guess he'd become comfortably numb.

Sadly, there was little hope to be drawn from the other legendary rock star Roger, (although Waters is technically a George, with Roger being his real name, whereas bandmate Syd Barrett was really a Roger with "Syd" being a nickname—I hope everyone's paying attention as there'll be ques-tions later.) **Roger Daltrey** (CBE) of **The Who**—apparently *not* affiliated with the World Health Organization, (although who really knows any more?)—appeared on the newly-launched *'GB News'* network in June 2021. (Although the channel claimed to be a breath of fresh air through "challenging" mainstream news, it turned out to merely reinforce official narratives, adding validity to the idea of Co(n)vid by presenting it as a very real threat. Why would anyone expect it to do otherwise when its high-profile assets include Andrew Neil, a "former" BBC man to the very core of his bone marrow?)

Daltrey appeared in a 20-minute interview with presenter Dan Woot-ton during which he revealed himself to be a supporter of Boris Johnson, and a true believer in the notion of Co(n)vid as a very real threat to the public, and needing to be addressed with government intervention. He also revealed himself to have fallen for the social-engineering psy-op that is Black Lives Matter, affiliated with and funded by, as it is, billionaire "elite" system-server George Soros through his Open Society Founda-tions. Daltrey supported that group's P.R. stunt of (controlled) activists uprooting the statue of slave-trader Edward Colston and dumping it in Bristol Harbour. Daltrey is also a patron of the Teenage Cancer Trust and, while he *seemed* sincere in airing his sympathy for sufferers, he must surely have come across the many natural and alternative cures for cancer which exist as an alternative to Big Pharma's brutal chemo and radiotherapy, yet has never endorsed these nor suggested that his charity might look into them.

The only issue on which Daltrey appeared to endear himself to the Truth community was in his criticism of "woke" culture among Generation Z "Zoomers," (those born between the late 1990s and the early 2010s.) Although he rightly condemned "cancel culture" and the "snowflake" mentality of this generation's heavily-brainwashed Social Justice Warriors, this was not enough to cement his credentials as a genuine rebel to the system, (despite his carefully cultivated image in the 1960s,) and, given the tyrannical nightmare futures we all face, this was hardly the most pressing issue of the day.

With speculation persisting as to The Who being products of Tavistock, like their contemporaries the **Beatles** and the **Rolling Stones**, Roger may be in a position to know a thing or two about how societal influence through popular culture works. The Who ticked many other "usual suspect"-type boxes, too. Late bassist **John Entwhistle** was a Freemason, drummer **Keith Moon** died in suspicious circumstances in the same flat as **Mama "Cass" Elliott** had four years previous, (as noted in *'Sound Bites'*) and there was **Pete Townshend**'s much-publicised arrest over his viewing of child pornography, (his father had been a part of a Royal Air Force dance band.) The film version of the band's rock-opera, the Ken Russell-directed *'Tommy,'* depicts the effects of Satanic Ritual Abuse and trauma-based mind control within military families, and controversially featured Moon portraying "Uncle Ernie," a paedophile babysitter.

Either way, both of these Rock Star Rogers have given out mixed messages, and are either confused and largely clueless as to the big picture themselves, or are continuing to push desired agendas way into their final years.

Honourable exceptions

Given the glaring omissions of many obvious big names, therefore, those who *did* speak out about the tyranny and totalitarianism "justified" by Co(n)vid, stood out all the more. They remain very few in number.

The most high-profile of these was **Van Morrisson**. His vocal opposition to governmental lockdown policies was all the more surprising given that he belongs in the ranks of "Sirs"; he was made a Knight Bachelor in the Queen's Birthday Honours List of 2015 for services to the music industry and to tourism in Northern Ireland. Those who have been inducted into these ranks tend not to make any public statements which go against official Establishment protocol, making it all the more newsworthy on the rare occasion that one does. Morrison had collaborated in 1989 with fellow "Christian" and fellow "Sir," Cliff Richard, on the song '*Whenever God Shines His Light On Me.*' Years later, relating an anecdote about recording the song with Morrison, and noting Morrison's reputation for being "irascible and difficult," the '*Daily Express*' reported Richard as recalling that Morrison "said that he thought he belonged to a purple-blood group, which seemed to be some sort of rarefied spiritual royalty," and that Richard "really wasn't quite sure what to say to that." (There's more on Cliff Richard in '*Musical Truth Volume 1.*')

Van Morrison, one of tragically few prominent musicians courageous enough to publicly challenge the treasonous Co(n)vid narrative—all the more surprising for a "Sir."

https://commons.wikimedia.org/wiki/File:Van_Morrison_at_Notodden_Blues_Festival.JPG

In September 2020, Morrison released three new songs, all lyrically critical of official Co(n)vid regulations—'*As I Walked Out,*' '*Born To Be Free*' and '*No More Lockdown.*' The former included the lyrics:

"As I walked out all the streets were empty,
The government said everyone should stay home.
And they spread fear and loathing and no hope for the future.
Not many did question this very strange move."

The latter contained the following:

"No more lockdown, no more government overreach.
No more fascist police, disturbing our peace.
No more taking our freedom and our God-given rights,
Pretending it's for our safety, when it's really to enslave."

It was surprising and refreshing to hear an artist of such stature make such direct and candid observations in an era where socially-engineered Political Correctness caused almost all others to self-censor for fear of alienating fans or industry executives, or causing harm to their career. 2020 was a *long* way from the 1960s and 70s fashionability of protest songs which meaningfully addressed the social and political issues of the day. "The Belfast Cowboy" had previously performed a handful of "socially-distanced" gigs, presumably reasoning that these were better than nothing and at least allowed him to remain musically active and engage in some small way with fans. He had been critical of the restrictions put in place at these, however, commenting in an article on his *'Save Live Music'* website:

"As you know, we are doing socially-distanced gigs at Newcastle-Up-on-Tyne's Gosforth Park, Electric Ballroom and The London Palladium. This is not a sign of compliance or acceptance of the current state of affairs, this is to get my band up and running and out of the doldrums. This is also not the answer going forward. We need to be playing to full-capacity audiences going forward."

Morrison went on to cite a surprising ally in another Sir, **"Lord" Andrew Lloyd-Webber**, who had likewise been critical of restrictions on audience capacities in music venues:

"Sir Andrew Lloyd Webber and myself appear to be the only people in the music business trying to get it back up and running again. Come forward. It's not economically viable to do socially-distanced gigs. Come forward now, the future is now."

Lloyd-Webber proved to be not quite the anti-official-narrative maverick that his stance may have suggested, however, when he went on to participate in a trial for the Oxford Co(n)vid vaccine. By May 2021, he had evidently been pulled back into line when he publicly compared "selfish" people who refuse to take a vaccine to drunk-drivers.

Morrison, meanwhile, further urged his peers to join him in his stance, adding:

"Singers, musicians, writers, producers, promoters and others in the industry . . . fight with me on this. Come forward, stand up, fight the pseudo-science and speak up."

His words evidently fell on deaf ears, however, as offers of collaboration were in short supply. But there was no such scarcity when it came to a predictable backlash to his stance from aspects of the Establishment. Amid calls for his Freedom of the City honour to be revoked by Belfast City Council, Councillor Emmet McDonough-Brown said that his lyrics were "undermining the guidance in place to protect lives and are ignorant of established science as we grapple with Covid-19."

Northern Ireland Health Minister Robin Swann, meanwhile, took the tired and lazy approach of associating Morrison with "conspiracy theorists." In a shameless appeal to emotion, writing in *'Rolling Stone'* magazine, (Yeah, rock 'n' roll!), he stated:

"We expected better from him . . . Some of what is he saying is actually dangerous. It could encourage people not to take coronavirus seriously. If you see it all as a big conspiracy, then you are less likely to follow the vital public health advice that keeps you and others safe . . . His words will give great comfort to the conspiracy theorists—the tinfoil hat brigade who crusade against masks and vaccines and think this is all a huge global plot to remove freedoms. . . . I only hope no one takes him seriously. He's no guru, no teacher."

Swann's words spoke to the influence that he recognised that musicians such as Morrisson generally wield. He seemed to have largely got his wish in his hope that few would take him seriously, through the backlash the musician received from "fans" on Twitter and other social media. Replies received via his Twitter page included:

"Sorry Van. Trust the art, not the artist. So sad. #WearAMask."

"We are all so disappointed in you."

"Van is a good songwriter and performer, a medical adviser he is not."

'Tinfoil lining in his hat, David Icke doing the warm-up for the next tour."

"A slap in the face to the hundreds of thousands who have died across the world from this virus. Shame."

"Retire already before you go on risking lives."

"This Irish loving Van Morrison fan—disappointed. I have had many people who have this virus (over 20,) all have said this is something they have never felt before."

"It's a marvellous night to wear no mask with the saliva droplets up above in your eyes, a fantabulous night to catch Co(n)vid 'neath the cover of October skies."

Singing the blues

In November 2020, an unlikely ally for Morrison stepped forward in the form of another British Empire award recipient, fellow blues performer **Eric Clapton**. It was announced that the pair had collaborated on a further anti-lockdown single, '*Stand and Deliver*,' proceeds from which would go to Morrison's Lockdown Financial Hardship Fund, aimed at providing aid to musicians who had been financially hit by the enforced ban on live music performances. The Morrison-penned lyrics, which demonstrated incisive knowledge of what the Scamdemic was really all about, pulled no punches, and included the lines:

"Stand and deliver, you let them put the fear on you.
Stand and deliver, but not a word you heard was true.

Do you wanna be a free man, or do you wanna be a slave?

...Do you wanna wear these chains

Until you're lying in the grave?

Magna Carta, Bill of Rights,

The constitution, what's it worth?

You know they're gonna grind us down, until it really hurts.

Is this a sovereign nation, or just a police state?

You better look out, people, before it gets too late."

Blues guitar legend Eric Clapton earned the respect of an entirely new fanbase when he publicly cast doubt upon the safety and efficacy of the Co(n)vid "vaccine."

https://commons.wikimedia.org/wiki/File:Eric_Clapton_-_Royal_Albert_Hall_-_Wednesday_24th_May_2017_EricClaptonRAH240517-30_(34987232355)_(cropped).jpg

Clapton was not done with his anti-Establishment ranting, however. In May 2021, researcher Robin Monotti posted a written message he had received from Clapton addressing the taboo subject of vaccines—a hugely controversial no-go subject area for 99.99 per cent of all "celebrities" concerned with keeping their careers intact and their fanbase placated. The message was later posted on the America's Frontline Doctors website. Perhaps surprisingly, Clapton revealed that he had taken one of the AstraZenica Co(n)vid vaccines and, (less surprisingly,) had suffered adverse reactions as a result. He wrote in his on-line post:

> *"I am an old-timer, I have survived, with great help, addiction and alcoholism, and stand now in the greatest dilemma of my life... I am a man of faith, albeit abstract, and what I felt and saw unfold in March '20 began to lead me away from govt rhetoric and the devotion of the general public to the PM and his cronies... I looked for heroes in the house, and found C Walker, Desmond Swayne, and in unfortunate retirement, Lord Sumption... On YouTube I found Hugotalks and Talk Radio... that was all....*

> *"Then I was directed to Van M, that's when I found my voice, and even though I was singing his words, they echoed in my heart... I recorded "stand and deliver" in 2020, and was immediately regaled with contempt and scorn... "*

The fact that Clapton addressed his age in the post suggests a man of advanced years with regrets, and the desire to make whatever amends he can and stand in Right Action while he still has time:

> *"In February this year, before I learned about the nature of the vaccines, (and being 76 with emphysema) I was in the avant garde. I took the first jab of AZ and straight away had severe reactions which lasted ten days. I recovered eventually and was told it would be twelve weeks before the second one...*

> *"About six weeks later I was offered and took the second AZ shot, but with a little more knowledge of the dangers. Needless to say the reactions were disastrous, my hands and feet were either frozen, numb or burning, and pretty much useless for two weeks, I feared I would never play again, (I suffer with peripheral neuropathy and should never have gone near the needle.) But the propaganda said the vaccine was safe for everyone....*

> *"Then I met a member of this group, who counselled me to be careful and to have a look at what goes on with you guys... I felt like a veil*

had been lifted, that I was no longer alone, that it was okay, in fact essential, to hold on to my intuition and follow my heart . . . "

Clapton went on, inspired by the track 'Where have All The Rebels Gone?' from Van Morrison's newly-released double-album 'Latest Record Project Volume 1,' to question where the "rock 'n' roll" spirit of rebellion had gone, and why virtually all of his peers were meekly and obediently complying with tyranny, and apparently muzzled from speaking up:

> *"I continue to tread the path of passive rebellion and try to toe the line in order to be able to actively love my family, but it's hard to bite my tongue with what I now know . . . I've been a rebel all my life, against tyranny and arrogant authority, which is what we have now, but I also crave fellowship, compassion and love, and that I find here . . . I believe with these things we can prevail."*

Eric went on to record a hugely-circulated interview with Oracle Films reinforcing his stances detailed above. What I took away from it is that, those of us who have been "Truthers" for years are so deeply ingrained in our worldview, that we can forget that those who have spent their entire lives engulfed in mainstream Organised Society, are only just starting to notice that the world isn't quite the way they thought it was. It can seem incredible to us that someone of Eric's advanced years is only just waking up to this obvious fact. Yet, assets of his ilk are surrounded by handlers and gatekeepers to make sure they stay in line, and A-list musicians live an entirely different lifestyle to the rest of us, which is dependent on an acceptance of "mainstream" ways of doing things, and official narratives. It does, therefore, take courage and conviction to speak out in this way.

Of great interest to me was being told by one of the organisers that Van Morrison had attended my lecture on the machinations of the music business delivered at the Glastonbury Symposium in Summer 2015, where I demonstrated how the industry fits into the wider picture of mind-control and social-engineering perpetrated through Organised Society. We later had a phone chat, in March 2021. Van was upbeat and friendly, and demonstrated great knowledge of current affairs, indicating that he was a man who had clearly done his research. We agreed in principle to record an interview where I would ask him to expand on what prompted him to write his anti-lockdown songs, but this ended up getting blocked by somebody at Van's company, Exile Productions, who stated by e-mail: "We'll be in touch if this interview is something we want to move forward with." A typical P.R. gatekeeper's response. I now have to wonder if Van was warned against giving the interview with someone like me, for fear of how it might harm the remainder of his career.

Morrison became something of a flag-bearer for the live music community, given that so few well-known names were prepared to stick their heads above the parapet and criticise government policy, and that he was by far the best-known of the very few that did. In a tweet dated 29th December 2020, Morrison wrote:

> "We spoke to musicians in Northern Ireland to find out how they are coping. We cannot expect musicians who have worked their entire lives in a career they love to abandon it. We urge the government to set out a plan, to recover the arts sector."

And nine days earlier:

> "Remember, those who are shutting down our economy haven't missed a paycheck since lockdown began. We are _not_ in this together."

He had earlier commented on a statement from the Northern Ireland Executive in September 2020 proclaiming that live music had been made illegal, replying:

> "Did you know that live music is ILLEGAL in Northern Ireland? No other region of the UK has imposed such detrimental restrictions on our sector. Where is the evidence to justify such a severe approach?"

In January 2021 came the announcement, via his solicitor Joe Rice, that Morrison was planning to start legal action against the Northern Irish government over its blanket ban on live music in indoor venues. Rice said:

> "We will be seeking leave for judicial review to challenge the blanket ban on live music in licensed premises in Northern Ireland. We're

not aware of any credible scientific or medical evidence to justify this particular blanket ban . . . and we're going to challenge this in the high court."

The War on Joy

Morrison's stance appeared to be in direct defiance of a claim, which quickly went viral, that a statement made by the UK Chancellor Rishi Sunak had advised people who had worked in aspects of the Arts and Culture sector to think about retraining for new careers. Sunak appears to have been widely misquoted in the matter, though certainly did make the implication. Asked in an I.T.V. interview in October 2020 whether he was advocating that actors, musicians and the like should consider their careers over, Sunak employed the classic politician's tactic of avoiding answering the question directly. What he did say was:

His actual comments were:

> *"As in all walks of life, everyone is having to adapt. So I'm getting e-mails and seeing how theatre companies are adapting and putting on different types of performances. It is possible to do theatrical performances on-line as well and for people to engage with them that way and for new business models to emerge. Plenty of music lessons are still carrying on. The same thing happens certainly in my household and elsewhere.*

> *"So yes, can things happen in exactly the way that they did? No. But everyone is having to find ways to adapt and adjust to the new reality and that is what we have to do. And that's why we're allowing that to happen but also providing new opportunity for people if that is the right vehicle for them."*

It is in this regard that another Honourable Exception stepped forward, in the form of **Garry Cobain**, frontman of **Future Sound of London**, which produced one of the most unique and fascinating dance records of the 90s in their *'Papua New Guinea.'* To his great credit, Cobain was able to see through the scam and exposed the Co(n)vid agenda for what it really was all through his 2020 social media postings. Addressing the issue of artists being urged to retrain, his Facebook post of 8th October 2020 read:

> "… *Many who choose a life in the arts have indeed studied and are qualified for other vocations at a higher level than privileged wankers with PPE back-entry pass' level cronyism politics. The fact we choose constructive lives for expression and art, rather than destructive lies for one's own greed and racketeering, doesn't mean we'll tolerate your … trying to demean the worth of "art" and your pretence that you somehow achieved ANYTHING through meritocracy—be under no illusion: you didn't … you CREATE nothing & destroy much.*
>
> *"Since there's no gigs and concerts at the mo—us artists and creatives, (you'll be pleased to know,) ARE indeed using our other "vocations" and training/ education and intelligence in FULL effect, studying your crimes against humanity and detailing your clear embezzlement of democracy and "science." In the meantime, until your crimes are fully exposed, (they are, but it won't be long now before mass awakening,) I will continue to live my life for humanity and art as I wish, and do everything I can to oppose and withstand your tyranny. Thus my intelligence and gainful employ are best served at the moment and no wonder we scare the living daylights out of your murderous one dimensional scheming minds."*

The outlawing of creative pursuits, and therefore enjoyable leisure activities is, tellingly, a major tenet of idealistic Communism—the removal of all pleasure from the daily lives of the populace, so that only labour, greyness and drudgery remains. Sound familiar? This gave as revealing a hint as was needed that Sunak and his fellow lackeys were following orders from higher up in fast-tracking Communism into his country—just as government officials in many other nations were doing at the same time. Yuri Bezmenov was a former KGB agent who became a whistleblower and divulged many secrets of Soviet infiltration into foreign cultures. In an interview as long ago as 1972, two years after he defected to the United States, he detailed a 42-point plan towards cultural subversion. These included the following:

- Gain control of key positions in radio, TV, and motion pictures.
- Control art critics and directors of art museums. "Our plan is to promote ugliness, repulsive, meaningless art."
- Eliminate all laws governing obscenity by calling them "censorship" and a violation of free speech and free press.
- Break down cultural standards of morality by promoting pornography and obscenity in books, magazines, motion pictures, radio, and TV.
- Present homosexuality, degeneracy and promiscuity as "normal, natural, healthy."

As a matter of interest, other comments made by Bezmenov go some way to explaining why so many people—even in the face of overwhelming proofs and evidence presented to them—were incapable of accepting that the Co(n)vid-19 Scamdemic was a tool of political manipulation, much to the frustration of those who realised that the agenda only continued to succeed due to the unquestioning compliance of the masses. And remember, these comments are from half a century ago:

> "...Exposure to true information does not matter anymore. A person who is demoralised is unable to access true information. The facts tell nothing to him. Even if I showered him with information, with authentic proof, with documents, with pictures—even if I take him by force to the Soviet Union and show him a concentration camp—he will refuse to believe it until he is going to receive a kick in his fat bottom. When a military boot crashes his butt, then he will understand, but not before that. That's the tragedy of the situation of demoralisation."

Honourable mentions in the dance music world must also go to singer **Baby D** of '*Let Me Be Your Fantasy*' fame, and DJs **Norman Jay (MBE)** and **Norris 'Da Boss' Windross**, who all called publicly for the re-opening of all businesses in Summer 2021, with zero Co(n)vid restrictions in place.

From the Reggae world, a tip of the hat has to go to Dub genre pioneer **Lee 'Scratch' Perry** who died on 29th August 2021 aged 85, but who, very early on in the Scamdemic, indicated that he was nobody's fool by Tweeting:

> *"Greetings, my dear fans. My shows have been postponed due to Babylon scare tactics. But fear can't stop me from moving forward. Do not let your hearts be troubled."*

Perry earned further respect when the ugly subject of vaccination passports being required to attend events like sports games and live music shows, and as a condition of international travel, emerged in early 2021. Having been forced to reschedule his planned live tour for the third time, he Tweeted:

> *"Hopefully we will be able to travel at least for this year without the shot passport! Once that gets required for traveling I will sadly have to say goodbye to live shows."*

Going on to question the moral integrity of many of his fans who purport to adhere to the Rastafarian religion, he added:

> *"But there is something I'm wondering about: isn't Rasta supposed to stand for freedom, against slavery and against Babylon system? How comes that some of them calling themselves Rasta are promoting exactly that system by telling people to mask up and get the shot, while we should know what that means?"*

Other opposition from the Reggae world came from singer **Buju Banton**, who publicly criticised the Jamaican government's stance on granting immunity from prosecution to vaccine manufacturers for any harm or deaths their products may cause. Banton wrote on his Instagram page:

> *"So the love for this nation and its people soooo great. They will allow there (sic) friends to kill you and it's perfectly ok#honest # Jamaica land they love # not the people,"*

He was supported in this stance by fellow Reggae performers **Spragga Benz**, **Mr. Lexx**, **Kabaka Pyramid** and **Koolface**, who posted similar messages of outrage. Banton had earlier called on Jamaicans to refrain from wearing face masks, writing:

"We waan done wid dis mask wearing bullsh-t inna Jamaica. Who fi dead ago dead and who nah go dead, haffi jus live. We tired of you intellectual fools trying to tell us how to live our lives, you are so smart why you haven't found the cure for cancer ... Jamaican people need fi wake up. Mi nah wear no mask cause mask nuh mek fi man."

(Translation for non-patois speakers—"what's the deal with these mask-wearing regulations in Jamaica? Those who are going to die are going to die, and those who are not need to continue living ... Jamaican people need to wake up. I will not wear a mask because a mask does not make the man.")

Banton's post came at a time when much evidence had already emerged of the Co(n)vid vaccines from manufacturers Astra-Zenica, Pfizer and Moderna having caused the deaths, or severe injuries, of many thousands of people who had trustingly taken it. The tragic irony was that many of these people would have been terrified of

being damaged or killed by "the virus," and so took a cocktail of unknown substances into their bodies ... only to end up experiencing the very damage or death they were seeking to avoid—and would have done if they'd just stayed as they were.

A contemporary of Buju Banton, the singer **Bounty Killer**, represented the mistrust towards Government and Organised Society that many Jamaicans—and particularly fans of Reggae music—instinctively feel with his song 'Conspiracy Theory' released during 2020, and featuring fellow artists **Serani** and **Agent Sasco**.

Tragically, the man regarded as the original pioneer of Reggae music, **Frederick "Toots" Hibbert**, became another Co(n)vid statistic when he died in September 2020 at the age of 77. The mainstream press reported dutifully that he had died "after contracting Co(n)vid-19" but without actually stating it was what caused his death. Hibbert's group **Toots & The Maytals**, who originally performed Ska and Rocksteady, is acknowledged to have spearheaded its fusion into the newer "Reggae" form with their 1968 single *'Do The Reggay.'*

Rolling on

A name which doesn't belong in the category of "honourable exceptions," but which justifies a mention in this chapter in the interests of completism, is the aforementioned (Sir) Mick Jagger. While bandmate **Ronnie Wood** was busy picking up his "Freedom of the City of London" accolade, in an unexpected collaboration with **Foo Fighters** frontman **Dave Grohl**, (more on *his* background in *'Musical Truth 2'!*) a tongue-in-cheek song and accompanying video titled *'Eazy Sleazy,'* Jagger presented an array of mixed messages—in one breath appearing to oppose tyrannical government regulations, but in another advocating just putting up with it, rather than taking any kind of action. Some of the short, sharp lyrical lines include:

> *"We took it on the chin, numbers were so grim,*
> *Bossed around by pricks, stiffen upper lips.*
> *"Shooting a vaccine,*
> *Bill Gates is in my blood stream.*
> *It's mind control,*
> *The Earth is flat and cold."*
> *"Looking at the graphs with a magnifying glass,*
> *Cancel all the tours, football's fake applause."*

Jagger left no doubt as to his motives for penning the single, telling *'Rolling Stone'* magazine that the lyrics represented "a piss-take on conspiracy theories." He also dismissed 'anti-vaxxers" as "irrational," saying: "They got what they believe in and they believe in that. And it doesn't matter what you say, they're gonna believe in it. And rational thought doesn't work." His lyric about Bill Gates being in his bloodstream turned out to be accurate, meanwhile, as he mentioned that he himself had taken a Co(n)vid vaccine.

And could the line "it's going to be a garden of earthly delights" possibly be a mocking reference to the "New World" that Jagger, through his inside connections, knows is in the plans? He did, after all, study at the London School of Economics, one of the major social-engineering think-tanks in the UK. What other career would anyone expect an L.S.E. graduate to pursue other than that of a sexually promiscuous, drug-taking, degenerate rock star, right?

Additionally the Stones retained, for almost 40 years, the financial management services of a bankster member of the aristocratic "elite" ranks whose official name must qualify as one of the longest ever. Rupert Louis Ferdinand Frederick Constantine Lofredo Leopold Herbert Maximilian Hubert John Henry zu Löwenstein-Wertheim-Freudenberg, Count of Loewenstein-Scharffeneck, more commonly known — thankfully — as just plain Prince Rupert Loewenstein — reportedly met Mick Jagger in the late 1960s, and was recruited to help release the band from their stifling contract with the notorious lawyer Allen Klein, (whose financial services were also employed by the Stones' "rivals," the Beatles.)

Loewenstein remained embroiled in the band for almost 40 years, helping them to become tax exiles, copyrighting their famous lips-and-tongue logo, (an evocation of the Hindu goddess Kali according to researcher Freeman Fly, rather than of Jagger,) and becoming Godfather to Jagger's son James. Despite this close relationship, Loewenstein maintained that he was never a fan of the band's music. Sounds like the ideal foundation for a business and personal relationship lasting four decades, right? As the *'Secret Sun Speaks'* blog wrote of the alliance on Twitter: "Boy, nothing says rock 'n' roll rebellion like "grand inquisitor of the Constantinian Military Order of St George and President of the Order of the Knights of Malta."

Indeed.

Back with *'Eazy Sleazy,'* Jagger complains insincerely about the "prison walls" of lockdown and how "way too much TV" is "lobotomising me." Yet, lest we forget, he was one of the prominent participants in the *'One World At Home'* concert, reinforcing the governmental instruction to "stay home," and leading by example by performing from his living room ... *on the very television that he claims is lobotomising people!* The entire Co(n)vid narrative has been replete with lies, contradictions, mistruths, self-conflicting data, gaslighting and Satanic mockery. Why would we expect any different from one of the most servile assets of the system with a facilitated career lasting decades?

Mick may have earned himself a better brand of dog biscuit for services rendered and for sitting when told to sit, but ultimately, as **Led Zeppelin** would say, the song remains the same. Same shit, different asset. Yawn.

She's <u>not</u> leaving home

So that's the Stones. What of their apparent "rivals," the remaining members of, arguably, the most successful and influential pop group of all time, the Beatles? Well, no grumbling about lockdowns from **Sir Paul McCartney**, who seemed to spend the early weeks of the "Pandemic" travelling between the UK and the United States, before hunkering down and recording his new album, '*McCartney III*.' By the time the mainstream narrative had shifted to the tediously predictable "solution" of the (Bill Gates-funded) vaccine, McCartney was fulfilling his Extra Curricular Activity commitments by telling the press he couldn't wait until it was his turn to have one.

His bandmate, Sir (as of 2018) **Ringo Starr** released a video message to his fans as 2020 gave way to 2021, meanwhile. He began behind his home drum kit wearing a face mask, going on to talk about his achievements for the year with much reference to "peace and love." (I'm not sure what's so peaceful and loving about a world take-over psychological operation aimed at reducing the world's population and engineered by the Chinese Communist Party, but maybe I'm missing something.) He finishes the video by reminding us to "play it safe" and "keep other people safe" as he replaces his mask. Starr (Starkey) later announced he was re-scheduling all the dates for his planned 2021 tour, which had already been re-scheduled from 2020, with the weak, virtue-signalling announcement that: "At the end of last year when we moved the tour to 2021 who would have thought this would be still going on?" (About the only relevant statement he has made.) "While I've had my vaccine," (there's a fucking surprise, eh?) "big gatherings are not yet safe and too many people will still be at risk." (Yawwwwwwwnnnn.) "So we will be moving the tour once again — this time to 2022."

In the Summer, Ringo announced the release of his new E.P. titled *'Change The World.'* Taking the fear muzzle off would be a good start. Paul and Ringo's stances tell us so much about how it is that they're still alive and well, when **John Lennon** and **George Harrison** shuffled off this mortal coil long ago.

McCartney/ "McCartney" wasn't the only senior system asset called upon to be of service in the vaccine agenda. Joining him were those other well-known Sirs **Elton John (Reginald Dwight)** and Michael Caine (Maurice Micklewhite,) who took part in an N.H.S. advertisement in early 2021 to encourage take-up of the Co(n)vid vaccine in the wake of disappointingly low take-up figures, (I can't think why.) These two wouldn't have been asked nicely if they fancied taking part. They would have been told they're doing it. This is what desperation looks like. And anyone dumb enough to allow an unknown, untested substance to be inserted into their body just because Elton John or Michael Caine said it was OK wholly deserves every "adverse reaction" they get.

Since we're on the subject of Elton, incidentally, some of the lyrics to his 1984 (of all years) hit *'Passengers'* become interesting in light of the very vaccine passport agenda that the complicity of he and his like are helping to bring about. As the hookline goes:

"Deny the passenger, who want to get on."

Which is exactly what the vaccine passports are intended to bring about for those that don't have them. And then:

"The spirit's free, but you always find,
Passengers stand and wait in line."

Almost as if mocking the societal group-think and uniformity that "socially-distanced" lockdown queues brought among inherently free spirits. Plus, as if referencing the theory that the vaccines may contain some kind of tracking mechanism, representing the Biblical "mark of the Beast":

"It's tattooed in your veins.
You're living in a blood bank,

And riding on this train."

Hmmmm . . . .

There wasn't much to be heard from Elton's contemporary Sir (are you keeping count?) **Rod Stewart**, but he did crop up in a tittle-tattle story in September 2021 when the *'Daily Record'* reported that he and his wife Penny Lancaster got surrounded by fans when they called into an Essex pub for lunch, and Rod had to ask them to disperse "over Covid concerns." When the truth gets out about what murderous lies these "celebrities" have been helping to push, they'll be getting surrounded for very different reasons, and won't want to be popping out to a local pub.

Rod did indicate his inside knowledge of "elite" plans on his 2016 track *'Walking In The Sunshine,'* however, which initially included the line, "Oh my, these are scary times. The New World Order is causing disorder on the borderline." Do a lyric search with that song now though, and you'll find the "New World Order" reference has been completely scrubbed as if it never existed. Why should that be, I wonder??

All roads lead to the V

Desperation from the system to prop up the failing vaccine agenda in the wake of disappointing uptake levels from the public occurred in February 2021, when vulture.com reported that Hollywood A-listers were apparently trying to use their influence to jump the waiting lists for the Co(n)vid vaccine. According to an executive from an entertainment publicity firm quoted:

> *"People are chartering planes from New York and L.A. to Florida for doses. I've had people telling me they're thinking about trying to get the vaccine. They ask, 'How bad will this look if I'm found out?' You could be dismissed from your position. You could see your personal stock tarnished. It would be worse than the college-admissions scandal. Nobody wants to take that risk. 'How bad will this look?' You'll be a fucking pariah immediately."*

The article also suggested that these self-serving sell-outs were more concerned with virtue-signalling to their fans, than with any genuine health benefits involved, however.

And it turns out that this dynamic was simply a modern-day reboot of one from decades before when, in 1956, Elvis Presley was recruited for a fake photo depicting him taking the Polio vaccine, to try and turn around the low uptake among young people that there had been up to that point. The phrases "there's nothing new under the sun," and "if it ain't broke don't try to fix it" didn't come about by accident. By the time free takeaways, taxi discounts and cinema tickets were being offered to try and incentivise the under-25s into taking the "jab," the desperation was palpable. After all, being paralysed for life is a small price to pay for being able to see the latest *Fast and Furious* flick for free, right, kids?

Back to music, (so many digressions, goddamit!) more enthusiastic vaccine-pushing came from **Toyah Willcox** who, even in her early 80s heyday enjoyed only fleeting fame, but appears to have been trading off it for the past 40 years by popping up as a talking head on any vaguely music-related television show going. Appearing in a bizarre head-dress alongside her husband **Robert Fripp** of the group **King Crimson** in a video posted on New Year's Day 2021, Willcox said:

> *"It might be running up the hill for the next two months. Just hang on in there, because once that vaccine is available to us, we're going to be on a rollercoaster of experiences. There's going to be no stopping us. The world will be ours, and this has been the great leveller. I believe we are a united world."*

Talk of a "united world" and "we're all in this together" sound to me like thinly-veiled references to Communism and the "elite" New World Order, (they would after ten years of deep-diving in the murky waters of conspiracy truth,) and echo messages put out by both the British government and the Queen, helping to propagate the deadly nature of "the virus" by insisting it does not discriminate between young or old, rich or poor. It least it's "inclusive." A suitably "woke" virus for the 2020s.

James Corden sang for his supper — or least his O.B.E. — when he performed a musical sketch for his American *Late Late Show* celebrating the lifting of most Co(n)vid restrictions in New York, of course down to the rollout of the vaccine. What else? He was joined for the musical merriment by an equally obedient and system-serving Ariana Grande. There was unfortunate timing in that British viewers got to see the "celebratory" sketch right after Boris Johnson and his fellow traitors had reneged on their pledge to finally remove all Co(n)vid restrictions in the UK on the Summer Solstice of 2021. To paraphrase **Miami Sound Machine**, "liars will be liars. Bad liar. Bad liar."

Long-time **Fleetwood Mac** singer **Stevie Nicks** was on board with the agenda when she was reported to have begged fans to wear a mask, offering the Appeal to Emotion that she'll "probably never sing again if she contracts coronavirus." (That's only *if*, mind.) In a post made to her Facebook page in August 2020 she wrote:

> *"This virus can kill you. It can kill me. Kill my chances of pulling on those boots and hitting the road. Kill the chances that any of us in the music community will ever get back to the stage, because we would never put you in danger."*

Annie Lennox showed she could be relied upon to stay on-message when she recorded a video for fans revealing that she had taken the Moderna vaccine. She gleefully reported that she had suffered "no side effects whatsoever." Phew! That's a relief then. But it probably won't be much comfort for the families of the many hundreds of thousands who *have* died or been seriously maimed through not being so fortunate with this grotesque biological experiment. Oh, did I mention that Annie is an O.B.E.? Not sure if that's important.

R.E.M. frontman **Michael Stipe** put out a series of videos to his fanbase early on in the scam, reinforcing the message to 'stay at home." In March he told his viewers, "we'll celebrate in four months." This would have been July, by which point many of the early restrictions in some of the US states had been lifted. Was this a lucky guess, or did he have inside knowledge of the plan? By the following year, Stipe and fellow R.E.M. musician **Mike Mills** were participating in Public Service Announcements encouraging Americans to take... as Rolf Harris used to say, can you tell what it is yet? Stipe even laughs as he delivers his. Because genocide is so funny, you know.

Stipe ticks many boxes in terms of being a likely mind-control candidate seeming, like so many other singers, to slip into alternative personas during his stage performances. He also ticks boxes in terms of military family links. Although reluctant to talk about his father in interviews—a scenario reminiscent of **Jim Morrison**'s claims that his Navy Admiral dad was dead when he was still very much alive—Stipe once revealed that his father "flew helicopters in Vietnam." Stipe himself grew up on military bases around the world. He is known for his socially-conscious lyrics which *appear* to be diametrically opposed to those one would assume his father held. *'Orange Crush'* is a scathing criticism of the use of the biological weapon Agent Orange during the Vietnam War, for example, while *'Man In the Moon'* mocks the idea that N.A.S.A.'s Apollo missions could possibly have landed there, (they didn't.)

But this is far from the first time we have encountered such *apparent* shows of rebellion, and anyone paying attention will surely realise by now that creating false "rebels" out of owned assets is a standard control system tactic. If there is going to be dissent, it may as well be controlled. R.E.M. were close to C.I.A. assets **The Police**, opening up for them at shows, and were signed to the Copeland brothers' I.R.S. (International Records Syndicate,) with F.B.I. (Frontier Booking International) booking their shows. (The Copelands' other venture was named Copeland International Artists—or C.I.A. Ever get the feeling you're being handed a clue?)

And could R.E.M.'s very naming—standing for the light sleep-state known as Rapid Eye Movement in which dreams are the most vivid and metaphorical, be a sly nod towards dream-like dissociation from reality induced by mind-control?

In the edition of the on-line newspaper *'The Hill'* which ran a story titled *'Paul McCartney: COVID-19 vaccinations are 'cool,'* the article also listed **Mariah Carey**, **Olivia Rodrigo**, **Eric Church**, **Ozzy Osbourne** and **Tony Bennett** as among other "entertainers" who had promoted vaccines in interviews or through social media.

Total recall

A ragtag bunch of assorted "celebrities" was put together at the very start of the UK's vaccine rollout, as reported by the '*Sunday Mirror*' under the title "*We'll Give the Jab a Stab.*" This motley crew of obedient pets included: Bob Geldof, (another big surprise, eh?); **Lulu**; Esther Rantzen; Michael Parkinson; Michael Palin and Eamon Holmes, (despite having had David Icke guest on his talk radio show several times warning of the N.W.O. masterplan, including the vaccine agenda. Eamon "Truther" Holmes. Yeah, right.) Just hazarding a guess, but I suspect one or two of this book's readers wouldn't mind administering a jab or two to some of the "celebrities" themselves . . . though not necessarily with a syringe. The public had already been forewarned to expect such stunts. An article in the '*Guardian*' in November 2020 titled '*N.H.S. to enlist "sensible" celebrities to persuade people to take coronavirus vaccine*' spoke of "influencers" who are "known and loved" being recruited. Apparently Lulu, Esther Rantzen and Toyah Willcox are officially deemed "sensible." Who knew?

There was very little surprise—for me at least—when Geldof was wheeled out later in the narrative, and stories emerged of him planning a new Live Aid-style concert, this time to raise funds for vaccinating people living in Third World countries. The only real surprise is that he was said to have been coerced into the project by former UK Prime Minister Gordon Brown. After all, who could be more relevant to politics and current affairs than the wildly charismatic party guy Brown, right? I guess Tony Blair was busy on some other genocidal agenda or other. Brown complained of "Medical Apartheid," maintaining that poor people in developing countries had as much right to a vaccine as their more fortunate counterparts. (Apparently it's "Apartheid" *not* to roll out killer vaccines in the developing world as in Western nations, but it's *not* "Apartheid" to limit people's freedoms of choice and movement based on whether they make the personal decision to take said killer vaccines into their own bodies. Right. Got it.)

In the same week came the announcement of the "Global" Citizen Vax Live concert, "the concert to re-unite the world," (though performed remotely via TV and on-line links, naturally. People actually assembling physically all in the same place is *soooo* 2019, darling.) Pet poodles ordered to sit, beg and sing at this one included **Jennifer Lopez**, **Eddie Vedder**, the Foo Fighters, **J Balvin** and **H.E.R.** Sounds like a real party. Apparently, pushing "the vax" had become the number one priority of the "entertainment" industry, (is anyone else getting bored with this yet?) and the natural/ herbal/ holistic plant-based cures for *all* diseases that are provided by Nature, and have been administered by Shaman the world over for millennia, can just be completely ignored.

There was "outrage" from *'The Sun'* newspaper when it reported that loathed, convicted paedophile **Gary Glitter** had received his Co(n)vid "jab" ahead of the staff at the prison where he was being held, reinforcing the idea that vaccination is a privilege and a lucky perk. I was told in conversation in early 2021 that certain well-known (if you watch TV, that is) "influencers" from the world of "reality TV" had been paid large sums of money to promote the official government line on Co(n)vid on their social media platforms, and—outrageously—to state that a family member had fallen ill from "the virus." Given that I trusted the veracity of the source, I submitted a Freedom of Information Act request to the Government's Cabinet Office. The request read:

> *"Under the Freedom of Information Act, I would like to request details of which celebrities/ public figures have received payments to promote the government's policy on coronavirus (Covid-19) on their social media sites, and which celebrities/ public figures have been paid to state that a family member has contracted Covid-19.*
>
> *"Please provide details of the amounts paid, and the dates on which the payments were made."*

After taking almost the full 30 days by which they are obligated to give a response, the Department's utterly disappointing, though not entirely unexpected reply was:

> *"This information is being withheld under section 40(2) of the Freedom of Information Act (personal data.) We consider that disclosure of the information would contravene principle A under article 5(1) (a) of the General Data Protection Regulations (GDPR), which*

requires that personal data should be processed lawfully, fairly, and transparently. I have considered the legitimate interests in disclosure and have found that, on balance, there is no overriding legitimate interest or necessity in disclosure that override reasonable expectations of privacy of the individuals concerned."

It seems the Government is capable of morality—on its own terms—when it deems it appropriate. Apparently a public figure's right to privacy is more important than the people's right to know whether they have been paid public money for reinforcing a provable criminal scam. On the question of whether payments have been made to state that a family member had contracted "the virus," meanwhile, the response was:

"The Cabinet Office does not pay celebrities/ public figures to state that a family member has contracted Covid-19."

A similar motley assortment of owned assets was assembled for a government-sponsored ad to push the Co(n)vid vaccine to black and Asian communities when the take-up had been especially lacking among ethnic minorities. (It's just a thought, but maybe it's because they're extra-suspicious—rightfully—of the motives of any government that claims to care about them following generations of subjugation and enslavement of their ancestors at the hands of Empire.) To her great discredit, singer **Beverley Knight** was among the those called upon for this sickening piece of propaganda. Who, really, was ever going to say, "well, I was adamant that I wasn't going to take the vaccine given the cocktail of toxic shite it contains. But if Beverley Knight says I should, well, that's different! I'm making my appointment right now."

All bases were certainly covered when veteran Country singer **Dolly Parton** emerged the same week, crowing proudly in the mainstream press about how she'd taken the Moderna vaccine that she had reportedly helped to fund, to the tune of $1 million...Is it just me, or is there a pattern emerging here? She even changed the words to her most popular hit, 'Jolene,' to: "Vaccine, vaccine, vaccine, vaccine, I'm begging of you, please don't hesitate. Vaccine, vaccine, vaccine, vaccine, because once you're dead, then that's a bit too late."

Then there was **Dave Bartram**, the former lead singer with **Showaddywaddy**, whose video insisting that "the only" way to "beat the virus" was vaccination appeared the same day. This was a master stroke. After all, who more relevant to the culture of 2021 than the singer of a band who had had their heyday 45 years previous, and even then were recycling the sounds and styles of the 1950s? It seems singers whose best years are decades in the past have no problem promoting the agendas of eugenicists, satanists, paedophiles, thieves and career liars if it means keeping themselves in the public eye. I'm sure the paycheque comes in handy too.

The joke's on us?

Jaz Coleman, frontman of the veteran British group **Killing Joke**, *appeared* to be taking an admirable stance when he stated on a video posted to his jazcoleman.com site in July 2020, that he was somewhere in Central America, (without elaborating on where or explaining why,) and that he might never leave since he in no way would be taking one of Bill Gates' vaccines. All along, Coleman has been heard *saying* all the right things, whether it's rallying against unimpeded "globalisation" or the lost art of critical thought, or, such as when addressing New World Order bagman Bono in a 2009 interview, he told writer Pippa Lang:

> *"Bono and his old boys' network — pah! I know what he's creeping out to do, flying round the world in his big jet. Did you know he's earned over one billion pounds tax-free?! This guy is not fit to even talk. And wearing those stupid fucking sunglasses all the time. He's a phoney. He's a fraud. I'd like to see him up in the dock with Tony Blair for war crimes!"*

So far, so good, right? And Coleman appears to have a particular bee in his bonnet about Bono, having called him out as "a fucking disgrace," a "motherfucker" and an "Irish piece of shit" in an interview for the BringTheNoise portal.

So often, however, it's not what's said but the way in which it's said that tells so much, and Coleman's protestations in the latter interview lacked sincerity for me, as if they were merely being recited on cue as he slouched nonchalantly in his seat. Then somehow we have to reconcile Coleman's apparent anti-Establishment stance with comments he himself made when discussing his own family background and upbringing. Like **Brian Jones** of the Rolling Stones he was born in Cheltenham, (home of British Intelligence's G.C.H.Q. agency.) His father Ronald Coleman is listed as a schoolteacher. It's through the line of his mother, Gloria Pandey, that the connections into British colonial India come. After revealing in an interview with loudersound.com that he was told from an infant that he would become a musician, Coleman added:

> *"My great, great, great grandfather was Mangal Pandey, who led the insurrection against the British in 1857, and is revered in Mother India as one of the great nationalists. Then there's B.N. Pandey who wrote 'The Break-Up of British India' and was very close to Gandhi. My grandfather was in the 1962 war with China; he executed two of his own men for not going forward, and he believed in global revolution."*

Another comment of his that takes some explaining away occurred during a 2015 interview for the Mike James Rock Show. After referencing "elite" bloodline families such as the Schiffs, Morgans, Rockefellers and Rothschilds, Coleman went on to note that there are "some wonderful individuals in these families," and, frustratingly unchallenged by the interviewer, that, "even one member of my band works for perhaps one of these great big families and flies in his private jet."

Coleman has long displayed a penchant for dressing in dark, Gothic attire—sometimes in a top hat out of the voodoo tradition, and with his face painted black and white to evoke the duality so often symbolised within Freemasonry. He has been no stranger to flashing some tried-and-tested hand signals over the years, too, notably the Masonic 'shhhh' sign—the index finger held to the lips to denote the telling of no secrets.

Given that dark occultists do adhere to the tenet of always giving we "profane" ones the opportunity to know, however—whether this represents spiritual mockery, or so that we can never make the (as they see it) legitimate claim that we didn't know—perhaps there's a clue as to the group's true nature from its name, which Coleman once explained as: "The killing joke is like when people watch something like '*Monty Python*' on the television and laugh, when really they're laughing at themselves."

Meanwhile, '*The Killing Joke*' also became the title of an edition of the '*Watchmen*' series of graphic novels created by artist, (and occultist/ Crowleyite) Alan Moore, and later a Batman animated adventure. It is a phrase which may well have been lifted from the opening lines of '*Onion Peelings*' from within Aleister Crowley's '*Book of Lies*,' which reads: "The Universe is the practical joke of the general at the expense of the particular, quoth Frater Perdurabo, and laughed."

The concept of controlled opposition is as widespread within the world of entertainment as it ever was in the world of the military. If voices of dissent in response to Establishment tactics are inevitable, goes the logic, then it may as well be the Establishment controlling said voices.

Getting one's money's worth

By this point, all hope for anyone who would actually respond to this cynical ploy in the way its architects had intended had been lost. If there were any hope to be had at all, though, it came from some very clear indications that the controllers were getting absolutely desperate by this point. Knowing that trying to mandate the vaccines would constitute a breach of all kinds of human, not to mention, Natural rights, they tried every propaganda trick in their arsenal to try and coerce the "useless eaters" into voluntarily taking the jab. This included getting the Queen to appear on-line, via a purported Zoom conference, to tell of how she had taken the vaccine, that it "didn't hurt a bit," that it was one's civic duty to take it for the sake of others, and that it would constitute self-ishness not to.

There's so much to say in response to this, but I'm wary of getting sidetracked into an epic rant of righteous indignation, So I'll just leave it at the observation that apparently, it's NOT selfish to have hoarded obscene, sickening levels of wealth for centuries upon centuries which could have eradicated all poverty, starvation and homelessness multiple millions of times over. Or indeed to harbour your son when he's accused of the sexual abuse of minors as facilitated by his serial paedophile and child-trafficking chum.

Oh, and it might not be important, but I guess I should mention it either way. THAT WAS NOT THE QUEEN! I'm no technical expert, but "Her Majesty"s appearance was one of the most blatant displays of deep-fake Computer-Generated Imagery that it's possible to get. Nothing about it was convincing; she had the air of a hologram about her; the face was too elongated; the words spoken didn't match with the mouth movements; the voice was clearly not that of the Queen but of a voice actor; she spoke at a far quicker pace than the Queen ever has; her responses were too quick and sharp to be natural, and — most telling of all — she smiled several times and displayed a full range of human emotions! There was more of the same when she purportedly appeared on a Zoom call at the time of the COP26 "Climate Change" conference in Glasgow. The images provided to the mainstream press were so blatantly faked it's almost as if those behind them WANTED to alert the public to the fact it wasn't her!

As a friend commented to me in an e-mail concerning those forever beholden to their overlords through the engineered careers that have been facilitated for them — a dynamic that applies to musicians, actors, television presenters, sports personalities, religious leaders, business leaders and politicians alike — and even monarchs, it would seem:

> *"Once the Mafia buys you a new expensive car; beware. Someday your involvement will find you unable to refuse your new friends' "just a little task here and there."*

The death of entertainment?

The speed with which all expressions of art, culture and leisure were shut down in the wake of the "Pandemic" suggests that these were considered pretty much redundant by 2020. Sunak's comments — evasive and as non-committal as they were — suggest an official position that the creative arts, and in particular the music industry, are now considered expendable. As my previous books have detailed, the music industry has been employed as a vehicle for psychological manipulation and the subliminal shaping of tastes and opinions for decades, and the agendas were demonstrably ramped up in the years since 2000. I've commented in interviews, half-jokingly, that every time you think the music industry's controllers have debased the art form to as low as it can go, they find new ways of plumbing the depths of the cesspit yet further.

But what if that point really *has* been reached? What if the social-engineers considered that they'd done such a successful job in making popular music as insidious, Satanic and destructive as they possibly could, and now the time has come to tank it? This—as far as their sick, psychopathic agendas are concerned—would have the additional demoralising effect of robbing young music fans of the product that they'd become so reliant upon, as harmful as it may have been, and traumatising them by suddenly making their lives feel empty and unfulfilled.

Brothers in arms?

One group which has always been presented as "edgy" is **Oasis**. Frontman **Noel Gallagher** didn't do any favours to his apparent "fuck the system" image when he was pictured hobnobbing with British Prime Minister/ warmonger Tony Blair at a champagne reception at Downing Street in June '97. Gallagher had been a highly vocal supporter of Blair. Even as recently as 2019 he was still claiming to be a fan. In an interview in November of that year with the *'Manchester Evening News,'* he told the reporter:

> *"I was out about two months ago and I happened to bump into Tony Blair in the foyer of a hotel. And I said: 'I bet you're glad you're out of it now, aren't you, mate?' And he said: 'Actually I'm not, I wish I was fucking back in it because it is fucked."*

> *"Still to me he's the only person when I hear him talking that makes any sense."*

Gallagher's anecdote rings true, since Blair still takes any opportunity he can to try to appear still relevant and hold influence. Towards the end of 2020, instead of having been hanged for Treason and Crimes Against Humanity years before, he seeped back on to TV screens like a rat scurrying out of a sewer, and was given airtime to promote the Co(n)vid vaccine, and insist that society should not be allowed to go back to normal until every adult in the land had taken it.

All of this makes Noel Gallagher's stance on the mask-wearing phenomenon during Co(n)vid rather out-of-character, therefore, since it would appear to contradict what his hero Blair would have been officially endorsing. In September 2020, Gallagher drew the scorn of the controlled press by stating that he won't wear a mask when on public transport, as it represents a violation of his personal liberties. Speaking on a podcast with Matt Morgan, who Gallagher berated as a "cowardly germophobe" he said:

> *"It's not a law. There's too many fucking liberties being taken away from us now . . . I choose not to wear one. If I get the virus it's on me, it's not on anyone else . . . it's a piss-take. There's no need for it . . . They're pointless.*

> *". . . I was going up to Manchester the other week and some guy's going, 'can you put your mask on,' on the train, 'because the transport police will get on and fine you a thousand pounds. But you don't have to put it on if you're eating.' So I was saying: Oh right, this killer virus that's sweeping through the train is gonna come and attack me, but see me having a sandwich and go, leave him, he's having his lunch?"*

But . . . is anyone really surprised? . . . it was mixed-message time when, on 1st June 2021, *'The Independent'* reported that Noel had taken a Co(n)vid vaccine upon the recommendation of his GP. If Noel really had been as clued-up on Co(n)vid fascism as his stance on masks suggested, it might be reasonable to assume that he would have fully researched the vaccine issue and concluded that it's just one more aspect of the New World Order agenda of which he would have wanted no part. Having initially resisted, he is alleged to have been swayed simply by his doctor telling him he would be "a fool" not to take it. Noel's argument, however, was that his taking the vaccine should not be used to sway anyone else from making what should always be a personal free-will decision, (even though there seems to have been little point in this article running if coercion wasn't its covert aim!) In an *apparent* railing against his peers, Noel ranted:

> *"I will say, it's a human right to decline (the vaccine.) And the people who are virtue-signalling, (with) their lofty wagging their finger at people who are declining it, can eff off. That's how fascism starts. When I sit at home and in between the football there's public information films with Lenny Henry (saying) 'take the jab', looking like an abandoned dog, I'm like: 'mate, you take the jab, it's up to you.'"*

Noel's brother **Liam** has always been thought of as the more "dangerous" and "rebellious" of the pair but did not back up his brother on the mask issue. In the same month as Noel's interview, a fan on Twitter suggested he "drop the mask and be a proper geezer," to which Liam replied: "I don't mind the mask mooch about no fucker knows who you are sweet as."

Liam went on to cement his reputation as a Co(n)vid opponent. At the time of a protest performance in front of Parliament by around 400 artists to draw attention to the plight of struggling musicians, Gallagher posted a series of Tweets related to the issue:

> *"So the dopes in gov telling musicians and people in arts to retrain and get another job, what and become massive cunts like you, nah yer alright.*

> *"This country would be beyond wank if it wasn't for the arts and the music and football show a bit of respect you little TURD.*

> *"If anyone needs to retrain it's them shower of cunts."*

Apparently, it wasn't just government ministers who resembled Liam's favourite vocabulary for the female genitalia; that status is reserved for 'the virus" itself too. In late December, evidently rather miffed that the football game between Everton and Manchester City had been called off due to players "testing positive," Liam possibly summed up the sentiments of the world—though in more characteristically colourful language—by Tweeting" "The footy is off GUTTED you fucking cunt of a virus be gone you fucking shit."

Liam returned with some more choice words—this time for a named individual—when Chief Medical Officer Chris Whitty added to the psychological torture, fraud and crimes against humanity already being visited on the British nation, with further bleak warnings about the ongoing spread of the "virus." Writing on Twitter, seemingly his favourite mode of expression, Gallagher commented "That Chris Whitty is getting on my titty he needs a slap!"

Later, Liam eloquently articulated his feelings on the latest country-wide lockdown with a Tweet dated 5th January 2021. *"Illegal to leave home FUCK OFF."*

A diss from a rose

A fellow Mancunian, less of a household name, but who has never had a problem with freely expressing himself, is **Ian Brown**, singer with the 90s "Madchester"-era Indie group the **Stone Roses**. As far back as the start of his solo career he was making songs like 1998's *'Corpses In Their Mouth,'* named after a quote from the book *'The Revolution of Everyday Life'* by the Situationist writer Raoul Vaneigem. By 2001, the album *'Music of the Spheres'* had appeared, with its single *'F.E.A.R.'* Here, Brown recited various phrases which make up the acronym of the title, such as "fallen empires are ruling," "fantastic expectations, amazing revelations," and "free expression as revolution."

His 2007 single alongside **Sinéad O'Connor**, *'Illegal Attacks,'* pulled no punches right from its opening lines: "So what the fuck is this UK? Gunnin' with this US of A, in Iraq and Iran and in Afghanistan." By 2018, he had become possibly the first artist with a mainstream background to address the issue of stratospheric aerosol spraying, known scientifically as geo-engineering, and colloquially as "chemtrailing" in his song *'Blue Sky Day,'* which includes:

> *"Whatever happened to a blue sky day?*
> *Planes overhead sprayin'*
> *All my blue sky day away*

... You think I'm crazy, would you rather I don't say?
Shall we pretend that it ain't happenin',
And it'll all just go away?"

Former Stone Roses frontman Ian Brown incurred the wrath of his own
"fan" base when he dared to exercise critical thinking, do his own research,
and express an opinion other than the one publicly approved by Organised
Society.

https://commons.wikimedia.org/wiki/File:IanBrownToronto2005.jpg

Brown confirmed himself to be an artist with a social conscience, courageous enough to fully express his sentiments without concerns of how it might "affect his career" throughout the "Pandemic." He Tweeted almost daily to expose Co(n)vid-19 as a monumental scam designed to take away individual rights and freedoms and usher in the New World Order's plans, to expose the agenda to justify mass vaccination as "the only solution," and to consistently decry government lockdown regulations as unscientific, cruel and unlawful. As if I didn't already like him enough, in February 2021 he endeared himself to me even further by Tweeting:

> *'I will NEVER sing to a crowd who must be vaccinated as a condition of attendance. NEVER EVER!"*

125

Brown stood true to his word when, shortly after this Tweet, he announced that he was pulling out from his headline slot at the 2021 Neighbourhood Weekend Festival in Warrington owing to the organisers' insistence that all attendees must provide proof of vaccination.

Kudos in this regard must also go to **Richard Ashcroft** of the **Verve**, who declined to appear at the 2021 Tramlines Festival when it became clear that his performance would be subject to certain government restrictions. Ashcroft complained that, despite his telling the organisers that he would not appear under such circumstances, they continued to advertise his name on the bill. **Supergrass** were happy to step in as Ashcroft's replacement. The festival had advised that ticket-holders must be able to provide a negative lateral flow test or proof of vaccination as a condition of entry. Explaining himself in an Instagram post, Ashcroft wrote:

> *"Apologies to my fans for any disappointment but the festival was informed over 10 days ago that I wouldn't be playing once it had become part of a government testing programme. I had informed my agent months ago I wouldn't be playing concerts with restrictions. The status of the festival was one thing when I signed up for it, but sadly was forced to become something else."*

Some weeks later, however, came the announcement via his official platforms that Ashcroft was pulling out of his headline slot at the Tunes In The Dunes festival in Cornwall with just two days' notice due to "contracting Covid" It's a safe bet that Ashcroft, being aware of the scam that is vaccine passports, would also know that the entire Co(n)vid debacle is a hoax, and that if he had indeed got ill, it would be from something other than "the virus." So a reasonable question would be: what the hell's going on here then?

His announcement came in the same week that comedian-turned-podcast host Joe Rogan, having picked up a reputation as a "Covid denier" and as "anti-vaccine," also claimed to have "contracted Covid." There is, of course, a morbid irony to someone who had previously doubted the veracity of Covid, then *just happening* to go down with it when less than 1 per cent of the population actually do, even according to official figures. This is, of course, the point. It's all propaganda and mockery. I personally never trusted Rogan's supposed credentials as a "truther," which were never any more convincing than Katy Perry's former mind-control handler Russell Brand's, and this incident confirmed for me his status as just another establishment tool.

Not that Katy fared any better. For Halloween 2021 she dressed up as a syringe, (with a goon mask, naturally,) while her husband Orlando Bloom dressed as a doctor, to push the idea of vaccinations. I can think of little more horrifying.

Anyway, that digression done, back to gig boycotts. Things just kept getting better in this regard with Eric Clapton, who announced a short while after Ashcroft's stance that he would refuse to perform at any venue which applied any form of medical Apartheid as a condition of entry. This stance smoked Queen guitarist **Brian May (CBE,)** (who looks more like the reincarnation of Sir Isaac Newton with every passing year) out of his hole when, in a *'Daily Mail'* article in August, he branded Clapton a "fruitcake" for his anti-vaccination sentiments, while insisting he still remained his hero:

"I love Eric Clapton; he's my hero, but he has very different views from me in many ways. Anti-vax people, I'm sorry, I think they're fruitcakes. There's plenty of evidence to show that vaccination helps. On the whole they've been very safe."

(There's only one slight problem with Brian's statement—the "plenty of evidence" *actually* shows that the Co(n)vid vaccines have been anything *but* safe, were never adequately tested and as such cannot even be considered "vaccines" in the traditional sense and have killed and maimed hundreds of thousands. Apart from that he's spot-on.)

May didn't miss another chance to shill for the hand that feeds him in a separate interview for *'The Independent'* where—aside from reinforcing the validity of Co(n)vid, he attempted to cement his credentials as an astro-physicist by insisting the Apollo moon landing hoaxes, so transparent a child of five could see through them, were real:

"I don't really want people spreading misinformation, especially if my kids are getting hold of it, or my grandchildren. It was all done in a Hollywood studio? Bullshit!"

(More likely the Nevada Desert actually, but still . . .)

Back with Ian Brown, meanwhile, a few months earlier in 2020, at the point at which many of the world's populations had been "given" back just a few of their freedoms, Brown had put out his song *'Little Seed, Big Tree.'* In a few minutes the song conveyed the truth of what the world was going through, (along with a sly reference to Bill Gates) as effectively and memorably as a two-hour documentary or 500-page document could, with lyrics like:

> *"Masonic lockdown in your hometown*
>
> *Masonic lockdown, can you hear me now?*
>
> *From the top down, soul shot down*
>
> *State shakedown, mass breakdown*
>
> *Global orders, riding over borders*
>
> *Get behind your doors for the new world order*
>
> *Doctor Evil and his needle*
>
> *Doctor Evil with a masterplan."*

With tedious predictability, the mainstream quickly rallied to diffuse any inspirational impact Brown's song may have had. A scoffing Mark Beaumont in the *'NME'* was quick to publish an article titled "Ian Brown's conspiracy tweets are pure Covidiocy. And he's not the only tinfoil hat-wearing rocker," and the sub-heading, "The Stone Roses singer joined the red pill-devouring ranks with a series of anti-lockdown missives. What is it with musicians and not believing the TRUTH?" His article goes on to assert that "The NO MASK part of Brown's argument is particularly idiotic," and ends with advice which could have come straight from an edition of any corporate-owned mainstream news bulletin, "Mask up, stay at home, get your jab when it arrives . . . " Robin Murray writing for *'Clash Music,'* described *'Little Seed, Big Tree'* as "woeful," "genuinely appalling" and "absolute entry-level local boozer open-mic nonsense."

As well as drawing scorn from virtue-signalling "fans," and even fellow Stone Roses bandmate **John Squire**, Brown's stand for common-sense, dignity and Truth drew mocking contempt from another quarter. The

Irish twin brothers **John and Edward Grimes**, known together as **Jedward**, had hardly set the world on fire and kept the public's tongues wagging since winning the *'X Factor'* "talent" show in 2009 and going on to release albums and present on TV. For some reason, however, they felt qualified to mock Brown on social media, trolling many of his posts drawing attention to the Co(n)vid scam with comments like: "Hi Ian, You discredited yourself with your backward views and non-logical actions," and "The Public have lost all respect and credibility for your views! Your music and cheekbones are a dream, but your tweets are a nightmare."

The pair also had a few choice words for those protesting their natural rights at one of the freedom rallies in Dublin, stating: "Dear Dublin anti-mask protest. Get the fuck inside you selfish low lives sincerely the rest of the country." With Brown being someone who has clearly taken the personal responsibility to research what is *really* going on behind the cover of a "Pandemic" which isn't one, and who has an inherent understanding of where Rights and Freedom *really* come from, I suspect the desperate attempts to appear relevant from a couple of talent-lacking and none-too-bright walking advertisements for Tavistock-style social engineering won't cause him to lose much sleep . . . and I won't be expecting any kind of Jedward career resurgence any time soon.

Jedward's stance was supported by an Irish music star of a rather different ilk, in the form of Sinéad O'Connor.

> *"Can I please ask that selfishly unmasked crowds standing shoulder to shoulder protesting and ignoring Covid protective restrictions not use my music as if to suggest I support you in any way. I do not."*

(See this book's *'Sound Bites'* section for more on O'Connor.)

Conscientious objectors

Jim Corr, of the Irish family rock band **The Corrs**, is clearly a man with a conscience and the capacity for independent research, and had already been publicly vocal about the anomalies surrounding 9/11 and many other issues prior to his commentary on the Scamdemic and associated vaccine agenda. A list of honorary exceptions of his nature would not be complete without Jim's name on it, therefore.

An entirely different reaction came from another *'X Factor'* contestant, meanwhile. Wales-born, Morocco-raised **Yousseph 'Chico' Slimani**. Following his appearance on the show, he went on to have a UK number one hit with the camp and cheesy *'It's Chico Time.'* Based on his public image, Chico was one of the last people anyone might have expected to turn up as one of the featured speakers at the protest events that took place with crowds of many thousands in London in 2020. Demonstrating that he had put in many hours of research and was prepared to go wherever the truth took him—and to stand up and be counted—his demo speech on 29th August was one of the most hard-hitting of all in Trafalgar Square. He had previously founded the Rainbow Child Foundation, which describes itself as a non-profit organisation helping under-privileged children around the world, and his speech—delivered as a poem—referenced institutionalised paedophiles and trafficked children a "the real Pandemic," a constant under-current to the "virus" narrative among truth-seekers.

If Chico, based on his pop music credentials alone, was a wildly unlikely name to be taking a stand against injustice and immorality, **Right Said Fred** certainly gave him a run for his money. Remembered for camp pop hits such as *'I'm Too Sexy,' 'Deeply Dippy'* and *'Don't Talk, Just Kiss,'* brothers **Fred and Richard Fairbrass** found out for themselves what it's like to go against any mainstream narrative or "approved" stance when they joined the crowds at the 26th September Trafalgar Square freedom rally. Presenting the notion that protesting against tyrannical incursions into basic human rights is a strange thing to do, rather than just silently and meekly accepting it, the mainstream media and many in the public rounded on the Fairbrasses, who subsequently went to lengths in the newspaper interviews that followed to insist they were not "Covid deniers." Tweeting in response to the initial round of public criticism, the pair stated:

> *"No need to erode free speech and the right to assembly in the process. Those rights were hard earned, give them away and we'll never get them back."*

Speaking to *'The Independent'* newspaper some weeks later, Fred Fairbrass said:

> *"My position is I'm not a Covid denier and I'm not anti-vax, but I defend those people's right to express their opinion. That's all it is. So there's another march at the end of this month and we'll be going to that as well for exactly the same reason, which is free speech."*

The Fairbrasses were particularly concerned at the impact that government-imposed lockdowns were having on the ability of musicians and performers of all kinds to continue making a living. They subsequently became one of the early acts to perform on *'That Was Then ... This Is Now,'* a new on-line TV concept created by **Mike Stock** of **Stock Aitken Waterman** fame, and presented by former Radio 1 DJ Mike Read. Mike Stock commented:

> *"These are heritage acts who have been largely ignored by the government and have been cut off from any income this year. We hope to provide some financial assistance as well as giving audiences something of real high quality to enjoy."*

The show, for which viewers pay an access fee, broadcasts via the TicketCo TV platform at 7pm on Thursdays—the timeslot traditionally occupied by the BBC's *'Top Of The Pops'*. **Kim Wilde**, **Limahl**, **Chesney Hawkes**, **Nik Kershaw**, **Paul Young**, **Sonia**, **The Fizz** (formerly **Bucks Fizz**) and **Toyah Willcox** (again!!) are some of the other names to have appeared.

The treasonous vipers in the mainstream press naturally had a field day when Richard Fairbrass was suddenly hospitalised in August 2021, gleefully delighting in his downfall as headline after headline, (of course, because they all just regurgitate their "news" from the same sources rather than actually going out and doing any *real* journalism for themselves—and I've seen this for myself through having worked in a radio "news" room,) gloated that he had "caught Covid-19" without missing the opportunity to cement his status as one of those irresponsible "anti-vaxxers" by adding, "but he's still against the vaccine." The gutter presstitutes love "poetic justice" stories like this, and a whole glut of them had been going around at the time, attempting to keep the simple-minded in line by saying, "See? This is what happens when you deny Covid and oppose vaccines. You end up getting it. Serves you right!"

It's not just from the world of music that *the* most unexpected names have been emerging as freedom fighters, meanwhile. No-one could have reasonably expected that status to have been fulfilled by Gillian McKeith given her unfortunate reputation as "the poo lady" from Channel 4's *'You Are What You Eat'* in which she examined participants' stool samples to assess potential dietary improvements. While television peers like Denise Welch and Carol McGiffin of the show *'Loose Women'* went *some* of the way in criticising the UK government's response to Co(n)vid, McKeith pulled no punches, going more balls-out than most men in fearlessly calling the Scamdemic out for the fraudulent outrage that it was on her social media, much to the chagrin of the mainstream shitrags, of course — always a good sign that you're on the right track.

Similar no-holds-barred real talk came from veteran stand-up comic Lee Hurst, who found himself a lonely voice in the world of Comedy when he courageously spoke out about the lies, corruption, medical Apartheid and genocide. His inevitable smearing by the press and ostracisation by his profession highlighted that the field of Comedy — just like Rock music in that it's *supposed* to be "edgy" and "anti-establishment" — is actually about as radical as a copy of *'Crochet and Knitting Monthly'* as his fellow "comedians" cowered meekly from behind their masks. Only when told it was OK to do so, mind. He would have been entirely alone in his field if not for the similarly brave and bold speaking out of comedian Alistair Williams, who deserves similar props and kudos for doing the right thing.

The roll call of wholly unexpected names to have spoken out about the Plandemic also includes Cuban/ American rapper/ singer **Pitbull**, who, on an episode of the *'Drink Champs'* show on the Revolt TV YouTube channel, spontaneously highlighted the connections between Co(n)vid and the worldwide implementation of Communism. He went further by referencing Bill Gates' involvement, and the Event 201 simulation exercise that he had spearheaded. With his entire body of music work being pure garbage, these comments represent the first worthwhile words to have come publicly out of his mouth. It suggests that many artists may be far more intelligent and capable of thinking for themselves than their public persona, or the extent to which they are muted and censored by their gatekeepers, would suggest.

The British rapper **Zuby** deserves some recognition for not being afraid to speak out about Co(n)vid fascism on his Twitter page. Answering one follower who had advised him that he should keep his political views to himself, Zuby responded:

> *"No. I'm a public figure so I need to do the exact opposite of what you suggest. So many sissies and cowards out there . . . I'm not joining them."*

In one of many other such messages, he also wrote:

> *"I am pro-freedom and personal decision-making. I am against governmental overreach and authoritarianism. If you want to wear a mask, take a drug, or stay at home, that is within your rights and I will support your rights. Don't trample everyone else's."*

Some plain talk—and the expected attempt at reputation-trashing that inevitably followed, came from veteran UK Grime MC **Wiley**. In the '*Metro*' newspaper of 6th May 2020, "journalist" Mel Evans opted for the predictable and supremely unimaginative headline of "Wiley shares bizarre coronavirus conspiracy theory as he suggests virus was 'created by China' as method of 'depopulation'."

These writers never think it relevant to go on and explain just *why* a theory is "bizarre," nor to actually research what the person in question is claiming to see whether there is validity to it. They merely parrot, just like every other controlled mainstream mouthpiece out there, the "official" line deemed to be "normal." Because what could be more "normal" than removing people's basic Rights and Freedoms of movement, assembly and protest, shutting down the borders of entire nations, forcing people to stay in their homes with threat of kidnap, violence or extortion if they fail to comply, forcing people to shut down businesses that they've spent their entire adult lives building up, forcing people to wear pieces of cloth over their noses and mouths which do nothing to keep them safe but rather *cause* infections and weaken immune systems, encouraging people to spy and report on their neighbours, dictating to people who they can and cannot have in *their own homes*, when they can and cannot go out, and where they can and cannot go, presenting flawed science and deliberate mis-information as "truth" and systematically suppressing alternative information that challenges the status quo, and hiring legions of mercenary thugs to beat up, kidnap and incarcerate those who assemble to peacefully protest their rights, all for a "virus" which, even according to provably inflated and manipulated "official" figures, has only affected less than half a per cent of the world's population? Nothing "bizarre" about any of that, right Mel? All perfectly normal and acceptable. Why on earth would anyone think otherwise?

(I have to note, though, that it is unfortunate that the lead picture accompanying the *'Metro'* article featured **Wiley**—real name **Richard Kylea Cowie**—making the tired and familiar "666" sign with his fingers that so many owned and controlled music industry assets have over the years. Realistically—and as reinforced so many times through these books—there's no way he would have achieved the level of influence he has without having been co-opted in such a way. He is, after all, an MBE. This may call into question the authenticity of his comments for some. The way I see it is that artists are allowed a certain degree of freedom to express personal opinions within clearly defined parameters. If they should step outside of these they get to know about it fairly quickly.

A couple of months later, Wiley earned himself a ban from Twitter and Facebook and the scorn of the mainstream after Tweeting comments that were branded "anti-Semitic," (which actually means anti-Arabic rather than anti-Jewish, when the etymology of the phrase is scrutinised, just as an aside) following a public fall-out with a former manager who happened to be Jewish, and later lashed out at critics, many of whom also happened to be Jewish. When asked what he would like to say to his fans, Wiley commented that, at 41, he was at the end of his Grime career and no longer relevant, which might explain why he felt so confident to speak out earlier about the "Pandemic."

The *'Metro'* article did its best to mock Wiley and make him sound unintelligent, and referred to a piece in that month's *'Q'* magazine, (which folded two months later after 34 years in business, with—iron-ically—a decline in circulation and advertising revenue blamed on the "Pandemic,") in which Wiley had commented:

> *"There's a deeper root. I wanna know why. I wanna know who is behind it . . .*

> *". . . Why are celebrities and famous people jumping out at this? How come I didn't get the memo?" Is there a special memo that 'if something like this happens, we follow the agenda?'. . . The famous people and celebrities who've popped up, 'Oh I've got it but no symptoms'. I don't believe 'em . . .'*

Smoking out the shills

One such "celebrity" to have claimed early on that he had contracted "the virus"—thus helping to push the initial first wave of hysteria and fear-based panic—was actor **Idris Elba**, a long-time control system asset. Graduating from British acting work, (his earliest roles were in murder reconstructions for BBC1's '*Crimewatch*' programme) to roles in American TV shows and movies, he collected an O.B.E. from Prince William in 2016.

In March of 2020, Elba alleged that he had "tested positive" for "the virus," despite having no symptoms. It's a shame Mel Evans over at the '*Metro*' didn't consider this claim rather "bizarre." Elba Tweeted that he was "self-quarantining" at home and urged others to do the same. He addressed fellow "celebrity" Tom Hanks' claim that he too had contracted "the virus" (more on Hanks in the chapter on Co(n)vid Predictive Programming,) by stating:

> *'I'm proud of Tom Hanks . . . who came out and said they have it, and been public about it. I was definitely motivated by Tom's move there. But also, I think, there's some transparency given to this situation when someone like Tom or myself is in this situation.*

Elba's comments came days after he had attended an event by the think-tank/ charity we.org, at which he had posed for photos with Sophie

Grégoire Trudeau, the wife of Canadian Prime Minister Justin Trudeau. Coincidentally enough, Trudeau was among a number of world leaders who claimed that they had "caught the virus", including the UK's Boris Johnson a short while later, and Prince Charles, thus reinforcing the desired view that the "virus" doesn't discriminate and "anyone can get it."

Elba has made inroads into the music world through his activities as a rapper, singer-songwriter, and DJ, often playing at "elite" celebrity events and private parties — or at least he did in the days when people were still "permitted" to have parties. He is a friend of veteran DJ-turned BBC asset Pete Tong (MBE,) with whom he has performed at many such events.

Miscellaneous other vaguely famous Co(n)vid naysayers are to be found, but they are few and far between, and reside very low in the pecking order of music industry fame and recognition. One such example is **Jez Williams**, guitarist with the Manchester band **Doves**, who opined in an *'Independent'* newspaper article on 11th September (appropriately enough for a conversation about conspiracies):

> *"I'm not into conspiracy theories. But I don't think the economy should've been totally locked down. The death rate is 0.04 per cent, so to close the whole world's economy down is fucking nuts... There's over 45 million people jobless now [in the US], going into poverty. It's fucked! They issue debt so they can own everything. It's part of the culling of businesses."*

American rapper **Wiz Khalifa** questioned the often-repeated claim that Co(n)vid was in some way connected to the planned roll-out of human health-harming 5G transmitters with the brief Tweet "Corona? 5G? Or both?" on 3rd April. This received a generally favourable response from his Twitter followers in contrast to the backlash that Brits Ian Brown and the Gallaghers had received, with comments like, "I feel like 5G caused corona. Every time we have a major advancement in technology there is a Pandemic," and, "I'm pretty sure the virus started because of the 5G radiation, for the sole purpose of population control."

It seems like a wry expression of the Satanic principle of inversion that, those influential artists who might have been expected to raise up and make a stand about tyranny and the loss of freedoms, put on their mask and stayed silent. On the other hand, many of those whose careers, and therefore widespread influence, had peaked earlier, and who might have been considered to quietly toe the official line—are the ones who stuck their head above the parapet to say what needed to be said. I guess that gives us yet further insight into an invisible line, above which any artists residing are silenced from having any public voice of their own, and where all comments need to be of the "approved" variety, whereas those who never crossed that line—or who are now considered spent and expendable by the industry—are still able to express themselves as individuals capable of conscious thought.

Rap responds

What of the British hip-hop scene? Would it not be unreasonable to expect arguably the leading voice when it comes to outspoken, conscious rap music to have something to say about such an obvious Scam as Co(n)vid? That leading status belongs to **Kareem Dennis**, a rapper of British and Iraqi descent better known by the artist name **Lowkey**.

In the past, Lowkey has never shied away from controversial subjects, addressing the genocidal military campaigns of Barack Obama's administration on the two-part 'Obama Nation,' the social injustice of London's Grenfell Tower fire on the two-part 'Voices of Grenfell,' the inhumanity of British colonialism with fellow conscious rapper Akala on 'Behind My Painted Smile,' the desperation of political refugees on 'Ahmed' and—perhaps the most contentious of all—Israel's murderous incursions into neighbouring Palestine on the two-part 'Long Live Palestine.'

For a period, Lowkey cemented his reputation as an activist by taking a hiatus from the music business during which he based himself in Palestine undertaking humanitarian work. In 2017 he earned himself the scorn of the Jewish community when, during a live freestyle for the 'Fire In The Booth' feature on **Charlie Sloth**'s show on BBC 1Xtra, he referred to "zombies and zionists." (Fellow UK rapper **Mic Righteous** had previously had the phrase "free Palestine" blanked out by a sound effect when the replay of his 'Fire In The Booth' freestyle was later published on the BBC's website.) Lowkey further clashed with the BBC when he publicly criticised long-time Radio 1 rap DJ **Tim Westwood** for presenting his show from a UK military base in Afghanistan.

Lowkey then, is clearly someone very capable of thinking outside the box, rejecting the propaganda of official narratives, and questioning the version of events that governments, the mainstream media and academia present to us. Indeed, he created an album alongside fellow rapper Logic titled '*New World Order*,' so clearly has an understanding of "elite" agendas to manipulate and control the masses. When he speaks in interview, he appears intelligent and well-researched, his accent far more refined than the "street" timbre he applies to his voice when on track. And yet, when it comes to the Co(n)vid Scamdemic, Lowkey has adhered to the official narrative throughout.

In April of 2020, he guest-wrote an article for '*The New Arab*' website in which he made multiple references to "the Pandemic," and reinforced the mainstream media's line on the effect that it was having on N.H.S. hospitals, (despite many citizen journalists at the time filming wards which were said to be "war zones" and finding them to be empty, the "Nightingale Hospitals" which were hastily constructed among doom-laden predictions of out-of-control casualty numbers which instead sat unused, and the internet awash with N.H.S. staff somehow finding the time to rehearse and perform complex dance routines on TikTok.)

The same month, Lowkey guested alongside comedian Tez Ilyas on Arabic TV station Al Jazeera's Facebook channel, on an episode of its '*AJNewNormal*' show. Given an opportunity to talk about the Co(n)vid situation which, by that point, had had the UK in the grip of its first lockdown for a few weeks, he again neglected to question any aspect of the official government narrative. At the end of the show, he was invited by the host to perform a live, spontaneous freestyle, the lyrics to which included the following lines:

> "*Warnings since last year, they should have been more prepared,*
> *We all know it would have been different if it was Corbyn there.*
> "… *It's depressing when they should have been investing in tests for all.*
> "… *Stay well, stay free, lockdown is just a state of mind.*

"... There are lessons in every crevice of this Pandemic.

"...Make sure you wash your hands and eat food from a clean surface.

"...Death hurts more when they ignore the experts, agendas and lectures.

Confusingly, there appears to be another UK act named Lowkey in the Grime/ Bassline genre, which did pass comment on the political agendas behind Co(n)vid. The track *'Pandemic 20'* was published on YouTube with the accompanying written message:

"It's 2020 and we face a new global threat—Coronavirus! A disease that has conveniently brought nations to their knees and paved way for a Brave New World. A world where the richest 1 per cent take control of everything and everyone, and the ordinary person has no rights to stop it!

"Do not be fooled into believing our governments have your best interests at heart with all the measures being taken. The virus may go away but the restrictions may stay. We are all in this together so lets stay strong, positive and unite to the sound of Lowkey and we can take back our freedom which we once took for granted!"

Kareem Dennis/ Lowkey's reputation as a politically-conscious British rapper is seconded by that of **Akala**, real name **Kingslee Daley**. Despite rallying memorably against the monarchs of Empire, "Globalist" bankers, morally corrupt religious leaders and third-world dictators on *'Thieves' Banquet,'* and regular rants against colonialism, he remained largely silent on the world-changing issue of Co(n)vid. His Twitter page throughout 2020 mainly concerned itself with various political and social struggles around the world, and football. His only comment on the Scamdemic was in a Tweet of 13th July concerning Jamaican politics, in which he wrote:

"The management of Covid was just another example in a wider Caribbean paradox—managing some really big things extremely

well, while still failing miserably on many basics, most obviously inequality and extreme levels of violence."

There's irony to be found from the fact that Akala's sister, **Niomi McLean-Daley**, is better known by the artist name of **Ms. Dynamite**. While Akala has regularly criticised the system of Empire, his sister was happy to accept an MBE from the Queen in 2018, an achievement which not hampered by her having been convicted in 2006 of assaulting a police officer and being sentenced to 60 hours' community service. Writing in *'The Guardian,'* she justified her decision in the wake of the renewed interest at the time in the Windrush, the first ship to bring Caribbean immigrants to the UK in the late 1940s:

> *"So as I sat, torn over my decision, it became clear and very simple. I would accept the MBE—not because I want to be part of the establishment, or had suddenly stopped caring about the damaging legacy of empire and colonialism, or that it was suddenly all OK, but because I wanted to honour my grandparents, and all of their generation, and the extraordinary sacrifices they made."*

Elsewhere, Co(n)vid and the UK rap scene converged devastatingly when **Benedict Chijioke**, better known by the artist name of **Ty**, a veteran rapper, died on 7th May 2020, aged 47. Though his official cause of death was given as pneumonia, many media outlets made much of the fact that he had received intensive treatment for Co(n)vid. The reports that he had "died after contracting coronavirus" echoed those of other celebrities such as comedians Eddie Large and Bobby Ball. Such phrasing doesn't actually mean that "coronavirus" had been the cause of death, otherwise it would have been stated more explicitly that they had died "*of* coronavirus."

A further casualty of the British hip-hop scene in that fateful year was the rapper known as **Black The Ripper**, real name Dean West. He had been one of the guest artists on part 2 of Lowkey's aforementioned 'Obama Nation,' and had similarly gained a reputation for political outspoken-ness. During the last days of his life, Black had made multiple posts on his Snapchat account linking the Co(n)vid Scamdemic to the electromagnetic radiation emitted by the 5G technology that was getting installed at the time, and the microchipping, vaccine and Bill Gates-endorsed depopulation agendas. One of his posts read:

> *"Vaccinations. microchips, 5G, Coronavirus are all part of the same plan. They are not separate issues. Use your brain. See how it's all linked."*

On 6th April, Black The Ripper was reported to have died while on holiday in the Caribbean island of Montserrat. Three months later his family stated that, according to his autopsy, he had died of a heart attack. With morbid irony, his peers in the rap community were unable to come out and pay tribute at his funeral due to bans on such gatherings put in place as a result of the very "virus" agenda that he had sought to expose.

Screen tests

The Scamdemic ticked so many boxes on the long-standing wish-list of the New World Order architects — and in the tenets of ideological Communism. One of the key demoralising tactics has been denying people the social contact with others that is so much an instinctive human inclination. The Co(n)vid scam came along at a time when most were already conducting vast swathes of their everyday activities via a phone, tablet or computer screen — from on-line banking and shopping, to making video calls to friends and family.

By convincing the bulk of a population that it was now dangerous to be outside of your own home, and that, through the very act of breathing, a stranger you might pass on the pavement could end up killing you, the controllers coerced the masses to conduct virtually every aspect of their daily activities via electronic screens. (Rather reminiscent of the omnipresent "telescreens" in the movie version of George Orwell's *'1984'* from which Big Brother spouts the propaganda and mind-control to the masses. But I'm sure that's just a coincidence.) "Instead of calling in on your mum, just wave to her on a Skype call," went the narrative. "It's just as good as being there!" Within only days of the first "Pandemic" lockdowns, people were sharing recipes and doing exercise classes all via video conferencing calls. The daily keep-fit classes of Joe

Wicks (MBE,) alternatively known as The Body Coach, became eagerly anticipated by millions of the domestically-imprisoned, and made him into a household name without him ever needing to leave his own home.

For the manipulators, this dynamic serves them on several fronts. It contributes towards the transition towards an Artificial Intelligence/ Transhumanist future, where people become ever more reliant on technology to perform basic functions for them. It erodes the natural inclination towards actual social contact with others. This, in turn, prevents unity, bonding and a sense of togetherness, and severely limits opportunities for any kind of organised pushback or resistance to the all-pervading tyranny. By restricting the bulk of interactions to electronic means, this also means that all calls can be monitored, surveilled and recorded, placing further challenges on any kind of effective solidarity.

The slow-drip mind-control to convince the easily brainwashed that video-calling was the way to go began early on in the scam. The Queen broke protocol by appearing in two special televised message "from home", (although many doubts persist about the authenticity of these messages—that's something for another time!) British Prime Minister Boris Johnson attempted to serve as an example to the nation when he announced that he had contracted "the virus" just days after imposing the first lockdowns, subsequently appearing "at home" in Downing Street, giving a message to the nation from his Smartphone. Before long, multiple TV advertisements broadcast images of families and "ordinary people" communicating with each-other via phone and tablet screens—all smiling and happy, naturally, because enforced house arrest and the erosion of natural rights is such FUN!!—while a voice-over delivers the vacuous message that "we're doing all we can to keep you safe during these unprecedented times." Yes. Just like every single other bought-and-paid-for corporation out there that's claiming exactly the same thing.

As a matter of interest, isn't it curious how quickly these corporations had their ads on the screen, all enforcing the "coronavirus" regulations within only days of the "Pandemic" having been officially declared? Professionals within the commercial production industry have told me that to create a new ad. from initial conception through to broadcast, takes a matter of many months minimum. And yet none of these corporations are supposed to have known about the UK government's Draconian lockdown measures until the general public found out about them in March?

The same scrutiny might be applied to shops and supermarkets, all of whom had their "social distancing" signage, tape and stickers for their floors marking out where people should stand, and perspex screens designed to "protect" their workers installed in all stores across the land, all at the same time as each-other, and all within only days of the "Pandemic" breaking." It seems, as has forever been the case, the public were the last to now.

This slow change in perception of how things must now be done, along with the mantra "The New Normal" endlessly repeated through government and mainstream media messages, all paved the way for new music gig conditions. "Who needs to go to a concert venue or stadium and get pushed and shoved around by others," went the unspoken implication, "when it's just as much fun to watch all the action from the comfort and convenience of a screen? After all, you run every other aspect of your life from your screen, so why not this too?! And this is *much* better than straining to see the tiny figure of a musician on a stage miles into the distance. It's like they're giving an intimate performance just for you in the comfort of your own home!"

And this became the rationale behind the *'One World: Together at Home'* "concert" on 18th April 2020, said to have been presented by the "Global" Citizen, and in support of the World Health Organisation, (the control-system cabal by any other name.)

This was a two-hour event, (preceded by a six-hour on-line marathon,) broadcast via T.V. and on-line, with the stated aim of bringing together performances by several household-name musicians, all supposedly playing from their own homes to constantly reinforce the endlessly-repeated mantra of "stay home, stay safe." While Jimmy Fallon, Jimmy Kimmel and Stephen Colbert hosted the show for its American broadcast, in Britain it was — naturally — aired by the B.B.C., which wheeled out its assets Clara Amfo, Dermot O'Leary and Claudia Winkleman for the occasion. The chosen line-up spoke volumes in terms of currently-serving poodles to the industry. Alongside newer names such as **Shawn Mendes**, **Taylor Swift**, **Billie Eilish**, **Maluma** and **Lizzo**, stood long-established veterans like **Stevie Wonder**, and a fair few "Sirs"—Paul McCartney, Mick Jagger and the rest of the Rolling Stones, Elton John and, for the UK version of the show only, **Tom Jones**. An endless array of other "celebrities," businesspeople, politicians and others in the pocket of the Cabal, made cameo appearances.

Perhaps the most telling aspect of the event was that it was curated by, and said to have been the brainchild of, **Lady Gaga**. She crops up again in the Adrenochrome chapter of this book, and there's plenty on her background in *'Musical Truth Volume 1.'* As I, and many other authors and researchers have asserted, Gaga's entire image is Satanic in nature, and she has shown herself to be one of the key purveyors of dark occult symbolism, themes and agendas during her years of fame. Whenever a "celebrity" is served up to us in the way Gaga was, and we become subliminally entrained to think of them as "the next big thing," a delve into their parentage often yields results. In **Stefani Germanotta**'s case, it is her mother who is of interest. Cynthia Germanotta, regularly described as a "philanthropist" and "activist," in 2018 launched the United for Global Mental Health initiative in conjunction with the Born This Way Foundation that she had co-founded with her daughter. The following year, she eliminated any doubts that she was Cabal-connected, by being named as Ambassador for Mental Health for the United Nations' World Health Organization.

So this means the world had a scenario where a concert promoting staying at home and avoiding natural human contact with others—a factor reported to have been responsible for untold numbers of suicides and mental health conditions, because no accurate figures of the scale of the problem have been kept—was curated by the daughter of an Ambassador claiming to represent the interests of those suffering from mental health issues!

You couldn't make it up. And in 2020, you didn't have to.

Hey, DJ!

Musicians aside, there is another breed within the ranks of the industry who, depending on the style and genre they represent, have also been thought of as being rather "radical" and "anti-Establishment."

This is the professional DJ. Not the Dave's Mobile Disco types who used to play weddings, birthdays and Bar Mitzvahs, (when such things still took place) and play anything from 'Y.M.C.A' to 'Summer of '69' on demand, but DJs who identify as artists in their own right—either those who produce their own tracks, or those who make a living from playing superclubs and festivals the world over.

As with "edgy" musicians, it might have been reasonable to expect some backlash from this community after several months of them being deprived a living, and the culture-shock of spending a year cooped up at home instead of jetting around the world to a non-stop barrage of parties. Businesses of all other types got an opportunity to open and trade in the UK in the months following the "Pandemic" announcement... except nightclubs. Where these had once been valued by the manipulators as dens of corruption and vice that suited their society-altering agendas, by March 2020, it seems they had run their course and were now entirely expendable.

Sadly, no such backlash took place, with the vast majority of DJs remaining entirely silent, and those who did speak up merely parroting the vacuous "stay safe" messages of the mainstream media propagandists.

There were only two honourable exceptions that I was able to pinpoint. The first was the British DJ and producer, (and original purveyor of the Acid House/ Rave scene) **Danny Rampling**. In his social media posts throughout 2020, Rampling was highly critical of the devastating effect the UK government's lockdowns were having on the economy, on the arts, and on people's mental health. He also attended one of the freedom rallies taking place in Brighton. On 18th September he posted the following to his Facebook fan page:

> "London's empty streets yesterday afternoon... the energy and soul has been ripped out of W1 and the city of London. Consequences of fear perpetuated upon society that has crippled the economy, and the confidence of people to go to the city... No more lockdowns, no more fear paralysis. Stop acquiescing to this new abnormal. Coronavirus is not lurking on every street corner to infect us all."

Danny also messaged frequently about the importance of keeping our immune systems boosted, and understood the significance of the planetary conjunctions happening at the Winter Solstice of 2020, contributing a music mix to mark the occasion. Whatever the case had been earlier in his long career, by 2020, it seems he was able to speak his mind freely without fear of repercussions. Incidentally, it was Danny who put me on to the first *'Zeitgeist'* documentary in 2008 when we were both stranded at Riga airport in Latvia following a gig and we got chatting. My viewing of the film was a key component in my "waking-up" process. I recorded a *'Good Vibrations'* podcast with Danny in June 2021, which can be listened to via the link in the Resources section at the end.

The only other DJ to have shown himself capable of critical thought and independent research — plus the conviction to share his findings publicly despite the inevitable backlash — was British Progressive House DJ **Steve Lawler**. By January 2021 he had begun challenging the official "virus" narrative on his Twitter page. Adding his comment to a video he had linked to which challenged the "official" statistics, he stated:

> *"I'm sure I'm going to get a lot of haters for posting this. But honestly, the amount of people deeply suffering now is just really not OK any more. It never was, but seriously. Enough is enough. Check stats. I did. they are true."*

As Lawler had predicted, a chorus of dissenting voices immediately jumped to a knee-jerk reaction and attempted to counter his points. Replying to one follower who had said, "maybe the BBC are in on it, eh," Lawler Tweeted:

> *"Oh, for God's sake. The BBC! Ha ha ha. Have you been asleep? I'm not going to waste any more time with you. You just lost any credibility you had left, which wasn't much in the first place."*

And later added in response to a message of support:

> *"Yup. Sounds about right. And all the accounts that get nasty are all accounts opened in 2020. Someone is spending time and money on trolling people who speak the truth."*

At a stretch, Jungle/ Drum & Bass pioneer **Goldie** *might* also be considered an exception as, in the wake of Rishi Sunak's patronising comments,

Goldie produced a video of himself performing various menial tasks like cleaning floors and windows, commenting sarcastically:

> *"Rishi Sunak suggested that I should re-train after 35 years of being an artist, because this isn't viable, even though I own my own art gallery . . . I think that doing art is a waste of time. I would rather do this job. Yes, re-train me as a floor cleaner or something."*

Five other DJ/ producers—**Fatboy Slim**, **Sherelle**, **Jyoty**, **HAAi** and **The Blessed Madonna**—joined Goldie in a video interview feature for '*Mixmag*', similarly decrying the government's lack of financial support for the nightlife sector.

By the time of this interview, October 2020, the UK's nightlife scene had already been shut down for over six months. The fact that this group took so long to publicly speak out suggests that they had been sitting tight up to that point, not wanting to be viewed as controversial or "irresponsible" and quietly hoping that they were experiencing only a short temporary blip in their livelihoods. By the six-month mark, it would have become obvious that there were no plans to re-open clubs and festivals any time soon. It seems that DJs—even those high-up the pecking order such as Goldie and long-time BBC asset **Pete Tong**, both MBEs—weren't privy to any advance knowledge that their club careers were about to grind to a crashing halt. I suspect the same would be true of many high-up musicians.

Elsewhere, idealistic stands from the professional DJ community against the loss of personal Rights, Freedoms, and the destruction of a way of life that brings joy and meaning to so many millions, were non-existent. But there was no shortage of household names parroting the official advice to "stay safe," and coercing their fans into wearing masks and observing "social" distancing. Behind these appeals to emotion would doubtless have been much desperate hopefulness that the nightmare of lockdowns would come to an end and the parties could start again soon, yet none wanted to be heard expressing that sentiment.

It would seem many others actually bought the lies and deceptions being peddled. Part of the Soviet subversion strategy involved infiltrating all aspects of the arts and filling them with Cultural Marxist ideology, and sure enough, at the time of the 2020 US election campaign, many from the dance music field could be seen joining the engineered mainstream media narrative of demonising Donald Trump, and praising his Democratic rival Joe Biden, whose policies would have done the bidding of his Chinese Communist Party controllers.

One such example of propagating a mainstream stance to his fans came from Richard West, better known as **Mr. C**, a member of the British dance/ rave group **The Shamen**, and best remembered for his vocals on the 1992 number one chart hit '*Ebeneezer Goode.*' When a debate erupted on his Facebook page over whether the UK government's lockdown responses to Co(n)vid could be justified, West (who now lives and works as a DJ in Los Angeles,) posted:

> *"The government is doing it all wrong. The Tube shouldn't run. The schools should remain closed. Pubs should remain closed."*

A separate Twitter post read:

> *"When I see people not wearing masks, I see them as uncaring, inconsiderate people who have total disregard for others and the severity of Covid. These people make me feel angry and unsafe."*

Personally, what makes me angry is people aged over 50 who *still* haven't figured out that governments and the mainstream media are there to lie and instil fear-based mind-control in the populace, and who put all their faith in whatever these career liars say without conducting wide-ranging research for themselves. It is these people's unwavering adherence to authority and officialdom that is taking away the natural-born Rights and Freedoms of others who DON'T consent to being ruled over by tyrants and deceivers.

West had earlier claimed, in all apparent seriousness, that Bill Gates should run as President of the United States, reinforcing the view always peddled by the mainstream of Gates as a selfless "philanthropist," and backed up with a Tweet stating:

> *"SARS-COV2 vaccines will not be mandatory. They will not contain microchips & they will stop people dying. Those who believe otherwise please have a tin foil hat."*

148

This viewpoint conveniently ignores the fact that Bill Gates comes from a family of stated Eugenicists; his father was a founding member of the Planned Parenthood operation, which advocates for abortion and significant population reduction. Gates himself talked in a 2010 TED presentation of his desire to lower the world's population through the use of vaccines. The Bill & Melinda Gates Foundation was behind the Event 201 "simulation" exercise in October 2019 which "predicted" the outbreak of a major Pandemic. Gates funded virtually all of the key organisations involved in the Co(n)vid agenda, including the GAVI vaccine group, the Center For Disease Control, the World Health Organization, the United Nations, and, most significantly, the World Economic Forum, which sought to introduce its society-changing "Great Reset" (the long-fabled New World Order by any other name) off the back of the "virus."

Despite having no medical or scientific training, Gates was also behind each of the vaccines as the only possible medical remedy to Co(n)vid, (natural cures for disease such as Hydroxychloriquine apparently don't exist,) and appeared on T.V. within days of the "Pandemic"'s outbreak claiming that the only way we would ever be able to get society "back to normal" and get our freedom of movement back is by everyone in the world taking one of his vaccines. Apparently he gets to decide such things.

West was either blissfully unaware of these facts about Gates' true nature and motives when lauding his hero, or was conveniently overlooking them in order to fulfil an agenda. What do readers think? Either way, he continued evangelising for the Co(n)vid vaccines long after truthful facts about how they had been killing and maiming many thousands of people had been brought to his attention in his chat threads, at which point he forfeited any right to later make the claim that "he didn't know." And he didn't stop there, later arguing for the further deletion of people's God-given Rights and Freedoms and the personal choice of how to conduct their lives so long as they are doing no harm, Tweeting:

> *"I've been saying from Day 1 that government guidelines & restrictions are nowhere near strong enough to get this Pandemic under*

wraps. Now stats are off the charts and I for one can't wait to get the vaccine."

It seems he wasn't entirely beyond a spot of partying and socialising himself, however, as by April 2021 he was excitedly announcing his involvement in a live-stream DJ festival at Lake Tahoe, (at which all in attendance, naturally, would be "testing for Co(n)vid" before coming.) Announcing his set, West went on to reveal that the proceedings would be kicking off at "6.66pm Pacific Time on Saturday evening."

The start time was later changed to 7.02pm

Others from the dance music world weighed in to offer further propping-up of the official Co(n)vid narrative. **Bushwacka**, of the duo **Layo & Bushwacka**, (**Layo** was West's business partner in the London nightclub The End in the 1990s) addressed the issue of young people organising illegal raves and dance parties during the "Pandemic."

> *"When we did illegal raves, it wasn't a potential threat to anyone's lives. Six months without any raves due to Covid and now the illegal raves are popping up everywhere. What's the difference? Well, I'll tell you what the difference is. When we got home from those raves 30 years ago we weren't potentially killing our grandparents. DJs and Promotors (sic) promoting this shit, get over yourselves. Selfish, self-centred beyond belief. That is what you are. This ain't no old man talk—this is the reality. You are taking the piss."*

In January 2021, Bushwacka engaged in discourse with other high-profile DJs, criticising their decisions to perform at the Zamna Festival in Tulum, Mexico—one of the few nations that was "permitting" such events at the time.

There was morbid irony to Bushwacka then posting a video concerning Suicide Awareness Day with his added comment, "a message that may help save lives," when the lockdown measures that he supports have been *directly responsible* for untold numbers of deaths that could have been prevented if these people hadn't been subjected to the trauma and desolation that comes through enforced home imprisonment, and the removal of Rights, Freedoms, essential social contact and joy. I often wonder if these individuals ever actually see the flawed logic and contradictory nature of such stances, or if they really do go through their entire lives unable to see that they're running mind-control programmes. Bushwacka later went all the way in confirming himself to have been totally brainwashed by the Establishment system when he revealed, in late January 2021, that he'd taken the Co(n)vid vaccine.

On 2nd February 2021, only days after criticising other DJs for taking part in the Mexico Festival, Bushwacka Tweeted that he himself was playing live at Cross Club in Prague, Czech Republic.

Similar hysteria about others exercising their Right to Movement and Assembly while causing no harm was in evidence from **Amadeus Mozart**, one half of the **Tidy Boys** hard house duo, and evidently another mainstream media believer, who in February 2021 Tweeted:

> *"Human nature to try and find a blame for tragic Covid spread, but as I have been saying since day one, a minority of the general public fucked things up. A report out today by the N.H.S. Track & Trace that shows up to 40 per cent of people who tested positive or advised to isolate have NOT self-isolated, which is absolutely crazy. Add this to silly house parties, random protests, poor social distancing, AND a new variant that spreads 55 per cent more rapidly, that's why we are were (sic) we are."*

Young people seeking to socialise and express themselves through music and dance is an inherent, natural experience as part of their development through life. This is a primal instinct built into the human psyche, which is why so many ancient cultures placed so much importance on music and dancing as a ceremony to connect their humanity with their spiritual aspect. The social engineers behind the worldwide explosion in electronic dance music, from its roots in the Acid House parties of the late 1980s, to the point it was at by the end of 2019, fully realised this, which is why they sought to steer the phenomenon off down their own desired path—to let weekly dance and music rituals become a staple part of the experiences of many millions of young people—but all, ultimately, on the industry's own terms.

That same anthropological understanding of this dynamic would have been in place when the decision was made to cruelly pull all that from under the clubbers, dancers, DJs, promoters, engineers, and all others reliant on the nightlife scene for a living, with barely a week's notice. The middle-aged dance music stars lecturing others about their lack of responsibility were fortunate enough to have enjoyed their formative years getting up to anything they chose. The generation with the misfortune to have been in their late teens or early 20s in 2020, will have missed out on a rite of passage not denied to any generation before them for 100 years.

The over-riding tendency among the dance music community to adhere to official Co(n)vid policy, and merely re-parrot everything the mainstream media has said about the 'Pandemic," will either be down to childlike naïvety on their part, overly liberal "woke" world-views, (shaped for them by social-engineers of whom they would have no knowledge — remember master Propagandist Edward Bernays' assertion, in 1928, that "we are governed, our minds are moulded, our tastes formed, our ideas suggested, largely by men we have never heard of,") or far too many mind-altering drugs consumed in decades past. Otherwise, they know only too well that an agenda is being pushed under the cover of Co(n)vid, and they've been paid or otherwise coerced into help perpetrate it.

For those for whom this is the case, by staying silent, they're confirming that their own salary and career is more important than everyone else's Freedoms, including those of *their own* children. If all in the entertainment industry who knew better but stayed silent for fear of a personal price to pay would instead unite, and use the colossal sway and influence they hold over the public mindset to call out Co(n)vid for the monumental scam it is, they could have destroyed its insidious hold on society overnight. It was all summed up neatly in a meme I saw doing the social media rounds in late 2020, stating:

> *"Imagine in a war in which the majority of one side didn't know they were at war, ridiculed those that did, and were blindly obedient to their enemy."*

Left. It's the new right

I commented to a friend at the time about how few liberal lefties would be able to see the irony of their having fallen for the lies of the Scamdemic, perpetuated by Tories and the Public School Old Guard against which they claim to be so passionately opposed. My friend observed:

> *"We've got mutual musical friends who have been the worse kind of compliant. One of them is in a Punk band which even has the slogan "Kick out the Tories." You can't make this shit up! The so-called 'progressive' and 'anti-establishment' have been the most compliant of all. Not only compliant, but actually against all of us speaking out too. It's like they've spent years defining themselves by their political beliefs, to the point if they question it, there will nothing left for them. Incredible really."*

The question of whether there was still even a glimmer of the once-rebellious Punk Rock spirit pretty much got answered when, in Summer 2021, a gig by **Teenage Bottlerocket** (me neither) taking place in St. Petersburg, Florida, offered pre-booked tickets for $18 for concert-goers who could provide proof of vaccination. The unvaccinated were being allowed entry . . . for a cover price of $999! When challenged about the blatant discrimination this scenario presents towards those who make the personal, free will choice over what to put into their bodies, (isn't "Punk" supposed to be opposed to fascism and tyranny, or did I miss something here?,) the band's singer **Ray Carlisle** responded, "perhaps put together a GoFundMe and all the other weirdo anti-vaxxers can help support you going to Teenage Bottlerocket for a thousand dollars. That's always an option." Leaving the group to wallow within the irrelevance and obscurity that such a supremely arrogant attitude warrants is, of course, another.

The same stance was shared by Dave Grohl, **Bruce Springsteen** and the **Strokes**, (or those that control them,) when glimmers of hope for opening venues back up in Summer 2021 emerged. All three acts announced gigs in New York City where only attendees who could provide proof that they had been fully vaccinated would be granted entry. As many observers commented, this amounted to Medical Apartheid and discrimination, yet, though such breaches of human rights would have had Social Justice Warriors decrying the unfairness if it were any other group in society being excluded, in the Brave New World of Co(n)vid-1984, apparently this was just fine.

Springsteen further cemented his status as an owned puppet when fronting a billboard campaign in his native New Jersey encouraging the public to continue to wear (completely useless) face masks throughout the Summer season. More "born to comply" than "Born To Run." As such, Springsteen, Grohl and all of their like can now take their places alongside the other treasonous sell-outs who have been openly pushing genocide—whether of their own accord or under the coercion of their handlers as it doesn't make a difference to the mechanisms of the Universe—and take the Karmic consequences that come with adopting such a stance.

And it wasn't much better with the UK's **Kaiser Chiefs** at the 2021 Isle of Wight Festival, (packed shoulder-to-shoulder with unmasked attendees, rather ironically,) where frontman **Ricky Wilson** paused the show to address the crowd, saying, "let me hear you if you've had the Pfizer vaccine, let's hear it for Moderna, AstraZeneca," before inviting agitation by adding, "let's hear it for the anti-vaxxers." Less "I Predict A Riot" and more "I predict a kickback." Maybe they should rename themselves the Pfizer Chiefs?

As a user named True Blue commented on a Twitter thread exposing the treachery:

> *"Imagine paying money to go see live music for enjoyment only to be lectured to using propaganda with intent to cause division and hatred amongst people."*

It was an exercise in futility to expect any exemplary pushback from veteran New York DJ/ producer **Danny Tenaglia**, meanwhile. No room was left for doubt when, for his 60th birthday in March 2021, he linked with music platform Beatport on a marathon fundraiser for … the United Nations! Well, they have been struggling to make ends meet lately, bless 'em. And after all, why fight against Totalitarian Tyranny in which personal Freedoms are destroyed and the State owns everything, when you can instead raise money for one of the very vehicles that helps get the job done, right, Dan? The fundraiser featured input from many other big-name DJs, including **Harry Romero**, **Hernan Cattaneo**, **Seth Troxler** and—perhaps puzzlingly for someone who has called out Co(n)vid as a scam but doesn't seem to recognise the U.N. as one of the main monoliths involved in it—the aforementioned Steve Lawler.

Meanwhile, the utter absurdity of the narrative that the vaccine is the only way out of the "pandemic" was highlighted when both **Bryan Adams** and **Jon Bon Jovi** had to pull out of concerts in late 2021 after testing positive for the you-know-what...despite both being fully vaccinated. That went well then.

Cox in the box

The veteran DJ/ producer frequently cited as a "legend," **Carl Cox**, who also participated in the above-mentioned U/N/ fundraiser, certainly wasn't about to do any harm to his 30-year-plus career by speaking out against the fascistic measures put in place by soulless psychopathic "Dictator" Dan Andrews, the treasonous Governor of Victoria State in Australia. Instead, Cox sat out several months at his Melbourne home under enforced house arrest, streaming the sets he would ordinarily have been playing at festivals around the world, via live on-line streams, frequently reminding his fans to "stay safe in the Pandemic," and on occasion appearing in video with fellow DJ **Christopher Coe** wearing a face mask...in his own home!

In a March 2021 guest appearance on **Lenny Fontana**'s *'True House Stories'* podcast, Carl endorsed vaccinations as the only route out of lockdowns and back to partying, and supported the Australian government's hardline Co(n)vid stance in the belief that this was necessary, and was the only way that "cases" were able to diminish. Cox did come across as confused, ill-informed and concerned only with not alienating his fanbase through sounding "politically incorrect" than running any malevolent agenda. But that last assertion was removed by the time *'Mixmag'* announced, in August, that Cox was fronting a campaign to encourage clubbers to get vaccinated. Not only that, but he also went on to participate in an ad for the N.H.S. encouraging clubgoers to take an untested experimental drug into their bloodstream in direct contravention of the very types of Rights and Freedoms that he once claimed to be so vehemently in favour of protecting.

Carl's obedient compliance becomes all the more frustrating considering that, during his lockdown months, he worked on his auto-biography, *'Oh Yes Oh Yes'* (seemingly echoing his reaction to tyranny.) In it, he reminisced about his days on the early UK rave scene, where it was commonplace for he and his peers to dodge police who were trying to raid and shut down the parties. He also spoke of considering it his "duty" to be at a 1990 rally in Trafalgar Square to protest about government plans to make rave gatherings illegal. So why did he not feel to protest during Co(n)vid when *way* more Rights and Freedoms were being taken away from all of us, not just ravers? His stance parallels that of former Punk Rockers, who positioned themselves as "anti-Establishment" in their youth, yet seem to settle into a comfortably numb neutrality as middle age creeps in.

The righteous indignation displayed disappointingly, but not entirely expectedly, by the majority of music's A-listers, speaks to some very interesting aspects of the human psyche that a keen anthropologist or social scientist could have a field day with. I can't better the way David Shepstone Strickland put it when addressing the cult of Co(n)vid in a Facebook post of January 2021, so I'll leave the words to him:

> *"The brainwashed Covid cult followers are nothing more than attention-seeking hypochondriacs, framing their cowardice as a virtue, promoting themselves as "selfless life-savers," as the hero protagonist in their own theatre of life, as their imagination has been captured by a televisual Pandemic narrative by design.*

> *"None of the perceived threat or danger is based in reality. These drones have such unimpassioned lives, this fear-porn sense of occasion gives their life this perverse sense of purpose.*

> *To the degree they can display their worship of authoritarianism masquerading as care in their community, is a perfect control device they can visit upon their contemporaries, and by extension, a sense of power they bask in, not understanding they are mired in complete*

righteous ignorance, such is the insidious success of the generational brainwashing.

"They don't give a damn about other people, yet can't wait to bleat how many people they know with "Covid," wearing self-indulgent misery as a badge of honour, and in a sadomasochistic frenzy DEMANDING MORE RESTRICTIONS!

"...when the entire premise of this "Pandemic" is rooted in falsehoods, that doesn't mean the world has to stop to make you feel safe... and the fact that anyone is happy to simply sit by and watch people's lives completely fall apart just to avoid any confrontation or personal responsibility, speaks to nothing more than sociopathy—the antithesis of the altruistic 'we're in this together, care for the community' rhetoric."

Expanding on this, my own webmaster had some incisive observations about why so many people have such a hard time admitting that they have been duped by sources they previously assumed they could trust. It is part of the ego's natural inclination to jump to its own defence when it feels it has been discredited, he considered, and most people don't want anything to upset their comfortable and convenient worldview—even when denying the existence of such a threat goes directly against their own self interests.

"As I see it, one of the biggest obstacles to ending this lie is people refusing to admit that they have been dead wrong in their compliance with every order, and believing every word on CNN and on the BBC. Refusing to admit that they have been completely conned like never before, refusing to admit that they have been on the side of evil and have helped to further the biggest lie in human history. Therefore they will continue to go along with the lie simply out of pride."

Resources:

Independent Ireland: Garda probe after Bono relatives die in house fire:

- https://www.independent.ie/irish-news/garda-probe-after-bono-relatives-die-in-house-fire-26197215.html

Swamp: Who Is Ireland's Barbara Hewson? Age of Consent to 13, Murder, and Bono. 1498 Til Now:

- https://vocal.media/theSwamp/who-is-irelands-barbara-hewson-age-of-consent-to-13-murder-and-bono-1498-til-now

Actress Scarlett Johansen is a bloodline descendent of Vladimir Lenin's wife:

- https://www.quora.com/q/worldhistory/Why-didnt-Lenin-have-children?ch=10&share=197e7b6a&srid=oXa6Z&fbclid=IwAR29Cvb7rpa5kUMKsNA9Bs7DFasIGtL0ayxOvNN-N7U2dfZYD2QOz9z6aMbQ

Van Morrison asks artists to speak out against socially distant concerts: 'Fight the pseudo-science':

- https://www.yahoo.com/entertainment/van-morrison-asks-artists-speak-out-against-socially-distant-concerts-fight-pseudoscience-175428889.html?guccounter=1&guce_referrer=aHR0cHM6Ly9lbi53aWtpcGVkaWEub3JnLw&guce_referrer_sig=AQAAAE7jHeejtQd3ALWv_-M-UhRmdV_ALPNk-HPa2R86dU6FjehgjZkwxyaYfo1iVJAI4G_ea1FSm--kWrvee0hnRSFy2RnY0Cm-7bcKqvA2Eu2t1DVjeqLV6hGaL0xKjJ5MMbQdPRiVnf8dQ6E2ed4qZ4Rg7b1yTpWpItLbhA0hQc7Ij

Fullfact.org: What did Rishi Sunak actually say about people in the arts?:

- https://fullfact.org/economy/rishi-sunak-arts-opportunities/

The Yuri Bezmenov Communist Goals of Infiltration and Indoctrination Reality Show 1972:

- https://colonelrobertneville.blogspot.com/2008/12/
  yuri-bezmenov-communist-infiltration.html?m=1

GHQ Magazine: Goldie Has A Message For Rishi Sunak:

- https://ghqmagazine.com/goldie-has-a-message-for-rishi-sunak/

Music Mxdwn: Morrissey Played a Show in London Amid the Coronavirus Outbreak:

- https://music.mxdwn.com/2020/03/17/news/morrissey-played-
  a-show-in-london-amid-the-coronavirus-outbreak-plays-the-
  smiths-london-for-the-first-time-in-13-years/

Ringo Starr's New Years Eve 2020 Message:

- https://youtu.be/SDzIHeeDCjg

Toyah Willcox and Robert Fripp push the Co(n)vid vaccine:

- https://www.youtube.com/
  watch?app=desktop&v=GOgKuCxcL2k

The Guardian: Noel Gallagher says he refuses to wear a 'pointless' mask despite UK laws:

- https://www.theguardian.com/music/2020/sep/15/
  noel-gallagher-says-he-refuses-to-wear-a-mask-de-
  spite-uk-laws?fbclid=IwAR3PPYMLUpw_tRa8HLsCNj_
  EU6KGB2bIwl_PpJ8LKYUe1xWUR6QIBMBuDkM

Manchester Evening News: Noel Gallagher says Tony Blair 'is only politician who talks sense' after chance meeting:

- https://www.manchestereveningnews.
  co.uk/whats-on/music-nightlife-news/
  noel-gallagher-tony-blair-politician-17282803

Liam Gallagher hits out at government 'dopes' as musicians protest near parliament

- https://news.sky.com/story/coronavirus-liam-gallagher-hits-out-at-government-dopes-as-musicians-protest-near-parliament-12091731

Liam Gallagher calls coronavirus a 'f***ing c***' after Everton v Man City match called off due to positive Co(n)vid-19 tests

- https://www.independent.co.uk/arts-entertainment/music/news/liam-gallagher-coroanvirus-everton-manchester-city-b1779644.html

Ian Brown shares anti-lockdown song 'Little Seed Big Tree' and hits out again over coronavirus:

- https://www.nme.com/news/music/ian-brown-hits-out-again-over-coronavirus-and-shares-anti-lockdown-song-little-seed-big-tree-2756322

Ian Brown's conspiracy tweets are pure Co(n)vidiocy. And he's not the only tinfoil hat-wearing rocker:

- https://www.nme.com/features/ian-brown-conspiracy-theory-tweets-anti-vax-coronavirus-2752532

Ian Brown responds to being called "conspiracy theorist" before attracting the wrath of Jedward:

- https://www.nme.com/news/music/jedward-hit-out-at-ian-brown-for-coronavirus-comments-your-tweets-are-a-nightmare-2752565

Ian Brown receives backlash online for apparent anti-vaxxer views:

- https://www.nme.com/news/music/ian-brown-receives-backlash-online-for-apparent-anti-vaxxer-views-2745994

Chico Time — London Protests Trafalgar Square 29/8/20:

- https://www.youtube.com/watch?v=Vy8D9dRmraY

The Independent: Right Said Fred say they are not 'Co(n)vid deniers' after appearing at anti-lockdown protest:

- https://www.independent.co.uk/arts-entertainment/music/news/right-said-fred-anti-lockdown-protest-b1759134.html

Daily Mail: We're too sexy for our MASKS! Right Said Fred are hit by backlash for joining anti-lockdown march in London:

- https://www.dailymail.co.uk/news/article-8780929/Right-Said-Fred-hit-backlash-joining-anti-lockdown-march-London.html

Stevie Nicks Begs Fans to Wear Masks as She'll 'Probably Never Sing Again' If She Contracts Coronavirus:

- https://uk.finance.yahoo.com/news/stevie-nicks-begs-fans-wear-032332243.html

Metro: Wiley shares bizarre coronavirus conspiracy theory as he suggests virus was 'created by China' as method of 'depopulation':

- https://metro.co.uk/2020/05/06/wiley-shares-bizarre-coronavirus-conspiracy-suggests-virus-was-created-china-method-depopulation-12661664/?fbclid=IwAR1tobppRrAi51gjJIIqTQnO9684n7JbTfgWpTSs1c7n0K4OB4z9zj5ArnE

Wiley apology for Tweets 'that looked anti-Semitic' after Twitter ban:

- https://www.bbc.co.uk/news/technology-53581771

Ty death: Rapper dies after contracting coronavirus aged 47:

- https://www.independent.co.uk/arts-entertainment/music/news/ty-death-coronavirus-rapper-age-cause-Covid-19-a9504771.html

The Jewish Chronicle: Rapper Lowkey attacks Zionists in performance on BBC Radio 1 show:

- https://www.thejc.com/news/uk/rapper-lowkey-attacks-zionists-in-performance-on-bbc-radio-1-show-1.449591

The New Arab: Rapper Lowkey writes on the Pandemic:

- https://english.alaraby.co.uk/english/comment/2020/4/7/coronavirus-is-killing-N.H.S.-workers-their-deaths-were-preventable-1

Lowkey's Pandemic rap on Al Jazeera's 'AJ The New Normal':

- https://www.facebook.com/7382473689/videos/525162204832458/

Lowkey: Pandemic 20 (Grime/ Bassline track):

- https://www.youtube.com/watch?v=sMzLIRy75WI

NME: Paul Weller says he hopes we "don't go back to normal" after coronavirus:

- https://www.nme.com/news/music/paul-weller-says-he-hopes-we-dont-go-back-to-normal-after-coronavirus-2703096

NME: Billy Bragg calls Glastonbury cancellation "a bit of a shock":

- https://www.nme.com/news/music/billy-bragg-calls-glastonbury-cancellation-bit-shock-2864308

The Guardian: Richard Ashcroft quits Tramlines festival owing to its Co(n)vid research:

- https://www.theguardian.com/music/2021/jul/06/richard-ashcroft-quits-tramlines-festival-owing-to-its-covid-research

Pitbull talks about Communism, Co(n)vid 19, Event 201, Bill Gates:

- https://youtu.be/V0xbdt-9v2M

Sir Elton John and Sir Michael Caine push the vaccine:

- https://www.youtube.com/watch?v=8kHYUq0_0YQ&feature=youtu.be

Vulture.com: The Biggest Shot in Hollywood Every A-lister wants a Co(n)vid vaccine, but are they willing to get canceled for it?:

- https://www.vulture.com/2021/02/celebrities-on-skipping-covid-19-vaccine-line.html

Celebrity advert urges ethnic minorities to get Co(n)vid-19 vaccine:

- https://youtu.be/jVlIEPwJb0Q

Lee Scratch Perry Will Say Goodbye To Live Shows If Co(n)vid Vaccine Becomes Mandatory:

- https://www.dancehallmag.com/2021/02/25/news/lee-scratch-perry-will-say-goodbye-to-live-shows-if-Covid-vaccine-becomes-mandatory.html

Buju Banton Slams Jamaican Gov't Over Plans To Give Immunity To Co(n)vid-19 Vaccine Makers:

- https://www.dancehallmag.com/2021/02/01/news/buju-banton-slams-jamaican-govt-over-plans-to-give-immunity-to-Covid-19-vaccine-makers.html

Bounty Killer, Agent Sasco, Serani—Conspiracy Theory (Remix) (Official Visualizer)

- https://www.youtube.com/watch?v=0sz37_jvg9E

The Sun: Paedo Gary Glitter gets Co(n)vid vaccine while his victims and prison staff wait for theirs:

- https://www.thesun.co.uk/news/13978055/paedo-gary-glitter-Covid-vaccine/

Sky News: Dolly Parton changes Jolene to vaccine as she gets coronavirus jab she helped fund

- https://news.sky.com/story/covid-19-dolly-parton-changes-jolene-to-vaccine-as-she-gets-coronavirus-jab-she-helped-fund-12234339

Eric Clapton, Bryan Ferry and others to play a pro-hunting concert:

- https://www.ilxor.com/ILX/ThreadSelectedControllerServlet?boardid=41&threadid=52136

The Express: Cliff Richard described Van Morrison as 'irascible and difficult' before hit breakthrough:

- https://www.express.co.uk/entertainment/music/1398154/cliff-richard-news-music-van-morrison-strange-difficult-chart-record-song-uk-spt

Jaz Coleman: Killing Bono:

- https://www.metaltalk.net/20101104.php

BringTheNoise: Jaz Coleman (Killing Joke) dislikes Bono (U2):

- https://www.dailymotion.com/video/x2rw6db

loudersound.com: Killing Joke's Fearless Leader:

- https://www.loudersound.com/features/killing-joke-s-fearless-leader

Jaz Coleman interview on Mike James Rock Show:

- https://www.youtube.com/watch?v=VC8xpCqt2hs&feature=emb_title

N.H.S. to enlist 'sensible' celebrities to persuade people to take coronavirus vaccine:

- https://www.theguardian.com/society/2020/nov/29/N.H.S.-enlist-sensible-celebrities-coronavirus-vaccine-take-up?fbclid=IwAR3SrnwKFzE9YBF6b6hEb1Nlyq4Clx-Pf9sWyKs0LAKl8A-xsC3StEKX0Syo

Freedom of Information Request: Payments to public figures to promote Co(n)vid-19 legislation:

- https://www.whatdotheyknow.com/request/
  payments_to_public_figures_to_pr_2#incoming-1740430

EAZY SLEAZY—Mick Jagger with Dave Grohl—Lyric video:

- https://www.youtube.com/watch?v=MN9YLLQl7gE

Pink Floyd's Roger Waters . . . The NWO SELL OUT

- https://153news.net/watch_video.php?v=KO9YKXY62OG1

'Good Vibrations' podcast with Martin Brown—'The Dark Side of the Floyd:

- https://www.spreaker.com/user/markdevlin/
  good-vibrations-podcast-vol-159-martin-b

BBC: Prince Rupert Loewenstein obituary:

- https://www.bbc.co.uk/news/entertainment-arts-27515395

Gordon Brown and Sir Bob Geldof discuss Live Aid-style project to help vaccinate world's poorest:

- https://www.standard.co.uk/news/politics/gordon-brown-bob-
  geldof-Covid-vaccine-live-aid-b929162.html

Michael Stipe: Athens, Georgia, was my home. Its leaders are letting Co(n)vid-19 wreak havoc:

- https://www.theguardian.com/commentisfree/2020/sep/17/
  coronavirus-georgia-michael-stipe-op-ed-failures

NME: Michael Stipe labels Donald Trump a "sack of lies" and calls for better Co(n)vid-19 strategies:

- https://www.nme.com/news/music/michael-stipe-labels-don-
  ald-trump-a-sack-of-lies-and-calls-for-better-Covid-19-strate-
  gies-2755535

Eric Clapton after Co(n)vid vaccination: 'I should never have gone near the needle':

- https://www.americasfrontlinedoctors.org/frontline-news/eric-clapton-after-Covid-vaccination-i-should-never-have-gone-near-the-needle?fbclid=IwAR0nDhXZ12rIHL-gLfBbFuyxRrGa8CjfMUIW2WO1YhY3GKB3H82yLggSw-5o

Andrew Lloyd Webber says 'selfish' people who refuse to have Co(n) vid jab are as bad as drink-drivers:

- https://www.dailymail.co.uk/news/article-9588893/Andrew-Lloyd-Webber-says-selfish-people-refuse-Covid-jab-bad-drink-drivers.html

Florida Concert Charging $18 for Vaccinated, $1,000 for Unvaccinated:

- https://www.theepochtimes.com/florida-concert-charging-18-for-vaccinated-1000-for-unvaccinated_3837785.html?utm_source=CCPVirusNewsletter&utm_medium=email&utm_campaign=2021-06-01&fbclid=IwAR-2A8vdrCR4I-iI3WNTlcPfm8j-f26NSWgcWmzS-O-bV-JW6qIrE1k7BNQ8I

21st Century Wire: Foo Fighters, Springsteen, Strokes Only Allowing 'Fully Vaccinated' to Attend NY Shows:

- https://21stcenturywire.com/2021/06/10/foo-fighters-springsteen-strokes-only-allowing-fully-vaccinated-to-attend-concerts/

Eric Clapton: Exclusive & Uncensored | Oracle Films:

- https://www.youtube.com/watch?v=4OHmMKrVbNk

Good Vibrations podcast, Vol. 192: Danny Rampling—The War on Joy:

- https://www.youtube.com/watch?v=8WScnXH_TQ4

Turning The Inside Out: Morrissey On-Line interview, June 2021:

- https://www.morrisseycentral.com/messagesfrommorrissey/turning-the-inside-out

RTE: Morrissey slams Pandemic as 'Con-vid':

- https://www.rte.ie/entertainment/2021/0706/1233475-morrissey-slams-Pandemic-as-con-vid/?fbclid=IwAR37eFBr95mwT-JzJPin9jsEEGoc028SldIR_SLrJkrE86a1dO7LvHWly8vU

Paul McCartney slams idea that wearing face masks infringes on civil liberties: "That is stupid":

- https://www.nme.com/news/music/paul-mccartney-slams-idea-that-wearing-face-masks-infringes-on-civil-liberties-that-is-stupid-2843307?fbclid=IwAR08CJBpDIgnTQtpU-LA8nCYMmrwFk5RpDmoFTzP6c-xZ6kxxaIeboY_iX_U

Queen's Brian May, 74, labels Eric Clapton, 76, a 'fruitcake' along with all other anti-vaxxers:

- https://www.dailymail.co.uk/tvshowbiz/article-9875775/Queens-Brian-labels-hero-Eric-Clapton-fruitcake-anti-vaxxers.html?fbclid=IwAR08hb1lFcPe_Aulqaj8x2Cb8FNu0ONT4X-KNEFNr0OzUJHJtrroPPEzZDvY

The Independent: Brian May talks about the Covid failures of the Johnson government, Eric Clapton and the anti-vaxxers:

- https://www.independent.co.uk/arts-entertainment/music/features/brian-may-interview-queen-b1896040.html

The Guardian: Bob Dylan accused of sexually abusing a 12-year-old in 1965:

- https://www.theguardian.com/music/2021/aug/16/bob-dylan-accusations-sexual-abuse-lawsuit

Paul McCartney: COVID-19 vaccinations are 'cool':

- https://thehill.com/blogs/in-the-know/
  in-the-know/565921-paul-mccartney-covid-19-vaccina-
  tions-are-cool?fbclid=IwAR16i1uqLf92pmsFhn5RfcVacn-
  Wv2Wrg0XI0FSOhNeqfXPQccTsqes5Ql2o

David Gilmour: "We're both double-vaccinated."

- https://www.guitarplayer.com/news/david-gilmour-im-hoping-
  that-i-will-have-an-album-ready-in-the-next-year-or-two?fb-
  clid=IwAR27THgIIfHJZ-bbljNAe5VhWckt3Sih2IMKTqYhZ-
  TeGi2XU51KjmYap9hI

Blabbermouth: Ian Hill Says All Members Of Judas Priest Have Been
Vaccinated: 'We're About As Protected As We Ever Will Be':

- https://www.blabbermouth.net/news/ian-hill-says-all-mem-
  bers-of-judas-priest-have-been-vaccinated-were-about-as-pro-
  tected-as-we-ever-will-be/?fbclid=IwAR3Ouh6aHIqFuoZ-
  2ph3xrIuxbWQRD7GCbCO3BKAgbzzd_NFZbX8bvxMaZqg

Mixmag: Carl Cox Teams Up With the N.H.S. To Encourage People
to Get Vaccinated:

- https://mixmag.net/read/
  carl-cox-N.H.S.-vaccinations-jabs-nightclubs-reopening-news

Dr Kishan Bodalia discusses the COVID-19 vaccine with Carl Cox |
N.H.S.:

- https://www.youtube.com/watch?v=1l_zyGLxvv0

Kaiser Chiefs' Ricky Wilson angers anti-vaxxers with onstage
comments:

- https://www.nme.com/news/music/kaiser-chiefs-ricky-wil-
  son-angers-anti-vaxxers-with-onstage-comments-3050231?f-
  bclid=IwAR2hNztvwLuWdqppUxPVB1DS-
  DZ7OeV80y1GTQ97yi8JQqSJAS-_xfnxRkPM

NME: Iron Maiden's Bruce Dickinson tells fans to "get vaccinated":

- https://www.nme.com/news/music/iron-maidens-bruce-dickinson-tells-fans-to-get-vaccinated-3034630

Bryan Adams, Jon Bon Jovi test positive for COVID-19, cancel events:

- https://timesofindia.indiatimes.com/entertainment/english/music/news/bryan-adams-jon-bon-jovi-test-positive-for-covid-19-cancel-events/articleshow/87424502.cms?fbclid=IwAR1-asUseayRr2qfkBSZls8cydYmbtCPYzrPJIX-I0qu7t1jnjFO0oyIqkgw&from=mdr

CHAPTER 4

SOUND BITES, PART 2

"When the truth is found....to be lies...and all the joy within you dies...."

> *Jefferson Airplane: 'Somebody To Love.'*

"The handshake seals the contract.
From the contract, there's no turning back.
The turning point of a career..."

> *Depeche Mode: 'Everything Counts.'*

In September 2020, the Electronic Dance Music world was shocked by news of the sudden death of **Erick Morillo**, one of the most prolific DJs and producers on the scene. Born in New York but largely raised in Colombia, Morillo went on to create tracks under several pseudonyms including **Reel II Reel**, and after working closely with the record label Strictly Rhythm, created his own Subliminal Records imprint. (True to its name, the label's artwork contained much symbolism pertaining to Freemasonry and dark occultism.)

What many fans found even more shocking, however, was that Morillo's death had occurred just three days before he was due to appear in court on charges of sexual battery after several women had accused him of rape, among them fellow DJs Empress and Ida Engberg. In a post on her Facebook page, Empress wrote about the sexual harassment she had received from Morillo, revealing that it dated back as far as to 1998:

> *"Erick Morillo used to sexually harass me like crazy when I worked as a buyer at a Record Store in NYC called Satellite when I was 17 years old. So much so that he even got my phone # out of the store's database without my consent and also a friend of mine's home # that*

170

I was at so he could call me & leave me harassing disgusting weird breathy, sexual messages."

Commenting in an Instagram post, Ida Engberg wrote:

"I met Morillo in Ibiza back in 2006. Once in an after party at his house I sat outside in a sunbed talking to a friend of mine when he approached me from behind, pulled my head back, held my forehead against the sunbed and poured a drink into my mouth against my will. I got upset and asked what that was. He laughed and said 'it's MDMA'. "

Morillo was found dead at his home in Miami Beach, Florida. No cause of death was immediately released, but Ernesto Rodriguez, a spokesman for Miami police, stated that there were no apparent signs of foul play. The report later released by the County Medical Examiner, however, concluded that Morillo had died accidentally of "acute ketamine toxicity," with MDMA and cocaine use listed as contributing factors. Fate, it would appear, is not without it sense of irony.

*

Life appeared to imitate art in the most morbid way when it came to the ultimate fate of the British reggae artist **Smiley Culture**, real name David Emmanuel. After making his initial impact with his single *'Cockney Translator'* in 1984, it was early the following year that he enjoyed mainstream recognition when his follow-up, *'Police Officer,'* made it into the national top ten. Its narrative light-heartedly depicts a fictional encounter between himself and an over-zealous police officer who had conducted an unwarranted vehicle search. The officer then excitedly realises who Smiley is and lets him go in exchange for his autograph.

Tragically, Smiley's ultimate encounter with the police was nowhere near as trivial. He was arrested in July 2010 and charged with conspiracy to supply cocaine. His trial was due to begin on 21st March of the following year. Six days before that, he received a visit by police to his home in Surrey. They were in possession of a search warrant in relation to the importation of Class A drugs to the UK.

The official account of what happened, as testified by the four officers present, repeated by the coroner, and accepted by the jury at his inquest, beggars belief. We are told that Emmanuel offered the officers a cup of tea and went into his kitchen on the pretence of making it. While there, he supposedly made the spontaneous decision that his life had no further meaning, and stabbed himself in the heart with a kitchen knife, dying at the age of 48 and leaving behind two children. The foreman of the jury said:

> *"David Victor Emmanuel took his own life. Although the tragic events of 15 March 2011 were unforeseeable, giving one officer the responsibility of supervising Mr Emmanuel and at the same time the premises search book was a contributory factor in his death."*

The Wikipedia entry on Emmanuel, meanwhile, notes that:

> *"...Emmanuel's family raised concerns about the investigation, claiming that the IPCC 'had let (them) down' and that many 'unanswered questions' remained. The conditions surrounding his death and the subsequent investigation were also questioned by members of the general public, his death often being considered in the context of police brutality and other black people dying in police custody."*

*

A further death of a music star no less suspicious in nature, is that of the Swedish Electronic Dance Music producer and DJ **Avicii**, real name Tim Bergling. In his case, he turned up dead on 20th April 2018 in a residence belonging to the Royal family of Oman, close to its capital city of Muscat. Upon "investigating," the Omani police stated that there had been "no criminal suspicion" or evidence of foul play in his passing. The cause of death was later announced to have been by blood loss caused by stabbing with a broken wine bottle. The verdict was that Avicii had committed suicide. He was 28.

Bergling—whose mother had been a film and television actress and whose father was listed as "a businessman"—had certainly been a troubled soul. Having achieved worldwide fame at the age of 21 through his debut single 'Levels,' a few years of constant worldwide touring and a solid schedule of productions later, he was said to have been completely burned out and ready to retire. His mental health is said to have suffered due to the punishing demands of his strenuous schedule, and in 2012, he had been hospitalised for 11 days with acute pancreatitis said to have been caused by excessive alcohol abuse. Three years later, he underwent surgery to have his appendix and gallbladder removed, and became addicted to painkillers. He is said to have felt pressurised by both management and his fans, who he feared letting down, to continue touring in spite of his ailing health. All these factors certainly suggest someone at an unhappy place in life, and sure enough, his own family issued a statement accepting the verdict of suicide.

Some anomalies remain, however.

In an interview given to 'USA Today' in 2012, Bergling revealed that his stage name of Avicii, minus the additional 'i' at the end, referred to "the lowest level of Hell" in Buddhist traditions. It is said to be the place where the dead who have sinned will, after receiving punishment, be reborn.

19th—21st April seems to be an unlucky period for music artists, given that Prince had died on 21st April two years before, and the Gang Starr rapper Guru on 19th April 2010, with suspicious elements to both departures. These were either side of the official birthday of the Queen of England on 20th April.

An article in 'Rolling Stone' magazine revealed that Avicii had been corresponding with his management by e-mail and conference call during his final days, and making plans for the guest artists he wished to have appear on his new music. Per Sundin, head of Universal Music Sweden, said of Avicii that, "all his notes were in happy mode." This seems to be a common factor in music industry "suicides," since both **Chris Cornell** and **Michael Hutchence** were said by family members to have been in good spirits and making plans for the future just before they are said to have taken their own lives.

(The same was said of **Cranberries** singer **Dolores O'Riordan** when she turned up dead in a bathtub in the London Hilton Hotel on Park Lane three months before Avicii's death in 2018. O'Riordan had travelled to London from New York to discuss an upcoming reunion album for the Cranberries, and to work on her side project D.A.R.K with the producer known as Youth. The coroner's report was delayed by several weeks, but eventually concluded that she had died of accidental drowning following consumption of alcohol and prescription pharmaceuticals. O'Riordan joins a group of music stars who have turned up dead in bathtubs over the years, including **Jim Morrison** and both **Whitney Houston** and her daughter **Bobbi Kristina**. Drugs and alcohol were blamed in each instance. Earlier in her career, O'Riordan sported a closely-cropped bleach-blonde hairstyle, a look which has been identified by researchers as a symbolic indicator of the presence of trauma-based mind control. Like a large number of other music artists, O'Riordan had spoken of having suffered sexual abuse as a child, and suffering depression.)

What many citizen researchers found most intriguing, however, came from the accompanying video to Avicii's 2015 single '*For A Better Day.*' Harsh and unforgiving—literally—it depicts international child sex trafficking, opening with a truck pulling up in the wilderness and a group of paedophiles examining the children that it contains. Two are then seen running through a crop field, desperately trying to out-run their pursuer, then jumping off a cliff into the sea. These same two, now adults, are next shown exacting brutal revenge on the paedophiles one by one, and crossing off their faces on a board as each is despatched. This was interpreted by some as an effort on Avicii's part to expose "elite" child trafficking rings—although to be fair, the amount of editorial control he would have been likely to have personally had over the contents of the video are likely to have been minimal. It's more likely that the decision was made from elsewhere within the Avicii camp.

Nevertheless, many researchers posited a link between the subsequent death of Avicii and those of American singers **Chris Cornell** and **Chester Bennington**, who are similarly reported to have "committed suicide" the year before, with suspicious aspects to both events. It was suggested that Cornell and Bennington had been investigating paedophile gangs operating within the music industry, and were seeking to expose what they had found. This joined persistent rumours that Bennington was actually the biological son of American politician John

Podesta, whose name was a constant factor in the Pizzagate child sex trafficking affair, and in witch Marina Abramovich's "Spirit Cooking" dinners. The same claim of wishing to blow the whistle on the "elite"s sordid activities was made of Avicii. Though it has to be acknowledged that two of the websites making the claim, Neon Nettle and Yournewswire, are both disinformation platforms, the latter having been operated by David Icke's former webmaster Sean Adl-Tabatabai. This, in my book, doesn't necessarily negate the idea.

*

The video to **Culture Club**'s breakthrough single '*Do You Really Want To Hurt Me*,' which would have made little sense to anyone viewing it upon its release in 1982, takes on some different connotations now that we are able to understand so much of the true nature of the music industry and the sordid lifestyles of the 'elites."

The video begins with **Boy George,** real name George O'Dowd**,** in a courtroom sporting a Jewish Rabbi's hat, and a long white shirt adorned with Hebrew writing apparently spelling out "Culture Club." The courtroom is adorned with Masonic decor. George is evidently being tried as he sings, "give me time to realise my crime." The jury is made up of politically incorrect "blacked-up" performers in the style of '*The Black And White Minstrel Show*.' The video was directed by Julien Temple, who has previous when it comes to revealing symbolism in pop videos.

The setting then shifts to what, according to the caption, is "The Gargoyle Club" in London's Soho in 1936. George, in modern dress, is seen dancing seductively around tables occupied by Bohemian and "society" types all dressed in 1930s garb, before being ejected by Security.

Situated at 69 Dean Street, the building that became the Gargoyle Club was originally a Georgian-era house, built in the 1730s. It began life as a nightspot in 1925 as the aristocratic socialite David Tennant established the Gargoyle as a private members' club which, in its early years, attracted a wealthy "elite" clientele. By the 1970s the venue's basement, and that of the neighbouring building, had been developed into a music club known as Billy's. According to Graham Smith and Chris

Sullivan's book '*We Can Be Heroes*,' this was "a rather seedy gay club frequented by rough lesbians and even rougher trannies." Billy's was attended by a young pre-fame Boy George himself, and many of the characters who would go on to the fabled Blitz club in Covent Garden, giving birth to the British "New Romantic" movement.

After Billy's, the basement of the Dean Street venue became the nightclub Gossips. This was the spot where the former BBC Radio 1 hip-hop DJ Tim Westwood first came to prominence, playing warm-up sets for the late Steve Walsh, and reggae supremo David Rodigan (MBE.)

Back to the video, and George is next seen emerging fully-clothed from a swimming pool at, what the caption states is "Dolphin Square Health Club" in 1957, where he continues to shock patrons. He is finally seen dancing out of his prison cell as the rest of the band performs.

Dolphin Square, in London's Pimlico, has hit the headlines of recent years in connection with paedophilia. Flats and apartments there are owned or rented by prominent MPs, and many have been implicated in accusations of child rape on-site. Scotland Yard confirmed in 2014 that they had launched a murder investigation connected to allegations of child sex abuse dating back to the 1970s and 1980s, involving three paedophile MPs and centred around flats in Dolphin Square. Among the politicians to have had attended parties there were Margaret Thatcher's former Home Secretary (Baron) Leon Brittan.

Brittan had been handed a dossier by fellow Tory MP Geoffrey Dickens detailing alleged paedophile activity by "people in positions of power, influence and responsibility," yet later claimed he had no recollection of receiving it. In June 2014, a few months before his reported death, Brittan was interviewed by police in connection with the alleged rape of a 19-year-old student in his central London flat in 1967. After his death, he was accused by Labour MP Tom Watson of "multiple child rape." A child sex abuse victim stated that Brittan was present when two men murdered a boy after sexually abusing him.

Brittan was alleged to have been a visitor to the Elm Guest House in South West London, reported to have been a den of child sexual abuse. In 2013 Mary Moss, a social worker friend of Carole Kasir, the Elm's proprietor from 1979 to 1982, posted on the internet a series of images claimed to be from the Elm's guest book, giving the names of many famous people said to have been regular visitors. Along with the names of many prominent politicians and civil servants, from the music world the list included **Sir Cliff Richard**, said to have used the alias 'Kitty,' actor/ singer **Jess Conrad (OBE)**, and former BBC DJ **Chris Denning**.

George reportedly turned down the offer of an MBE in 2004.

One further curiosity comes from the Culture Club song. Although he doesn't appear wearing it in the video, in photographic stills from the shoot, a "Star of David" symbol, (also the sigil adopted by the House of Rothschild,) appears on George's shirt. Years later, he was pictured with the same sigil having been painted on to the crown of his head. Although known as Gerry, George's father's name was Jeremiah, and though there is no biographical information available to confirm this, the name suggests he may have been of Jewish stock, which could explain George's Star of David sigils. George's Culture Club bandmate and occasional lover **Jon Moss**, is Jewish.

Muddying the waters yet further, however, in 2007, George publicly criticised fellow pop star **Madonna**'s embracing of the Jewish mystery school tradition of Kabbalah, stating that the faith is intolerant of gay and lesbian relationships. He had previously described Madonna as "a vile, hideous, horrible human being with no redeeming qualities."

George's father is said to have been physically abusive towards his wife. George himself described him as "a terrible father and a terrible husband." In 1995, George's youngest brother Gerald, who suffers from schizophrenia, was convicted of killing his wife. After years of heavy drug addiction, George himself was convicted in New York of the assault and false imprisonment of a male escort, who he was said to have handcuffed to a radiator and beat with a metal chain.

All these factors considered then, the question has to be asked: was the viewing public getting subtle clues as to the world of child sexual abuse at the hands of the world's "elite" through this enigmatic pop video? Another expression of Placing the Truth in Plain Sight, even though virtually nobody in 1982 would have been able to identify it as such? And could it have been hinting that George himself had been subject to such abuse in his younger years? Indeed, could this, in fact, explain the origin of the 'Boy' tag in his artist name? Particularly considering the song includes lyrics such as "this boy loves without a reason," "precious kisses, words that burn me, lovers never ask you why," and "wrapped in sorrow, words are token, come inside and catch my tears"?

Oh, and one last thing, as Columbo would have said: according to an article in the '*Scottish Daily Record*,' an early name for the band before changing it to Culture Club was . . . Sex Gang Children.

*

For anyone wondering how to disappear into obscurity after achieving fame as part of a much lauded band, a look at the life of **Mark Hollis**, singer and primary songwriter for the group **Talk Talk**, provides a master study in the subject. Indeed, an article on him published in '*Vice*' magazine was titled '*How to Disappear Completely: When Musicians Retire For Good.*' The ending is far from happy, though.

Talk Talk started out as participants in the New Romantic movement, supporting **Duran Duran** on one of their early tours in 1981. As the decade progressed, their sound and style evolved to the point where they picked up the genre label of Post-Rock. The group split up following the release of their fifth album, '*Laughing Stock.*' After a few absent years Hollis returned with a self-named solo album in 1998, but then disappeared from the music industry completely. He stated that he wished to raise his children, commenting at the time, "I choose for my family. Maybe others are capable of doing it, but I can't go on tour and be a good dad at the same time."

Hollis' retracting from the business puts me in mind of the situation with **John Deacon**, the bassist with **Queen**, who had very little to do with the band following the death of **Freddie Mercury** and disappeared into retirement, leaving his bandmates **Brian May** and **Roger Taylor** to continue without him. Virtually no photos of Hollis appeared on the internet following his retirement, with few posts being made to his Facebook page.

Gaining an understanding of Hollis' motives is made difficult through little information being available on his life pre-fame, and the fact that he rarely gave interviews, and was considered elusive and "difficult" on the occasions that he did. A 1988 article in '*Q*' magazine noted:

"Mark Hollis is aware that he is perceived as 'a difficult geezer' at times. This, he says, is because he won't 'play that game' of hand-shaking and pleasantry-exchanging. But rather than giving the impression of being a terse, rapier-tongued weasel, he comes over more as a nervous, pensive individual with a few ideas of great import to unleash upon the populace."

At this point, a delve into the Talk Talk back catalogue pays some dividends. Much of their sleeve artwork contains the esoteric and occult symbolism that has come to be such a tell-tale sign of artists who have been completely absorbed by the industry machine. This all turns out to have been created by the veteran illustrator/ designer James Marsh, who worked extensively in the record business since the start of his career in the 1960s. His sleeves for Talk Talk are based on many of his paintings, in the surrealist style of Salvador Dali. Various creatures, particularly birds, adorn most of the covers. *'Life's What You Make It'* and *'The Colour of Spring'* feature butterflies, (though not Monarchs,) which often signals the presence of trauma-based mind control. A butterfly re-appears, along with a single eye, on *'History Revisited.'* *'The Party's Over'* features a face with a tear falling from the left eye.

Hollis' disillusionment with the music industry appears to have been triggered by the band's record label EMI attempting to sue him over their 1988 album, *'Spirit of Eden,'* not sounding commercial enough. This lawsuit set the precedent for the clause that a band's recordings have to be of a commercially satisfactory nature. Further legal issues ensued between Hollis and the label.

He is reported to have died suddenly in February 2019, aged 64. Different dates were given by different media outlets. Some reported that it was on the 18th, others that it was the 24th or 25th. He is said to have died after a "short illness" but with no further details made public. The only family member to have made a public quote appears to be his cousin-in-law, Anthony Costello. Old photographs were used in his obituaries, and there was no mention of his wife or children; similarly, there appear to be no photographs of any of them on-line.

The last 20 years of his life remain an enigma, therefore, and an outside observer is left to wonder whether his sudden departure is entirely innocent, or is somehow connected to his falling out of love with the industry that nurtured him.

*

When **Aretha Franklin** passed away of Pancreatic Cancer on 16th August 2018, it whittled down yet further the amount of veteran black music legends still left in the world. One of the last remaining was **Stevie Wonder**, but sadly, Aretha's passing led to him confirming his true nature as yet another agenda-pushing system asset. In comments made to CBS's '*This Morning*' programme, Stevie opined that "Global Warming deniers" were partly to blame for his soul sister's death:

> *I just feel that all these various diseases that we have and all that is happening in the world, in part is because there are those who don't believe in Global Warming, don't believe that what we do affects the world.*

While Stevie is right that our thoughts and emotions affect the mood and energy of the world we live in, the rest of his comments avoid the fact that "Global Warming" is yet another "Globalist" scam designed to sow fear and lay a guilt trip on the general public in order to extort yet more of their money through "green" tax hikes. Records show that throughout its history the Earth has undergone rhythmic cycles of heating and cooling, and its current status is entirely in line with this. In fact, "Global Warming" is now more commonly referred to as "Climate Change" in the absence of any reliable evidence to support the former term. The mainstream media always seems to forget to mention this.

It's a tragedy that such a musical genius should end up as just another mouthpiece-for-hire in this way. But quite simply, Stevie Wonder would not have had the long-lasting and influential career that he has if he weren't singing to the control system's song sheet. No-one can, as I hope this book series by now has shown.

By the way, have you heard the one about Stevie Wonder possibly not really being blind? This suggestion has come from several fellow celebrities, including singers **Lionel Richie, Chaka Khan**, basketball star Shaquille O'Neal, and comedians Anthony Anderson and Steve

Harvey. Though they would doubtless play the plausible deniability card if challenged by saying they were only joking, their comments join several anomalies such as Stevie being pictured taking a photograph of **Michael Jackson**, pictured watching television and looking at the screen of a phone, sitting courtside at several basketball games, and catching a microphone stand knocked over by **Paul McCartney** at a live show at the White House.

16th August turns out to be a rather unlucky date for air passengers. Separate plane crashes on that date in 1987, 1991, 2005 and 2015 resulted in the collective deaths of 591 people. It's also a rather unlucky date, it turns out, for musicians—particularly those who have been crowned with "royal" titles. **Robert Johnson**, dubbed "The King of Blues," died on that day in 1938, **Elvis Presley**, "The King of Rock 'N' Roll," is said to have departed this realm on the same date in 1977, and as mentioned Aretha Franklin, "The Queen of Soul," left this mortal coil 41 years later. In the ancient Pagan calendar, 16th August represented the Festival of Minstrels and Vesta, a celebration of poetry and songs. It also happens to be Madonna's birthday.

*

Johnny Rotten's was a carefully cultivated image, crafted by the Bohemian mogul and impresario **Malcolm McLaren**, (about whose bizarre life there was much discussion in '*Musical Truth Volume 2.*') Once past the snarling, contemptuous persona which largely created a blueprint for the British "Punk" attitude of the 1970s, however, there are a few anomalous aspects to the character of **John Lydon**.

In 2014, Lydon/ Rotten revealed in his autobiography '*Anger Is An Energy*' that he had attended late-night drinking sessions in the House of Commons in his teenage years. There, he witnessed well-known MPs cavorting with escort girls and heading off with them at the end of the night. Lydon wrote that he thought many of the MPs present would have assumed that he was a male escort, due to his unconventional way of dressing. Lydon says he was introduced to the parties by his friend Linda Ashby, whom he described as "a working girl, basically." Lydon and Ashby shared a flat close to Buckingham Palace at the time; synchronistically, the father of Lydon's **Sex Pistols** bandmate, **Sid Vicious,** worked for a time as a guardsman at Buckingham Palace. He and Vicious' mother met when both spent time in the Royal Air Force. Hardly the family backgrounds one might expect from an anti-Establishment Punk Rocker.

At one kinky Commons session, Lydon says Ashby introduced him to the politician Jeremy Thorpe. This was in 1976, the year that Thorpe was forced to resign after finding himself at the centre of a sex scandal, and a short time before Lydon exploded on to the music scene under his alter-ego of Sex Pistols frontman Johnny Rotten. Given the Pistols' *apparent* "anti-Establishment" image and the contempt they *apparently* displayed for British convention through songs like '*God Save The Queen,*' the House of Commons might be considered an extremely unlikely place for Rotten to have been hanging out in.

John Lydon. A masterclass in a crafted enigma.

https://commons.wikimedia.org/wiki/File:John_Lydon_at_the_Hammersmith_Odeon,_2008-09-02.jpg

Credit: Ed Vill from Caracas, Venezuela

In 1978, Lydon/ Rotten appeared to demonstrate knowledge of the sordid activities of BBC presenter **Jimmy Savile**—common knowledge now, but still a best-kept secret at the time. In an interview for an upcoming film where he sneeringly stated that there were several people he'd like to kill, he announced that Savile was among them, stating:

> *"I think he's a hypocrite. I bet he's into all kinds of seediness that we all know about but are not allowed to talk about. I know some rumours. I bet none of this will be allowed out."*

Lydon complained that he was banned from BBC radio airplay as a result of making the comment.

Decades later, Lydon appeared on an episode of '*Piers Morgan's Life Stories,*' on which the audio clip was aired. While Morgan and the crowd celebrated the fact that Lydon had displayed knowledge of Savile's activities so far back, when asked if he'd ever done anything about it, Lydon replied that he felt he'd done his bit by simply making the comment. Several BBC presenters of the time admitted, once the revelations about Savile's paedophilia had come out in 2012, that they had all heard stories of what he'd been up to—much of it in his BBC dressing room—but that it was the culture within the BBC not to speak openly about such things.

Ten years on from the Savile comment, Lydon's name came up in further unlikely circumstances. On 21st December (the Winter Solstice) of 1988, the infamous Lockerbie bombing occurred when Pan Am Flight 103 exploded mid-air, and crashed to the ground close to the Scottish border town of Lockerbie, killing all on board. The bombing was blamed on Abdelbaset al-Megrahi, an intelligence officer from Muammar Gaddafi's Libyan regime.

In 2018, a TV documentary on the disaster, '*Lockerbie: The Unheard Voices,*' revealed that a handful of celebrities had been due to be travelling on the flight, but had changed their plans at the last minute, thus saving their lives. Among these were the British-Canadian actress Kim Cattrall, best known for her role in TV's '*Sex And The City,*' who said she had changed her flight after spending time in Harrods in London buying a teapot for her mother. Detroit group **The Four Tops**' lives were reportedly saved by a last-minute change in the recording time for their slot on TV's '*Top Of The Pops,*' causing them to catch a later British Airways flight. Lydon, meanwhile—also reportedly booked on the flight—explained that his wife had spent so long packing that it had caused them to fortuitously miss the departure. (A musician who *was* on the flight and perished along with all the others, was **Paul Jeffreys**, who had been a bass guitarist on the group **Cockney Rebel** in the 1970s.)

This story is curious in its own right, but becomes even more so when factored in with other, similar accounts. In the wake of the 9/11 events of September 2001, claims emerged of several famous people who had been scheduled to be on one of the doomed flights, but whose plans changed at the last minute. Among these were said to be singers **Michael Jackson** and **Patti Austin**, actor Mark Wahlberg, Leighanne Littrell, actress and wife of **Backstreet Boy** Brian Littrell, and Seth MacFarlane, creator of '*Family Guy*' and '*American Dad.*' **Paul McCartney**, (if we'd started a drinking game for every time his name gets mentioned in this book we'd all be under the table by now,) has stated that he was onboard a plane at New York's JFK airport waiting for take-off as the disastrous events in Manhattan were unfolding.

At other death-laden disasters, meanwhile, individuals who would later *go on* to become famous *just happened* to be present. A young **Chrissie Hynde**, yet to find fame with the group **The Pretenders**, was a student at the site of the Kent State Massacre of 1970, in which the boyfriend of one of her friends was among the four victims shot dead by the Ohio National Guard at a "peace" rally. Against what must surely be incredible odds, also witness to the same event was *another* future music star in the form of **Gerald Casale**, the singer and bassist with the New Wave/ Rock group **Devo. Bob Lewis**, a fellow founding member of Devo, also attended Kent State University and graduated shortly after the shooting. The event is said to have inspired the formation of the band, its name being derived from the theme of the "de-evolution" of mankind.

The story puts me in mind of the Altamont Free Festival on 6th December 1969, which became infamous for all the wrong reasons when the Hell's Angels who were providing "security," stabbed to death one of the attendees, 18-year-old Meredith Hunter, right in front of the stage as the **Rolling Stones** performed. '*Gimme Shelter,*' the film released in the wake of Altamont and documenting the Stones' 1969 US Tour, includes a credit for a young camera operator by the name of

George Lucas. He would go on to become one of the most celebrated movie directors of all time with 'Star Wars' a few years later, but at the time of Altamont, is said to have captured the murder of Meredith Hunter on film. None of Lucas' footage was included in the film's final cut.

The presence of Chrissie Hynde, the Devo founders, and Lucas at these horrific events — and them going on to achieve fame some years later — has caused some to question whether these incidents constituted some kind of morbid initiation into the upper ranks of their respective industries.

When you add to these events the near-misses enjoyed by Lydon and the others in the wake of Lockerbie and 9/11 — and then consider what the odds are of so many famous people *just happening* to be involved one way or another in these stories — it tends to suggest that this goes way beyond the realm of coincidence, but rather bears the hallmarks of pre-planning.

The dynamic was taken yet further by the Co(n)vid-19 Scamdemic of 2020 — as detailed in the earlier chapter — when an unfeasible number of famous people just happened to contract "the virus." What, really, were the odds of Prime Minister Boris Johnson, Health Secretary Matt Hancock, Prince Charles and Prince William *all* being unfortunate enough to catch Co(n)vid, many asked, when most ordinary people would be hard-pressed to find one person in their entire circle of family and friends who had done the same?

As evidenced so many times throughout these books, it seems a Lifetime Actor's work is never done.

*

One of the most unpopular Tory government ministers during the Co(n)vid-19 Scamdemic, (and *think* of the competition!) was the sickly, quesy Secretary of State for Transport Grant Shapps. Among his claims to fame in that time were his suggestion that taking a vaccine should be a condition of being allowed to travel internationally.

In 2012, an investigation by '*The Guardian*' found that Shapps had personally altered his entry on Wikipedia, deleting information about financial donors to his private office. A man you can trust.

Anyone coming across Shapps for the first time could be forgiven for assuming him to be just another greasy, self-serving liar, finding it improbable that there should be any family links whatsoever into the music industry... unless they'd first read either of the other two '*Musical Truth*' books, that is. Anyone who has *won't* need to sit down to recover from the shock of finding out that Shapps' brother, Andre, was a keyboardist member of the group **Big Audio Dynamite** (BAD) between 1994 and 1998. BAD's frontman was **Mick Jones**, who had been a founding member of **The Clash.** Jones also turns out to be a cousin of Grant and Andre Shapps through his Russian Jewish mother Renee Zegansky. Jones attended Strand School in South London, a boys' grammar school noted for its induction of young men into the British Civil service.

This is not the only familial connection between The Clash and the British Establishment, either. The father of fellow founding member Graham Mellor, better known by his stage name of **Joe Strummer**, was Ronald Mellor (MBE). Born in colonial India, Ronald attained the rank of Second Secretary in the British Foreign Office. Graham/ Joe was born in Ankara, Turkey as a result of Ronald's posting there, and attended the private City of London Freemen's School. Like Jones and Clash manager Bernie Rhodes, he hails from a Jewish family, in his case, through his great-grandmother.

Strummer's brother David committed suicide in 1970; according to Strummer himself, he had been interested in the occult and had been a National Front "Nazi." Strummer died suddenly of what was reported to be a congenital heart defect on the Winter Solstice, 22nd December, of 2002, aged 50.

The Clash, being one of the principal acts to populate the British Punk and New Wave scenes, have always been portrayed as representing the antithesis to Establishment values and the societal status quo, as per the "punk" ethos. The strong family links of its two most prominent members into expressions of the very Establishment they claimed to oppose, however, speak for themselves.

*

Another improbable link between music and politics comes from the fact that **Grace Slick**, frontwoman of the San Francisco group **Jefferson Airplane**, hugely influential during the LSD-laden psychedelic scene of the 1960s, attended Finch College in Manhattan, the same school as Trish Nixon, daughter of the 37th President of the United States, Richard Nixon. It was this connection which led to a bizarre story involving Slick attempting to dose Nixon with LSD, in the hope of opening him up to a spirit of love and inclusion. Nixon had been a fierce opponent of Counter-Culture values—particularly recreational drug use—and was facing huge opposition to his Vietnam war policies.

In April 1970, Trish Nixon arranged a social event at the White House for alumni of Finch, and Slick—having attended ten years before Trish—was on the list, albeit under her maiden name of Grace Wing. Slick decided to attend and to bring along a friend, who turned out to be political activist (and future ally of **John Lennon**,) Abbie Hoffman. Slick planned to slip Acid into Nixon's afternoon tea once inside the event.

Unfortunately for Slick and Hoffman, their infamy as anti-government protestors saw them being recognised and refused entry at the door. The plan would have fallen flat anyway, as it turned out the President wasn't due to have been present at the event at all.

*

Any younger or newer users of social media may be unaware that before there was Facebook, (an apt choice of name considering it stands as a CIA/ NSA tool for data gathering,) Twitter, Instagram, Tik Tok or Snapchat, there was a short-lived, but very popular site known as Myspace. As well as rudimentary social networking opportunities, this offered a platform for music makers to share their output independently, with facilities for uploading audio and video files, and promoting live shows and events.

Many up-and-coming bands, singers, rappers and producers held out hope of making it big through being discovered as a result of their output. Though the vast, overwhelming majority did not, there are two names that were cited by the mainstream as having broken through to the big time purely as a result of being "discovered" thorough Myspace.

One was singer **Lily Allen** who, we're told, only became popular as a result of large numbers of fans sharing her songs far and wide on Myspace. The fact that her father is the TV and film actor Keith Allen, who appeared in '*Trainspotting*,' and the videos for Blur's '*Country House*' and New Order's '*World In Motion*' (which he co-wrote,) apparently has no bearing on the matter, and is pure coincidence. Keith seems to enjoy appearing naked in public as often as possible, as Beat poet Allen Ginsburg did; in his early career as a stand-up comedian he would perform entire routines naked without making any reference to the fact; in 1976, he lost his job as a stage-hand after rushing on-stage during a Max Bygraves performance and linking arms with the chorus line, completely naked. He donned the birthday suit again for his cameo in the movie '*Shallow Grave*,' and ditched the garms one more time in 2019 as the nude model for a BBC painting show.

Lily gave an insight as to where her moral compass lay when, in her auto-biography '*My Thoughts Exactly*,' she revealed that she had lied about miscarrying the baby she had conceived with **Ed Simons** of electronic dance duo **The Chemical Brothers** to garner public sympathy, when in fact no such miscarriage had occurred. In the same book, she confessed that she had an affair with **Liam Gallagher** when he was married to former **All Saints** member **Nicole Appleton**, among other infidelities.

The Allen family is another with career military connections—hard to believe, I know. Lily's grandfather was a Royal Navy submariner. Many in the extended family have, like Keith and Lily, followed careers in the arts. Lily's brother Alfie, (subject of a song on her debut album '*Alright, Still*' teasing him for his habit of sitting around smoking weed all day,) is an actor, as is their uncle, Keith's brother Kevin Allen, who is also a director. Lily's mother, Alison Owen, is a film producer. Lily turns out also to be a third cousin of singer **Sam Smith**. (Smith helped push the Transgender social-engineering agenda when he announced that he was "non-binary" and wished to be addressed as "they" rather than "he."

The other act which, industry lore has it, launched their career off the back of Myspace exposure, was Sheffield-formed group the **Arctic Monkeys**. According to an article on the officialcharts.com website, (which also attributes the success of **Calvin Harris, Adele, Kate Nash, Sean Kingston, Sandi Thom** and **Owl City** to initial Myspace exposure):

> *"Arctic Monkeys got their first big break on Myspace, but there's a twist. The Sheffield band were decidedly old-school, concentrating on writing, gigging and distributing demo CDs, so it was actually friends of theirs who set up their Myspace page, with fans later taking it upon themselves to share bootleg versions of tracks on forums. The band's growing following caught the attention of multiple major labels, but they ultimately signed to independents Domino in 2005."*

The band's debut album '*Whatever People Say I Am, That's What I'm Not*' is said to have become the fastest-selling debut album in British history, and was ranked at No. 30 on '*Rolling Stone*' magazine's list of the greatest debut albums of all time. I'm sure the millions of other bands who have posted demos of their songs on-line over the years and hoped to hit the big time would love to know how they achieved this.

Some fans have found it intriguing that the image of group frontman **Alex Turner** was completely transformed in 2011, where he went from a mop-haired, relatively shy frontman, to rocking a greased-out rock star persona, a contrast highlighted by his appearances at that year's T In The Park and Loopzilla festivals.

While it remains possible that these acts were co-opted by the Industry machine following their initial breakthroughs, what seems far more likely is that, in the early years of the 2000s, the popularity of Myspace was used as a cover story for how these acts became so popular and influential so quickly, with the truth of why it was them over and above any other contenders, lying elsewhere.

*

A further apparent breeding ground for UK music acts who would go on to become hugely popular and influential—a physical location this time, rather than an on-line portal—has been the Brit School in Croydon. Reserved for students of 14 to 19 years of age, it describes itself as "Britain's only free Performing Arts & Technology School. It is an independent, state-funded City College for the Technology of the Arts, the only one of its kind dedicated to education and vocational training for the performing arts, media, art and design and the technologies that make performance possible."

Founder Mark Featherstone-Whitty is said to have been inspired in his idea for the Brit School by the 1980 American movie '*Fame.*' He went on to work with **Sir Paul McCartney**, (take another swig,) on establishing the Liverpool Institute of Performing Arts. With Establishment asset Sir Richard Branson as an early backer, the Brit School went on to achieve funding from the British Phonographic Industry, including proceeds from the annual Brit Awards event.

In the same way that most British Prime Ministers and senior politicians of the past several decades will have been "educated" at the same small select group of institutions, (Eton, Oxford, Cambridge,) the list of Brit School students who have gone on to enjoy fame, success and influence, is truly dizzying. A small list of such names includes; **Adele, Amy Winehouse, Bashy, Jessie J, Ella Eyre, Jamie Woon, Lynden David Hall, Katie Melua, Kate Nash, Katy B, Leona Lewis** and **Dane Bowers.**

*

Just how did **Ed Sheeran** (MBE) go from obscurity to becoming arguably the most successful British singer-songwriter of the 2010s, picking up countless industry awards, (including three nominations at the 2012 Music of Black Origin Awards, despite his music bearing no relation to black sounds or styles,) as well as film roles and almost universal critical acclaim? Organised Society would have you believe that this kind of career path is open to anyone, so long as they posses the required skill, work really hard, and have a bit of good luck in their hustle.

As we have come to discover, however, that particular fairytale isn't how it actually works. But who your Dad is, often can be. A delve into Ed's old man's activities, therefore, pays dividends. Hailing from

Northern Ireland, John Sheeran is listed as an art curator and lecturer. Along with his wife Imogen, a culture publicist-turned jewellery designer, he ran an independent art consultancy, Sheeran Lock, from 1990 to 2010. This set-up saw them score some important affiliations, including curating the official 50th Birthday Exhibition of Prince Charles, and the United Nations Millennium Exhibition, 'Our World in 2000,' at the U.N. headquarters in New York. Promotional pictures of a young, pre-fame Ed show him covering up one eye. Is anyone really surprised?

In other eyebrow-raising connections, Ed reportedly revealed himself to be a distant nephew of Frank Sheeran, the Irish-American mobster portrayed by Robert De Niro in the film 'The Irishman.' This claim came from actor Stephen Graham who starred in the same movie. "They're related, you know," Graham told 'The Sun.' " ... That's what Ed said—he says it's his distant uncle."

A family link that's much easier to establish, meanwhile, is that Ed is a second cousin of the broadcaster Gordon Burns, who used to present ITV's 'The Krypton Factor.'

It sure is a small world.

*

While the hippie/ Psychedelic scene was taking hold in America in the mid to late 1960s, its Counter-Culture values appealing to those of a Liberal/ leftist political persuasion, it was known that those of a more conservative/ Christian/ patriotic mindset would find the loose morals of that movement wholly reprehensible. Conveniently, the Country & Western genre was available in direct opposition.

On the surface, Country appeared to espouse wholesome, Christian, "All-American" values. In the music industry, however, appearances can be deceptive ... as we well know. And so it is that a closer inspection of the genre reveals some familiar MOs and calling-cards.

The C&W scene was very much centred around Nashville, Tennessee. An entire district of the city, known as Music Row, is comprised of businesses directly linked to the industry, including record labels, recording studios, artist management companies and live music venues.

On reflection, this is a very similar dynamic to the one found in the Laurel Canyon district of Los Angeles, home to an unfeasible number of musicians populating the Counter-Culture/ Psychedelic rock scene, as documented in David McGowan's landmark book 'Weird Scenes Inside The Canyon.'

Sure enough, the same links to aspects of the military and military-intelligence that were found in the LC, are also present in Music Row. Both areas had drug-addicted artists who showed signs of having undergone mind control; both areas had artists with direct family ties to the military ranks; both areas created entire scenes with their own lifestyles and fashions; both scenes controlled and dominated radio for decades and introduced new technology for listening. Whereas Laurel Canyon's heyday coincided with new advances in FM radio, allowing the music to be heard more clearly and widely, in Music Row's case, it led to the industry introducing different formats and speeds (one being "33"!) for vinyl records, as well as the use of 8-track recording techniques.

Among Music Row's most celebrated sites are Studio A and Studio B owned by RCA Records, where hundreds of prominent musicians have recorded tracks. RCA stands as a great example of a record label with direct military ties. Standing for the Record Corporation of America, it was developed out of the US Navy, and before becoming home to recording artists like **Elvis Presley, Glenn Miller, Harry Belafonte, Perry Como, Paul Anka, Neil Sedaka, Waylon Jennings, Nancy Sinatra** and **Benny Goodman**, held the status of the dominant electronics and communications firm in the United States for over five decades, pioneering the introduction of radio and television broadcasting.

It was a radio broadcast that was largely responsible for popularising Country music to many of the 50 states. Started in 1925 and recorded a few blocks from Music Row, 'The Grand Ole Opry' show still broadcasts and stands as a showcase of artists from the genre. By the 1930s it was broadcasting at a groundbreaking 50,000 watts, and it had become a tradition for families to gather round their radio sets every Saturday night to hear it.

As researcher Sean McCann noted in the 'Good Vibrations' podcast I recorded with him on the subject, The "Opry" would never showcase anyone from the Counter-Culture, *except* for Laurel Canyon-ites **The Byrds**. Somehow this band alone managed to span both scenes.

Country fans harboured nothing but contempt for what they perceived to be the degenerate morals of the Counter-Culture longhairs, and so another successful pitting of one tribe in society against another was achieved in line with the controllers' Divide and Conquer strategy. And all adding yet further weight to the notion that popular culture and entertainment have long been a military-grade weapon in the mind-control of the masses.

*

A dubious fashion trend sported by a handful of "celebrities" in recent years has been the wearing of red-tinted sunglasses in public. It's a look commonly employed by the previously-mentioned **Bono**—though he appears in blue-tinted pairs also. Others in this motley assortment have included **Jimmy Savile, Elton John** and Robert Downey Jr. Despite a '*Wall Street Journal*' article asking the question '*Why Do So Many Ageing Stars Wear Tinted Glasses?*' then going on to answer it by suggesting it's simply to make them look cool and disguise their wrinkles, a more conspiratorial theory is that the glasses act as a visual indicator that the wearer belongs to some kind of secret society.

A more practical explanation, however, is that the tinted glasses are worn to block the blue light which is emitted from street lights and car headlights after dark, and from the plethora of electronic devices routinely used and which, according to some, is harmful to human health; blue light is said to damage mitochondria, hinder melatonin production, and hinder the body's ability to produce and uptake vitamin D. It can also throw Circadian Rhythms out of synch, resulting in insomnia. Blue blocking glasses and blue screen filters come recommended for people who spend many hours a day looking at a device screen.

This theory posits that, far from making a fashion statement, these "celebs" have been clued-in on this aspect of the "elite" agenda to harm human health, and are merely taking steps to avoid the same pitfalls faced by their fans.

As ever, it seems, the public are the last to know.

*

I've been asked at various points since the appearance of '*Musical Truth 1*' if I've discovered any nefarious aspects of Swedish national exports **ABBA**. Not having taken a deep dive into that group's history, I've always replied that I don't have anything specific on them, but that there would be no way a group could have achieved the level of success and influence that they have without being completely beholden to the industry's controllers.

I've now taken a rudimentary look at certain aspects of the group. There will surely be more to know, but this will do for starters. First off, the group's name contains some word magick. In Hebrew the word means "father," and the reversibility of it has overtones of the adepts of Aleister Crowley's Thelema philosophy training themselves to read backwards. The group's Eurovision Song Contest-winning breakthrough hit, '*Waterloo*,' has Masonic overtones given Napoleon's Freemasonry. The Waterloo event has also become infamous as far as the Rothschild banking dynasty is concerned, given that Nathan Mayer Rothschild is said to have learned early through his own personal couriers of Napoleon's defeat, and used his unfair advantage to bid on the London Stock Exchange and make himself a fortune.

Another early hit, '*Dancing Queen*,' was written in tribute to Silvia Sommerlath, the new bride of the King of Sweden, Carl XVI Gustaf, beginning a long association between ABBA and the Swedish royals. In 1993, ABBA's Anni-Frid Lyngstad was recruited to sing the song at the 50th birthday ceremony of Queen Silvia.

The lyrics to the band's body of hit songs seem, auto-biographically, to chart the breakdown of the two in-group marriages as the years progressed, going from happy in tone in early songs, to what is often described as "Swedish melancholia" by the end of their career. While these lyrics have been both praised for their incisive honesty, and derided as kitsch, on closer examination some social-engineering appears to have been achieved. The group could be accused of popularising, or "normalising" the idea of divorce. Many of their lyrics also espouse loose moral codes, which appears to be in contrast to their family-friendly image and the commercial accessibility of their songs.

Things just stop short of taboo on '*Does Your Mother Know*' where an underage girl attempts to seduce an older man at a disco, but the man seems to do the right thing by begrudgingly rejecting her advances and declaring "you're only a child."

ABBA's songs also helped to take Disco music into the mainstream, along with its associations with gay culture and drugs. On the sleeve to the single '*Voulez Vous*' the group appear in a cube housed inside a pyramid. A pyramid re-appears on the American 2014 issue of their '*The Singles*' compilation. For 1977's '*Abba: The Album,*' half of the group's faces appear in shadow, as the **Beatles**' did on their '*With The Beatles,*' an effect repeated in some of their videos, and a motif associated with embracing one's "shadow self," or egoic, material aspect. The odd pentagram crops up from time to time too.

The issue of Anni-Frid's parentage became a talking point late in her career. Born to a Norwegian mother, it emerged that her father had been a sergeant in the German Wehrmacht army which was involved in the occupation of Norway after World War 2. Such mothers and children were shunned in Norwegian society of the time, becoming known as the "*Tyskerbarnas*" or "German children." Anni-Frid and her mother, Synni, were forced to emigrate to Sweden, where Synni died of kidney failure before Anni-Frid was two. In 2002, the '*Guardian*' reported that a group of 12,000 offspring of Norwegian mothers and German soldier fathers planned to fight for compensation in the European Court of Human Rights.

For most of their visually striking videos, (plenty of one eye symbolism) and for '*ABBA: The Movie,*' the group recruited the Swedish film director Lasse Halstrom. We get more Establishment connections here through his maternal grandfather Ernst Lyberg having been Minister of Finance in the first cabinet of Prime Minister Carl Gustaf Ekman, and leader of the Liberal Party of Sweden in the 1930s.

After ABBA's break-up in 1983, **Bjorn Ulvaeus** and **Benny Andersson** went on to pick up countless awards and merits, both from the record industry and from aspects of the Swedish Government and academia, cementing their position as darlings of the Establishment. They began writing musicals. one being '*Chess*', with that game's obvious ties to occultism and Freemasonry through the black-and-white checkerboard symbolism. Prior to the formation of ABBA, Bjorn and Benny were in a Swedish group called the **Hootenanny Singers**, an obviously Scottish-sounding name; could this be a veiled allusion to the Scottish Rite of Freemasonry?

While this book was being written, the news came of ABBA's sudden and unexpected reunion in September 2021 for *'Voyage,'* their first album in 40 years, and the accompanying single *'Don't Shut me Down.'* What could be the reason for this shock re-appearance—particularly if we consider the question from the point-of-view of system agendas, and that ABBA's "farewell" in 1983 with *'Thank You For The Music'* did seem very, well, final? Well, how about the fact that ABBA have long been beloved of the Australian nation, largely down to a strategic single release and touring schedule there during their peak in the 1970s? At the time of the group's re-appearance, Australia was in the grip of some of the most extreme tyranny of anywhere in the world, and pockets of resistance were beginning to build in the form of protest rallies, and a blockade of ports and key distribution routes by truckers. Could ABBA have been instructed to exhume themselves to distract the Australian public and keep their attention away from other more important things happening in their own nation?

Or am I just being overly conspiratorial here?

*

A video missing from my analysis of 1980s pop videos in the last book was *'These Dreams'* by the American group **Heart**. It should have made the selection, as its array of symbolism doesn't disappoint. The whole sequence has, appropriately for the title, a dream-like quality. This is evocative of the dissociation from reality that subjects of trauma-based mind-control encounter, and is further enhanced by a view of the singer through a mirror frame—a common motif for mind-control—flanked by two sinister hooded figures.

The rest of the video doesn't disappoint as the band performs surrounded by Masonic pillars, a sea of hands reach out towards the singer as if trying to molest her, and the same sea of hands is seen emerging from a cage in the floor...as if they're being kept captive in an underground facility, perhaps? The only thing missing is the black-and-white checkerboard floor—a rather disappointing omission.

Though their biggest hits were in the mid-1980s, Heart were formed in Seattle as far back as 1970. From shortly afterwards the group was fronted by sisters **Ann** and **Nancy Wilson**. Could any reader really encounter any surprise by this point to learn that their father was a Major in the US Marine Corps, with postings at various American military facilities around the world?

*

While I could go on listing the nefarious aspects of pretty much every household name group of the past 50 years—a task which would see at least another ten volumes of '*Musical Truth*,' which is not something I relish the thought of spending my remaining years labouring away at—one act which has come across my radar enough times, and ticks so many boxes as to be worthy of special mention, is Genesis. A quick run-through some of the main points becomes worthwhile.

Of interest straight off the bat are the circumstances surrounding the band's formation. The group's founding members, **Peter Gabriel, Tony Banks, Anthony Phillips, Mike Rutherford** and **Chris Stewart**, were students at Charterhouse Public School near Godalming, Surrey. It was here that the young hopefuls are said to have been "discovered" by music mogul and Charterhouse alumnus **Jonathan King**—later exposed as a serial child-rapist who had used his fame to seduce scores of young boys. Not the most admirable of mentors. When the BBC decided to make a documentary on Genesis in 2014, they caused outrage by insisting on including an interview from King, despite him having already served jail time and been convicted of several offences. Apparently no-one else would do and the BBC considered King's inclusion more important than the insult that would be caused by giving airtime to a child-rapist in a programme funded by public licence payers, despite having already been embroiled in paedophile scandal for two years following the Savile revelations.

We get into familiar territory with the father of singer/ songwriter/ guitarist Mike Rutherford, who was a Captain in the Royal Navy, (well, you didn't really expect him to have been a lorry driver or a brickie, did you?)

In original vocalist Peter Gabriel's case, his father's profession throws us somewhat off-track, his having been an electrical engineer with numerous patents to his name. However, we're back on the money when we move to his great-great-uncle, Sir Thomas Gabriel, 1st Baronet, who served as Sheriff of London and Middlesex, and later Lord Mayor of London from 1866 to 1877. We're on the bloodline trail.

(On the subject of mayors and sheriffs, incidentally, would anyone be surprised to learn that the grandfather of Coldplay's **Chris Martin**, John Besley Martin (CBE), was once a Sheriff and Mayor of Exeter? Or, come to that, that his aunt, Elisabeth Jane Martin, was the wife of Julian Sandys, son of Diana Spencer-Churchill and grandson of Winston Churchill? Nothing unusual about rock musicians having connections to Lawmakers, the aristocracy and British prime Ministers. No, really. There isn't. Still think Coldplay's instant rise to fame and critical adulation off the back of their successful debut album was just random and could have happened to anyone?)

Anyway, back to Gabriel. A barmaid or a toilet cleaner was never going to make the grade when it came to Pete's first marriage, and appropriately that honour went to Jill Moore, the daughter of Philip Moore, Baron of Wolvercote, a real piece of Establishment furniture. He was Private Secretary to the Queen for nine years, as well as serving the First Lord of the Admiralty and holding the Deputy British High Commissioner post in Singapore.

Outside of his two marriages, Gabriel has been romantically linked with **Kate Bush (CBE)**, **Sinead O'Connor** and actress Rosanna Arquette.

In terms of extra-curricular activities, Gabriel has been seen to be among the most politically active of all musicians. What this actually means, however, is that like **Bono, Sting, Annie Lennox** and the like, he is often called upon to lend the familiarity of his name to various "Globalist" charities and NGOs to further certain social-engineering agendas.

Which just leaves us with Genesis' most recognisable frontman, drummer-turned-singer **Phil Collins**. Though Phil has clearly played the music industry game and been rewarded with the kind of career that comes when you toe the line and don't rock the boat, (he started early, cropping up as a teen extra in the **Beatles**' 1964 movie '*A Hard Day's Night*,') there's little nefarious about him that's crossed my radar thus far. I can't, however, get a particularly unsettling facial expression out of my mind when hearing his name.

In 1993, ITV screened an episode of '*This Is Your Life*' in tribute to boxer-turned pantomime entertainer Frank Bruno. Worryingly, Bruno had been a close friend of Jimmy Savile, and was interviewed, alongside BBC radio DJ **Mike Read,** at Savile's funeral, where he spoke of him having been "a good man, a one in a million," adding that Savile had helped him "in a lot of ways that I can't talk about on the television," and that Savile had "done a lot of special things that people don't even know." (This was a year before Savile's serial paedophilia became public knowledge.) Through his often child-like demeanour, Bruno has shown signs of possibly having been subjected to trauma-based mind control.

Phil Collins was one of the guests on the '*This Is Your Life*' episode. In his recorded message he talked of Bruno's involvement in the Prince's Trust charity, and went on to mention "all the kids whose lives you've *touched*." At the point that he makes the comment, he gives an expression of pure evil.

Were we getting a truth-in-plain-sight double meaning from one in the know? (You can view Collins' look at the 19:41 mark in this video—https://youtu.be/vg-utVgibVQ)

*

Given the other prominent artists who turn out to be cousins of **Madonna,** (**Celine Dion, Lady Gaga,**) it's something of a surprise to discover that **Cyndi Lauper**, who was pitched as Madonna's rival upon the release of her debut album '*She's So Unusual*' in 1983, *doesn't* share the same family links, (though Lauper did jokingly refer to Madonna as her "evil cousin" on Australian TV show '*The Project*' in 2016.)

Besides Madonna, Lauper also credited **Boy George** and **Prince** as friends and influencers when asked about her early career, and does seem to share a trait, in that they have all shown signs of having been subjects of MK-Ultra-mind-control programming.

Cyndi Lauper. Though married to a man and with one child, a non-stop feature at Gay Pride events around the world. That's what happens when your handlers instruct you to prop up agendas.

https://commons.wikimedia.org/wiki/File:Cyndi_Lauper_SF_Gay_Pride_2008_(cropped).jpg

Author: Bastique

Lauper's early life echoes that of Madonna in that they were both born into staunchly Catholic families. While Madonna's father was Italian-American, in Lauper's case, the Italian influence comes from her mother, (who appeared as herself in the video to Cyndi's first hit '*Girls Just Wanna Have Fun,'*) while her father, about whom little information seems to be available, was of German and Swiss descent. Five years older than Madonna, she grew up in the Ozone Park neighbourhood of Queens, New York. Her father left the family when she was ten and her mother re-married a man described in her book '*Cyndi Lauper: A Memoir,'* as a "violent bully" who threatened to sexually assault Cyndi and her sister. Turbulent home lives involving violent and threatening father figures are present in the early lives of all the above 80s icons — Boy

George, Prince, (as portrayed in his auto-biographical movie *'Purple Rain,'*) and Madonna, (as chronicled in her song *'Oh Father'.*)

Lauper faced poverty and hardship—just like Madonna—after running away from home at 17. Her pre-fame years involved her terminating a pregnancy, and becoming the survivor of a sexual assault. In her memoir, she talks of becoming alcohol-dependent and having contemplated suicide. Why are these themes so prevalent in the world of popular music, so much more so, proportionately, than in regular walks of life, or in other professions? And could they be planted into official biographies as accounts of early-life trauma to explain away what may have *really* caused certain personality traits?

Several indicators of mind-control programming of the type detailed in this book's first volume, appear throughout Cyndi's career. Her flamboyant and exuberant style is present in her videos and stage performances—such personality changes are often a by-product of Multiple Personality Disorder—as is her frequently dyed hair—just like Madonna. Pink hair is a motif associated with Monarch Programming, as detailed in the many articles on the subject on the Vigilant Citizen website, (www.vigilantcitizen.com.)

Several clues appear in the video to her 1989 song *'I Drove All Night.'* In it, she appears with the peroxide-blonde hair that is a visual indicator of the phenomenon known as Beta Sex Kitten Programming. (More here—https://hollywoodsubliminals.wordpress.com/project-monarch/sex-kitten/) Marilyn Monroe popularised that archetypal look. In the video to her follow-up, *'My First Night Without You,'* (complete with a black-and-white checkerboard floor, would you believe?) Cyndi reprised the peroxide look and rocked a white dress of the type Marilyn famously wore in *'The Seven Year Itch.'* (Madonna rocked the exact same look at about the same point in her career, and has talked of being the "reincarnation" of Marilyn Monroe. Given that she was born in 1958 and Marilyn isn't said to have died until 1962 that doesn't quite work out—unless she was speaking symbolically of being another Monarch fashioned in the *style* of Marilyn??) Beta slaves are symbolised by cat imagery, and sure enough, Cyndi cavorts in a leopard-print dress in the video. Multiple versions of Cyndi appear on-screen at the same time, suggestive of the Multiple Personality Disorder that is produced by trauma-based programming. She also appears to be bound and trapped as images are projected on to her body.

Later in her career, Lauper began pushing the social-engineering agendas for which artists are so often used—particularly when they've passed their peak. In particular, she has pushed the LGBT and Transgender agendas which *aren't* about standing up for the rights of people from those communities, but rather cynically exploit them to mould public attitudes and perceptions in line with much wider-reaching goals of mass mind-control and societal manipulation. *That's* social-engineering. Besides Madonna, (no great surprise there,) **Kim Wilde** and **Samantha Fox**, (memories of 80s schoolboy fantasies are rushing back here with the mention of these names,) have also been wheeled out to prop up the same agendas in more recent years, (and all rocked the blonde Beta sex kitten look.) Despite heterosexual relationships, Fox now professes to be a lesbian, while Lauper, Wilde and Madonna all married men.

Ian Fleming wrote in the James Bond novel '*Goldfinger,*' "once is happenstance. Twice is coincidence. Three times is enemy action." A similar dynamic may be considered with all these artists. One example suggestive of trauma-based mind control is happenstance. Two examples may be considered coincidence. Three—and way, *way* beyond—becomes a trend that only an individual in a heavy state of denial or cognitive dissonance would write off as random and meaningless.

Sadly when it comes to Monarch-style programming, with the sick, diseased entity that is the corporate music industry, it's just another day at the office. And Cyndi Lauper represents just another brick in the wall.

Resources:

DJ Mag: Two DJs publicly Accuse Erick Morillo of Sexual assault and Inappropriate Behaviour:

- https://djmag.com/news/two-djs-publicly-accuse-erick-mo-rillo-sexual-assault-and-inappropriate-behaviour#:~:tex-t=Morillo%20was%20accused%20of%20rape,tested%20positive%20for%20his%20DNA.

Jury returns suicide verdict at Smiley Culture inquest:

- https://web.archive.org/web/20140820040044/http://www.london24.com/news/jury_returns_suicide_verdict_at_smiley_culture_inquest_1_2260856

Avicii: 'For A Better Day' video:

- https://www.youtube.com/watch?v=Xq-knHXSKYY

Culture Club: 'Do You Really Want To Hurt Me' video:

- https://www.youtube.com/watch?v=2nXGPZaTKik

Scottish Daily Record: Five things about Boy George and Culture Club you might not know:

- https://www.dailyrecord.co.uk/entertainment/music/music-news/five-things-boy-george-culture-12343244

The Elm Guest House: List of Visitors Courtesy of Mary Moss:

- https://cigpapers.blog/2013/04/29/the-elm-guest-house-vip-paedophile-party-list/

Aangirfan blog: Leon Brittan Named as Child Rapist and Witness to Child Murder:

- https://aanirfan.blogspot.com/2015/01/leon-brittan-disap-pears.html

Guardian Obituary: Mark Hollis, lead singer of Talk Talk, dies aged 64:

- https://www.theguardian.com/music/2019/feb/25/ mark-hollis-lead-singer-of-talk-talk-dies-at-age-64-reports-say

The Guardian: Wherefore art thou Mark Hollis?:

- https://www.theguardian.com/music/musicblog/2008/apr/09/ markhollis

Vice: How to Disappear Completely: When Musicians Retire For Good:

- https://www.vice.com/en/article/j5be53/ mark-hollis-talk-talk-retire-disappear-reunions

Interview with James Marsh on his album cover work for Talk Talk:

- https://albumcoverhalloffame.wordpress.com/2012/11/07/ james-marsh-talk-talk-interview/

RT: Global warming deniers partly responsible for Aretha Franklin's cancer, says Stevie Wonder:

- https://www.rt.com/ usa/436417-aretha-franklin-global-warming-wonder/

BBC bans Johnny Rotten in 1978 for outing Jimmy Saville:

- https://www.youtube.com/watch?v=v4OzI9GYag0

Daily Mail: Johnny Rotten's VERY scandalous nights in the Commons: Sex Pistols star reveals how he attended drinking sessions with MPs—and watched them head off with escort girls at the end of the night :

- https://www.dailymail.co.uk/news/article-2780889/ Johnny-Rotten-s-VERY-scandalous-nights-Commons- Sex-Pistols-star-reveals-attended-drinking-sessions-MPs- watched-head-escort-girls-end-night.html

Lockerbie Bombing: Victims nearly included Four Tops, John Lydon and Kim Cattrall:

- https://www.mirror.co.uk/news/
  lockerbie-crash-victims-could-included-13645196

The Independent: Sex & drugs & herring rolls: Punk's Jewish roots revealed:

- https://www.independent.co.uk/arts-entertainment/music/
  news/sex-drugs-herring-rolls-punk-s-jewish-roots-re-
  vealed-9155498.html

How Grace Slick Planned To Dose President Richard Nixon With LSD:

- https://ultimateclassicrock.com/
  grace-slick-president-nixon-acid-1970/

Myspace acts who found success on the Official Charts:

- https://www.officialcharts.com/chart-news/
  myspace-acts-who-found-success-on-the-official-charts__25882/

NME: How Arctic Monkeys' isolation album 'Tranquility Base Hotel & Casino' predicted pandemic life:

- https://www.nme.com/features/arctic-monkeys-tranquili-
  ty-base-hotel-casino-pandemic-2745473

Famous People: John Sheeran profile:

- https://www.thefamouspeople.com/profiles/john-
  sheeran-48454.php

The Guardian: Torment of the Abba star with a Nazi father:

- https://www.theguardian.com/world/2002/jun/30/kateconnolly.
  theobserver

Tragic Details About Cyndi Lauper:

- https://www.youtube.com/watch?v=54XNYS0GM2o

CHAPTER 5

IT MUST BE TRUE—IT WAS ON TV

The controllers of Organised Society—and therefore the Scamdemic—continue to adhere with religious fervour to their tenet of Placing the Truth in Plain Sight. And the amount of slow-drip subliminal programming in the years up to 2020 gives a shocking insight into just how far back this was all getting cooked up.

> *"Anything built upon lies and deception cannot last. Failure is built right into it."*
> Commenter to my YouTube channel.

> *"They have the guns, We have the poets. Therefore we will win"*
> Howard Zinn

> *"They would not listen, they did not know how.*
> *Perhaps they'll listen now?"*
> Don McLean: 'Vincent'

To put everything into its true context, it's necessary for this chapter to deviate from the music world for a while -although it does play its part in the story later on! But it would not be doing this complex and far-reaching psy-op justice, to not examine the methods and tactics by which it was able to control the thoughts, emotions and actions of the vast, overwhelming majority of the world's population, coercing them into behaviours and ways of life that would have been unthinkable a year before and which, if anyone had suggested at that time that these would be the circumstances in which we would all be living, they would have been dismissed scoffingly as a "conspiracy theorist," or be told, 'You've been watching too many movies and TV shows, mate!"

That latter phrase is very telling, because it addresses the means by which so much of the mind-control was able to be implemented. A malevolent control system which has all other bases covered—complete domination and control of banking and finance, politics, academia, science and medicine, big business and mainstream news—would never pass up the vast opportunities for thought-entrainment, behaviour-modification, and other tactics perfected through the science of Social Engineering and Psychological Manipulation that popular culture vehicles present. Though this book's previous volumes have focussed on popular music's role in this dynamic, the worlds of television and Hollywood movies are just as much strategic weapons in the "elite"s arsenal. While these individuals are psychopathic and lacking so many of the faculties that constitute full humanity, they are incredibly clever and efficient in planning, and then executing their evil deeds. Unlike regular members of society—as the experiences of 2020 and 2021 taught us—they <u>are</u> able to make a plan and stick to it, putting any in-fighting or ego clashes to one side in the interests of getting the job done. This chapter will examine some of the ways in which they achieve it.

While the "Musical" part of this book's title may not apply so much in this section, the "Truth" part certainly does!

I predict a psy-op

I covered the phenomenon of Predictive Programming (PP) at length in Chapter 12 of *'Musical Truth Volume 1,'* but just by way of quick recap to set the scene—this is the act of placing a visual depiction of an event yet to happen but known to be coming, into works of popular culture, where they will be absorbed by many millions of people, but only on a subliminal level. The vehicles used to convey these ideas include movies, TV programmes, cartoons and commercials, and, in the music world, large-scale concerts, awards shows such as the *'Grammys'* or *'MTV VMAs,'* and music videos. This wide array of outlets, through which thousands of examples of PP have been pinpointed, serves as confirmation that, at their very upper levels, all these industries are ultimately controlled and directed by the same people, or groups.

There are three main reasons why Predictive Programming is employed. The first is that it conveys a familiarity with the narrative that the perpetrators wish to get across. This might be, for example, a "false-flag" terror event using crisis actors. (See the work of the foremost researcher in this subject area, Ole Dammegard at www.lightonconspir-acies.com for in-depth analysis of many such "news" events over the years.) The aspects of the storyline in question that the viewing public has absorbed—albeit unknowingly because most visuals to which we are exposed get taken in below the threshold of conscious thought in the subliminal mind—are then in place ready for when the treacherous mainstream media reports the "real-world" event that it was designed to foreshadow. Because there is already a familiarity with the narrative in the mind of the perceiver, the news version of the event is much more likely to be accepted as "real" and to "sound right."

The second reason comes from the recognition by the sick ones that we humans possess the innate ability to create our own experienced reality according to the consciousness we apply to it. We can literally create what happens with our thoughts, when our Will and inten-tion are applied. There is also a recognition of the maxim that "energy flows where attention goes." By getting, potentially, millions of people through the combined audience of a movie, TV show or music video, to pay attention to a certain narrative—or a sign or symbol which itself carries a unique energetic frequency and a meaning, or intention—the manipulators seek to have their desired outcome brought into manifes-tation through the collective conscious energy that they have harvested from the viewers.

The third reason is, I suspect, the principle one behind why this practice has been so widely employed for decades. The controllers are very well-studied in occultism and have a deep comprehension of the principles of Natural Law. In their arrogance and hubris, they grudgingly accept that the God of Creation installed these universal mechanisms into this reality, and that chief among them is the Non-Ag-gression Principle of Do Not Harm. They recognise that, through the law of cause and effect, or what many would term "Karma," there are consequences for violating this principle—to not cause harm to another against their will.

They therefore feel that they can avoid the Karmic debt that would otherwise come down upon them, by announcing to us in advance what they intend to do. They choose to use the popular culture vehicles which they control as a means of achieving this. So, to take the events of September 11th 2001 as an example, there were endless films, TV shows, cartoons, advertisements and record sleeves in the years, and even decades leading up to that event, which depicted aspects of what we saw unfold in the news coverage of that fateful day.

These only came to light through vigilant researchers, however, AFTER the horrors of 9/11 had unfolded, and this exposes the fatal flaw in the thinking of the psychopaths. In their sick, diseased minds, (never forget that the "elite" ranks are comprised of the sickest, most diseased abominations to have ever infested Earth,) because they announced, in their own chosen way, what they intended to do at some point in the future, the burden no longer falls on them, but on us instead. As they (mistakenly) see it, because we didn't find some way of communicating back to them, "we've seen what you plan to do on September 11th and we're not having it!" we've voiced no objection, Therefore—as they see it—they're not violating our rights. To not say no—as they see it—is as good as saying yes.

The writing's on the wall

The "elites" have never been backwards in coming forwards when it comes to revealing their dastardly plans in advance, and often openly disclose them in their own writings. Before we get into movies, TV shows, music videos and such, let's first consider some of the documentation at our disposal.

Despite apparently having no prior knowledge that "the virus" was going to emerge in late 2019 and go on to decimate the entire world, World Economic Forum supremo Klaus Schwab, (who sounds *way* too much like a bad James Bond villain to ever be taken seriously, and who I always envisage stroking a white cat whenever he appears) was able to work remarkably quickly on his book, '*Covid-19: The Great Reset*' which was published by July 2020. In all seriousness, Klaus asks readers to believe that the W.E.F.'s entire Great Reset initiative to restructure the worldwide economy—an arrangement in which, naturally, "Globalist" corporations would benefit—was only hatched *after* the world became decimated by "the virus."

World Economic Forum psychopath-in-chief and caricature James Bond villain Klaus Schwab. All that's missing is a white cat.

https://commons.wikimedia.org/wiki/File:Klaus_Schwab_WEF_2008_ (cropped).jpg

A large part of the Great Reset's proposals advocate that, in the near future, private ownership of items like homes and cars should be abolished; everything should be owned by the state, with individuals given a Universal Basic Income on which to live, this placing all regular members of society on an even financial footing, with the super-rich retaining the cream of the world's wealth for themselves . . . just like they've always done, come to think of it.

This is as blatant a tenet of idealogical Communism as it's possible to get, and sounds like a cross between the plots of the movies *'Metropolis'* and *'The Hunger Games.'* It was James Bond villain Blofeld who told Bond he was "the author of all your pain," but it might as well have been Schwab saying it to the rest of the world.

As an Amazon review of Schwab's spill-the-beans book, (co-authored with fellow "Globalist" and WEF affiliate Theirry Malleret) by Sam Meredith observes: "the book looks ahead to what the post-coronavirus world could look like barely four months after the outbreak was first declared a pandemic."

In Schwab's writings, we get it straight from the horse's mouth as to what the real objective behind the Co(n)vid agenda always was.

"In one form or another, social- and physical-distancing measures are likely to persist after the pandemic itself subsides, justifying the decision in many companies from different industries to accelerate automation. After a while, the enduring concerns about technological unemployment will recede as societies emphasize the need to restructure the workplace in a way that minimizes close human contact. Indeed, automation technologies are particularly well suited to a world in which human beings can't get too close to each other or are willing to reduce their interactions. Our lingering and possibly lasting fear of being infected with a virus (Covid-19 or another) will thus speed the relentless march of automation, particularly in the fields most susceptible to automation.

" . . . From the onset of the lockdowns, it became apparent that robots and AI were a "natural" alternative when human labour was not available. Furthermore, they were used whenever possible to reduce the health risks to human employees."

Funny how mainstream media "journalists" all around the world never picked up on any of this stuff or deemed it worth reporting to their audiences. The book concludes with an official admission that the threat from the "virus" has been hyped out of all proportion by fear-mongering governments and media:

"There is no denying that the Covid-19 virus has more often than not been a personal catastrophe for the millions affected by it, and for their families and communities. However, at a global level, if viewed in terms of the percentage of the global population affected, the corona crisis is (so far,) one of the least deadly pandemics the world has experienced over the last 2,000 years. In all likelihood, unless the pandemic evolves in an unforeseen way, the consequences of Covid-19 in terms of health and mortality will be mild compared to previous pandemics. At the end of June 2020, Covid-19 has killed less than 0.006% of the world population. To put this low figure into context, the Spanish flu killed 2.7% of the world's population and HIV/AIDS 0.6%"

Access Hollyweird

The complexity—and evil—of the 9/11 operation doesn't even come close to the level of planning involved in Co(n)vid. Even the two World Wars, occurring as they did at times when the world's population was significantly smaller—did not directly affect the lives of as many people. Indeed, the Scamdemic and everything that it has been used to "justify" in its wake, has accurately been described as representing World War 3. We now live in an era where war can be declared without a single bullet being fired or a single soldier deployed. Nations are no longer pitted against nations. What we now have is Information Wars; wars for the collective mind of mankind. We, the people, in our billions, have been declared the enemy of the "elite" ruling class—infinitesimally small in number by comparison. Psychological weapons have replaced tanks and guns. The pieces have been slowly assembled over the decades, while the vast majority were distracted and entranced by mainstream media lies and the popular culture offered seductively by Organised Society.

The Hollywood film industry pretty much ground to a screeching halt as soon as the Co(n)vid hoax first started generating the planned-for fear and hysteria in America. Very few films got churned out and thrown on the normally relentless conveyor belt. Not that there would have been any means of screening them had any movies been made, given that cinemas in many of the US states and many other countries remained closed for months. The fortunes of the 25th James Bond movie *'No Time To Die,'* (a starkly prophetic title, as it turns out,) Daniel Craig's swansong in the role, gave an indication of this. Originally slated for a Spring 2020 release, this was then moved to Autumn of that year, then rescheduled for Spring 2021, then finally, the latter months of that year. This final rescheduling was announced at a time before government restrictions had officially been extended to late 2021, indicating some potential inside knowledge on the part of the film's producers and distributors. We now know that one of the reasons for its delay would have been down to the aspect of the plotline in which Rami Malek's villainous character has developed a biological weapon as a means of massive depopulation. A little bit too close for comfort?

Hollywood output being deliberately trashed was a factor the architects of the Scamdemic narrative could afford to bear, given that this vehicle had already delivered much of its true value within a Co(n)vid context—years of subtle, subliminal programming through "fictional" storylines, creating an unknowing yet effective familiarity with certain ideas, so that when they suddenly cross the line from "fiction" to reality, they are more readily accepted by a suitably entranced populace.

"Pandemic" programming was already in place, possibly with the Co(n)vid masterplan having already been devised by that point, in 1995's 'Outbreak,' directed by Wolfgang Petersen and starring Dustin Hoffman, and based on the previous year's novel 'The Hot Zone: A Terrifying True Story' by Richard Preston. (A separate novel, titled 'Outbreak,' concerned with the spread of the Ebola "virus" in the US, was authored in 1987 by Robin Cook—not the one who just happened to fall to his death while hiking in remotest Scotland shortly after blowing the whistle on Tony Blair's governmental involvement in falsifying evidence to go to war in Iraq and Afghanistan. You know, like you do.) Here, a "virus" which causes a deadly fever, quickly spreads across America. The source is said to have been a monkey from Africa, (echoes of A.I.D.S.?) which was sold on the black market for animal testing. The "virus" is said to cause influenza-like symptoms and to be airborne. The California town most affected is placed into quarantine and martial law is imposed. An experimental serum is created which cures the 'virus's original strain. A rogue military general plans to conceal the virus's existence so it can later be used as a biological weapon.

Any of this sounding familiar?

As Wikipedia observes: 'Outbreak's plot speculates how far military and civilian agencies might go to contain the spread of a deadly, contagious disease.

I think we all know the answer to that question now, don't we?

A somewhat similar plot was the subject of the Steven Soderbergh-directed 'Contagion,' released in 2011, and featuring Matt Damon heading up an all-star cast. Familiar elements are present in the plot: a "virus" becomes transmitted by respiratory droplets and fomites; government agencies are forced to impose radical restrictions to "contain" the pandemic, and a vaccine becomes the miraculous cure that saves the day. Screenwriter Scott Z Burns is said to have consulted with officials from the World Health Organization to ensure the accuracy of what the story depicted, as well as Larry Brilliant, the Chairman of the Board of Ending Pandemics. (I'd say some improvement is needed on that front.)

The real-life Centers for Disease Control and Prevention (C.D.C.) features in the plot as an agency whose input is vital to combatting the "pandemic." 'Contagion' depicts social disorder, including panic buying at stores, caused by multiple cities being placed into lockdown and "quarantine" orders being imposed. A tracking facility seeks to trace all who have been in close contact with anyone who has contracted the "virus." Computer modelling attempts to predict the infection rate. A character portrayed as "conspiracy theorist" (yawn,) claims to have cured himself from infection using a homeopathic cure.

The idea of the "virus" being used as a sinister bioweapon is also presented. The film's closing flashback sequence shows the origin of the "virus"; a bat from a rainforest in China drops an infected piece of banana into a pig farm. The pig that consumes it then goes to slaughter and is prepared by a chef in a Macau casino. He subsequently transmits "the virus" via a handshake to a character who flies from Hong Kong to the United States.

Incredibly, some way into the Scamdemic, UK Health Secretary Matt Hancock admitted to basing part of his vaccination strategy on the plotline of 'Contagion,' giving us as close an admission that we have all been living through a scripted movie as it will likely ever be officially acknowledged. Speaking to LBC Radio, Hancock commented:

> *"In the film it shows the moment of highest stress around the vaccine programme is not in fact before it's rolled out—when actually it's the scientists and the manufacturers working together at pace—it's afterwards when there's a huge row about the order of priority. I insisted we ordered enough for every adult to have two doses . . ."*

The Wachowskis, the driving force behind the 'Matrix' movies, clearly have much inside knowledge of "elite" agendas, (and even helped prop one of the key ones up when they became Transgendered.) Of interest within the "virus" context is their 'V For Vendetta,' based on the earlier graphic novel by artist (and occultist and Crowley devotee) Alan

Moore. The story finds the UK in turmoil, ravaged by civil unrest and a raging "pandemic." "Undesirable" members of society—homosexuals, Jews, immigrants—are imprisoned and executed, (Bill Gates-style Eugenics, anyone?) A concentration camp has been set up at Larkhill, a very real military garrison close to Stonehenge in Wiltshire. The media pushes constant fear propaganda, and the government uses the "virus" threat to its political advantage, while constantly reinforcing to the public that "this is all being done to keep you safe." The only part of the story which, sadly, has not yet come to pass is the climax, where society has woken up to the lies and corruption and vast hordes have joined V, the movie's protagonist, in an anarchist showdown against the controllers. Funny how only the dark and devastating parts of such stories come into physical manifestation, rather than a happy ending like that. While the original novel had set the story in 1997, the film version is set in 2027.

Only more astute viewers spotted a couple of subtle symbolic renderings in 'Captain America: The First Avenger,' also from 2011. But the fact that they were spotted at all shows that virtually nothing slips under the radar any more, given the armies of eagle-eyed truthseekers now deployed all over the world. A freeze-frame of a scene set in New York's Times Square shows what resembles a "coronavirus" symbol on a background billboard, opposite another which is advertising Corona beer. A third billboard depicts a face mask. A close-up of a fourth reveals an ad bearing the slogan, "By George, we Did It."

The George Floyd event, which showed all the signs of being yet another state-sponsored false-flag psy-op, occurred in the midst of the "pandemic" in America, causing yet further civil unrest and chaos. Another George—the billionaire financier and key "elite" asset George Soros—was heavily involved in the Antifa and Black Lives Matter movements, both of which were embroiled in the Floyd narrative. A slogan popularised in the wake of the Floyd incident was "I can't breathe," supposedly Floyd's last words as his alleged killer, police officer Derek Chauvin, knelt on his neck and blocked his airway, but a phrase equally attributable to the idea of a pneumonia-like illness that causes respiratory problems ... or indeed to the problem of being forced to wear a face mask for hours on end.

Those who have lapped up the avalanche of "Dystopian" and "post-Apocalyptic" sci-fi flicks that have been churned out on the Hollywood meat grinder of recent years, might find themselves enjoying them slightly less when they realise that these films have been revealing the type of future that the sick controllers have in mind for all of us in the not-too-distant future. It would appear that this dynamic was at play in 2013's '*World War Z*' starring Brad Pitt, described as a "zombie pandemic" movie. Pitt's heroic character is a former United Nations agent, (helping to frame that organisation as benevolent and virtuous, when in fact it is one of the key architects of the nightmarish New World Order Agenda 2030.) The movie reveals that the zombie influx has been caused by a "virus" (surely not?) and that the only cure is going to be... a vaccine! A former CIA operative has access to a "safe zone" operated by Israel's Mossad, also presenting both of those murderous and treacherous organisations in a benevolent light. Israel is portrayed as working in league with Palestine, and with huge walls being erected to keep out the zombies, (as opposed to the real reason for the wall separating Israel from Palestine—collective punishment and genocide.)

Have you noticed how "zombie" movies have been so *en vogue* in recent times? What could have been the motive behind putting images of brain-dead golems besieging towns and cities in a trance-like state into so many plots? A glance at the masked hordes wandering the average High Street or shopping mall in 2020 and beyond provides the answer. This was more morbid mockery of *us*, (well, those who allowed themselves to be coerced into wearing a face-nappy, anyway.) The "zombies" in these movies are designed to represent the general public. The mask-wearing was known to be coming years in advance. These movie-makers were mocking you and me, and how they knew we were going to be forced to live. This is how sick, depraved and evil these 'people" really are.

Have you also noticed how these Hollywood movies and TV shows never seem to depict a future where people live in co-operative/ voluntaryist societies, standing in Truth and Right Action, and living free of coercion, mind-control, and tyrannical control systems seeking to erode their personal sovereignty? Can't have *that* type of existence being observed, absorbed and imagined by the world's populace, can we?

Anyway, back to some intriguing aspects of '*World War Z.*' The climax of the movie finds Pitt's character in a World Health Organization lab, where he has to retrieve vials of deadly "viruses." The number of the lab storing these "viruses" is given as V-139. With C being the 3rd letter of the alphabet and inserted instead of the number, a slight rejig of the characters gives us CV-19, as in "Covid-19." This may seem like a bit of a stretch to some, which I can understand. But how about this? An eagle-eyed viewer of my videos pointed out that the security code for the "virus" storage area is given as 56964. If these numbers are added together, we get 30. Then, if the same numbers are subtracted from each-other, we get -20. So we have a 20 and a 30. As in 2030, possibly? As in the United Nation's Agenda 2030 masterplan? Reaching too much, and just coincidence? Or yet more subliminal entrainment dressed up as "fiction"?

A vast number of movies containing predictive aspects of what life in 2020 and beyond has turned out to be were produced in the preceding 20-year period, so memories of their content—albeit buried deep in the subliminal mind—would still be accessible in the consciousness of the viewing public. Examples abound from not just Hollywood but many nations around the world and include, but are by no means limited to: the '*Cabin Fever*' series (beginning 2002,) the '*Resident Evil*' series (beginning 2002,) '*28 Days Later*' (2002,) '*Smallpox 2002: Silent Weapon*' (2002,) '*The Paradise Virus*' (2003,) '*Dawn of the Dead*' (2004,) '*The Coming Pandemic*' (2005,) '*Mulberry Street*' (2006,) '*Virus*' (2007 and 2019 versions,) '*I Am Legend*' (2007,) '*I Am Omega*' (2007,) '*28 Weeks Later*' (2007,) '*Have Mercy On Us All*' (2007,) '*Planet Terror*' (2007,) '*Virus Undead*' (2008,) '*Blindness*' (2008,) '*Pontypool*' (2008,) '*Quarantine*' (2008,) '*Doomsday*' (2008,) '*Happy End*' (2009,) '*Autumn*' (2009,) '*Carriers*' (2009,) '*The Crazies*' (2010,) '*Stakeland*' (2010,) '*Rammbock*' (2010,) '*Retreat*' (2011,) '*A Virus Called Fear,*' a documentary examining how fear distorts our perception of the world (2012,) '*Deranged*' (2012,) '*Fedz*' (2013,) '*93 Days*' (2014,) '*The Returned*' (2013,) '*Flu*' (2013,) '*Cargo*' (2013,) '*Antisocial*' (2013,) '*Battle of the Damned*' (2013,) '*The Hive*' (2014,) '*Wyrmwood*' (2014,) '*What We Become*' (2015,) '*Hidden*' (2015,) '*Body Team 12*' (2015,) '*Containment*' (2015,) '*Maggie*' (2015,) '*Extinction*' (2015,) '*Embers*' (2015,) '*Here Alone*'

(2016,) 'Zoombies' (2016,) 'Pandemic' (2016,) 'Train To Busan' (2016,) 'Seoul Station' (2016,) 'Hilleman: A Perilous Quest to Save the World's Children' (2016,) 'Viral' (2016,) 'Anna and the Apocalypse' (2017,) 'What Still Remains' (2018,) 'Redcon-1—Army of the Dead' (2018,) 'Patient Zero' (2018,) 'Zombieland' (2019,) 'The Beach House' (2019,) 'Light of my Life' (2019,) 'Only' (2019,) 'Alive' (2020,) 'Before The Fire' (2020,) and 'Block Z' (2020.) There were also many movies depicting "viral" outbreaks in the decades prior to 2000.

I wonder if any of those involved in making these movies—those who *aren't* among the high-level ranks who understand the agenda, that is—at any point in 2020 or beyond looked back on any of these, made the connection, and thought to themselves, "My God! What *is* it that I've been a part of?"

Probably not many, eh?

Vaxx Hell

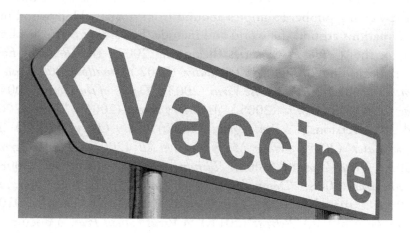

The entire Co(n)vid debacle was only ever intended to point in one direction.

http://www.wakeforestlawreview.com/2020/12/shots-for-all-the-legal-background-and-implications-of-mandating-flu-vaccines-on-college-campuses/

And so it was with the trilogy of *'Maze Runner'* movies produced between 2014 and 2018 and based on an original James Dashner novel from 2009. For some reason, movies depicting hellish, "Dystopian" future worlds where murder, mutilation, pain, suffering and anguish abound, became popular in the first two decades of the 2000s. Those seeking such titillation would not have been disappointed with the *'Maze Runner'* films. Though I wonder if their content would be deemed quite so thrilling now that certain aspects of the narrative have become our own daily existence?

The first film depicts the spread of—you got it—a deadly "virus" named 'the Flare.' A group of characters must navigate their way through a hellworld which has been ravaged by an Apocalyptic event caused by solar flares, followed by the "pandemic." The second instalment, *'Maze Runner: The Scorch Trials,'* includes a scene in an abandoned shopping mall where the group encounter a horde of humans zombified by the "virus." Sounds like my latest trip to my local Aldi. In the climax, *'Maze Runner: The Death Cure,'* the protagonists head for "The Last City," the base of operations for the "World In Catastrophe: Killzone Experiment Department (WICKED)." What's in a name, eh?

This is a sinister organisation concerned with controlling, subjugating, experimenting on, and significantly reducing the world's population, (See any government of choice in 2020 and beyond.) It deploys troops wearing gas masks to do its bidding. (Reminds me of the thug police unleashing their violence on the peaceful protestors in Trafalgar Square in late 2020.) The "virus" is now destroying humanity faster than ever before. There is talk of "immunes" to the "virus" and of a "serum" (vaccine) needing to be found as a cure. (Vitamin C and Zinc would probably do it—but what do I know, I'm just a DJ.) A cure found, a character is seen to be interested only in saving himself and others who he deems worthy, (Eugenics.) The series concludes with a small number of survivors (Georgia Guidestones-style population reduction) escaping to a safe haven by the sea.

No need to assume movies aimed at children have been left out of the mix. The 2016-released Netflix cartoon *'Hedgehogs'* steps up for duty on that front. With a Chinese screenwriter and director, this weapon

Mark Devlin

of psychological manipulation concerns a respiratory virus spreading among humans.

I think readers can probably guess for themselves the word beginning with V that is proposed as *the only* solution to the "pandemic." An exact quote from the film's ending runs: "I'm happy to announce we've discovered a vaccine. We no longer have to live in fear. Everyone can go back to their normal lives."

An interesting comment appears on the International Movie Data Base site (IMDB,) under the section labelled "Goofs," where a contributor has written:

> "… *In reality, vaccines are never discovered, but they have to be developed, which takes at least five years, which in the past took an average of about 20 years, and which in some cases could not be achieved even after decades.*"

Great point. Someone should tell the millions who have already taken a Co(n)vid "vaccine" into their bloodstreams, despite these products not even being "vaccines' in the traditional sense according to many medical professionals, — including Dr. Mike Yeadon, the former Vice-President of Pfizer, one of the Co(n)vid vaccine manufacturers — but representing "experimental gene therapy" instead, given that they have reportedly been developed within a matter of months, and not undergone the usual tests that any new "vaccine" has previously been required to before being released to the public.

Still, at least millions of children were subliminally entrained through a piece of "innocent" escapism to accept the mantra that vaccines represent *the only* way out of the "pandemic" ready for when this narrative would be rolled out in schools a few years later, so there's that box ticked on the agenda.

By the time talk had moved to the "mutant strains" and "variants" of the "virus" to justify yet further lockdowns in Summer 2021, it was just the right time for another piece of subtle programming courtesy of the Disney movie *'Loki.'* in which the main character sports a distinctive jacket with the word "variant" emblazoned across the back.

Not to be outdone by the movie world, meanwhile, and in the interests of having all bases covered, the 2018 *'Marvel's Spider-Man'* video game includes among its plot constructs, a deadly "virus" pandemic, "The Devil's Breath," released upon New York City by the villain, Mister Negative (!), (elderly Aunt May is one of the victims and dies, — though not in a death-trap "care" home,) quarantine, mask-wearing. mass civil unrest, martial law and Transhumanism. The ultimate happy ending occurs when a vaccine, (stop me if you've heard this one before,) is developed to "cure" the infected masses.

I really think these script-writers need to broaden their horizons and get out more. Maybe go world travelling . . . oh . . . wait . . . .

Perhaps the most devastatingly damning "prediction" piece came from the 2007 Japanese animated movie titled "Vexille" (vaccine/ ill??) because this went all the way to the ultimate goal of the Scamdemic, which was always to roll out an international vaccination agenda.

The story is set in a Japan of the 2060s, a time where cybernetics/ robotic technology has become fully fused with human activity, largely at the hands of a monolithic technology giant, Daiwa Heavy Industries, (a hybrid of Google and the Bill & Melinda Gates Foundation, seemingly.) The United Nations, (portrayed as the good guys!) imposes a ban on further robotics research, leading to Japan, in protest, cutting itself off from the rest of the world. The country is blanketed in an energy field broadcast from 270 off-shore installations, (5G transmitters,) and international travel and immigration is banned, (watch this space!)

By 2067, a deadly disease has struck Japan, and a vaccine, (stop me if you've heard this one before,) is the only proposed solution. It turns out that the "virus" had been deliberately created by Daiwa as a bio-weapon, with the "vaccine" used as an excuse for Transhumanist experimentation on human subjects. All Japanese citizens are said to have been reduced to forms of synthetic life, with the capacity for free will lost. Readers will note that this plotline tallies with the previously-mentioned writings of Jacques Attali, and the comments from some who had received one of the Co(n)vid "vaccines" and stated afterwards that "they've destroyed God" as they felt a complete disconnectedness from their spiritual side and from the rest of Creation.

This represents another act of evil genius on the part of the psychopaths; a society where the majority have been reduced to little more than flesh robots operating on base consciousness, is one where any mass "awakening," as so many gurus and researchers have promised us we've been on the cusp of, will have been neatly stifled. Those who have known better than to take one of the "vaccines" will be too few in number to effect any kind of sea change in society, by reaching a critical tipping-point of the numbers.

That's the version of events according to the sickos, anyway. If this most dark and disturbing of films offers any hope at all, it's in the closing comment of the titular character, who remarks that humanity's spirit can never be taken away. Maybe the fact that, even in spite of all that the "elite" class have unleashed on humanity—all the propaganda and mind-control, the poisons in the food, the water supply and the air, and the sea of unseen electro-magnetic radiation in which we exist—even in spite of all that, still the innate human capacity towards Right Action and the instinctive sense of connectedness to all else in Nature continues on. It seems—in some of us at least—there is that Divine spark that can never be destroyed. Although 'Vexille' was a cultural weapon of the control-system, its closing sentiments appear to indicate that the "elites" recognise this inherent Godly capacity; a light that, though it may be dimmed, will never be extinguished. Speaking of the fate of one of the main characters, the voice-over reveals:

> "Maria and her people were wiped out. But what they did, their sacrifice ... it won't be forgotten. They will live on in our hearts, a shining example to the world. It was Maria who taught us, what we are is more than just flesh and blood. As long as we have our spirit, nothing—no-one—can ever take away our humanity."

Legacy of the Idiot Lantern

There will doubtless be many other movie mind manipulations, but at this point we'll divert our attention towards TV series, and a rewarding place to start is with an episode of 'The Dead Zone,' a series which ran from 2002 to 2007, based around the book of the same name by Stephen King. (Notice how many of these key movies' scripts are based around earlier novels, suggesting that original creative ideas are frequently lacking among Hollywood screenwriters.) One particular episode of this series is concerned with—can you tell what it is yet, as TV entertainer (and convicted paedophile—he was on the BBC, what do you expect?) Rolf Harris used to say? That's right. It's a deadly "virus" which mutates and quickly spreads across the United States.

This one really could be mistaken for an episode of CNN or MSN-BC's Evening News, as the "virus" is said to have originated in China, and the desperate measures which the authorities have no choice but to implement, (all they're interested in is "keeping us safe," remember?) include quarantine and "lockdowns," (referred to by that name,) closures of schools and all public buildings, swab tests, mask-wearing, tracking and tracing of those affected, constant reinforcement that "this is for everyone's safety," the idea that the "virus" is being exploited by government for political means, the suggestion that "viruses" originate from animals and are spread by airborne transmission, the notion that the "virus" is spread by international air travel.

There is a reference to it taking 34 days to isolate the "coronavirus" said to have caused SARS, (which is more than has been achieved with Co(n)vid-19, which has *never* been isolated and therefore proven to exist.) An eventual cure is found to lie in "chloroquine," just one step away from Hydroxychloroquine, the anti-malarial drug put forward as a very real cure for Co(n)vid, and endorsed publicly by President Donald Trump. Another happy ending which, sadly, has not come to pass in this reality. Only the bad stuff does that, it seems.

Some rather darker scenarios were presented through an episode of the bleakly comedic '*The Last Man On Earth*' screened on the Fox network on 5th March 2017. Stop me if you've heard this one before, but the plot involves the outbreak of . . . well, you know. Tellingly, this is brushed off by one of the characters as simply "a bad flu season." Despite this, cities are locked down, streets are seen deserted, supermarket shelves are decimated, characters are seen wearing face masks, including babies and pet dogs. Again a vaccine is presented as *the only* hope for ridding society of the you-know-what. The story makes reference to 'President Pence' as the 46th President of the United States. At the time of the episode's airing, Mike Pence had just become Vice-President to Donald Trump. Disturbingly, the show depicts Pence as having died, aged 61. (He turned 61 during 2020.)

The YouTube uploader Angel White has noted that the period from this episode's transmission date to the date of the first alleged Co(n)vid patient, 1st December 2019, was 1,001 days. And also that the notorious occultist Aleister Crowley died on 1st December of 1947—72 years before Co(n)vid, and at the age of 72. Those looking for dark occult elements to this narrative, serving as Satanic mockery of the ignorance of the masses, will not be disappointed.

A 2018 sci-fi horror movie from Dark Sky Films, released on Netflix and titled '*Await Further Instructions,*' sees a family trapped inside their home by malevolent forces, with instructions communicated via the TV set, and with harmful vaccines becoming part of the storyline. These include the messages "Stay indoors and await further instructions" and "use trial vaccination kits, atmosphere polluted" similarly delivered. Subliminal programming much?

Intriguingly, a friend has pointed out that 2021, the year when the vaccination agenda really got underway, is recognised as the Year of the Ox in the Zodiacal system of—where else?—China. An ox is a cow and the French word for cow is *vache,* from which we get the word 'vaccine' harking back to Edward Jenner's work on smallpox with cows.

The final episode in series 2 of '*Siren,*' a show available on Amazon Prime Video and first aired in 2019, is titled '*New World Order,*' and themes portrayed include martial law, concentration camps, riots, (there's nothing like a nice, cheery bit of light escapism to unwind and relax with after a hard day at work, is there?) I.D. chips, and a mermaid wearing a face mask, 2020-style.

It seems the TV vehicles which "predicted" the events of 2020 and beyond were trying to "out-dark" each-other in how far into Dystopia they could take their storylines. Indeed, a viewing of the mockingly-named '*Utopia*' series, (not to be confused with the Channel 4 TV series of the same name from some years earlier,) could hardly be described as a feel-good heart-warming experience. This plotline includes—ready?...a "viral pandemic" (naturally,) white rabbits, (see separate chapter on "Adrenochrome,") a "green" agenda which advocates ceasing human reproduction for three generations in the interests of "the environment," (hold tight for the next manufactured "crisis" of "Climate Change," by the way, once the Co(n)vid scam has served its purpose—remember where you heard it first,) the taking of the knee by members of the public, Black Lives Matter/ George Floyd-style, vaccines that kill, (go figure) the demonisation of "anti-vaxxers" as "far-righters," and a Eugenicist character highly reminiscent of Bill Gates who sells laboratory-produced "meat."

In February 2021, Gates publicly stated that "all rich countries should move to 100% synthetic beef." Apparently he gets to decide what we should all eat now, as well as what we should have injected into our bloodstreams. Do you remember voting for this guy or consenting to any of these suggestions? Me neither. Gates and fellow tycoon (Sir) Richard Branson had already invested heavily in companies that produce synthetic meat. Anyone who has not viewed the prophetic 1973 movie 'Soylent Green' starring Charlton Heston—available for viewing on this link—https://www.dailymotion.com/video/x3dq3ef—really should do so at this point. It depicts New York in the year 2022, (go figure!) where over-population and all the pollution and strains on natural resources that it brings, has become an Extinction Level Event.

With access to natural foods now limited only to the super-rich, and the masses living in crowded slums, the state has taken to producing synthetic protein foods named Soylent, (the name being a combination of the main ingredients, "soy" and "lentils." Does this remind you at all of the plethora of "plant-based" foods that are now filling supermarket shelves to cater for the ever-growing vegan community? For the most part I'm a vegan myself on moral grounds, yet I recognise that these multi-national corporation mass-produced "foods" are not the best for human health and are anything but "natural" by the time they've been through their mass-market factory production. And why, if such brands as Wicked Kitchen and Heck (a minced curse-word euphemism for "Hell") are all about morals and ethics, do they have such demonic names?? Could we be getting told the truth, yet again in plain sight, of what these products are *really* all about?

The latest product, "Soylent Green," is said to be derived from ocean plankton, yet Heston's cop character discovers by the end of the movie the terrible truth of how this "food" is really being made. I won't spoil it for anyone who wishes to watch the film, but it seems likely that those behind it—director Richard Fleischer, (which means "butcher" in German—you couldn't make it up,) producers Walter Seltzer and Russel Thacher, and screenwriter Stanley Greenberg—would have had some idea that what they were making was more "science" and less "fiction," and was actually depicting "elite" agendas which would be coming into play almost 50 years into the future.

Read 'em and weep

Any cultural vehicle with the potential to manipulate mass audiences is fair game for the mind-sorcerer class, and so books join films, TV shows, video games and music in serving their purpose. I've no idea how anyone actually discovers such things, but it became realised very early in the Co(n)vid Hoax that aspects of what we were all being told had been presciently "foretold" by American author Dean Koontz in his novel 'The Eyes of Darkness', published almost 40 years earlier in 1981. Koontz' missing-person thriller includes a reference to a man-made biological weapon unleashed on society. In early editions of the book, this was named as Gorki-400 and is said to have been developed in laboratory facilities in the Russian city of that name. With the Cold War era having come to an end, however, in post-2008 editions the weapon was renamed as Wuhan-400 and said to have originated out of the Chinese city with which the entire world is now familiar. It's reasonable to assume that Koontz did not have any inside knowledge of the coming agenda back in 1981, but it would be interesting to know if it were he personally who chose Wuhan as the replacement city, or if it was other interested parties.

Only a year after Koontz' title, another novel depicting the outbreak of a deadly pathogen appeared. 1982's 'The Virus' just happens to have been penned by Stanley Johnson, father of Boris, British Prime Minister at the time of the Co(n)vid episode. But I'm sure it's just a coincidence. Amazon certainly seems to consider it just that, writing in its review of the title, "Stanley Johnson's 'The Virus' is more than astonishingly prescient, with uncanny parallels to the current Covid-19 pandemic." Johnson lays out the necessity of a virus in the eyes of an insidious elite to curb population growth. His comments can't help but bring to mind those of "elitist" Prince Philip, said to have died aged 99 right in the midst of Co(n)vid, who had famously mentioned in a 1988 interview with *'Deutsche Press-Agentur,'* "In the event that I am reincarnated, I would like to return as a deadly virus, to contribute something to solving over-population."

There was something about the outbreak of deadly viruses forming the basis of novel plots in the early 80s. Joining the last two in 1980 was *'Disposable People'* by authors Marshall Goldberg M.D. and Kenneth Kay. As its sleeve description puts it:

> *"Consolvo's Ulceration—a disease more horrifying than the Black Plague—was raging out of control. The leaders of the country thought they could confine the deadly epidemic to the remote area of the South West where it started. But they were wrong. When they finally ran out of volunteers for a vaccination program that had killed almost as many people as the disease itself, the government began to think the unthinkable."*

Sounds like just another day in the office to me.

A different kind of book, meanwhile, came from the psychic and paranormal author and TV personality Sylvia Browne. Though Browne, who died in 2013, was frequently criticised for the inaccuracies of the many predictions she made, she appeared to have some lucky strikes with her 2008 tome titled *'End of Days'* In it she wrote:

> *"In or around 2020, a severe pneumonia-like illness will spread throughout the globe, attacking the lungs and bronchial tubes and resisting all known treatments. Almost more baffling than the illness itself will be the fact that it will suddenly vanish as quickly as it arrived, attack again ten years later, and then disappear completely."*

I'm not so keen on the bit about it re-appearing ten years later, but the last part sounds good.

Right around the time that Stanley Johnson's "novel" was released, comments had been made by the "Globalist" bankster and Eugenicist Jacques Attali, giving an insight into the mindset which permeates the "elite" class, and the utter contempt they hold for the expendable masses of "useless eaters." Speaking to interviewer Michel Salomon in

1981 when he—Attali—was a senior advisor to French President Francois Mitterand, he said:

> *"Too large a population, and for the most part unnecessary, is something economically too expensive. Socially, it is also much better for the human machine to come to an abrupt halt rather than gradually deteriorating. We won't be able to run intelligence tests on millions and millions of people, you can imagine!*

> *"We will find something . . . or cause it. A pandemic that targets certain people, a real economic crisis or not, a virus that will affect the old or the fat. It doesn't matter. The weak will succumb to it, the fearful and the stupid will believe it and ask to be treated. We will have taken care to have planned the treatment, a treatment that will be the solution.*

> *"The selection of idiots will thus be done on its own: they will go to the slaughterhouse on their own."*

Nice chap, huh?

Attali's comments speak to the same sentiments towards the Great Unwashed held by Margaret Sanger, one of the founding members of Planned Parenthood, a Eugenics operation which advocates for significant population reduction through deciding which sectors of human society should be allowed to procreate, (them,) and which shouldn't (us.) Sanger, who was tellingly named as a personal hero by Hillary Clinton when she received Planned Parenthood's Margaret Sanger Award, described regular members of society as "human weeds," and observed that "the most merciful thing that a large family does to one of its infant members is to kill it."

The aforementioned Stanley Johnson has direct connections back into Planned Parenthood; after studying at Columbia University in the US, his biography states that he worked "directly" with J. D. Rockefeller III, as well as serving "on the staff of the World Bank and the International Planned Parenthood Federation." Stanley stated in an interview that the ideal population of the UK should be around 10 million and has made no secret of his contempt for the "illiterate" working classes.

Nor indeed has his son Boris, who during his time as editor of '*The Spectator*' wrote:

> "*The modern British male is useless. If he is blue collar, he is likely to be drunk, criminal, aimless, feckless and hopeless, and perhaps claiming to suffer from low self-esteem brought on by unemployment.*"

Boris gleefully announced his alliance with Bill Gates' GAVI vaccine alliance in the midst of the Co(n)vid scam, and, as mentioned in the earlier chapter, through Gates we get another link back to Planned Parenthood.

With a Prime Minister, and the public face of the worldwide vaccination agenda, both having direct family links to an organisation known for its desire to dramatically lower the human population, both in office at the time of a "pandemic" and the resulting vaccine roll-out... and with Gates having remarked during a 2010 TED Talk that: "the world today has 6.8 billion people. That's headed up to about nine billion. Now, if we do a really great job on new vaccines, health care, reproductive health services, we could lower that by, perhaps, 10 or 15 per cent"... what could possibly go wrong?

Muzzles for the muggles

The benefit for the sick controllers in employing popular culture vehicles for their mind-control and thought-entrainment tactics, is that their effects completely fly below the threshold of conscious recognition. No-one is expecting to have their thoughts, perceptions and behaviours shaped and moulded for them by other interested parties when they switch on the T.V., listen to some favourite music, or go to the cinema. Though the word "entertainment" can be broken down and seen to mean "to enter in and take the mind," (to "enter," "tain" from the French verb "*tenir*" meaning "to hold," and "ment" derived from the Latin for "mind,") to the average member of society, the word simply stands for some simple-minded escapism from the everyday pressures of the world, and a chance for some relaxing enjoyment.

Unfortunately, a relaxed mind is one wide open for subliminal programming, and this is how so much of the magicians' trickery gets achieved. Who, from regular, everyday society, would have consciously registered the large number of entertainment vehicles which featured the concept of mask-wearing in the years leading up to 2020, and connected that to the governmental coercion towards face masks becoming the "norm" in public at that time? Yet, when armed with the knowledge of how such dynamics work we can clearly comprehend how mask-wearing was turned from something bizarre and freakish, to something considered completely "normal," in the minds of most in society, with very few ever questioning the narrative.

Anyone walking into a pub wearing a medical-style blue face mask in 2019 would have received some questioning looks at the very least and may well have been asked to leave by the landlord on the grounds they were making the other customers feel uncomfortable. Anyone wearing the same face covering while entering a bank would likely have alerted security immediately to a potential robbery. This dynamic was reinforced by a recent episode of the long-running American "reality" show 'Candid Camera,' in which restaurant diners were secretly filmed as the staff—from the waitress to the chef to the manager—all appeared in face masks. This scenario, considered "weird" at the time, made the diners feel uneasy, causing some to make their excuses and leave.

Yet, in 2020 and beyond, *not* wearing a face nappy when walking into one of these establishments, (when they're "allowed" to be open, that is) is now deemed strange, and likely to cause uncomfortable feelings among others. The ease with which the dark occult sorcerers have been able to achieve such a sea change in societal attitudes is an achievement of pure genius—albeit evil genius—and the arsenal of mind weapons which comprise mainstream 'entertainment' have been prime tactics in how it has been achieved.

At times, having dipped their toe in the water to gauge just how much they can get away with without being widely called out, the sickos like to get cute and really rub the noses of the profane masses in it by taking their morbid mockery to record levels. As was the case with an episode of the fashion-based American "reality" T.V. show 'Project Runaway' from 4th April 2019, where an effeminate-looking male models a Tartan suit complete with matching face mask, which he is invited to take off after a few seconds on the grounds he "must be hot" underneath it; shame the same considerations aren't afforded to employees who are strong-armed into wearing one consistently for eight hours or more at work.)

And the name of the model showing off the fashion mask? Kovid. Is it even *possible* to take the piss any more than this? (Maybe it is. The mainstream press reported in 2020 that Tom Hanks had written a "heartfelt letter" to a bullied Australian boy who had written to him after Hanks and his wife Rita Wilson had "tested positive." The name of the boy? Corona. Well, we all know one. Hanks had earlier been in the news after becoming one of the first "celebrities" to contract "the virus," when it was reported that he travelled to a filming assignment in Australia with a typewriter in his luggage. The brand? Corona, of course. Well, we all do it, don't we? Pyjamas, toothbrush and a vintage typewriter are essential luggage items for any overseas trip.)

Young people were prepared for the coming mask agenda that was known to be coming. Tik-Tok, Snapchat and Instagram were all complicit in making the idea of face masks "cool" by presenting them as a fashion trend. For two years leading up to the Scamdemic, Snapchat had been offering its users random face coverings to add to their pictures on-line. British TV viewers were subliminally prepared through the launch of the BBC show *'The Masked Singer'* on Saturday evening primetime. The show, imported from South Korea, involves a "mystery" celebrity appearing in masked costume and performing, and a studio panel having to guess which famous person is behind the mask before they reveal themselves. The UK version was first shown on 4th January 2020, giving it two months to work its subliminal magic concerning mask-wearing before the Co(n)vid agenda made its first real impact.

Mask mandates are a virtue-signaller's dream. Now, people who have never really achieved anything in life, never held any kind of sway or influence on others through their own merits, can outwardly express their status as a "good person" and exert their (imaginary) authority on others by implying that they're "bad" if they don't follow the rules like they do, knowing they have Government and mainstream media propaganda on their side. Result! This dynamic was summed up beautifully by the YouTuber known as WhatsHerFace in her video *'Why I Wear My Mask,'* where with razor-sharp sarcasm, she stated:

"I love my mask. It's a simple and effective way to display my righteousness. Am I concerned that two children in China died because they were forced to wear a mask in gym class? NOPE! Am I concerned that I'm contributing to an impending socialist technocracy that will enslave the global population? NO! Am I concerned that my mask is symbolic of my compliance to the social conditioning that will eventually lead to the forced vaccination of every man, woman, and child on planet earth? Not a chance!

"Why am I not concerned, you ask? Because I decided a long time ago that shallow insignificant gestures are a much easier way to showcase my morality than actually being moral. Because in order to be a really good person, I need to stand up to a really bad person, and I don't like standing up for anything. It's much easier to trick my mind into thinking compliance is a virtue instead of what it really is—cowardice."

Bring out the gimps

And so—finally—we get to the music world's role in conditioning the easily-manipulated masses into unknowingly accepting the coming agenda.

Many would have considered **Madonna**'s performance at the *'Eurovision Song Contest'* in May 2019, to have been rather strange at the time, but viewing it now with the benefit of context, it makes much more sense. The *'Eurovision'* used to be considered cheesy and camp, though "innocent" enough. But in more recent years, it has joined other mass-audience events such as the 'Grammys,' the *'US Super Bowl Half-time Show,'* and the *'MTV'* and *'VMA Awards'* in being laden with dark occult imagery and ritualistic performances. This event was used to unveil Madonna's "Madame X" persona, (a mind-control alter,) which saw her appear with a patch, adorned with an "X," over her left eye. Her *'Madame X'* album was released in June, followed by an international tour, which came to an abrupt end in March 2020 due to . . . well, you know.

Bloodline Lifetime Actor and performing stooge Madonna "predicted" the Co(n)vid Scamdemic months ahead of time in one of her "Madame X" performances. What a lucky guess!

https://commons.wikimedia.org/wiki/File:Madame_x_-_London_Palladium_I.jpg

Following some straight Satanic imagery disguised as an homage to Catholicism, (is there a difference?) for a blood red-illuminated performance of '*Like A Prayer*,' Madonna was joined by "singer" **Quavo**, whose voice was so distorted by Autotune that he sounded like a malfunctioning Alexa, (helping to push the Transhumanist agenda—they never miss a trick.) Prior to their song '*Future*,' in which they declared "not everyone is coming to the future, not everyone that's here is going to last" (because of the killer vaccines, perchance?) Madonna delivered a monologue that had very telling overtones—particularly when factoring in the so-called Q "Plan" which posited that a group of "white hats" was working secretly behind the scenes to arrest and hold to account certain high-level politicians and celebrities for their complicity in crimes against humanity. (Like **Diana Ross**, I'm Still Waiting.)

She said:

> "*They are so naïve. They think we are not aware of their crimes. We know, but we are just not ready to act.*"

Bringing in the "pandemic" programming, she then adds:

"The storm isn't in the air. It's inside of us."

At this point, she blows on her dancers, who are decked out in creepy gas masks, and they all fall down as if dead.

Once the Scamdemic was in full flow, Madonna obediently joined other "celebrities" in stating she had tested positive for "coronavirus antibodies," and donated $1 million to the Bill & Melinda Gates Foundation to fund "research" into creating a new vaccine, (which had already long been in existence waiting to be unleashed.) I'm sure Bill was very grateful for the generous donation. I hear he's now down to his last $131 billion.

We might now do well to re-visit the **Arctic Monkeys**. Something which has been considered curious in recent times is the group's 2018 album '*Tranquility Base Hotel & Casino*,' where **Alex Turner** envisions a run-down resort on the moon where many people have gone to escape some form of an apocalypse on Earth. It contains some eerily prescient lyrics, the most striking being: "No-one's on the streets, we moved it all online, as of March." This even got picked up on by an article in '*NME*' magazine, titled '*How Arctic Monkeys' isolation album 'Tranquility Base Hotel & Casino' predicted pandemic life.*'

Was this just "happenstance" or "coincidence"? Or were we being given yet another subliminal glimpse of Co(n)vid-related events to come, two years ahead of time, indicating some inside knowledge of future agendas from within the Arctic Monkeys camp?

90s rap superstar **Busta Rhymes** certainly has previous when it comes to an apparent uncanny knack of foretelling world-changing disastrous events. He began his fortuitous run with his 1996 and 1997 albums '*The Coming*' and '*When Disaster Strikes*,' but it was the following year's '*Extinction Level Event: The Final World Front*' which really took things to the next level. The front cover image. credited on the sleeve to artist Stu Maschwitz and 'Alli,' shows a view of New York's Manhattan Island from the Hudson River being engulfed in an inferno. Some three years later, the events of 9/11 unfolded in the same location.

In late 2020, Rhymes, real name Trevor Smith, who is a stated member of the Five Per Cent Nation religious order detailed in this book's previous volume, was back with 'Extinction Level Event 2,' the follow-up to the first volume of over two decades previous. The sleeve design featured a skull wearing a medical-style face mask. Though Busta had announced the album as far back as 2013, it finally appeared in the wake of the Co(n)vid agenda having already been unrolled, yet, as if second-guessing those that might pick up on it, Busta addressed his apparent status as a sage and seer in the lyrics:

> *"That being said, we can stop pretendin' that I'm mental,*
> *Like all the shit we witnessed be happenin' coincidental.*
> *See, back in '98 when I dropped the first Extinction Level,*
> *I was fightin' inner demons with personal scores to settle.*
> *They put it in a movie 'cause they knew that we ain't really know.*
> *Funny how they tried to tell us 22 years ago.*
> *What deeply impacted how watchin' a flick really moved me.*
> *As the world was ending, Morgan Freeman was prez in a movie."*

(His latter reference is to the portrayal by Morgan Freeman of the American President in the 1998 asteroid disaster movie 'Deep Impact.' Here, the world was being subliminally prepared for the unveiling of America's first black president in Barack Obama, who had already been selected for the role. By the time Obama was in office, Danny Glover portrayed another black president in the movie '2012,' an observation picked up on by Busta Rhymes:

> *"Then I questioned why they reiteratin' the same plot,*
> *Should we be a little para' now that they gave us Barack?*
> *In 2020, the message I'm sending,*
> *Now that my president gone, how convenient the world has ended."*

Elsewhere on 'Extinction Level Event 2,' Busta demonstrated having done extensive research into (or having inside knowledge of?) the "Globalist" NWO masterplan:

> *"One world language, one world religion, one world order.*
> *We have learned nothing (one.)*

Making the keys to Heaven a gift to the Devil.
Those who desire to supplant God.
Illuminati who tempt and horrify us as the most perfect angel Lucifer.
Seek to rebirth a New World Order upon the flesh, blood, and bones of all humanity."

In an interview streamed live on YouTube on 31st October 2020 on the Revolt channel, Rhymes fuelled further speculation as to what "inside" connections he might have.

> *"And the information I was stumbling on, I would just incorporate in the albums that I felt . . . at the time that information reflected what was going on the most. And because that information is infinite, I could go on forever taking about this type of shit. Because, 'in '96 'The Coming' came out. We dropped 'Everything Remains Raw' in '96 and I'm getting information that's saying some shit is going to change forever five years later as far as the world is concerned as we knew it . . .*

> *". . . Again, I'm not prophesying shit; I'm just looking at the information I'm getting, because, believe it or not, this information was out there and they was tellin' niggas. And the best way to hide some shit is by putting it in your face, right?*

Frustratingly, Rhymes neglected to go any further into what parties that information had come from, and the interviewers failed to press him to reveal any more.

In an interview of around the same time given to *'NME'* magazine, Busta further hinted at his knowledge of the "elite" ruling class and their plans for humanity. While he didn't go as far as to call Co(n)vid out as a scam, he did at least indicate that the public was being played and that Truth was being suppressed:

> *"There's obviously something wrong and some other agenda going on—a lot of it is political. It feels super-imbalanced and unfair. We're getting caught up in the overwhelming abundances of propaganda*

that's keeping us distracted from realising that there's some truth we need to start working towards and getting to the bottom of."

Busta had clearly experienced yet more frustration by the time he was able to start performing live shows again in June 2021, telling the crowd at one of his resumed concerts:

"All these little, weird-ass government mandates and policies—suck a dick! They're trying to take our civil liberties away . . . It feels good to be outside, for real. It's called the God-given right of freedom, right? No human being's supposed to tell you you can't even breathe freely. Fuck your mask!"

The creators of the track *'Pandemic,'* meanwhile, credited to **Dr. Creep** and released in 2013, were remarkably on-point with their lyrical reference to *"2020 Coronavirus,"* in a video that features characters in hazmat suits and gas masks being sprayed with disinfectant.

As were Japanese/ American DJ/ producer **Steve Aoki** and **Linkin Park** when they put out the video to their track *'Darker Than Blood'* in 2015. Five years ahead of Co(n)vid this depicted . . . deep breath . . . the outbreak of a deadly virus, an Apocalyptic society ravaged by marauding zombies, a futuristic Smart Grid-type cityscape, nanobots, and—what else—vaccines offered as *the* only solution. The storyline is set in 2052. Aoki's associated symbolism has long marked him out as a Masonic key asset of the industry machine. Linkin Park's **Chester Bennington** had only two years to live at the time of this song's release.

And British veterans **Killing Joke** (more on them in the *'Sound Bites'* section,) were ten prophetic years ahead of their time when they put out *'The Great Cull'* in 2010, its lyrics referencing the Georgia Guidestones' tenet of reducing the world's population to half a billion, The song referenced the *Codex Alimentarius* project, and others that described life a decade into the future with uncanny accuracy:

"Thin the herd, thin the herd.

The great cull is coming down.

The great cull is coming down.

Develop virus market cure, exploit the panic.

Contaminate by guile and stealth, a quick strum of the harp.
Depopulate, initiate pharmaceutical companies."

Pretty much the content of any random '*BBC Evening News*' bulletin of
2020 and beyond. Now here's Bill with the weather . . .

What the papers say

There will always be those sceptics of a more scientific left-brained persuasion who would wholesale reject the notion that meaning could be
found in anything as trivial as a movie, TV show or pop video. Maybe,
therefore, these types would like to consider the odds of the many real-
world "drills" and "preparedness exercises" which have taken place over
the years, "predicting" the outbreak of a "deadly" virus, and considering
what measures might have to be taken *should* one—you know, just on
the off-chance—happen to occur?

Among these were '*Dark Winter*' in 2001, staged by, among others,
the Johns Hopkins Center for Civilian Biodefense Studies, and the
same year's Global Health Security Initiative, with the World Health
Organization listed as a "technical advisor." Then there was 2003's
'*Global Mercury: An International Bioterrorism Exercise*' staged by the US
Department of State, and more recently, '*Clade X*' in 2018, a "pandemic
tabletop exercise" coming from those nice people at The Johns Hopkins
Center for Health Security whose only concern is to keep us all safe.

Then, the icing on the cake, Event 201 in New York City in October
2019, just weeks before a man ate a bat in a Chinese wet market and
caused the entire world to shut down. What lucky timing that Johns
Hopkins were available again alongside the World Economic Forum,
with funding from big-hearted Bill and Melinda Gates, and had worked
out what we all needed to be doing. Sure enough, there was good old Bill
on TV within just a few weeks, in a nice pastel sweater, (you can always
trust a man in a nice pastel sweater, after all—psychopaths wear suits,)
telling us how we wouldn't be able to get our lives back until everyone
had taken shots of unknown substances, (from which he stands to make
billions—but that's neither here nor there,) into their veins. Bill doesn't
come with any medical qualifications whatsoever, incidentally, but it

seems you don't need any when you're a billionaire from a family of Eugenicists.

Perhaps the most damning of all the documents that were uncovered by vigilant researchers, was the one originating from the Rockefeller Foundation in 2010, *'Innovating for a Bold Future,'* known alternatively as the *"Lockstep"* document, which detailed how a widespread "pandemic" could be used to control a population. It "simulated" the idea of 20 per cent of the world's population being killed by "the virus" in 2012, wiping out eight million people in just seven months.

As the Foundation's own website now proclaims, with no apparent sense of irony:

> *"Now that we're well into a real pandemic, we see some chilling similarities between our current Zoom-centered world and Lockstep. The report predicted that telepresence technologies would "respond to the demand for less-expensive, lower bandwidth, sophisticated communications systems for populations whose travel is restricted." Other predictions were off, including the emergence of M.R.I. technologies to detect abnormal behavior with anti-social intent."*

Along similar lines, coming out of the Johns Hopkins (yawwwn,) and Bloomberg School of Public Health-controlled Center for Health Security, in 2017 we had the catchily-titled *'The S.P.A.R.S. Pandemic 2025-2028: A Futuristic Scenario to Facilitate Medical Countermeasure Communication.'* Despite its seemingly benevolent-sounding aims, this was merely another blueprint, or "how to" manual, detailing how the Co(n)vid-19 Scamdemic would be rolled out—particularly as it appeared in March 2020 right at the start of it. Its claim to cover a "fictional" timeline of 2025-2028 was merely a cover, as it would appear to have instead been addressing what was planned for the period 2020-2023. A friend of mine took on the unenviable task of trawling through this spirit-crushingly dull document to extract the most cogent points, which include:

> *"P4—C.D.C. recommends hand hygiene and frequently disinfecting surfaces.*

P6—S.P.A.R.S. fatality of only 0.6%.

P14—Emergency use authorisation of drug/ vaccine.

P16/17—Getting minority groups to accept Government narrative by fear-based news : "S.P.A.R.S. can kill you."

P24—Public interest in S.P.A.R.S. wanes—only fatal in 0.6% of cases. Development of new public health messaging campaigns and the forthcoming vaccine called Corovaccine.

P24—Enlisting help of well-known scientists and celebrities, including that of a former President and BZee, a popular hip-hop star—with the campaign having mixed results, eg, BZee receiving some backlash.

P43/ 44—Critics claim vaccine inadequately tested and had unknown long-term side effects. Special efforts to get Muslims to embrace S.P.A.R.S. vaccine using prominent imam.

P45—African-American distrust and legacy of Tuskegee syphilis experiments—aggressive vaccine campaign but repurposing hashtags like #blacklivesmatter. Some African-American pushback.

P55—New aggressive advertising campaign by Government. If some-one searches Google for 'corovaccine side effects,' a sidebar will appear to explain the benefits of the vaccine. Anti-vaccine videos on YouTube required them to mention pro-vaccine benefits. Vaccine rates increase in nearly all the targeted groups.

P63—Government delays to act, saying "we have to wait for the data." Government pushes behavioural health guidance to strengthen public's coping skills and support for grieving individuals. President talks about recovery after pandemic and the sacrifice vaccine recip-ients had made to hasten the end of the pandemic, (the dead and badly injured essentially become "heroes.")

P66—AFTERMATH—several high-ranking officials at C.D.C. and F.D.A. forced to step down 'to spend more time with their families.' (Some pawns and higher-value chess pieces have to be thrown under the bus by these psychopaths.)"

Anyone *still* residing within the delusion that "this could all just be coincidence and proves nothing," are finally invited to explain how it could be—*if* there really were no Establishment foreknowledge whatsoever that the "pandemic" was coming—that biometric tests for Covid-19 were patented in 2015 in the Netherlands and the US in 2017. In both cases the individual applying for the patent was named as Richard A. Rothschild of the Rothschild "elite" banking dynasty. In both cases, "Covid-19" is named, years before it is supposed to have come into usage.

We also have the quandary of how the American Congress's C.A.R.E.S. Act—Coronavirus Aid Relief and Economic Security Act—which speaks of responding specifically to the "Covid-19" outbreak, is on record as having been registered on 24th January 2019 when the "pandemic" didn't emerge until the end of that year.

Meanwhile, notice too how the much-vaunted Public Health Emergency of International Concern, one of so many outfits set up in the wake of Co(n)vid, spells out PHEIC . . . pronounced "fake." The more you look, the more you see!

Not to be left out, meanwhile, less than a year before the Event 201 "preparedness exercise," the treasonous Australian government had already laid the foundations for that nation to become the testing ground for full Orwellian, New World Order tyranny, with the publication of a document catchily titled *'Australia's National Action Plan For Health Security, 2019-2023.'* What serendipitous timing that they *just happened* to get all this in place *just* before a major "Global pandemic" hit. Phew!! Isn't random chance and coincidence a wonderful thing?

You can read this psychopaths' wet dream—if you can stomach it—via the URL at the end of the chapter.

Anyone still insisting that "the virus" came out of nowhere and took the world's governments and powerbrokers by surprise after being presented with the above mountains of evidence is, frankly, in such a calcified state of denial and under such heavy mind-control, that they are beyond all hope and redemption in this life and wouldn't wake up to Truth if it were to beat them savagely around the head with a nail-stud-ded baseball bat while screaming through a bullhorn, "I am Truth! I am Truth! Wake the FUCK UP, you ignorant BASTARD!"

Standing on ceremony

There has never been a point in human history with so much potential to ensnare the hearts, minds and souls of billions, as that offered by the combination of television and the internet. And indeed, this potential has not gone unexploited by the Hidden Hand. It is terminally naïve to assume that a dark death cult would pass up the opportunities offered by mass-audience events like the *'US Super Bowl Half Time Show,'* the *'Grammys',* the *'MTV and BMA Awards',* and now even the *'Eurovision Song Contest'*—particularly when, if you go high enough up the chain of command, it becomes clear that the very same forces are pulling the strings of all these vehicles. The above-mentioned events, and many others of a similar nature, have become so saturated in Satanic/ dark occult symbolism in recent times that they've even sparked the atten-tion of the owned-and-controlled mainstream media. In response to **Katy Perry**'s demonic *'Dark Horse'* performance at the *'Grammys',* for instance, *'E! Online'* mainstream entertainment news Tweeted: "Um, did we just witness *actual* witchcraft during Katy Perry's Grammys performance?"

The controllers going so all-out either indicates their psychopathic assumption that they have the general public so far into mind-control that they can now mockingly rub our noses in it and get away with it . . . or it indicates that the New World Order wet dream that they've fantasised about for so long is now so close to completion that they need to employ every trick in their book to get the final pieces into place, with no time to worry about how, in doing so, they might expose their true nature, this having to necessarily be chalked up as "collateral damage."

Which brings us to what may be the strangest aspect of what *appears* to be Co(n)vid-19 pre-programming of all. The synchro-mystic aspects here are so all-pervading that they truly boggle the mind, and the fact that this event occurred eight years before the unleashing of the Scamdemic—and would have required many years of planning prior to that—has got me wondering whether it's even *possible* for this degree of *human* planning to take place for such an event—or whether we need to consider forces and phenomena other than flesh-and-blood mortals sitting around a meeting table plotting to be the only realistic way in which all of this could have been brought into physical manifestation.

By the time of the Opening Ceremony of the London Olympics on 27th July 2012, conspiracy researchers were already well attuned to dissecting the occult ritual-fests that these events had become, and sure enough, vigilant students pored over every aspect of this spectacle, shining a spotlight on all the symbolism contained. Many truthseekers had had their minds blown by the astounding work of Rik Clay in this regard. In his landmark interviews with Red Ice Radio in June 2008, Rik had outlined how the numerology and symbolism involved in the London event—all the way down to the street names within the vicinity—hinted at the "elite" plan to use it to usher in a New Age, with connections to the concept of "Zion" very much in evidence.

In 2012, much anxiety was focused on the mythical date of 21st December, representing the end of an era as foretold in the ancient calendar of the Mayans. It had been strongly speculated that ahead of this, some major "false flag" terror event might be triggered while the eyes and minds of the world were focused on London, ("the new Jerusalem.") The late researcher Ian Crane mused afterwards on whether the scale of warnings offered by truth researchers in this regard just may have caused the would-be instigators to rethink their plans, given how obvious it would have been if they had still gone ahead.

Rik Clay never lived to see if his predictions about 2012 would come to pass. He is said to have taken his own life on 28th August 2008, just two months after exposing his findings on Red Ice. His family accept the verdict, affirming that he was no longer able to cope with the magnitude of the discoveries that he had made. Inevitably, however, suspicions persist that there was foul play involved in his death at the tragically young age of 26. His ashes were scattered on Ilkley Moor in West Yorkshire on the symbolic date of 11th September that year.

Despite the thorough analysis of the Olympics Opening Ceremony, however, upon the breaking of the 2020 Scamdemic narrative, many researchers suspected that there had been yet more detail intricately encoded into the ritual to mark apparent foreknowledge of what was to come.

Supposedly representing everything that was "great" about Britain and held in a stadium flanked by pyramids complete with illuminated capstones, the Ceremony, (it's not like we weren't being told!) began with a "celebration" of the National Health Service. This involved troupes of doctors and nurses performing dance routines very similar to the ones we saw in 'Tik-Tok' videos from 2020, *purporting* to be genuine doctors and nurses who, despite being "rushed off their feet" in Co(n)vid "war zones," somehow managed to find the time to rehearse complicated dance routines, (though in reality, blatant Satanic mockery of the stupidity of the masses.) This piece had been preceded by an appearance from veteran multi-instrumentalist **Mike Oldfield** performing '*Tubular Bells,*' best known for its inclusion on the soundtrack to the movie '*The Exorcist,*' and just one of so many Satanic overtones.

Next in the sequence the mood turns decidedly darker as night descends on groups of children in hospital beds, and Harry Potter author J.K. Rowling reads a passage from '*Peter Pan*' by J.M. Barrie, (consistently accused of having been a predatory paedophile.) Children read under the bed covers by torchlight, including one girl who bears more than a passing resemblance to child "activist" Greta Thunberg—unknown in 2012, but very much in the public consciousness by 2020. Creepy figures begin stalking the hospital beds; the children become visibly scared as Cruella de Vil from '*101 Dalmations*' and The Child Catcher from '*Chitty Chitty Bang Bang*', (played by mind-controlled system asset Russell Brand,) taunt them menacingly.

The most significant part of this sequence, however, is an inflatable figure bearing a resemblance to Boris Johnson seen rising from a hospital bed. Just days after placing the UK into lockdown in March 2020, it was reported that Johnson had contracted "Co(n)vid" and had been committed to an N.H.S. hospital—as if someone of Johnson's position and wealth would *not* go into private care. In reality Johnson had not contracted anything other than a terminal case of treachery, his "hospitalisation" standing as a sinister propaganda stunt to terrify the public into conforming with the all-new Draconianism that had just been dumped on them. At that time, Johnson was serving his second term as Mayor of London. *If* the figure in the bed is intended to represent him, it suggests it had already been decreed that he would be in place as British Prime Minister at the time of the Scamdemic, and that the story of his hospitalisation from "the virus" would be spun early in the narrative ... almost eight years ahead of time.

A week prior to the Olympics event, the Batman movie '*The Dark Knight Rises*' had been released and absorbed into the subconscious of millions. This is responsible for a whole raft of Predictive Programming of its own — not least the sequence where the character Bane is poring over a map which bears the name "Sandy Hook." Months later, a week prior to the fabled Winter Solstice of 2012, a "mass shooting" at Sandy Hook Elementary School in Newtown, Connecticut is said to have taken place at the hands of a "lone gunman' (aren't they always?) Adam Lanza. (Although it didn't; the title of Jim Fetzer's banned-by-Amazon book '*Nobody Died At Sandy Hook*' is an accurate one.)

According to occult researcher Michael Wann, appearing on an episode of Greg Carlwood's '*The Higherside Chats*' podcast in September 2020, even this movie was displaying advance knowledge of what was known to be coming, with more synchronistic overlaps at every turn. As Wann commented:

> "*The Dark Knight Rises*" *is a wordplay to the 'dark night of the soul.' And the dark night of the soul, in my opinion, is a very good explanation of what we're seeing everyone being brought through right about now. Here's a definition ... 'There can be no rebirth, without a dark night of the soul — a total annihilation of all that you believed in and thought that you were.'*

> "*So from a higher spiritual perspective, the dark night of the soul is where everything collapses down. So you can see all of the illusion in your life, and so that you can find who you truly are. But the dark night of the soul is also a recognition of the destruction of everything*

of what you thought of your life. And that is very much tied into this narrative.

"...Everything must be destroyed, and then rebuilt. So when we're talking about the Dark Knight rising, the dark night of the soul, yes, there is an individual element. But there's also a cultural element, which this is about, that must be destroyed. And they're telling us this is going to happen through the virus."

Wann went on to observe that Boris Johnson, London Mayor during one of that city's most pivotal periods, appeared to be paraphrasing villainous Bane from the Batman movie in his first speech after being appointed Prime Minister in July 2019. Johnson had said:

"The time has come to act, to take decisions, to give strong leadership and to change this country for the better. My job is to serve you, the people."

Whereas Bane's quote had gone:

"We take Gotham from the corrupt, the rich, the oppressors of generations who have kept you down with myths of opportunity, and we give it back to you, the people."

A strong visual characteristic of Bane, meanwhile, was that he wore a face mask. And when he was asked in the movie what would happen if that mask were to be ripped from his face, he responded that he would probably die...which had become the way many of the general public felt about their own face masks during the Co(n)vid era.

Greg Carlwood took the baton from Wann on '*THC,*' adding:

"I just want to reiterate that when you watch those ceremonies, they have synchronised lights or dancers, and they form an exact Coronavirus! The pattern that synchronised swimmers make with these rounded shapes. It is the exact thing! If you tried to tell people to make one they couldn't do a better job. And just that 'Dark Knight' thing where James Holmes is basically mirroring a scene from the Frank Miller comic book where an orange-haired psycho shoots up a theatre,

and then they're doing this here also in the Olympic ceremonies. Both Batman running around and a group of orange-haired gymnasts are making a human pyramid!

"And again, Aurora/ Corona; this is that sun symbolism. It's nuts, man. And the Boris Johnson thing. I mean, Jesus, he's the Mayor of London in 2012, and then Prime Minister in 2020, quoting Bane, a guy who wears a mask, and is the first dude to get Coronavirus as a major politician. These threads are not thin, you know. They're deep!"

The 2012 opening sequence was completed by several dancing Mary Poppins' complete with spinning umbrellas—a common motif associated with trauma-based mind control programming. A popular song from the Mary Poppins movie is the one with the lyric "a spoonful of sugar helps the medicine go down." The song's principal lyricist, Robert Sherman, is said to have been inspired by his son having received the polio vaccine at school, so now a link to another key aspect of the Co(n)vid agenda emerges! Insane coincidence? Or some kind of unseen higher powers at work making all this stuff happen?

What's in a name?

Throughout the fear and doom-laden mainstream media reports during the "pandemic," there was constant fluctuation between "the virus" being referred to as Co(n)vid-19, by its alternative identity of SARS-COV 2, and simply "coronavirus." We saw the same dynamic at play during the years of the (manufactured) "terror" threats from I.S.I.S., who were alternatively referred to as "I.S.", "Islamic State," or sometimes "Daesh."

These are examples of a well-worn psychological tactic. References to differing names gives the impression that the "threat" is all-pervasive, complicated, and way too dangerous for the likes of us "little people" to even contemplate taking on. Far better to "leave it to the experts" who understand all these complicated terms.

There was another tactic at play with the interchangeability between "Co(n)vid" and "coronavirus" too. Coronaviruses are a group of diseases comprising multiple variants and include, tellingly, influenza and the common cold. They are nothing new, having been known about and referenced for decades, and many household cleaning products have boasted for years on their labels that they are effective in killing "coronaviruses." Because of the way some news bulletins have referenced "the virus" as "Co(n)vid-19" and others have talked in the same way about "coronavirus," it has "justified" rules and restrictions that have been put in place, nominally, to combat *any* "coronavirus" (including the common cold,) rather than specifically addressing Co(n)vid-19. This is knowing and deliberate deception of the public by the architects of this treasonous scam. It is this blurring of the lines that enabled the treacherous "Coronavirus Act" to be put through the UK's Parliament, "justifying" the removal of the rights and freedoms of the public. This Act stands to be reviewed every six months, and could conceivably be renewed in perpetuity, given that it addresses "coronaviruses" that have been, and will be, around forever.

Few seem to have questioned why it is that "coronavirus" is always presented as one lower-case word, rather than the more sensible "Corona virus" with a capital C. Or why it is always "coronavirus" rather than "*the* coronavirus" in the news. All of these questions become answered by the preceding paragraph.

"Coronavirus" also becomes an interesting word to conjure with in the circumstances, given that it is an anagram of both "carnivorous," (remember the farcical initial claim of how it had mutated from a bat in a "wet market" in Wuhan, China, where anything that moves is sold and eaten as 'meat"?) and of "virus or a con" (which speaks for itself.) As does the fact that "face mask" is an anagram of "fake scam." And could the Universe be displaying its own dry, sardonic sense of humour through "Dr. Fauci" turning out to be an anagram of I C Fraud?

Through some seemingly mind-melting sorcery, meanwhile, if a numerical value is ascribed to each of the letters of "corona" through their position in the alphabet—so 3 for C, 15 for O, etc, the total value comes to 66. With 6 letters in "corona." The dark occultists' favoured number of 666 is with us again, and never seems far from the surface in these manufactured psy-op narratives. And in more fun with words, Covid reversed becomes "Divoc,' which in Hebrew just happens to mean "possession by an evil spirit." You couldn't make it up. And you don't have to.

It would also be remiss not to observe that "coronavirus" is often shortened in common parlance to simply "CV." Ascribing numerical values here, we find that C is the 3rd letter of the alphabet, and V the 22nd. So we get 322. Not only is March 22nd (3/22,) a key date in the dark occult calendar, being the date on which, in 1980, the Georgia Guidestones were first unveiled,) 322 is also the revered number of the Skull & Bones mystery school from within Yale University, known alternatively as the Brotherhood of Death or Order 322, the ranks of which are reserved only for those of key "elite" family bloodlines.

*

As noted in the earlier chapter, the architects of this outrage have departed from their usual methods of operation in over-reaching spectacularly. We can speculate as to whether this is down to supreme arrogance and hubris, or to desperation and sheer panic at the notion they no longer have the time they once felt they did to put the final pieces of their demonic jigsaw puzzle in place, owing to the speed with which empowering information is now leaking forth. Either way, the cat is out of the bag/ the genie is out of the bottle/ Pandora's Box has been opened, depending on which analogy you prefer, and the point of no return has been reached. From here on out it is a spiritual war between the forces of Good and Evil, and one thing about the lies and deceptions which accompany Evil, is that they always get found out and exposed in the end. It might take decades, or even centuries, but by their very nature, lies cannot stand the test of time. Truth, meanwhile, requires no defending, because it just *is*, and can always be shown to be so.

This eternal dynamic ensures that the Co(n)vid Scamdemic *will* be shown to be what it really is, and when it does, all those who actively and knowingly perpetrated the lies, will stand fully exposed for the part they played. A phrase used by the brilliant British researcher Phillip Day in one of his Situation Report newsletters summed up this state of affairs succinctly: "When it dawns on the public what these lunatics have done, pray for their souls, because they won't find mercy in this world."

The same might also be said of all those mainstream media "journalists," TV and film directors, scriptwriters and actors, and complicit "celebrities" who similarly helped facilitate genocide. When payback day comes, I wouldn't trade Karma with them for all the gold in the world.

Resources:

The Guardian: Matt Hancock's vaccine rollout was inspired by Contagion:

- https://www.theguardian.com/film/filmblog/2021/feb/04/contagion-film-matt-hancock-covid-vaccine-policy-hollywood

Absolute proof the Co(n)vid Scam Was Planned Long in Advance—Mark Devlin at Truth Juice, Part 1:

- https://www.youtube.com/watch?v=INTzkFHJxew&t=2760s

Clues and pointers in 'The Last Man on Earth':

- https://www.youtube.com/watch?v=65YbGJ3sr54&t=19s

Await Further Instructions movie trailer:

- https://www.youtube.com/watch?time_continue=63&v=cEx-GHt350NE&feature=emb_title

Digital Spy: Bill Gates: Rich nations should shift entirely to synthetic beef:

- https://www.digitalspy.com/tv/ustv/a34242025/utopia-season-2-release-date-amazon/

Wikipedia: Films about viral outbreaks:

- https://en.wikipedia.org/wiki/Category:Films_about_viral_outbreaks

Vexille (2007) [English Dub]:

- https://www.youtube.com/watch?v=7PG5-SJ6fkk

WhatsHerFace YouTube channel: Why I Wear My Mask

- https://www.youtube.com/watch?v=0tH1p8Bnmwc

Lyrics: Dr. Creep: 'Pandemic':

- https://genius.com/Dr-creep-pandemic-lyrics

Madonna at Eurovision 2019:

- https://www.youtube.com/watch?v=VG3WkiL0d_U

Busta Rhymes on his apocalyptic album covers (from 12 minutes in):

- https://www.youtube.com/watch?v=i7nieCNVbE4&feature=share&fbclid=IwAR0yMrPdpzvVGv2pWFf7voQbB4W-ZIq6caRb6Y1NHmkB2gXvAsXiPPjoLqd4

Vigilant Citizen: Busta Rhymes' Album "ELE2": It's Messages About the New World Order and the Five-Percent Nation:

- https://vigilantcitizen.com/musicbusiness/busta-rhymes-album-ele2-its-messages-about-the-new-world-order-and-the-five-percent-nation/

ATOMIC BOMBSHELL: ROTHSCHILDS PATENTED Co(n)vid-19 BIOMETRIC TESTS IN 2015. AND 2017:

- https://silview.media/2020/10/04/atomic-bombshell-rothschilds-patented-Covid-19-biometric-tests-in-2015-and-2017/

Dark Winter "preparedness exercise':

- https://www.centerforhealthsecurity.org/our-work/events-archive/2001_dark-winter/about.html

Global Health Security Initiative 'preparedness exercise':

- http://ghsi.ca/

Australia's National Action Plan For Health Security, 2019-2023:

- https://www1.health.gov.au/internet/main/publishing.nsf/Content/054D7F36DA7F8F72CA2581A8001278EB/%24File/Aust-Nat-Action-Plan-Health-Security-2019-2023.pdf

Rik Clay's interviews on Red Ice Radio—All Four Hours:

- https://redice.tv/news/
  rik-clay-s-interviews-on-red-ice-radio-all-four-hours

The Rik Clay Foundation:

- http://www.rikclayfoundation.org/rik-clay.html

2012 London Olympics Opening Ceremon/ Co(n)vid-19:

- https://www.youtube.com/watch?v=vkgGz5n14NY

The Baron Trump novels on Wikipedia:

- https://en.wikipedia.org/wiki/Baron_Trump_novels

People: Billion Dollar Baby: Welcome to the World of Barron William Trump:

- https://web.archive.org/web/20150925091754/http://www.
  people.com/people/archive/article/0,,20175764,00.html

Newsweek: Did an Author From the 1800s Predict the Trumps, Russia and America's Downfall?:

- https://www.newsweek.com/donald-trump-predicted-inger-
  soll-lockwood-adventures-barron-melania-last-644284

Newstarget: Patent document shows that DARPA built Co(n)vid with the help of Bill Gates, WHO:

- https://www.newstarget.com/2021-06-29-darpa-built-Covid-
  help-bill-gates-who.html

Steve Aoki Feat. Linkin Park—Darker Than Blood (Official Video):

- https://www.youtube.com/watch?v=i1P1ClJcSPc&t=45s

CHAPTER 6

DONALD THROUGH THE LOOKING GLASS

The strangeness continues. Trump, Tesla and time travel, apparently all foretold.

"Nobody told me there'd be days like these.
Strange days indeed.
Strange days indeed."

John Lennon: 'Nobody Told Me.'

Even in spite of the unlikeliness of everything in the previous chapter, perhaps the most mind-blowing of all apparent examples of the fore-shadowing phenomenon doesn't involve the "virus" at all, but concerns a sub-plot to the entire Co(n)vid saga. Though it took long enough to become clear, and though it ticked many other boxes on the agenda, it does appear as if the "pandemic" was created, in very large part, to derail Donald Trump's chances of gaining a second term in office as President of the United States, (POTUS.)

Part of the thinking of the psychopathic architects was that, by ter-rifying the American populace into believing they could catch a deadly airborne virus at any time if they dared to set out on to the streets, a great many could be coerced into casting their vote in the 2020 election by post. This dynamic offered far more scope for vote-rigging and elec-toral fraud of the type that did indeed occur. Trump *appeared* to be a major thorn in the side of the cabal control system since his unexpected victory at the polls in 2016—an election in which Satanic system-server Hillary Clinton, (as previously noted, a cousin of Trump!) was fully expected to sweep the vote. According to a popular school of thought within alternative research realms, had this occurred, the New World Order control system of which most of the world's population got a free sample in 2020/ 21, would have been fast-tracked into place much quicker, and even more severely.

Or were there other forces at play here?

In 1889, the American lawyer-turned-novellist Ingersoll Lockwood wrote a children's novel titled *'Travels and Adventures of Little Baron Trump and his wonderful dog Bulger.'* This was followed by its sequel four years later titled *'Baron Trump's Marvellous Underground Journey.'* The stories follow the exploits of its central character, a German boy named Wilhelm Heinrich Sebastian Von Troomp, known alternatively as "Baron Trump." In the adventures, the boy discovers a secret portal that allows him to time-travel, and he encounters strange underground civilisations along the way.

Having remained obscure for over a century, in 2017 the novels gained something of a resurgence when it was noted that they bore an uncanny amount of parallels to aspects of the then-President Donald Trump's life and activities. The most obvious was the fact that POTUS had named his youngest son, and only child with his wife Melania, Barron. A 2015 article in *'People'* magazine confirmed that Donald chose the boy's first name. Writing in *'Newsweek'* magazine in 2017, Chris Riotta noted the following crossovers:

> *"Trump, an aristocratically wealthy young man living in Castle Trump, is the protagonist of Lockwood's first two fictional novels ... The little boy, who has an unending imagination and "a very active brain," is bored of the luxurious lifestyle he has grown so accustomed to.*

> *... Trump's adventures begin in Russia, and are guided thanks to directions provided by "the master of all masters," a man named "Don."*

While the protagonist of the novels lives in Castle Trump, POTUS Donald's New York residence and business premises is the similarly self-named Trump Towers. Relevance has been placed on the Russia setting owing to the (since discredited) claims of Russian interference in the 2016 US election.

Three years after the second Baron Trump novel, Lockwood penned another story, this one titled *'1900'*, or alternatively, *'The Last President.'* This concerns a wealthy man with premises on New York City's 5th Avenue, who ran for President and was not expected to win, but against all the odds did. Once in office, he began signing Executive Orders to right the wrongs of the previous administrations. As Chris Riotta notes:

> *"The story begins with a scene from a panicked New York City in early November, describing a "state of uproar" after the election of an enormously opposed outsider candidate.*

> *"The entire East Side is in a state of uproar," police officers shouted through the streets, warning city folk to stay indoors for the night. "Mobs of vast size are organizing under the lead of anarchists and socialists, and threaten to plunder and despoil the houses of the rich who have wronged and oppressed them for so many years."*

Trump Towers is situated in New York City's 5th Avenue.

Many of the President's staff are named in the novel. Among them is a Secretary of Agriculture named Lafe Pence.

Donald Trump's Vice-President during his first term was Mike Pence.

At this stage, these amazing "coincidences" bring to mind another series of baffling correlations between US Presidents Abraham Lincoln and John F. Kennedy, both recognised as having gone up against the "elite" control system cabal of their day and challenged its stranglehold over Organised Society, 100 years apart, and with both having paid the price for their bravery by way of assassin's bullets. Although "fact-checking" sites like Snopes have taken apart the full list and debunked many of the claimed correlations, even after this process, that which is left remains mind-boggling.

As matters of verifiable fact, Lincoln was elected to Congress in 1846, while Kennedy was elected to Congress in 1946. Lincoln was elected President in 1860, and Kennedy in 1960. Both wives lost a child while living in the White House—Willie Lincoln in 1862, aged 11, and Patrick Bouvier Kennedy in 1963, two days after he was born prematurely. Both Presidents were shot on a Friday, in the head and while seated. Both were succeeded by their Vice-Presidents, who were both Southerners named Johnson; Andrew Johnson, who succeeded Lincoln, was born in 1808. Lyndon Johnson, who succeeded Kennedy, was born in 1908. Lincoln was shot in Ford's Theater, and Kennedy was shot while riding in a Lincoln Continental 4-door convertible made by Ford Motor Co.

At what point do the mathematical odds of all this being "random" become simply impossible, and an acknowledgement that other, unknown forces must be at work to form these patterns becomes necessary?

(Incidentally, the Baron Trump stories were published right around the time of a novel by the American writer Morgan Robertson who, in 1898, published a story named '*Futility*.' It told of an ocean liner, The Titan, crossing the Atlantic at great speed during the month of April, colliding with a iceberg and sinking, with too few lifeboats for all the passengers. 14 years later, the Titanic, (though it was really another in White Star Line's fleet, the Olympic—see British author John Hamer's work on the subject!) sank in almost exactly the same circumstances as The Titan. It was speculated at the time that Robertson possessed some kind of psychic or clairvoyant gift, which he denied.

The only other possibilities are that this was a very early example of Predictive Programming through popular culture, with Robertson somehow having foreknowledge of the event which would occur in 1912, that he had somehow been able to time-travel or "remote-view" the future—a claim applied to Lockwood—or that it was an extraordinary coincidence at odds of probably several billion to one.

Going back to our Trump story, the narrative now gets even deeper and moves on to encompass the life's work of the genius Serbian scientist and inventor so beloved of the Truth and Freedom community, Nikola Tesla. Two days after Tesla died alone in Manhattan's New Yorker Hotel in January 1943, the FBI ordered the government department known as the Alien Property Custodian to seize and analyse Tesla belongings and notes, in the hope of getting up to speed on his life's work. This department brought in a well-known professor and electrical engineer to advise on possible applications for Tesla's technology if they were to fall into enemy hands. The professor was one John G. Trump, the paternal uncle of the future President Donald Trump, who stated in his official report:

"(Tesla's) thoughts and efforts during at least the past 15 years were primarily of a speculative, philosophical, and somewhat promotional character often concerned with the production and wireless transmission of power; but did not include new, sound, workable principles or methods for realizing such results."

John Trump himself was noted for developing rotational radiation therapy, and together with Robert J. Van de Graaff, he developed one of the first million-volt X-ray generators.

Along with his work on Free Energy — the tapping-into the energetic field in which all things exist and the harnessing of it as a power source to surpass electricity and fossil-fuel energy — Tesla is thought to have worked on technology involving time travel — the ability to enter and exit at will, different points along the time-space continuum.

The Trump family involvement in acquiring Tesla's discoveries, and the uncanny connections to time-travel motifs coming from the Baron Trump books, have led many researchers to question whether Donald Trump and those he had worked with were able to see into the future way ahead of time, to know what the outcome would be of world events in 2020/ 21. This notion is strengthened, according to many, when factoring in the technology thought to exist within the Intelligence community named Looking Glass.

This appears to be a variation on the concept of Remote Viewing, practiced by many psychics and mediums, and weaponised by organisations such as the C.I.A., where a "viewer" is able to undergo an out-of-body experience and "travel" to a different point on the timeline and a different geographical location, observe, then return and report back their findings. Could the Trump family, interested researchers have asked, have inherited a technology facilitating the viewing of future timeline playouts from the work of Nikola Tesla?

Another motif entered the picture regarding research into Trump's true nature sparked by world events of 2020. Always a character who divided opinion, his many detractors — generally those of a Left-leaning "Liberal" political persuasion — saw Trump as nothing less than the

Antichrist. Certainly, this viewpoint was strengthened by the almost universal demonisation of him by the ("elite") corporate-controlled mainstream media. Conversely, Trump's legions of fans viewed him as nothing short of a Messianic figure, and a saviour sent into troubled times on a mission from God to take on the darkness and Evil of the world. It becomes interesting in this regard, therefore, to consider that Donald was born on the night of a total lunar eclipse, on 14th June 1946, that his mother's name was Mary, and that his father, Fred, had the middle name of Christ. (The original family name in the German was Drumpft before it was Anglicised to Trump.) After he was dumped from Twitter in the midst of a big-tech media backlash against him in early 2021, many suspected that Donald had returned to the platform under a new account, using the name John Barron.

Meanwhile—back with music—the lyrics to '*Say It Ain't So, Joe,*' the 1975 single from British actor and singer **Murray Head** make for interesting reading when placed in the context of the 2020 US election. This surely is that rarest of phenomena, "a coincidence." Yet nevertheless . . . Head said of the song in 1994:

> *"Say It Ain't So, Joe" was provoked by a seventies documentary on Richard Nixon prior to his resignation. The presenter was asking the editor of a small town newspaper outside Washington, how, in the face of conclusive evidence and proof, his readers could still show such undying support for the president they elected . . . The song is about heroes and their 'clay feet'. It is also a plea from myself to the kind of 'Joe Public' who, in fear of losing face, refuse to relinquish their faith in a fallen idol."*

Considering "Joe" to be a reference to Joe Biden, and with the word "trump" cropping up, at a stretch it could be considered that Head was foreshadowing events 45 years ahead of time.

> *"Say it ain't so, Joe, Joe please.*
> *Say it ain't so.*
> *That's not what I want to hear, Joe,*
> *And I've got a right to know.*

They told us that our hero has played his trump card.
He doesn't know how to go on.
We're clinging to his charm.
And determined smile.
But the good old days are gone.
The image and the empire may be falling apart.
The money has gotten scarce.
One man's word held the country together,
But the truth is getting fierce."

It doesn't stop there. The lyrics to **David Bowie**'s song *'Saviour Machine'* from *'The Man Who Sold The World'* album also raise some eyebrows when placed in a 2021 context:

"President Joe once had a dream,
The world held his hand, gave their pledge.
So he told them his scheme for a Saviour Machine.
They called it the Prayer, its answer was law."
Then later:
"A plague seems quite feasible now
Or maybe a war
Or I may kill you all"
"Don't let me stay, don't let me stay.
My logic says burn, so send me away."

Upon assembling all of the above, I was reminded of the opening monologue from Paul Thomas Anderson's fascinating movie *'Magnolia'* where the narrator, Ricky Jay, states:

"It is in the humble opinion of this narrator that this is not just 'something that happened.' This cannot be 'one of those things.' This, please, cannot be that. And for what I would like to say, I can't. This was not 'just a matter of chance.' . . .
"These strange things happen all the time."

Resources:

Lyrics to David Bowie's 'Saviour Machine':

* https://genius.com/David-bowie-saviour-machine-lyrics

CHAPTER 7

SOUND BITES, PART 3

"I wonder to myself,
Will life ever be sane again?"
The Smiths: 'Panic'

"Whenever the people need a hero we shall supply him."
Albert Pike, 33rd Degree Mason

It can be difficult to accept that any scene which produces art of a quality and finesse that genuinely uplifts the soul could in any way be contrived, or part of some larger, more nefarious agenda. Vigilant research and maturity of mind teaches us that this can indeed be the case, however. Such examples abound in the movie world; *'Schindler's List'* contains some of the most emotive scenes in movie history, for example (I relate so much to the ending where Schindler's assistant Stern tells him he did so much, yet Schindler himself laments not doing more, as this is how I always feel myself about my own output,) yet was clearly a propaganda vehicle from director Steven Spielberg to reinforce the official accounts of the Jewish Holocaust when so much evidence has come to light in recent years to challenge that accepted narrative. And that's before getting into the frequent allegations of paedophilia against Spielberg himself, most notably in an essay from *'Back To The Future'* actor Crispin Glover.

Along similar lines, you'd be hard-pressed to find any monologue more moving than Charlie Chaplin's (KBE) speech on morality and Right Action in his magnum opus *'The Great Dictator.'* Yet we have to somehow reconcile this with his proclivity towards sexual relations with underage girls, most famously with Lita Grey whom he made pregnant when she was 15, before marrying her some months afterwards.

Which brings us to Philadelphia International Records, the label set up in 1971 by songwriters and producers Kenny Gamble and Leon

Huff, alongside their producer and musician partner Thom Bell. Over the next few years the trio were the masterminds behind some of the most celebrated records in soul music. The highly distinctive "sound of Philadelphia" which they pioneered largely added a disco tinge to their soulful output, producing critically-acclaimed hits for the likes of **The Three Degrees, The O'Jays, Harold Melvin & The Bluenotes, Thelma Houston, Billy Paul, Teddy Pendergrass, Lou Rawls** and **The Intruders**.

It's not that there was anything nefarious about Gamble and Huff themselves—at least not that I've been able to find—the pair having met through being jobbing musicians in the 1960s. They seem to have been sincere and well-meaning in putting out the music that they did. The circumstances in which their label really made its presence felt, however, is where the dubious input of both the Columbia Records Group and music industry mogul Clive Davis come in.

By the early 1970s, having viewed the success of rival labels like Motown, Stax and Atlantic, Columbia (later absorbed into the Sony corporation) decided that it wanted to harness the lucrative black music market. Though this scene was populated largely by black musicians, a large part of the consumer demographic consisted of middle-class white people with plenty of disposable income.

With little experience of black music culture, the Columbia executives commissioned a study into the likely requirements for a black music subsidiary of their own to succeed. With money no object, the corporation approached the Business School subsidiary of the ivy-league Harvard University to thoroughly research the scene they wished to penetrate. The highly scholarly result passed into legend as "The Harvard Report," officially known as *A Study of the Soul Music Environment*, and recommended that Columbia establish a subsidiary specifically dedicated to the soul music genre. With Gamble & Huff's Philadelphia International Records imprint already on board, this was the vehicle through which Columbia sought to exploit the market.

Columbia/ Sony, as anyone who has read *'Musical Truth Volume 1'* will know, has previous when it comes to dubious business practices and—possibly—a hand in the premature demise of some of its key artists, **Michael Jackson** being the most obvious. Serving as an executive for Sony at the time, meanwhile, was veteran music industry mogul Clive Davis, now most infamous for his suspect behaviour at the time of **Whitney Houston**'s death in 2012. As of 2007 Sony Music Entertainment has owned all rights to the Philadelphia International Records catalogue.

The music world became a far better place as a result of the glorious output from Philadelphia. I include this story only to highlight the cynical background to its success, and the master label's interest only in financial gain and societal exploitation. This is far from an isolated example of white-run corporations seeking to financially and culturally exploit the black soul music scene, however, as we will see from our next story.

*

Though all genres show evidence of having been infiltrated and manipulated, the black music scene in particular appears to have been in the crosshairs of the industry's sick controllers more than most others. This possibly speaks to the contempt that the "elites" have always held for people of colour and their associated cultures. Leaving aside the rap and hip-hop scene, covered at length in this book's first volume, the body count among soul music's artists—particularly those whose songs espoused messages of love and unity—is way higher than could be reasonably attributed to random chance or happenstance. The casualty rate also appears to be perversely out of all proportion when it comes to artists who attempted to stand up to their record companies and take steps towards reclaiming their rightful song royalties and publishing fees. Enter **James Brown, Sam Cooke** and **Otis Redding.**

According to multiple accounts this trio, already dismayed at the manipulative and unjust behaviour of their respective record labels, made moves in the 1960s towards forming their own publishing company to handle all royalty payments from their songs, and to gain ownership of the master tapes of their own recordings. News of this evidently leaked back to the Industry Machine, and it resulted in the violent and premature demises of both Cooke and Redding as a devastating warning to any others in the industry who may have had similar ideas.

Sam Cooke is said to have been shot to death by Bertha Franklin, the manager of a Los Angeles motel, on 11th December 1964. The official story is that he had been at a restaurant earlier that night, where he had been drinking heavily and had met a young woman, Elisa Boyer, (named as 'Lisa' in some reports.) The pair then went to the motel. According to Boyer, Cooke had taken her to the motel against her will, and when he had started to molest her she feared he was going to rape her. Accordingly, she scooped up her clothing, also grabbing most of Cooke's in the process, and was able to run to the manager's office for help. When the manager took too long to reply, she fled the building. Cooke is then said to have angrily run to the manager's office, dressed only in a jacket and one shoe, forced his way in and grabbed Franklin, demanding to know where the girl had gone. A struggle ensued, in which Franklin, in self-defence, shot Cooke once in his torso, and struck him on the head with a broom.

Cooke's family and friends immediately dismissed this account of the story—even more so when the coroner's jury delivered a verdict of justifiable homicide. Although robbery was presented as one possible motive for Cooke's killing, given that he had reportedly been seen at the restaurant flashing a large amount of cash, the more widespread suspicion was that that Boyer, Franklin, and the motel's proprietor, Evelyn Carr, were complicit in a plot to have Cooke murdered. Fellow singer **Etta James** cast doubt on the official verdict when she viewed Cooke's body prior to his funeral, and wrote that his injuries were way more severe than could have been sustained at the hands of the motel manager. She noted that he had been so badly beaten that his head was nearly separated from his shoulders, his hands were broken and crushed, and his nose mangled.

There appear to be some Masonic-themed calling cards in Cooke's story. He was 33 years old at the time of his death, (33 being an important number in the degrees of Freemasonry, and the music industry being controlled by Freemasonic networks, as detailed in Volume 1.) His reportedly being dressed in just one shoe correlates with certain Masonic rituals. Researcher Ole Dammegard has detailed how, in so many recent (staged) false-flag "terror events," apparent "victims" have been pictured wearing just one shoe in an element of Masonic/ Satanic mockery of the profane masses looking on. Furthermore, Cooke is said to have burst into the manager's office and been shot at 3am, this being "the witching hour" when many dark occult rituals take place.

Some immediate suspicion fell on Cooke's manager, Allen Klein, who would later go on to handle the **Beatles'** financial affairs when they formed their Apple Corps music company, at the same time as he was managing their "rivals" the **Rolling Stones.** (The Stones later complained that Klein had withheld royalty payments, stolen the publishing rights to their songs, and neglected to pay their taxes for five years.) According to the 2019 documentary *'Lady You Shot Me: The Life and Death of Sam Cooke'*—based on the words Cooke is reported to have said after being shot by Bertha Franklin—Klein extorted all royalties from Cooke's music during the period he "managed' him. Cooke's family stated that they had received no royalties or benefits from his output, and that Klein had seen to it that these would instead go to his company. The documentary also suggested that Klein had conspired to have Cooke murdered so he himself would become the sole beneficiary of his music.

Almost three years to the day after Cooke's death, singer/ songwriter **Otis Redding**, with whom Cooke had collaborated in forming an independent music publishing company, died, along with four members of soul group **The Bar-Kays** and two others, when the light aircraft they were travelling in crashed into Lake Monona in Wisconsin. Redding was 26 years old, and his death came just three days after recording what would become his biggest hit, '*(Sittin' On) The Dock Of The Bay.*' Interestingly, fellow artist and collaborator James Brown claimed in his 1986 autobiography '*The Godfather Of Soul*' that he had warned Redding not to fly that day.

In 2015, an article posted to the naturalrecordsstudios.com website titled '*The Blues—Conspiracy or Curse?*,' cited the near-identical case of 30-year-old **Jim Croce**, noting that a plane carrying the Blues singer crashed in Louisiana and killed him and five others the day before his new song '*I Gotta Name*' was due to be released, and just a few days before his planned retirement from music. Like Redding he had performed a show shortly before boarding the plane. The article goes on to proclaim: "Far too many young musicians die in plane crashes to be a coincidence, not to mention those young musicians who died in other circumstances," and goes on to list the plethora of artists who fall into this category including, (besides Redding): **Ricky Nelson, Aaliyah, John Denver, Patsy Cline, Stevie Ray Vaughan, Ronnie VanZant**, guitarist **Steve Gaines**, vocalist **Cassie Gaines, Buddy Holly, Richie Valens, The Big Bopper, Jim Reeves** and **Harold "David" Box.** As the article observes of Jim Croce: "Not only did his death ensure that his newly-released single would be a hit, it all but guaranteed he would never be forgotten, hence securing future sales."

Cooke and Redding's legal wrangles over their publishing deals echo those made a generation later by **Michael Jackson**, **Prince** and **George Michael** against their respective labels, with all three performers ending up dead in their 50s within a few years of the clashes.

James Brown. A lifetime of service to the hand that fed him. His friends Sam Cooke and Otis Redding suffered their fates much younger.

*https://www.flickr.com/photos/heiner1947/4430588088/in/
set-72157623613839496/*

Author: Heinrich Klaffs

In 2016 James Brown's son Daryl, who himself had worked in the music industry, appeared in an interview with Sean Stone, the son of movie director Oliver Stone. Two years previous, Daryl had published a book, '*Inside The Godfather.*' The same year the biopic '*Get On Up*' had been released, with Chadwick Boseman starring as James Brown. In the interview Daryl related the story of how his father had planned with Sam Cooke and Otis Redding to break away from the majors and create a distribution company of their own, and how this had resulted in Cooke and Redding's deaths. The parties responsible, Daryl claimed, had decided that his father was worth more to them alive than dead, so he was the only one of the three to survive. Sure enough, James Brown went on to put in another four decades' worth of service to his overlords. It's not for nothing that he became dubbed "the hardest-working man in showbusiness."

Daryl referenced the fable of "The Crossroads" as attributed to the legend of Blues singer **Robert Johnson**, and the concept of "selling your soul for fame and fortune." "When you look at the industry today, it's very demonic," Daryl observed, "the way they place things. It just doesn't make any sense." He went on to acknowledge that his father had indeed sold his soul in exchange for his continued success, and that he became a major money-making asset of the Industry Machine. Daryl stated that to the industry, artists are "like Barbie and Ken—they're commodities." James had reportedly admitted openly that he had "gone to the crossroads."

This idea was reinforced by a short film commissioned for BMW in 2002 and directed by Tony Scott, brother of prolific director Ridley, who served as an Executive Producer. In it, a young James Brown is seen, Robert Johnson-like, at a remote desert crossroads. The caption advises that this is November 1954, the time when James, then 21, supposedly made his deal with the industry. Modern-day James' voiceover says, "I traded sunrise for sunset, that's what I did. If I knew then what I know now . . . nah . . . Darkness is death's ignorance and the devil's time."

The film then fast-forwards to November 2002, where an ageing James is taken by his driver, played by actor Clive Owen, to a hotel named "Crossroads." Once inside he attends a meeting with an eccentric 'Prince of Darkness,' or 'the Devil,' played by actor Gary Oldman. James tells the Devil, "I want to renegotiate my contract." The Devil replies, "our deal was your soul for fame and fortune. Didn't I deliver?" James responds, "Yes. But the ageing process . . . we didn't address it. I can't do the splits any more...Our original deal no longer stands. The ageing process has lessened my ability to perform...I can't maintain my fame and fortune."

James then proposes a new deal—another soul for another 50 years, as he offers up his driver. The film goes on to show a drag race along the Las Vegas strip and out into the desert between James and Clive Owen, and The Devil and his driver, (hence the BMW relevance.) James and Clive win the race with Oldman's car going up in flames as it's struck by a speeding train. At the end of the film, however, Oldman is seen to have survived and gets a visit from dark occultist and Church of Satan member Marilyn Manson, of whom the Devil says "he spooks me out." Ten years after directing the short film Tony Scott died of apparent suicide after jumping from a bridge in Los Angeles.

Elsewhere in the Sean Stone interview, Daryl Brown expressed the view that Otis Redding was actually beaten to death, rather than having died in the plane crash. This claim was reinforced by researcher Yash Qaraah in his 2016 YouTube video *'The Music Industry (The Honest Truth.)'* Daryl also claimed that the death of his older brother Teddy, who was James Brown's first-born son, did not occur from a car crash as official accounts had always claimed, but that he was in fact sacrificed as further "payment" for James' continued engineered success. In his book Daryl writes that Teddy was actually shot "Gangland-style" before the car crashed. The sacrifice of first-born children in exchange for career success is a theme which has cropped up endlessly in conspiracy research, and was examined at length in the first *'Musical Truth.'*

James Brown eventually died on Christmas Day of 2006 at the age of 73, meaning that he, Cooke and Redding all passed away in the month of December. The official cause of death was given as congestive heart failure resulting from complications of pneumonia after he had been hospitalised in Atlanta. Daryl, however, does not accept the official claims, instead suspecting that his father was poisoned. The claim that Brown was murdered goes way beyond only Daryl's personal opinion; in 2019 an investigation by TV network CNN and other journalists caused more than a dozen people to call for a new inquiry into both Brown's death and that of his third wife Adrienne. Marvin Crawford, the doctor who signed Brown's death certificate, told CNN he had suspicions over the swiftness of his deterioration, stating: "He changed too fast. He was a patient I would never have predicted would have coded... But he died that night, and I did raise that question: What went wrong in that room?"

Crawford added that a nurse had told him drug residue was found in a tube helping Brown to breathe, and said "somebody perhaps could have given him an illicit substance that led to his death." Daryl Brown stated that his father's skin had turned grey, consistent with the idea that he had been poisoned. (Black comedian and political activist Dick Gregory, who first presented the legendary Zapruder Film of the JFK assassination to the American public in 1975, is said to have died in very similar circumstances to Brown in hospital in 2017, leading some to suspect similar foul play.)

Among others to have alleged that Brown was murdered are his friend the Reverend Al Sharpton, Brown's fourth wife Tomi Rae, his manager Frank Copsidas, and his daughter LaRhonda Pettit and son-in-law Darren Lumar, both of whom have since died. LaRhonda had made the claim that her father's body had gone missing from the crypt where it was being held, in order to prevent any opportunity for a post-mortem to prove he was murdered. Brown's son-in-law, Darren "Chip" Lumar, told Atlanta news outlet CBS 46 that James Brown had been murdered. In 2008, Lumar was shot dead in the garage of his Atlanta home. Police said they suspected the incident to be a contract killing.

Charles Bobbit, his long-time friend and personal manager, was reportedly at Brown's bedside when he died. Michael Jackson is said to have remained there for two hours afterwards. Jackson and Brown were close friends. Jackson had adopted Brown as something of a father figure given the abuse and manipulation he suffered at the hands of his biological father, Joe. Jackson learned many of his dance steps and performance techniques from Brown. Daryl says, "everything he did was because of what my father taught him," and that both Brown and Jackson had talked of "getting out" of the industry before they died.

Brown died exactly ten years before George Michael, who turned up dead on Christmas Day 2016. (See 'Musical Truth 2' for a thorough examination of this case.) In a never-ending labyrinth of curiosities and "coincidences," George's birthday was 25th June, the date on which

Sony label-mate Michael Jackson turned up dead in 2009. 25th June is said to be celebrated as 'anti-Christmas' by certain Satanic groups, marking the beginning of the sun's decline from its highest to lowest point in the sky (in the Northern Hemisphere,) whereas conventional Christmas celebrates the opposite.

Incidentally, Charlie Chaplin died on Christmas Day (of 1977,) as did, from the music world, Rat Pack member **Dean Martin** in 1995 and **Eartha Kitt**, (famous for the song '*Santa Baby*') in 2008, while those born on Christmas Day include The Pogues' **Shane MacGowan**, **Annie Lennox** and **Dido**.

*

The soul/ R&B music world seems to have had a particularly raw deal when it comes to the early departures of so many of its prominent performers from one cause of death or another, (eclipsed only by the insanely high body count in another expression of black music culture—the world of hip-hop.) **Aaliyah, Tammi Terell** and **Lisa 'Left Eye' Lopes (TLC)** were all dead by the age of 30, **Minnie Riperton** only made 31, **John Coltrane, Donny Hathaway, Charlie Parker,** (see below,) **William Powell (O Jays)** and **Paul Williams (Temptations)** by the age of 40, **Gwen Guthrie, Whitney Houston, Charmayne 'Maxee' Maxwell (Brownstone,) Sylvester, Billie Holliday, Jackie Wilson, Phyllis Hyman, Sharon Redd** and **Bernard Edwards (Chic)** before the age of 50, **Barry White, Curtis Mayfield, Michael Jackson, Prince, Teena Marie, George Michael, Harold Melvin, David Peaston, Dave Prater (Sam & Dave,) Harold Melvin, Teddy Pendergrass** and **Eddie Kendricks (Temptations)** all died in their 50s. **Isaac Hayes, Donna Summer** and **Gil Scott-Heron** were gone by the age of 65.

Would the casualty list be this high—proportionately speaking—in any regular work, I wonder? Say, in the fields of lawyers, lorry drivers or supermarket cashiers? Given that some of the artists above died of apparent drug overdoses it could be argued that this aspect of artistic life determines a higher body count than that of other professions. But even so, there are some real tragedies within soul music's ranks. Aaliyah was killed in a plane crash aged only 22. **Mel Appleby**, one half of the 1980s pop/ dance duo Mel & Kim, was dead from a form of cancer by 23. **Tammi Terrell** was only two years older when she succumbed to brain cancer after a devastating illness. Terrell's singing partner, **Marvin Gaye**, after becoming a purveyor of conscious protest songs, was shot dead by his own father one day shy of his 45th birthday. **Teddy Pendergrass** was left paralysed from the waist down after a car crash in 1982, in which his car is suspected to have been tampered with. (There are allegations that Pendergrass became unwittingly entangled in mafia/ organised crime wars within the music industry.

Another such tragedy is that of **Donny Hathaway.** The official line is that he committed suicide on 13th January 1979 by jumping from the 15th-floor balcony of his New York hotel room. He was 33 years old. His "suicide" is said to have occurred following severe bouts of depression and erratic behaviour. He had been diagnosed with paranoid schizophrenia eight years earlier. It is reported that between 1973 and 1977, Hathaway's mental instability necessitated several hospitalisations, (in New York City, a hotbed of MK-Ultra mind-control activity rather than in his native Chicago,) and placed extreme strain on his home life and recording career.

Anyone who has researched the true nature of the music industry and the fates of many of its artists will immediately notice some red flags hinting at the possible presence of mind-control programming. Unconventional, and particularly paranoid behaviour—Hathaway had told producer **James Mtume** shortly before his death that white people were trying to kill him and wanted to wire up his brain to a machine so as to steal his creative output—often identifies mind-control subjects, as does severe depression as the victim's mind attempts to deal with the multiple personality dissociation which the programmers have induced. Fans of Hathaway have questioned how a man who made songs such as '*Thank You Master (For My Soul,)*' and was clearly a man of faith, would elect to end his own life.

Hathaway was also said to possess almost supernatural spiritual qualities. According to a blog article titled '*Donny, The 1st Movement*' on the Mind Control Black Assassins website:

"Donny was very, very special. He was "paranormal." Donny was a brilliant musician, arranger, songwriter and vocalist...He was exploring melodies, soft and elegant voices. He talked about exploring classical music and "melodic" patterns and motions, repetitive patterns that can be used with any scale. The use and practice of "melodic" patterns go back to the dawn of civilization, the Lands of Sumer and Kemet.

"...He was able to recapture some of the mysterious ancient "melodic" patterns surviving in Africa/ Black spiritual gospel music, and in silky smooth eloquence incorporate it in our everyday lives and struggles. They say that Donny literally sat in the studio and cried when he heard the playback of his final mix of the song 'Someday We'll All Be Free.'

According to musician/ producer **Reggie Lucas**, who was present at Hathaway's final recording session with James Mtume, Hathaway was accompanied everywhere by David McCoy Franklin, an attorney with political connections employed by Hathaway's record label, Atlantic, (plus a handler?) Lucas had said that Hathaway appeared heavily drugged on the evening of his death.

The writer of the Black Assassins article concludes:

"But we are now quite certain that the technology existed then, and the white knights of the CIA were very, very active in that very same thing—the paranormal, psychotronics, and mind-control, clandestinely. And we know somebody had taken complete control over Donny's mind and thoughts at the time of his death. He talked too much, and they threw Donny Hathaway out of the window.

"Donny's death was consistent with the CIA Assassination Manual. His death was primarily meant to not only permanently silence him, but also send a terrifying message to others to keep their mouths shut about Donny, "white people" and "psychotronic mind machines."

It turns out that the hotel from which Hathaway is said to have leapt to his death, New York's Essex House Hotel—on an adjacent side of Central Park to the Dakota Building in which the Satanic Ritual Abuse-depicting 'Rosemary's Baby' was set—has a reputation for being something of an MK-Ultra safe house, (rather like Manhattan's Chelsea Hotel, detailed at length in the previous 'Musical Truth.') Early on in 'Rosemary's Baby' a young woman falls to her death from the Dakota in suspicious circumstances. The glass from Hathaway's hotel window had been carefully removed—a specialist operation—and placed on the bed. The Essex was owned by hoteling tycoon J. Willard Marriott who was extremely well-connected to the CIA and other Government departments, as well as being a Freemason, (Anyone surprised?) Marriott was a board member of the Mayo Clinic, one of the key hospitals involved in the CIA's MK-Ultra mind-control experimentation. The Essex was the place in town where visiting Washington DC officials regularly stayed.

As in all areas of research, one or two apparent "coincidences" or nefarious connections could be written off. But when several come together, and patterns and trends that have been seen many times before emerge, other conclusions can reasonably be drawn. And so, all the evidence points to Donny Hathaway having been yet another music industry mind-control subject who seemingly outlived his usefulness to his controllers, and so was "suicided" away.

*

Black/ "urban" music fans received two jarring reminders within days of each-other in September 2021, of just why it's a mistake to have *any* kind of role models or "heroes" in the public eye. These people are *not* our friends, they're *not* there to enrich our lives in any way—quite the opposite in most cases—and we never *really* know who they are. But occasionally we get a few clues.

The most high-profile of the two examples was Robert Sylvester Kelly, better known by his artist name of **R. Kelly**. As both a singer and a producer Kelly enjoyed great success through the 1990s and early 2000s, attracting the reverence of fans who appreciated his fusion of soulful R&B, with nuances borrowed from the worlds of hip-hop and reggae. He also courted mainstream appeal through radio-friendly songs like 'I Believe I Can Fly' and 'Ignition.'

Allegations of sexual improprieties dogged his career almost from the start, however, the most infamous being his illegal marriage to singer **Aaliyah** when she was just 15 years old. This was later annulled, and Aaliyah died in a plane crash in the Bahamas a few years later. The accusations continued, including one high-profile claim that he had video-taped himself urinating on an underage girl. Despite these claims leaking into the mainstream from time to time, Kelly always seemed to avoid legal action suggesting that he might be protected by friends in high places.

By the time the claims that he was effectively running a "harem" and a kind of mind-control sex cult had emerged, however, it seems the tsunami of controversy could no longer be held back—particularly upon the airing of the cable television documentary *'Surviving R. Kelly'* in January 2019, in which several women alleged sexual abuse at his hands. The series resulted in Kelly's record label, RCA, severing his contract, and caused many artists with whom he had previously collaborated, such as **Lady Gaga**, to renounce their affiliations and remove their works from streaming services. (I just *love* the irony of someone like Lady Gaga feigning morality and decency, given her track record of pushing Satanism to her teenage fans!)

Kelly's eventual trial involved nine charges of sex trafficking, saw eleven accusers—nine women and two men—describe sexual humiliation and violence over a prolonged period of more than 20 years, and saw him face spending the rest of his life in jail. A guilty charge of racketeering joined a further eight of sex trafficking. The court heard how managers, security guards and other entourage members worked to assist him in his criminal enterprise.

The charges were almost identical in nature to those levelled against another musical pioneer. This book's previous volume detailed the claims of sexual molestation against **Afrika Bambaataa**, consistently worshipped as one of the three "founding fathers" of hip-hop culture. These came from two male former members of the Universal Zulu Nation organisation which Bambaataa had founded, who claimed he had forced himself on them sexually when they were still minors. Despite the story being thoroughly documented by investigative journalist Leila Wills of Chicago's *'Metropolis'* newspaper, there was a complete blackout from the mainstream press, with even those publications specialising in the genre of Hip-Hop and its associated cultures opting not to touch it.

In the podcast interview that we recorded together in 2016, Leila and I asked why this should be, at a time when prominent celebrities such as Harvey Weinstein, Bill Cosby and Kevin Spacey were getting "outed" as sex pests as part of the hysteria whipped up by the "Me Too" movement. We speculated on whether Bambaataa could have been receiving immunity from on-high, given that a pioneer of any cultural movement being doubly accused of sexually abusing minors would constitute headline news under normal circumstances. Leila's investigations for her documentary 'TRAPped In A CULTure' revealed that Bambaataa's real name was *not* Kevin Donovan, as had been reported in his official biographies for years, but was in fact Lance Taylor. One of the interviewees for the film, the Zulu Nation's one-time Minister of Information known as TC Izlam, was shot dead on an Atlanta street a short while after giving his testimony about Bambaataa's penchant for paedophilia and its covering-up by certain elements within the organisation.

It seems these were far from isolated incidents, however; some months later, 'Metropolis' broke the story of a lawsuit being issued against Bambaataa in New York's Bronx Supreme Court, claiming he had sexually abused and repeatedly trafficked a 12-year-old boy for sex with other men. His accuser had taken advantage of a one-year window during which alleged victims of historic sexual abuse could make their claims outside of the normal Statute of Limitations which would otherwise have barred them upon their 22nd birthday. The lawsuit claimed that one of the locations at which the abuse took place was Bambaataa's Bronx River apartment, which doubled as the headquarters for the Zulu Nation.

As 'Metropolis' reported of the case:

> "According to several alleged victims, Afrika Bambaataa considered himself an intergalactic being who had to protect himself from wicked forces. He put tape over his VCR and Betamax to prevent Big Brother from spying on him, and believed all phones were tapped. A New World Order would soon be here, and Bambaataa believed he gained superpowers by swallowing the semen of young boys.

His song, 'Planet Rock,' perfectly emulated his world; aliens, hip-hop, and rock (sex). His apartment was a mix of an office and an LSD trip. On the walls were images of spaceships. Vinyl records strewn all over the floor and photo albums of naked male Zulu Nation members and naked New York DJs were always in close reach. Gay and heterosexual porn played often on his floor model television."

Together, the Kelly and Bambaataa stories cast unhappy and unsettling overtones on not just these two previously lauded "heroes," but on the genres they pioneered, and the entire corporate industry machine. Many questions emerge; How is it possible they got away with these crimes for so long? Why did the media stay silent on these stories until the weight of evidence had become so strong that it could no longer be held back? What is the true nature of an industry in which incidents such as these—very far from isolated—can continually occur? What is the true nature of an industry which attracts—or breeds—characters of this nature?

*

Occasionally, the most unexpected candidates emerge to—in all apparent sincerity—expose the true nature of the industry of which they're a part. Actor Randy Quaid went public a few years ago with his claims of "star-whacking"—the idea that the dark controllers of Hollywood take out one of their own from time to time, either as a way of getting rid of "loose cannons" who have become a liability, or in line with their twisted religious rituals. He highlighted David Carradine and Heath Ledger as examples of this phenomenon. I don't know if anyone has noticed, but Randy's career hasn't exactly sky-rocketed since making those comments. He and his wife Evi have been in trouble with the US and Canadian authorities over various felony, trespass and vandalism charges. In 2020, Quaid claimed that the outcome of the US election, in which Joe Biden is *said* to have beaten Donald Trump, was fraudulent and the vote clearly stolen. (It was, as multiple damning evidence—tellingly rejected by the US Supreme Court—proves.)

Mel Gibson is another big name to have blown the whistle on — in his case — the mindblowing scale on which institutionalised paedophilia is endemic in Hollywood (Similarly, Mel's output of late has been a little lacking, Funny, that?)

In the music industry, however, the position of most unlikely whistle-blower and activist has gone to **Brian Harvey**, the former lead singer with the pop/ R&B band **East 17**. During that group's peak in the 1990s, Harvey evidently lived the high life that most stars of his prominence do. He had apparently struggled with depression and mental illness through his adult life, however, and these conditions became exacerbated as the group's short-lived success began to wane.

Controversy has never been far from Brian Harvey. He was sacked from East 17 in 1997 after endorsing the use of MDMA/ Ecstasy in an interview. His chances of remaining in the group became practically zero when the matter was addressed in a Prime Minister's Question Time session in Parliament. Harvey claims that he was set up by a journalist, in collusion with the rest of the band and their manager, and that he was coerced into making the comments in order to justify his planned removal. He had already received a police caution for the possession of cannabis four years earlier. The year after the Ecstasy incident he was convicted of assaulting a press photographer outside a London nightclub and fined £1,000. In 2001, he himself fell foul of an assault outside a nightclub when he was left needing surgery after being attacked by a man wielding a machete. That year, his five-year marriage to dancer Tash Carnegie, with whom he had a daughter, came to an acrimonious end, and Harvey announced that he was quitting the music business. He was later jailed for 56 days after breaching an injunction taken out by his estranged wife.

In 2005, Harvey was involved in a bizarre incident where he was hospitalised after being crushed under the wheels of his own Mercedes. It was speculated by the mainstream press that this constituted a suicide attempt, though Harvey later gave the improbable explanation that he had felt ill after eating a load of jacket potatoes, and fell from the car when he had opened the door to be sick.

Not even these events constituted Harvey's most extreme brushes with controversy, however. In more recent years, he has used his YouTube channels to make consistent references to the child sexual abuse that he says is rampant within the music industry. In 2014, he turned up at London's Downing Street and demanded to speak to then-Prime Minister David Cameron. Some months later he received an audience with Labour MP Simon Danczuk. The MP later called for an inquiry into allegations of child sexual abuse within the industry, commenting:

> *"He feels quite passionately about protecting children and really wants to make a contribution. We know that showbusiness is an industry that's had a number of abusers within it. He's providing a number of leads that I'm keen to follow up and that's exactly what I'll do. I'm pleased he's done the work he's done."*

Harvey's claims got the attention of multiple mainstream media outlets when, in January 2015, he posted a video of himself, titled '*Fuck The Industry 2*,' in which he is seen in an alleyway holding the plaque he had received to mark East 17's debut album, '*Walthamstow*,' achieving a million sales. Turning to the camera to say: "East 17, one million sales—here's what it fucking means," he proceeds to smash the plaque violently against a bin. As he walks away he says, "that's what I think of your fucking music industry." The caption accompanying the video reads:

> *"This is what I think of you all. Fuck your record industry, and fuck your weird paedophile world. Fuck you."*

And added was the message:

> *"One day you will all understand, but for now you can call me mad, nut job, loser, has-been, whatever. But when you find out what's really been going on, I want you all to ask yourself if you could take it??? Love to all victims who are never heard out there. I'll be your voice."*

By early 2021, Harvey had released a multitude of videos, in some becoming visibly distressed and apparently suffering mental breakdowns. He has repeatedly told an anecdote of having been taken to Browns in the early 1990s, a "gentleman's club" in Shoreditch, London, by former '*Eastenders*' actress Danniella Westbrook, with whom he was in a relationship at the time. Westbrook has said that she herself was groomed and sexually abused as a child, and that it was through this process that she "got my fame."

Harvey says she took him to the manager's office in the club, in which there was a concealed doorway controlled by a lever which gave access to a warren of secret upstairs rooms, all decked out in red decor with red lighting. There, Harvey says he saw a young woman in an intimate setting with a man but that upon glancing at her, something struck him as strange about her exposed stockinged knee. He later realised, he says, this it was too small to have been the knee of an adult, and that she must have been a child. He also says he remembers seeing a young boy in an adult's suit with four adults around him, and that drugs were being sold from the upstairs room.

Harvey has spoken of how the image of the girl has haunted him, how it was the igniting spark that began his unwitting exposure to the ugly side of the industry, and how Westbrook's having taken him there had ruined his life and singled him out for ongoing surveillance and harrassment. In early 2021, he also claimed that he had seen Ghislaine Maxwell in the club that night. Maxwell is the daughter of media mogul (and Israeli Mossad spy) Robert Maxwell, and the former partner of convicted paedophile and child sex trafficking fixer to the rich and famous, Jeffrey Epstein. (Robert Maxwell disappeared off his yacht in 1991 in what was a suspected murder. Epstein is said to have killed himself in his cell after being arrested in 2019. The phrase 'Jeffrey Epstein didn't kill himself" subsequently became one of the most popular memes on the internet. Ghislaine Maxwell was herself arrested in July 2020, accused of procuring and sexually trafficking underage girls.) Harvey has accused Westbrook of having set him up by taking him to the club, and of working in collusion with MI5 and Special Branch police, addressing her by saying "you're in with the Establishment. You're in with people."

Harvey's claims have been extremely hard to follow as he fails to present his points in chronological order or in any coherent fashion, and frequently becomes distracted and side-tracked. Piecing together his haphazard claims, however, he has stated that he has been targeted out of fear that he knows too much about paedophilia in the music industry's upper levels, and involving some very prominent names. Those that he has called out have included former band manager turned TV executive **Simon Cowell**, and former manager of **The Pet Shop Boys, Bros**, and **East 17**, **Tom Watkins**, (who died in February 2020, aged 70 after some years of illness.) In a February 2021 live-streamed video, Harvey claimed that Watkins frequently sent Danniella Westbrook and TV presenter Dani Behr out to buy tampons for his rectum "because he's been fucking pummelled like a cunt." (I know readers will be grateful for that image.) This video was titled '*There's A Price on my Head Right Now... Ghislaine!*' Midway through, Harvey breaks down in tears and is rendered speechless for several minutes.

(Simon Cowell stumped up £50,000 of the £150,000 bail money for **Jonathan King** when King was first jailed for sex offences against young boys. Cowell's publicist, Max Clifford, (who also managed Danniella Westbrook,) is said to have been angered by Cowell's actions and subsequently "set him straight about what kind of man King is." I guess he was in a position to know, since Clifford himself was sentenced to eight years' imprisonment after being found guilty of indecent assault against several girls and young women. Clifford died in prison, aged 74.)

In the ugly, tangled web of vice and depravity, Harvey has accused campaigner Bill Maloney of Pie N Mash Films, of being a plant for the intelligence services, and serving as a gatekeeper to prevent revelations of child sex abuse at the hands of prominent people becoming public knowledge. Harvey has said that at first he offered to work alongside Maloney, (who says he himself was abused as a young boy in social care) in producing his films, before coming to realise Maloney's true malevolent nature. Harvey has claimed that Maloney sought to undermine and derail the Operation Yewtree enquiry into Establishment paedophilia launched in the wake of BBC asset Jimmy Savile's exposure as a serial child abuser. Harvey has also claimed that a friend of his in whom he had confided, ended up getting murdered.

Other names Harvey has called out include the Queen, Prince Andrew, former Metropolitan police Vice Squad officer Jon Wedger, activist John Harris, (since deceased,) plumber-turned-activist Ian Puddick, and podcast host Shaun Attwood, along with several other well-known names within the "Truth"/ "alternative" media as being shills and insiders. He has alleged collusion in the plot against him from several newspapers, including the '*News of the World,*' which he claims illegally hacked his phone in the 1990s. An investigator working for the newspaper was later accused of having hacked the phone of murdered schoolgirl Millie Dowler, leading to the closure of '*News of the World*' after 168 years. Harvey has consistently claimed that the security services intend to kill him and has spoken of having a price on his head and of being a "dead man walking."

In 2017, Harvey returned to music-making to get his message across. In a track titled '*You'll Never Stop Me,*' (later re-released under the title '*Checkmate,*') and referencing the "Pizzagate" scandal of 2017 which alleged institutionalised paedophilia within the American political establishment, he raps:

> "*If you're gay, then you're gay. Don't pretend to be straight. You're a dirty politician who fucks kids every day. You're not an authority, I ain't got no respect for you, mate. Take a trip to Comet Pizza, have a slice at the gate.*
>
> "*...I can't believe this is what I'm finding out now. Calling out the industry, a madman.*"

A possible clue to the connectedness between the various strands of this bewilderingly complex story—and a potential insight into to how all its allegations have avoided the glare of the public through exposure in the mainstream media—comes from the image which accompanies the video as it appears on YouTube.

It shows the twin pillars of Freemasonry, Jachin and Boaz, along with a Masonic square and compass and two gavels and a trowel. An all-seeing eye appears above the image of two hands gripped in a secret Masonic handshake.

*

An alarmingly high number of music artists have claimed to have suffered sexual abuse as children—way beyond the rate that might reasonably be expected in other walks of life. In a 2021 HBO documentary on **Alanis Morrissette**, for example, she claimed that she was raped by multiple men when she was 15, (though she neglects to name them) just as her music career was beginning.

Their number also includes **Terry Hall**, frontman of the Two Tone/ska group **The Specials**, and later **Fun Boy Three** and **The Colourfield.**

In a 2019 interview in front of a live audience as part of Richard Herring's Leicester Square Theatre podcast, and reported on by '*The Sun*' newspaper in an article titled '*Pop Star's Paedo Ordeal*,' Hall revealed that he was abducted and abused for four days by a paedophile gang in France when aged 12, and had suffered years of depression and anxiety as a result. Herring neglected to push him for further details, though the incident appears to have been addressed many years earlier in the lyrics to the Fun Boy Three single '*Well Fancy That*,' which alleges abuse at the hands of a teacher. The song begins:

> "*You took me to France, on the promise of teaching me French.*
> *We were told, to assemble, to meet up at 10,*
> *I was 12 and naïve.*"
>
> *and later:*
> "*If I could have read, what was going on inside your head,*
> *I would have said, that I was blind to your devious mind,*
> *There's no excuse, but your abuse, and the scars that it leaves,*
> *Where do you draw the line?*
> *On school trips to France,*
> *Well, fancy that,*
> *You had a good time,*
> *Turned sex into crime,*
> *Well, fancy that.*"

The most shocking aspects of Hall's recollections were when he said they he could "laugh about it now" and that, "you know, going back to my abduction, it's like you can let that eat away at you, but then, well, you know, it's paedophilia and it's, like, part of life really."

Paedophilia certainly isn't part of life in the minds of most regular members of society. Perhaps Hall's perception of the phenomenon has been shaped by decades spent on the inside of the corporate music industry machine.

*

It's been straightforward enough to deduce the inspirations behind some of **Morrissey**'s songs; '*Last of the Famous International Playboys*' is an ode to London gangsters Ronnie and Reggie Kray, for instance, while '*Suffer Little Children*' was a devastating examination of the crimes of Moors Murderers Ian Brady and Myra Hindley. It seems **The Smiths** frontman has never shied away from controversial topics, or from addressing despised criminals.

The story behind the 1986 Smiths single '*Panic*' seemed clear-cut at the time, as the band freely offered an explanation for its "hang the DJ" refrain. Guitarist **Johnny Marr** recalled hearing a news report on BBC Radio 1 about the Chernobyl nuclear disaster in Russia, then straight afterwards DJ Steve Wright coming in with a jolly tone and introducing Wham!'s '*I'm Your Man*.' According to Marr, "I remember actually saying, 'What the fuck has this got to do with people's lives?'" Steve Wright may well be the DJ that the song had in mind, therefore.

An alternative explanation began circulating in the conspiracy world, however, in the wake of **Jimmy Savile**'s true sordid nature becoming public knowledge in late 2012. An internet rumour suggested that the song portrayed inside knowledge of Savile's crimes decades before everyone else found out, (particularly ironic considering the Smiths performed '*Panic*' on '*Top of the Pops*,' the BBC show which Savile hosted for many years.) The rumour pointed to the lyrics referencing panic on the streets of various British cities, but in particular the line "the Leeds side-streets that you slip down." Savile hailed from Leeds and maintained a property near the city's Roundhay Park. It was close to here that one of the victims of Yorkshire Ripper Peter Sutcliffe was discovered, prompting Irish researcher Thomas Sheridan to speculate that Savile may have been Sutcliffe's accomplice in some of his murders. The pair are known to have been friends, with Savile visiting Sutcliffe in prison.

The lyric "on the Leeds side-streets that you slip down" is repeated later in the song, followed by "provincial towns you jog 'round," prompting exponents of the theory to remind us that one of Savile's methods of getting close to children was to hide behind a facade of "doing a lot of great work for charity," and in particular, undertaking many fun-runs and marathons throughout the land.

Morrissey sings, "burn down the disco, hang the blessed DJ." Savile is credited with having been Britain's prototype disc-jockey, having pioneered the playing of gramophone records in dancehalls as far back as the late 1940s, where only bands had previously performed. It has been noted that he was "blessed" by The Pope amidst his various accolades. It is also suggested that of one of the song's more obscure lyrics, "hopes may rise on the Grasmere,

but, honey pie, you're not safe there," the 'honey pie' part could be a veiled reference to PIE, the controversial Paedophile Information Exchange, a platform through which child sex offenders could communicate with each-other and trade tip-offs to avoid capture, (and the use of "honey" traps.) A chorus of children join in the "hang the DJ" refrain in the song's final part, and the group featured a schoolboy on stage with them when they performed 'Panic' on the 'Eurotube' TV show.

The "Grasmere" part seems more ambiguous, though a paedophile named Paul Evans, who was convicted of a string of sex attacks against young girls in 2014, had also been convicted of sex offences resulting in a jail spell in 1990, four years after the release of 'Panic.' His address at the time of the 2014 offences was given as Grasmere Avenue, Padiham, Lancashire.

In the same way that Johnny Rotten displayed inside knowledge of Savile's crimes as far back as 1978, could Morrissey have been demonstrating the same, in an albeit oblique way, some years later? If he was, the "hang the DJ" sentiment would not have been entirely misplaced.

Jimmy Savile. Could he really have been the veiled lyrical subject of The Smiths song 'Panic'?

https://commons.wikimedia.org/wiki/File:Jimmy_Savile_PICT6249a.jpg

Source: Transferred from en.wikipedia to Commons.

Author: The original uploader was Jmb at English Wikipedia.

The odd synchronicities don't stop there, and I'm grateful to Jamie Drummond for bringing many of these to my attention. For a start it turns out Smiths guitarist Johnny Marr shares his 31st October/ Halloween birthday with Savile.

Though the main video for *'Panic'* features the group performing, there was a second promotional video created by film-maker Derek Jarman as part of his short film to accompany the release of the album *'The Queen Is Dead.'* The fast-moving black-and-white imagery from Jarman's version was super-imposed over the band's performance in what was deemed the "official" video.

Among shots of slum housing and industrial wasteland, Jarman's composition features several images of the Houses of Parliament and of Buckingham Palace, (on fire.) Could these be knowingly alluding to Savile's connections with prominent Establishment figures such as Prime Ministers Edward Heath and Margaret Thatcher, and Prince Charles? There's an image too of a spinning crown. There is no clear reason why a song ostensibly about DJs should otherwise feature images of these locations.

There is a creepy outstretched hand cropping up a few times during the video, which seems to be suggestive of a predator chasing after his prey.

Towards the end of the video there is what could be construed as a reference to necrophilia—a charge levelled at Savile—where a man is seen lovingly kissing a skull. Like the other images, this has no relevance to the surface content of the song.

When the "hang the DJ" line is first sung, there are images of very young girls shown.

The '*Queen Is Dead*' short film was shown before cinema screenings of the '*Sid and Nancy*' movie, which gives us a curious return connection to Johnny Rotten, (who, as we learned earlier, used to attend kinky sex parties in the House of Commons just along from the aforementioned Parliament.)

We get the all-too-familiar military links when it comes to Jarman, whose father was a New Zealand-born Royal Air Force officer. Jarman is said to have contracted AIDS and died of a related illness in 1994 aged 52.

The sleeve image for the '*Panic*' single was of Richard Bradford. He was an obscure American actor and the Smiths had no real reason to include his face on the cover. Are we reaching too much to wonder whether he was chosen because of Bradford's geographic proximity to Leeds, and with Savile alleged to have committed many of his crimes in Bradford?

The 1980s TV satire '*Spitting Image*' once included a sketch that featured Savile, the Smiths and Princess Diana. This doesn't tie in directly to the wider story that the Smiths themselves revealed the truth about Savile—but it does provide another public connection between the group and Savile, and it also ties in to the British Royals, as Savile is said to have been retained as a "counsellor" to Prince Charles and Princess Diana when their marriage was on the rocks. The ruse for the sketch was that a member of the public had written in to Savile's *'Jim'll Fix It'* show asking for him to play a Smiths song, but to arrange for some-one other than Morrissey to sing it. So Savile recruits Diana to sing it instead. The song turns out to be, for no apparent reason, the band's *'Heaven Knows I'm Miserable Now.'*

An odd sidenote to this is that the Smiths only ever played one con-cert on the date of Diana's death, 31st August. This was in 1986 when they performed just outside of Phoenix, Arizona. They're credited as having played just two songs in their set that night — *'Heaven Knows I'm Miserable Now,'* and *'Panic.'*

So to recap; In the early 90s, Spitting Image brought the strange combination of Morrissey, Diana and Savile together for a spoof version of *'Heaven Knows I'm Miserable Now.'* The Smiths are widely consid-ered to have revealed the truth about Savile in their single *'Panic,'* and the band performed both songs, and no others, exactly 11 years before Diana's untimely death.

Just in the interests of completism, there is an odd tie-in between The Smiths and Savile through the actor Nigel Havers. His father was a very prominent barrister, becoming Attorney General for England and Wales. In this role, Lord Havers played an important part in the trial of the aforementioned Peter Sutcliffe, the Yorkshire Ripper, to whom Savile is known to have paid frequent visits while Sutcliffe was an inmate in Broadmoor Hospital.

Nigel Havers once appeared on a TV show called *'I've Never Watched Star Wars.'* On this, he was seemingly introduced to The Smiths for the first time when the host forced Havers to listen to three Smiths songs — *'This Charming Man'* (Could the "charming" part allude to the casting of spells?,) *'How Soon Is Now'* and ... *'Heaven Knows I'm Miser-able Now.'*

Coincidentally/ synchro-mystically, Nigel Havers appeared in one of the few movies produced by Princess Diana's lover at the time of her death, Dodi Al-Fayed — the Oscar-winning *'Chariots of Fire,'* released in 1981 (and set in Paris, the city of Diana and Dodi's deaths.)

So, to recap again, the son of the man who presided over the trial of the Yorkshire Ripper appeared on a TV show being asked questions about a pop group that he claimed to know nothing about, yet are a group who have allegedly dropped the truth in their song *'Panic'* about Jimmy Savile who, in turn, has some sinister connections back to Peter Sutcliffe, whom Havers' dad helped controversially convict!

At the risk of falling too far down multiple rabbit holes—but in the interests of thoroughness—for the sleeve of their *'The Queen Is Dead'* album, The Smiths posed outside Salford Lads Club, a former sports and recreational venue established by Robert Baden-Powell, the founder of the boy scout movement. Allan Clarke and Graham Nash of the Hollies attended in their youth. Paedophilic activity is said to have occasionally occurred at the venue. It turns out that Savile had a working connection to Salford also, first arriving there in 1957 to take up the assistant manager's post at the Plaza dancehall on Oxford Road. He was back in the city to present the very first episode of *'Top Of The Pops'* in 1964 from the BBC's studios in Rusholme. In the wake of the allegations against Savile becoming public knowledge, Greater Manchester Police began investigating multiple claims that he had committed sexual abuse in Salford and Manchester during his time living there.

In the 1960s, Savile and fellow 'Sir,' Cliff Richard, (see Elm Guest House connection detailed earlier,) were known associates. With the BBC having seemingly covered up Savile's crimes for decades, a different relationship occurred between the Corporation and Cliff Richard in 2014. A police raid on the singer's Berkshire home in connection with the allegation of a historic sexual assault, was deemed inadmissible when a BBC camera crew had turned up at the house before the police had had a chance to arrive. Richard subsequently threatened to sue the BBC, (though didn't have any problem with appearing on a BBC2 programme in late 2021 documenting his early backing band The Shadows.)

And we're right back round to Morrissey again! In 2014, it was revealed that the Smiths frontman had asked—of all people—Cliff Richard to open up for him at a concert in New York on 21st June, the Summer Solstice. A more ill-fitting musical combination is hard to imagine, (although Eminem and Elton John did once perform together, come to think of it,) particularly as Richard admitted to barely knowing who Morrissey was. In the event the show was cancelled, with Morrissey later revealing he had been suffering from Barrett's oesophagus cancer and double pneumonia.

*

A contender which didn't make the selection of 1980s pop videos containing dark occult and esoteric symbolism detailed in '*Musical Truth 2*,' but which warrants a mention of its own, is the one for '*Duel*,' the 1985 hit single from the German Synth Pop/ New Wave band **Propaganda**. The group's name may carry more meaning than was originally thought. Their genre was described at the time as "Avant-pop," and one critic described the two girl, two-boy band as "like ABBA from Hell."

The video begins with singer **Claudia Brücken** stepping out of a car and crushing a red rose underfoot. Straight away the tone of the piece is set by a motif pertaining to nature and beauty being wilfully destroyed. Brücken then enters what appears to be a Chinese bar or opium den with 1930s decor, and takes a table opposite a man dressed in the garb of the time, (the band's **Michael Mertens**,) in stark contrast to Brücken's own spiky-haired punk look. These scenes are cross-cut into a dreamlike sequence, (dissociation,) in which the band are performing on a black and white checkerboard floor. Anyone who did read the section on video symbolism in the last book will not need to sit down to recover from the shock of hearing this.

An usherette arrives at the table and pops a pill into each of the pair's champagne glasses. This is where the video takes on an extremely sinister vibe. Brücken is seen falling unconscious before the viewer witnesses a young child in a nightgown walking along a corridor, traumatised as a sea of hands reach out to try and molest her. We then see the child inside a mirror frame; this quickly changes into an image of Brücken, then to an old lady, still in a nightgown, who takes the doll she is holding and smashes the mirror.

What the audience in 1985 was viewing—though virtually no-one at the time would have been aware of it as the opportunity to research such topics was completely absent then—was a depiction of lifelong Satanic Ritual Abuse (SRA) and trauma-based mind-control. Mirrors—especially smashed ones—are common images associated with the dissociation from reality that victims experience . . . as are dolls. Most undergoing the horrors of SRA do so from young childhood. In the video, Brücken's falling unconscious through being drugged, seems to be triggering deeply hidden memories of her abuse.

Next in the video, we see Brücken and Mertens having been imprisoned in a cage, being guarded by the group's **Susanne Freytag** in leather Nazi-style regalia. Mertens frees himself from his ropes, unties Brücken, and the pair overpower Freytag to get the keys to the cage. They escape along a tunnel of light and appear to have been kept captive in the basement of the opium den. As they emerge, Mertens begins duelling with one of his captors, (portrayed by the band's remaining member, **Ralf Doerper**.) Knocking him unconscious, they win their freedom.

This part seems to represent freedom from SRA being finally attained. Though most remain lifelong victims of their programming, some, (as exemplified by real-life survivors like Cathy O'Brien, Jay Parker, Jeanette Archer, Fiona Barnett and Jade Bidwell) do manage to break free of their captivity.

The video was directed by **Paul Morley**, Brücken's future husband, alongside **John Scarlett-Davis.** It's unclear whether the SRA depictions were designed to show that Brücken herself had undergone such treatment. If there had been any information available on her parents this might have offered further clues, but no such detail is to be found on-line. (She had joined her first band, Haarsträubend, aged just 14.) Morley had his own traumatising parental issues; in 2013 he co-operated with the 'Guardian' newspaper on an article examining the suicide of his father, Leslie, who had driven 140 miles south from Stockport to Stroud to kill himself. Morley revealed that his father had suffered from mental illness and depression, and that though he had held jobs with British European Airways and BP, he was never entirely sure what he did there.

The imagery in this video is cryptic and coded and would bypass the conscious mind of anyone unfamiliar with the subject matter. But there was little room for ambiguity from Propaganda's previous video for their debut single 'Dr. Mabuse,' named after a fictional character invented by writer Norbert Jacques and featured in three films by German director (and Freemason) Fritz Lang. As with 'Faust', this speaks of the legend of selling one's soul to dark forces in exchange for fame and fortune, a dynamic—either metaphorical or literal—more widespread among household-name musicians than anyone would ever dream possible. The lyrics to 'Dr. Mabuse' spell out the scenario being depicted in no uncertain terms:

> *"The man without shadow promises you the world,*
> *Tell him your dreams and fanatical needs.*
> *He's buying them all with cash.*
> *Sell him your soul, sell him your soul, sell him your soul.'*
> *Never look back, never look back."*

And:

> *"He's a Satanic gambler, but you just the fool,*
> *And you've already lost the chance of your lifetime.*
> *So don't be a fool, don't be a fool.*
> *Kein Zurück für dich, there's no way back.*
> *Sell him your soul."*

The follow-up to 'Duel,' was the distinctly Kraftwerk-esque 'P-Machinery,' whose creepy video contains hints of Transhumanism. While Brücken cavorts disturbingly with a lobster and a snake on plates, the rest of the band are depicted as marionettes having their strings pulled.

After forming in 1982, Propaganda got signed to ZTT Records, a label set up by producer **Trevor Horn** (CBE,) (best known as frontman of the group **The Buggles** of 'Video Killed The Radio Star' fame,) his wife Jill Sinclair, and the aforementioned Paul Morley. ZTT stood for "Zang Tumb Tuuum,' the title of a poem written by Italian futurist Filippo Tommaso Marinetti, and said to represent the sound made by a machine gun being fired, though the label claimed it represented the sound of a drum and cymbal being struck. 'Dr. Mabuse' was released in 1984 and Propaganda's debut album, 'A Secret Wish,' was due to follow soon after. Horn and Morley got sidetracked by the sudden runaway success of **Frankie Goes To Hollywood**, however, another group signed early to their label. FGTH dominated the UK singles charts through 1984 with their singles '*Relax*' and '*Two Tribes*,' necessitating the ZTT creative team's maximising of their success. More label attention was given to Propaganda the following year when '*A Secret Wish*' was released, reportedly inspiring producer **Quincy Jones** in some of the sounds and techniques he used on **Michael Jackson**'s '*Bad*' album.

In February 1985, Paul Morley married Claudia Brücken; they went on to have two children together. The pair's marriage is said to have led to a strained relationship between the group and their label. The group split for the first time shortly afterwards, and Brücken and Morley's marriage dissolved. Years later she began working, and entered into a relationship with, **Paul Humphreys**, one half the Synth Pop group **Orchestral Manoeuvres in the Dark.**

*

These three videos give a really outstanding overview of how social engineering and culture-creation have been achieved throughout the decades, on both sides of the Atlantic, and with the same military intelligence-affiliated individuals and organisations cropping up time and time again.

In particular, the second video (The Chaos Era) covering the LSD-laden counter-culture of the 1960s—a creation of the CIA from start to finish—is particularly thorough, summing up a complex story in highly succinct and thorough terms.

HOW MEDIA SHAPED THE GENERATIONS—RADIO & THE TEENAGER (2017)

https://www.youtube.com/watch?v=blYD_o9uQn8

HOW MEDIA SHAPED THE GENERATIONS—The Chaos Era (2017)

https://www.youtube.com/watch?v=J55DAItrtzA

HOW MEDIA SHAPED THE GENERATIONS- Do what thou Wilt (Sex, Drugs, and Aliens) 2017 https://www.youtube.com/watch?v=suwRg7tYSfM

*

Being very familiar with the process of research, I can't even begin to imagine the amount of hours it would have taken the proprietor of the following YouTube channel, mk2007al, to assemble this vast archive of videos on the Satanic side of the entertainment industry. The host is German, and while most of the videos are spoken in his native tongue, many have been re-done in English. These are presented from a Christian perspective, but it would be a shame if this aspect put off any non-Christians, since many of his observations are highly incisive. Several music A-listers get subjected to a very thorough examination here, including Pink Floyd, Abba, Queen, David Bowie, Bob Dylan, Kiss, Peter Gabriel and Depeche Mode.

https://www.youtube.com/channel/UCMXLaZu9k5Ey8vae9eAZLLw/videos

Resources:

The Telegraph: 'Perverted, degenerate and indecent acts': Charlie Chaplin and the original A-list divorce scandal:

- https://www.telegraph.co.uk/films/0/
  perverted-degenerate-indecent-acts-charlie-chaplin-original/

Popmatters: Rhythm And Bullshit: The Slow Decline of R&B, Part One:

- https://popmatters.com/050603-randb-2496103718.html

Remember the Sound: An Oral History of Philadelphia International Records:

- https://tidal.com/magazine/article/
  philadelphia-international-records-50/1-77247

How James Brown Really Died & The Death Of Sam Cooke and Otis Redding (James Brown Son):

- https://www.youtube.com/watch?v=EBiFUDzl07I

Buzzsaw: Sean Stone talks with Daryl Brown, son of James Brown:

- https://www.youtube.com/watch?v=8xMTTVZ2ueU

The Guardian: Call to investigate James Brown's death after murder claims:

- https://www.theguardian.com/music/2019/feb/06/
  james-brown-death-investigate-murder-claims

Yash Qaraah: The Music Industry (The Honest Truth):

- https://www.youtube.com/watch?v=deyc5tp6Y64

James Brown — Beat The Devil (2002) Directed by Tony Scott:

- https://www.youtube.com/watch?v=gfh7NBIh4hg

Mind Control Black Assassins: Donny Hathaway & MK-Ultra Mind Control:

- https://mindcontrolblackassassins.com/category/donny-hathaway/

BBC News: R. Kelly found guilty in sex trafficking trial:

- https://www.bbc.co.uk/news/entertainment-arts-58714203?fbclid=IwAR2wm5h0WNjkyOL0lrPeohb4qGCL9c0SzfCjB0IHsdCSfoeIT3LfQGt6G24

Metropolis Newspaper: Afrika Bambaataa and the Zulu Nation Sued for Child Sex Trafficking:

- https://www.metropolisnewspaper.com/articles/afrika-bambaataa-and-the-zulu-nation-sued-for-child-sex-trafficking?fbclid=IwAR2HJl-Sg8afBdzRWH5Rs3ZHOYkPuR8cQ9RtwGkcXOvDCUzJ3yzLM5roZn8

Leila Wills' 'TRAPped In A CULTure' video playlist:

www.youtube.com/c/leilawills

BBC News: Life of troubled pop star Brian Harvey:

- http://news.bbc.co.uk/1/hi/entertainment/music/4598937.stm

Brian Harvey: 'You'll Never Stop Me.':

- https://www.youtube.com/watch?v=Szaco7zDu9M

The Express: Brian Harvey smashes his platinum discs in outburst against the music industry:

- https://www.express.co.uk/celebrity-news/551807/East-17-s-Brian-Harvey-smashes-platinum-discs-outburst-music-industry

Brian Harvey: THERE IS A PRICE ON MY HEAD RIGHT NOW . . . GHISLAINE!!!:

- https://www.youtube.com/watch?v=_a6YbJG6qk4

Brian Harvey Exposes Browns Paedophile Red Room.:

- https://www.youtube.com/watch?v=NvtSAKw4S_A

Alanis Morissette says she was raped by multiple men in new HBO documentary 'Jagged':

- https://www.insider.com/alanis-morissette-says-raped-by-multiple-men-hbo-documentary-jagged-2021-9

BBC News: Terry Hall: 'At 12 I got abducted by a paedophile ring':

- https://www.bbc.co.uk/news/entertainment-arts-47088000

Lyrics: Fun Boy Three: 'Well Fancy That':

- https://songmeanings.com/songs/view/3530822107858675293/

Society X: Hang The DJ:

- https://5ocietyx.wordpress.com/2012/11/08/hang-the-dj/

Official video to Propaganda: 'Duel':

- https://www.youtube.com/watch?v=nnQ2zOmb6Hg

Official video to Propaganda: 'Dr. Mabuse':

- https://www.youtube.com/watch?v=px4xHQd9h14

Official video to Propaganda: 'P-Machinery':

- https://www.youtube.com/watch?v=660ZCEhvbnw

The Guardian: Paul Morley: 'Why did my dad drive south to kill himself?':

- https://www.theguardian.com/lifeandstyle/2013/jun/15/paul-morley-why-did-dad-kill-himself

CHAPTER 8

FORBIDDEN TERRITORY

The Adrenochrome agenda has gained major public recognition since 2020. Although it remains the "elite's" darkest and most devastating secret, still the usual array of blatant references has appeared in movies, TV shows and music videos.

> *"It reminds me that it's not so bad, it's not so bad."*
> Dido: 'Thank You'

> *"And I try,*
> *Oh my God, do I try,*
> *I try all the time, in this institution.*
> *And I pray,*
> *Oh my God, do I pray,*
> *I pray every single day,*
> *For a revolution."*
> Four Non-Blondes: 'What's Up?'

I never imagined, after including chapters in the first book on demonic possession, Satanic Ritual Abuse, and institutionalised paedophilia, that I would ever find myself having to conclude that I didn't take things far enough in including those subjects, and that in fact, even worse activities evidently go on behind the respectable veil of Organised Society—and with the music industry playing its own part in not only participating in the activities, but in flagrantly placing symbolism that promotes it right in our faces under the guise of "entertainment."

This is the world of Adrenochrome, and there's no way in Creation that any chapter addressing this subject head-on could be cheery and joyful. Readers should take this as a disclaimer, therefore, that this chapter will, by necessity, be a journey into doom and darkness, and will be a tough read for many. Reticent as I always am to delve into such heavy, low-density material—and much as I prefer to dwell on the positive whenever there is any to be found—this unspeakably horrific industry is closer to being fully exposed for all to see than it ever has before. I keep in mind the maxim "the night is always darkest just before the dawn." Turning away from it because it's too devastating to look at is *not* going to bring it to an end. That attitude only ensures that untold numbers of children will go on suffering. Shining light on the murkiest and most devastating of subjects is the only way to make them stop. And readers should stay with this book to the very end to get its full message. These kinds of subjects don't represent any kind of note on which I wish to leave things.

Though I've known for years of the trauma-based mind-control and ritual abuse that routinely takes place within "elite" bloodline families—and is applied to owned assets of the entertainment industry—the Adrenochrome aspect is one that I only caught up with in more recent times. The deluge of information that got shared in the wake of Co(n)vid and all the narratives associated with it, saw many millions becoming aware of this dread-filled activity for the first time.

How low can you go?

Let's get the really grim stuff over with to set the scene then—and again, it's necessary to stray somewhat from the music industry here in order to tell the full story—though this institution is of course involved.

According to multiple survivor witness statements, leaked intel, and a wide array of documentation, there are secret tunnel systems under the earth. These exist under most major cities on all continents, many of which are directly connected. Many of these, in turn, are connected to D.U.M.B.S.—Deep Underground Military Bases. There is no disputing that these facilities exist. They are controlled by the military and are ostensibly there for secret technology experiments, and are fully equipped to be able to sustain humans for long periods should the need ever arise for them to head underground to escape some catastrophe happening up above. (The humans concerned don't include you and me, of course—these are intended only for approved "elite" occupation.) This was a theme explored in Stanley Kubrick's 1964 satirical dark comedy *'Dr. Strangelove.'* We'll be visiting the various films of Kubrick *a lot* in this chapter.

As well as reportedly housing suppressed technology apparatus, the extensive information that has been leaked talks of children being forcibly imprisoned in these underground tunnels and bases. Some will have been kidnapped, and the official figures for the number of children who "go missing" every year all around the world are truly staggering. The constant coverage of the Madeleine McCann story in the UK mainstream press is (partly—because there's *way* more to know about the McCann story than the mainstream will ever reveal!) there to create the impression that children going missing is a rare occurrence, whereas this couldn't be further from the truth. The globalmissingkids.org site reports that over 112,000 children are reported missing in the UK each year, with the figure at 460,000 in the United States, 100,000 in Germany, 45,000 in Canada and 20,000 in Australia.

Others will have been kept captive from birth and will never have seen natural daylight, and—to return to the machinations of the music industry quickly—the public seemed to get an insight into this from the 1983 Russell Mulcahy-directed video to **Duran Duran**'s *'Union of the Snake.'* The band are seen in a remote desert location, with strange lizard-type creatures crawling over the sand dunes. A bellhop suddenly appears and beckons Simon Le Bon into an elevator, which proceeds to descend several storeys below ground. They emerge into an underground base in which children in nightgowns are being kept captive in cages and are later led away in a trance-like state. (See the *'Sound Bites'* story on Duran Duran for more of their highly questionable elements.)

Decoding Kubrick

The so-called "elites" that humanity has allowed to gain so much power and domination within this world—in spite of the ridiculously small number of them when compared with the rest of us—have, for generations, kept women captive as sex slaves and as "brood mares," specifically to be impregnated and to spawn endless supplies of new babies.

This dynamic was alluded to in *'Eyes Wide Shut,'* the final film of Stanley Kubrick. In his presentation for the 2021 S.E.E.D. 4 Growth on-line conference, American researcher Sean McCann, presented a highly astute analysis of how Kubrick was revealing—in coded, cryptic form as ever—how "elite" circles operate. Kubrick's movies have been endlessly analysed since the advent of the internet, and many students of his work concur that he had inside knowledge of the New World Order agenda and was privy to information that the general public wasn't. Most opine, however, that Stanley didn't entirely approve of what the "elite" class had planned for the rest of humanity, (rather like George Orwell with '1984,') and so attempted to appease his conscience by placing as much truth into the narratives of all his films from 1962's 'Lolita' onwards. By necessity, these revelations had to be covert and likely to only be picked up on by a very small few with their Eyes Wide Open. But the truth bombs are all there, cleverly woven into the sur- face narratives of these masterpieces. Stanley's movies depict aspects of MK-Ultra-style mind control, "elite" paedophilia, the "space" lies of N.A.S.A., the savagery and absurdity of war, and so much more.

Just one example from 'Eyes Wide Shut' presented by McCann, which would have gone over the heads of 99.9 per cent of the viewing audi- ence at the time of its release, involves Alice, played by Nicole Kidman, having been a sex slave at the hands of the cult in the years before she paired up with Dr. Bill, the character played by her then-husband Tom Cruise. During the scenes of the dark occult ritual, (tellingly filmed at Mentmore Towers in Buckinghamshire—a Rothschild mansion!) the women, who are used by the cult to birth new children for ritual abuse, drop their dresses in a certain manner as they prepare to be impregnated by the men.

In a scene where Alice is undressing for her husband, she drops her dress in the same manner, as she has been trained to do. Alice was a brood mare for the cult, and the daughter she now has with Bill is considered their property. Indeed, in the toy shop scene at the end of the movie, in blink-and-you-miss-it style, Helena, the daughter, is seen being led off by two men that we have viewed earlier as stooges of the cult. Alice distracts Bill with chat while this happens, indicating that she is complicit. She then tells him there's something very important they need to do. When he asks what, she replies, "fuck." At face value it seems like a crude note on which to end, the last word ever uttered in a Kubrick movie being "fuck." But reading between the lines, she is telling Bill that they need to create a new child for use by the cult now that Helena has been reclaimed.

Kubrick's choice of casting in these roles is interesting given Tom Cruise's strong ties to the mind-control cult of Scientology, and Nicole's father, Dr. Antony Kidman, having been an MK-Ultra doctor in Washington D.C. and Australia, and with several accusations of paedophilia levelled at him before he turned up dead in 2014 in Singapore. Though the official cause of death was a "heart attack," many suspect that he was taken out by his higher-ups as he had become a liability.

Kubrick died of a reported heart attack in March 1999, just one week after 'Eyes Wide Shut' had been released, and after executives at Warner Brothers had ordered several minutes of the original footage to be deleted. Given what the cut that we *have* been able to see reveals when it is fully decoded, the mind boggles as to what the deleted material contained!

Either way, given that induced heart attacks have long been an assassination method within the capabilities of the military-intelligence community, it would seem that Kubrick was finally considered to have gone a step too far with what he revealed in 'Eyes Wide Shut,' and that it cost him his life.

The 'Eyes Wide Shut' example is just one of so many clues that were placed in Kubrick's movies, giving an insight for those with the eyes to see and the fortitude to handle it, into the sick practices of this world's "elite" groups. This is the stuff of our worst nightmares for those of us with our full human faculties intact but are just another day at the office for the demonic scum.

Subterranean nightmares

The captive children in these underground facilities are reportedly used as supplies for Adrenochrome. This is a hormonal chemical which is secreted by the adrenal glands when a child is in an extreme state of fear and terror, and most potent when they are about to lose their life. It is the body's automatic way of trying to keep itself alive. I have no desire to go into graphic detail about what is done to these children in the harvesting rituals. It is, of course, horrific.

The Adrenochrome that is collected is then consumed by the ritual's participants, or stored for sale further down the line. Because it represents the body's way of desperately trying to keep itself alive, Adrenochrome is said to have live-giving properties, and when consumed in large quantities, to offset the effects of ageing and keep the participant looking fitter, healthier and younger than they ordinarily would. Reportedly, well-known figures such as Royals, world leaders, politicians, religious leaders, and all kinds of "celebrities" engage in these rituals. Anyone wondering why "elite" banksters, oligarchs and Royals seem to live so long compared with regular members of the public may just have found the answer. They may also have found the truth as to why certain celebrities — particularly women — are frequently praised in "newspapers" and celebrity magazines as looking "great for their age."

Adrenochrome is said to be highly addictive — more so than heroin according to some accounts — and sudden withdrawal after years of use is said to severely take its toll, reversing the anti-ageing process and causing the body to deteriorate rapidly. Have we just found the reason why so many "celebrities" pictured in their homes during lockdown looked like shit? Could a worldwide shut-down of the supply of Adrenochrome possibly be the cause?

We'll look at how the Adrenochrome industry has been conveyed symbolically in popular culture vehicles in due course. First though, just for any doubters or naysayers, we have some "real world" documentation that stands as close to indisputable proof of this industry as it's possible to get, short of a world-famous participant coming forward and telling all on mainstream T.V. And I won't be holding my breath for that one.

Decoding the data

The mainstream media has got as close as it can to revealing that Adrenochrome extraction routinely goes on in "elite" circles, only just stopping short of revealing how it's really done. A *'Sky News'* article in 2018 titled *'Young blood an elixir that prevents age-related diseases, study reveals,'* talked of how blood from a young person, if consumed, could stem off the effects of old age, (implying also that it could be given to animals, as well as humans.) The article notes:

> *"The trials by US start-up Ambrosia involved 70 participants—with all involved aged at least 35. After being given plasma—the main component of blood—from volunteers aged 16 and 25, researchers noted improvements in biomarkers for various diseases. Ambrosia currently offers teenage blood plasma to older customers at a cost of $8,000 (£6,200) for two and a half litres."*

Similarly, 'Newsweek' published an article in 2021 titled 'Can Blood from Young People Slow Aging? Silicon Valley Has Bet Billions It Will.' It quoted Nir Barzilai, the founding director of the Institute for Aging Research at Albert Einstein College of Medicine of Yeshiva University, as saying: "You have no idea how many people are interested to invest money in longevity. There are billions of dollars." The idea of "elites" desperately trying to stave off the effects of ageing, (could they be trying to prolong their death through fear of the judgement that lies beyond it for the behaviours they have employed in life?) ties into their belief in the concept of Transhumanism—the merging of humanity with technology to, in their thinking, cheat physical death and remain "immortal."

The subject of child sex trafficking ran concurrently with those of the Scamdemic and the Q "Plan" narratives on alternative sites and social media throughout 2020, with the frequent claim that all three were linked, and that the Covid scam had—at least in part—been concocted to provide a smokescreen for the paedophilic practices of the "elites." In the midst of this emerged the claim that Wayfair, the American furniture and home goods on-line retailer, was involved in worldwide sex trafficking via its fleet of container ships, and that many of the furniture items offered for sale on its website were, in fact, children, with coded language being used for those in the know.

Researchers pointed to several examples of furniture items bearing the names of children who had been reported missing, and being offered at exorbitant prices way beyond what anyone would expect to pay for such advertised items. Though the company naturally denied such claims, stating that the furniture items in question were priced so-high because they were specialist, niche items—and the "fact-check-ers" were naturally on-hand to "debunk" the claims—many such entries did get amended overnight once the claims were made public, with advertised prices plummeting, or entries disappearing altogether.

Fascinatingly, we're back to the films of Kubrick here. In the opening sequence to '*Lolita*,' where James Mason's character has tracked down Peter Sellers' with the intention of killing him for his having stolen the underage Lolita from his clutches, Sellers tells Mason:

> "*I got some nice friends, you know, who could come and keep you company here. You could use them as pieces of furniture. This one guy looks just like a bookcase. I could fix for you to attend executions. How would you like that? Just you, nobody else there. Just watching. You like watching, Captain?*"

Was all this meaningless babble, (which seems unlikely, as every line of dialogue in perfectionist Kubrick's movies tends to serve some pur-pose.) Or does it stand as another example of Kubrick, (who co-wrote the screenplay) placing the truth in plain sight? Is it possible he could have been telling us, as far back as 1962, of the coded language linking sacrificial humans with pieces of furniture?

Earlier in the scene, Quilty (Sellers) invites Humbert (Mason) to join him in a game of "Roman ping-pong." (Both are paedophiles.) Intriguingly, Comet Ping Pong was the name of the pizza restaurant in Washington D.C. that was at the centre of the Pizzagate scandal of 2016, with the claim that it was a front for child trafficking involving very high-profile politicians including Barack Obama and Hillary Clin-ton. "Ping-pong" has been identified as code language for the passing around of children for abuse within paedophile rings.

The Wayfair claims and counter-claims notwithstanding, the Ali Baba on-line retail site (www.alibaba.com,) has not been shy in coming forward, and has been blatant and unambiguous in its offerings. This company appears to be offering Adrenochrome and related products for sale on the internet, "legally" and without any consequences. On the day of writing this chapter, the site was offering "2021 made in China wholesale children harvested epineprine Adrenochrome" at a cost of £6,062,73 per unit. (Epinephrime is another term for adrenalin.) This was being offered by shipment from ports in Shanghai and Lianyun-gang at a rate of 30 units per month. The colour of the product is described as "red." On the same day, the site was offering "lot coated children Adrenochrome 100% polyester taffeta," and a "sound module Children Adrenochrome for plush toy." All these products are offered from China.

There have been seemingly few attempts to hide an official patent—detailed on the Google Patent site at https://patents.google.com/patent/US4501923A/en—of a "process for preparing Adreno-chrome" and credited to its inventor, Deryck F. Boot. The assignee is listed as the Minnesota Mining and Manufacturing company, better known as 3M, makers of Scotch Tape and Post-It Notes. The entry goes heavy on chemical terminology and, neglecting to mention human extraction, appears to represent a method of synthesising the human-originated compound.

Perhaps the most in-your-face example of all comes from the all-dom-inating tech giant Google—an extremely dark and Satanic organisation when it comes down to it. Most will be aware of the company's indus-try-standard web browser, Chrome. But fewer will be aware of a series of graphics processing units developed by the Qualcomm corporation, compatible with some Google technology, titled Adreno. The naysay-ers will claim it's just random and coincidence, as they always do. But seriously—ask yourself what are the odds of two products from two tech giants *just happening* to, between them, spell out "Adrenochrome," These products represent yet another way of rubbing the noses of the profane masses right in the "Elites" sick, depraved activities, knowing that it will go right over the heads of the vast majority, at the same time driving the small number of us who *do* recognise the coding, crazy from our frustration at the evil not being fully exposed for all to see.

Astonishingly though, the subject of Adrenochrome harvesting *did* break the mainstream surface in Summer 2020 when it became the subject of a news report on '*TGRT Haber,*' a nationwide mainstream TV station in Turkey. In it, the host spoke of Adrenochrome extraction as a reality, and even went so far as to name many politicians, celebrities and other famous people said to consume it. Those names, pictured on a screen behind the host, included Prince Philip, The Pope, George W.

Bush, John Kerry, Johnny Depp, Brad Pitt, Kate Moss, **Pharrell Williams** and **Lady Gaga**. The report presented pictures of many of these names "before and after" alleged Adrenochrome consumption, showing the apparent anti-ageing effect it has.

We were so close to this vile subject breaking cover and becoming a talking point within mainstream society via this Turkish report, and I—perhaps naïvely—truly thought we'd reached a breakthrough at the time. Tragically, however, nothing further came of it and it simply fizzled out, the way all "unwelcome" news that doesn't suit the controllers of Organised Society does. The fact that this wasn't picked up on by other TV networks and broadcast in every country around the world is one of the greatest travesties in human history, and the number of children that would have suffered and died between that day and this as a result of the inaction, can only be imagined in our worst nightmares.

The Black Eye Club

From around 2018, the number of celebrities and other famous people who were appearing in public with black rings around their eyes, as if they'd been punched in the face, became a talking point. The most obvious contender was Prince Philip who was photographed multiple times sporting shiners—most frequently under his right eye, but sometimes under both. And yet this was never picked up on by the mainstream press who, in "The Emperor's New Clothes" fashion, acted as if it were perfectly normal for him to appear this way, with no reason to ask any questions as to why. According to insiders, the black-eyed appearance is an after-effect of the withdrawal from Adrenochrome consumption.

A UK '*Daily Mail*' article in July 2018 attempted some damage-limitation by laughing the phenomenon off as the product of "conspiracy theorists" (so original) and using the word "bizarre" four times to describe the idea. (After all, why apply any investigative journalism to a claim to establish whether or not it does have any merit when you can simply brush it off as "bizarre" and avoid that need altogether?) Though it did cite some potentially credible esoteric explanations—such as mentioning the Egyptian sun god Horus whose left eye, (which he lost in a fight with his brother Set) was black and represented the moon, and the 1879 Freeman's Journal *'A Black Eye'* which decried the sight as "the devil's mark." It stopped short of attributing the black eyes as being the after-effects of Adrenochrome.

Prince Philip. Always the most prominent member of the "elite" Black Eye Club.

https://www.flickr.com/photos/12587661@N06/2316586995

Author: Michael Gwyther-Jones

Instead, the *'Mail'* presented the idea that it's a calling-card to show that these celebrities are "part of the Illuminati." It went on to cite the claims of the late author Sherry Shriner that the black eyes mark out those that have taken part in "soul scalping"—the ritualistic removal of their souls which are sold to "the Devil" in exchange for their fame and fortune. After picturing many celebs sporting the black eye look, the *'Mail'* went on to cite some of the weak and utterly unconvincing explanations that have been given for the black eyes; **Boy George** said one of his was simply "fashion make-up," while **David Bowie** brushed his off as "theatrics."

The Pope claimed to have got his after crashing in his Pope-mobile; Adam Sandler claimed he was punched by a pregnant Drew Barrymore's child through her stomach; George W. Bush has given multiple excuses for his, including being hit in the eye by a snowball, falling off his bike and being hit in the face by a microphone stand; Prince Philip was said by a Buckingham Palace spokesperson of just one of his many black eyes to have "just woken up with it." And since we're on the subject, what, I wonder, could have been responsible for the strange black rings under **Paul McCartney's/ "Paul McCartney's"** (delete as appropriate . . . and take a swig) eyes in the video message he recorded to commemorate Rolling Stones drummer Charlie Watts in late August 2021??

Are we all buying it? Or were we being given, as ever, the opportunity to know the true nature of those who garner the public's adulation, and therefore empowering energy, should we ever have the Will to go searching for the truth of the matter?

Nudge nudge, wink wink

In retrospect and with the benefit of hindsight—ever noticed how that's always the way?—it appears that the public has been given various clues and opportunities to know about the Adrenochrome in-joke over the years. The aforementioned Turkish news report began by including a clip of actress Sandra Bullock appearing on an episode of Ellen DeGeneres' TV chat show, in which she speaks of using the "foreskin" that came "from a young person" from "far, far away" as a beauty product to keep herself young. DeGeneres smiles knowingly as Bullock hesitantly reveals the details. A similar apparent admission of these sick practices came from a recently-exhumed 1975 TV interview with Rat Pack singer **Dean Martin** on Johnny Carson's '*Tonight*' show. In it, a visibly drunk Martin is asked by Carson if he got his friend **Frank Sinatra** anything nice for his 60th birthday, to which Martin replies, "how do you wrap up glands?" and the audience erupts into hysterics. Carson doesn't find it necessary to ask what he meant, acting as if he already knew and simply adding "glands to go" before asking Martin, "you don't . . . ?" to which Martin replies, "no, I quit that."

In the music world, the black eye makes an appearance in the video to **Blondie's** '*Atomic*' where a woman sports the look at the 2:52 mark. (Debbie Harry was a participant in the "Spirit Cooking" dinners of Satanic witch Marina Abramovich around the time that the "Pizzagate" scandal broke in 2016, where she was pictured in a blood-red dress plunging an apparently bloodied knife into a cake fashioned in the form of a human. A cake of very similar appearance had appeared decades earlier in the 1973 movie *'The Wicker Man'* which detailed the human sacrifice rituals of certain sun-worshipping Pagan traditions.

We also get a group of children all sporting black eyes in the 2009 video to the **Manic Street Preachers** song *'Little Baby Nothing.'* They all wear white T-shirts bearing various slogans, including "We Are Your Sacrifice." The same video includes an allusion to cannibalism, with a naked woman marked up for cuts of meat. Coming from the band who, the same year, declared "if you tolerate this then your children will be next," you have to wonder what they—or those that control them—knew.

Model and TV star **Chrissy Teigen** doubtless regretted a Tweet she had made in 2015 when, five years later, she found herself fighting off accusations of being implicated in child sex trafficking and Adrenochrome. Teigen had felt confident enough in an era before such matters were getting fully investigated by the alternative media community, to brazenly Tweet: "Johnny and I are on our way to thehollydale. Karina Belenoff is serving a nice 4 year old cheese pizza with Adrenochrome." The translation of this, given what we know about the food-related code words identified by the F.B.I. as being used by paedophile networks, is that Teigen was on her way to indulge in the Adrenochrome of a four-year-old child. The "Johnny" to whom Teigen refers is her husband, the R&B singer **John Legend**. On the face of his public image, Legend is one of the last music stars anyone might suspect of being implicated in such sordid activities—which gives an indication as to how carefully-cultivated personas are created to entrain the public in how to think of a certain artist.

Karina Belenoff is the daughter of Somerset Belenoff, the "royal" witch detailed in one of the *'Sound Bites'* stories elsewhere in this book. Karina is the proprietor of Cannibal Cravings at the Hollydale, to which Teigen's Tweet was referring. Despite openly endorsing cannibalism, this establishment has never been shut down and remains in operation. One of Belenoff's Tweets from January 2020 read: "#KentuckyViperMilitia celebrate alliance with Amish Underground Brotherhood by joining us at The Hollydale for the Witching event. 8 witches will be eaten for our eternal nourishment." Her Twitter profile advertises the website peoplearemeat.com, which now appears to have been taken down.

Along the same lines as the above is the purported Cannibal Club in Los Angeles, a venue which states that it serves human flesh. **Katy Perry**, CNN's Anderson Cooper, (son of Gloria Vanderbilt, whose name has come up frequently in the claims made about Adrenochrome extracted from children,) Chelsea Clinton and Meryl Streep are said to be among its patrons. The restaurant's website (www.cannibalclub.org) does not give its location, instead advising visitors to "introduce yourself through our contact page and we will send you information about our membership process. It is necessary for us to operate privately and to vet our members in order to avoid disruption from the less enlightened." Attempts have been made by Reuters and Snopes to "debunk" this establishment as "an old hoax." The Reuters article shows that the photographs which purport to be of the restaurant's staff, are in fact recycled stock photos. If the Club is really a hoax, it's difficult to understand why its website has not yet been shut down by some concerned agency. If it really is someone's idea of a joke, it is in extremely sick taste in light of what is known to be true about the unspeakably evil ritual practices of the "elite."

Less concerned about being cryptic than Teigen, it might seem, was **Sean Combs**, better known through the years as **Puff Daddy**, **P. Diddy**, and simply **Diddy**. Combs is the proprietor of Bad Boy Records and was the mentor to the doomed **Biggie Smalls**, aka **The Notorious B.I.G.** In the last book I detailed some of the evidence for Biggie having been an industry "blood sacrifice" to further Combs' ascent up the ladder to fame and fortune, the occult ritual that **Public Enemy's Professor Griff** claims Combs had to undergo to become such a key player, (Forbes has estimated him to be worth just under a billion, behind only **Kanye West** and **Jay-Z** in the hip-hop field,) and his family background. His father Melvin Combs, was a street hustler in New York affiliated to Frank Lucas, the character portrayed by Denzel Washington in *American Gangster.*

In May 2020, a book purporting to be written by Combs, and titled *'The Adrenochrome Witch,'* appeared for sale via the Nook section of Barnes & Noble and other retailers, (though was notably absent from Amazon.) According to its promotional blurb, "The Adrenochrome Witch is a true story about the elite secret society, and their bizarre eternal youth rituals. Not for the faint of heart." The book, written as if a fairy story, claims that the women of Hollywood and other "elite" types had searched for years to find the secret to preserving their youthful looks before discovering Adrenochrome. It talks of the rituals that take place among these communities and claims that the best way for the public to get a handle on it is to consider the lyrical content of The Eagles' 'Hotel California.'

It's difficult to know whether this book genuinely came from the mind and the pen of Sean Combs. For a start it's only seven pages long. It certainly has the air of a hoax in poor taste to it, in which case it's puzzling as to why his would have been the celebrity name to be put to this project over all others. The book, still showing as available on Barnes & Noble's site, retails for the hefty price of $100.00—around $14 per page—putting it out of the range of those merely curious to take a quick peek. Either way, it stands as more revelation—albeit restricted in likely reach—of Adrenochrome practices, and it's interesting to note that it emerged right in the midst of all the "conspiracy" talk surrounding child trafficking, Q, Trump, Covid, etc, at a time when, under lockdown tyranny, most in the world had been confined to their homes with nowhere to go, and plenty of time on their hands to research all manner of esoteric topics.

Sick flicks

What beggars belief is the sheer number of Hollywood movies—shown to mainstream audiences in the hundreds of millions—which have blatantly placed the sick rituals of Adrenochrome right under the noses of the viewing public. In so many cases these have been in the form of movies aimed at children or passed off as "comedies." Let's look at some of the worst offenders. Let's also consider the level of sickness and depravity required of a scriptwriter to convey the torture and murder of children—albeit in allegorical form—into a popular culture vehicle, knowing that the audience will believe it is merely indulging in an enjoyable leisure pursuit, rather than having such unimaginable horrors communicated to them. With that in mind, let's call out the screenwriters involved in each of these by name.

The obsession of Hollywood types with stemming off the physical effects of ageing is the central premise of 1992's 'Death Becomes Her' starring Goldie Hawn and Meryl Streep. As the film's Wikipedia entry notes: "The film focuses on a pair of rivals who drink a magic potion that promises eternal youth, but experience unpleasant side effects when they physically die, becoming walking, talking corpses as a result." As direct a reference to the practice of consuming Adrenochrome as it's possible to get without coming right out and saying so. Tellingly, Isabella Rossellini's character is said to be 71, but fools others into assuming she is decades younger due to her youthful appearance. The very same observation was made of "performance artist" (witch) Marina Abramovic when she first came to public attention through her "spirit cooking" dinners in 2016 and it was revealed that she was 70, despite most assuming her to be much younger.

This one was directed and produced by big-time Hollywood insider Robert Zemeckis, who had previously placed a treasure-trove of symbolism related to 911 in his 'Back To The Future' movies, indicating foreknowledge of that event. The writers were David Koepp and Martin Donovan — real name Carlos Enrique Varela y Peralta Ramos — who turns out to be the great-great-grandson of the founder of the Argentinian city of Mar del Plata, and whose uncle was a spiritual teacher to the future Pope Francis, so a couple of Establishment connections there.

Would anyone familiar with the true, Satanic nature of the Disney corporation be surprised to find it behind another main contender? 1993's 'Hocus Pocus' stars Bette Midler, Sarah Jessica Parker and Kathy Najimy as three witches from 17th century Salem, Massachusetts, who are reborn into the modern era and go on a mission to "suck the souls" out of children. The original 'Hocus Pocus' script came from Mick Garris, best known for his work within the horror genre and for collaborating with author Stephen King. The screenplay was adapted by Neil Cuthbert and David Kirschner. Bette Midler has commented that the making of 'Hocus Pocus' represented the most fun she had had in her career up to that point.

Also coming from the Disney camp — and with one of its animated characters sporting a single eye just to throw in some more "Illuminati" symbolism — is 'Monsters Inc.' The organisation of the title is involved with generating power by terrifying young children and feeding off the fearful screams that they produce. As Wikipedia's plotline puts it: "At the Monsters Inc. factory, skilled monsters employed as "scarers" venture into the human world to scare children and harvest their screams, through doors that activate portals to children's bedroom closets." Mention is also made of the "Scream Extractor," a large machine capable of forcefully extracting screams from kidnapped human children. Just more good, clean, family fun from those lovely folk over at Disney, right, parents? Original story credits for this one go to Pete Docter, Jill Culton, Jeff Pidgeon and Ralph Eggleston, with screenplay adaptation from Andrew Stanton and Dan Gerson.

Those involved in these movies would doubtless play the plausible deniability card, and say that the claim their plotlines refer to Adrenochrome is mere speculation, But even *if* they don't, a valid question might be—why are stories involving children being terrified considered "entertainment" anyway? What kind of psychological effect does this have on the children viewing it, and what kind of diseased minds would want to dream up such ideas?

In the *'Teenage Mutant Ninja Turtles'* film and TV series, the turtles keep children in the underground sewer in which they live, and have a fondness for "pizza." Go figure. Comments made in the movie include: "you are teenagers. The mutagen in your blood is of great value to them," and "inside those turtles is the most precious compound on earth. We will drain every last ounce of their blood to get it."

Will Ferrell has appeared in a disproportionately high number of movies covertly depicting aspects of child sexual abuse. Why could that be?

Meanwhile, Mel Gibson's outspoken comments about institutionalised paedophilia being rampant in Hollywood is put into context by his appearance in *'Daddy's Home 2.'* At one point his character references a child, saying: "and then you smack her on the ass and tell her what a lucky girl she is," and tells a young boy, "now you get up there and grab those balls."

And would you believe it, we've circled right back round to Stanley Kubrick again. 1971's *'A Clockwork Orange'* made clear references to MK-Ultra-style mind-control programming, but also suggested inside knowledge of the Adrenochrome agenda all those decades ago. We learn from narrator Alex that he and his fellow "Droogs" enjoy hanging out in the Korova Milk Bar, which "sold milk-plus, milk plus vellocet or synthemesc or drencrom, which is what we were drinking."

What other references might have been hiding in plain sight all these decades? Well, how about *'The Rocky Horror Picture Show'*—both the original stage show and movie that followed? It's almost a case of pick a social-engineering agenda and you'll find it pushed through this vehicle. Satanism, transgenderism, transvestism, hedonism, homosexuality, space aliens, it's all there.

More worryingly, however, so, it would appear, are the hidden references to Adrenochrome-laced blood drinking.

'Rocky Horror' was the creation of Richard O'Brien, who becomes yet another "interesting" character to study. In interviews he has claimed that he knew he was a transgender when he was six, (you know, like you do,) and correlates that with his bisexuality. He now takes regular oestrogen shots and sports a small pair of breasts, referring to himself as "the third sex."

Incredibly, Adrenochrome featured in an early episode (in 2007) of British TV drama *'Lewis,'* (of which there were 33 instalments,) the sequel series to *'Inspector Morse.'* As D.I. Lewis and his sidekick D.S. Hathaway investigate a murder, they stumble across an Adrenochrome extraction scheme. As Hathaway states: "to harvest Adrenochrome you have to go to Hell itself. You have to murder for it." (Hathaway was played by Laurence Fox, the son of veteran British actor James Fox, and became something of a political activist during the Scamdemic, attending anti-lockdown rallies, and going on to run for the role of London Mayor.)

Video games have not been exempt from the programming either—and why would they, given the wonderful opportunities they offer to the sick demon ghouls who run these industries? For some reason, young people feel compelled to play a PC, PlayStation 4 and Xbox One game titled *'Little Nightmares.'* Its promo blurb describes it as "a dark whimsical tale that will confront you with your childhood fears! Help Six escape The Maw—a vast, mysterious vessel inhabited by corrupted souls looking for their next meal'"

I think we can probably guess by now what this is alluding to.

Signs and symbols

Just as there are common motifs associated with childhood trauma-based mind control, such as broken mirrors, dolls, teddy bears with broken limbs, and pink hair—and just as the Pizzagate affair revealed the food-related terms that are used for sex-trafficked children such as "pizza," "hot dog," "pasta" and "chicken"—so it is with the Adrenochrome industry. Common symbology includes water melons, avocados, (both symbolising children,) and flowers—particularly carnations—thought by some to reference 'carnism' or cannibalism. Spilt milk symbolises children and Adrenochrome, and it's no random accident that missing children have been featured on milk cartons in America for years. Carnation is the brand name of the spilt milk featured in the movie *'Home Alone,'* said to document child star Macauley Culkin's personal abuse. Fish are another icon, which brings to mind a seemingly agitated **Madonna** singing into her hairbrush that "we need fried fish" during the 2020 lockdown, when a supply of Adrenochrome from China was said to have been deliberately tainted.

Another frequent symbol, meanwhile, is that of white rabbits. This brings to mind the "follow the white rabbit" phrase from author (and paedophile) Lewis Carroll's surreal Alice stories, which themselves are said to be commonly used as mind control triggers. A white rabbit similar to the one pictured in the Carroll stories is featured on the sleeve to the *'Beatles Ballads'* album. Much was made of the notion of "follow the white rabbit" in the first 'Matrix' movie, and this also became a popular slogan within the "Q Plan" narrative of 2017 and beyond.

The use of the rabbit theme is thought to derive from the molecular formula of Adrenochrome—$C_9H_9NO_3$—which is produced by the oxidation of adrenaline. When represented in the form of a diagram, it is said to resemble the front view of a rabbit with its protruding ears. I'm sure it's just meaningless happenstance that Jefferson Airplane's *'White Rabbit'* was chosen as the background song to the trailer for the new *'Matrix Resurrections'* movie.

316

The diagrammatical formula involves two hexagons, and these are another commonly-used symbol. These are the six-sided shapes featured on the soccer balls frequently used by young boys—again, something considered not to be any coincidence. (Intriguingly, "hexagon" contains the word "hex," a spell used in witchcraft, which often utilises the number 6.)

Would you believe it—we're back to Stanley Kubrick again! In 1980's 'The Shining,' the audience gets a close-up of the carpet in the Overlook Hotel as 10-year-old Danny cycles through the corridors. This bears a very distinctive hexagonal pattern. Another "coincidence"—or another coded clue from a very much in-the-know Kubrick? In an appearance on my 'Good Vibrations' podcast series, Isaac Weishaupt, the proprietor of the Illuminatiwatcher.com website, reminded listeners of the eventual sequel to 'The Shining,' 2017's 'Dr. Sleep.':

> "Dr Sleep basically continues the story of 'The Shining,' where sexual abuse by a handler has the ability to unlock powers of the mind, fractures of the mind... It's sort of super-powers of the Shining, this E.S.P. thing that they've got going on."

This story features a grown-up Danny who is now working as a caretaker in a residential home, still suffering the trauma of his childhood abuse at the hands of his father, Jack, as hinted at in 'The Shining.' Isaac points out that in one scene Danny is seen thumbing through the very same issue of 'Playgirl' magazine that his father was reading in 'The Shining,' and which carries an article on incest. The narrative features a sinister character named Crow Daddy, which Isaac feels may be a sly reference to Aleister Crowley. He went further on 'Good Vibrations' in suggesting how the influence of Crowley and his rituals has been tied into the activities of the "elites" for decades.

> "I think that to understand why these people do what they do is to understand Aleister Crowley, because, you know, Crowley was this sexist, animal-torturing rapist, and he's a devil worshiper, and abuses women and he's a complete sociopath. And he himself advocated for the killing of children. He talked about it in 'The Book of the Law' and 'Magick in Theory and Practice.' He talked about how to create

the Gnostic Mass Eucharist. It required the blood of a newborn, and he talked about how the blood of a baby is the purest ... This is something that they've been doing for hundreds of years. And I would argue that the elites are, you know, in support of this idea.

"If you look at 'Liber 77,' a Crowley book, he says things like, 'there's no God but Man,' and 'the slaves shall serve.' And that's the attitude of these elites ... they don't care if a baby gets killed if it makes them feel better. They're completely off-the-rocker, insane people! And in 'Magick in Theory and Practice,' Crowley said the whole planet must be bathed in blood before Man is ready to accept the law of Thelema; the Great War must be fought, and I don't think there's any lengths they wouldn't go to.

"And I think this ties into the ancient Babylonian religions and the sacrificing babies to Moloch and all that stuff. This is something that's like an esoteric occult doctrine that is no longer popular. It's only traded sort of on the underground. And for those in the know, it's something that happens when you reach a certain level of elitist, I believe."

Gaga for it

And so—appropriately considering this book's title—we circle back around to the music industry once again ... finally!. Like its evil Hollywood cousin, the music game has, of course, played its part in subliminally implanting the concept of Adrenochrome consumption into the unwitting minds of the public. How could it not when it was, after all, complicit in pushing the food-related terms depicting "elite" paedophilia as exposed by the "Pizzagate" affair? **Lady Gaga,** as noted, has previous when it comes to pushing agendas, so was a likely candidate for this one, and went for it in a none-too-subtle way when, in the midst of the Scamdemic in May 2020, she released her sixth studio album titled ... *'Chromatica.'*

The cover art was suitably dark in tone, depicting Gaga seemingly trapped against a pink wire grille in some kind of torture chamber by some entity resembling a metallic sperm; Transhumanism is hinted at.

Though the promotional blurb made much of a "concept" album that saw Gaga adopt a "cyberpunk" persona, and Gaga was quoted as saying she was "in a dark place" during the album's recording, (just like the rest of the world then,) the chances of *Chromatica' not* making a sly reference to this most forbidden yet topical of subjects, was, in this author's view, virtually zero. Wikipedia offers us the following by way of a cover story:

> *"Gaga proposed 'Free Woman' as a tentative working title from her fondness of the identically-named album track, but the singer felt her internal struggles called into question the proposed title's integrity. She instead chose 'Chromatica' . . . the product of her concept of a distant fantastical planet of in-fighting warrior tribes that come together for healing and peace through dance. Gaga describes the synthesis of color and sound as the framework for planet Chromatica and her shared vision with BloodPop."*

Nothing to see here, move along.

https://commons.wikimedia.org/wiki/File:Lady_Gaga_-_Chromatica_Logo.png

The latter, incidentally, warrants some further attention. **BloodPop** is the artist name of Michael Tucker. With collaborators having included Madonna, **Skrillex**, **Beyonce**, **Kendrick Lamar**, the aforementioned John Legend and the late **Avicii**, he clearly moves in the right circles. Besides BloodPop he also performs under the monikers Blood, Michael Diamond and Blood Diamond. According to researchers into Adrenochrome, a sub-section of the extraction process involves the incorporation of children's blood into fashion accessories such as jewellery, and into shoes. "The Red Shoe Club," like "The Black Eye Club," is said to mark out those celebrities who are firmly embroiled in this most wicked of enterprises. See the link in the Resources section to the Pizzagate blog article for more on this subject.

A small handful of survivors of Satanic Ritual Abuse (SRA) and Adrenochrome extraction have come forward to share their stories, one of whom is American Jessie Czebotar. Her insights compare with those of the likes of Cathy O'Brien and Jay Parker, outspoken survivors of trauma-based mind-control programming. Like Jay, she was born into a high-up bloodline family and chosen to be a 'Mother of Darkness." She claims, however, that she was "saved." She's now a Christian Chaplain working with victims of sex trafficking and SRA, and has stated that she is on a mission to take on the evil system from which she escaped and to bring it down.

Another is Jeanette Archer, who says she is a survivor of a childhood spent under Satanic Ritual Abuse. As she commented when addressing the crowd at the London freedom rally in Hyde Park on 26th June 2021:

> *"If you don't stand up and we don't fight back and start talking the truth about what's going on with the Satanists that are running this country, it's game over for our children. They want a lifetime's supply of Adrenochrome. It is the most addictive drug on this planet. they will do whatever they need to keep getting their supply . . . but they're not getting it."*

A counter-claim occasionally heard to the Adrenochrome allegations, is that the entire thing is, in some way, a hoax, designed to ritually mock and taunt those that look into it. This claim will be received in response to *any* alternative research subject, and in this case, I don't accept it owing to the overwhelming glut of evidence to suggest that it's very real.

But even *if* it were a hoax, another question that should then be considered is this: what level of diseased sickness and unfathomable evil does it take for human minds to be able to dream up as cruel a hoax as this, and foist it upon well-meaning, conscientious people who just wish to do the right thing, faced with apparently colossal levels of Evil? Just as we can wonder how it's possible for human beings to unleash the unspeakable evils of the Adrenochrome industry on children, so we can ask ourselves how it's possible for anyone to stoop so low as to be OK with perpetrating these deceptions for a pay check.

Whatever the case it indicates that there is serious cause for concern about the true nature of the world in which we live, and those who—for the moment—control it.

But not for much longer.

Resources:

(Warning—many of the links below are likely to be extremely upsetting and traumatising to some.)

Young blood an elixir that prevents age-related diseases, study reveals:

- https://news.sky.com/story/drinking-young-blood-could-prevent-age-related-diseases-study-reveals-11493276

Sean McCann's 'Waking The Dead' podcast series, including multiple episodes decoding the hidden symbolism within Stanley Kubrick's movies:

- https://open.spotify.com/show/0avYSUf7VFPfDdOQasWLOm

Turkish National Television—Adrenochrome—English Translation:

- https://www.bitchute.com/video/cNhuZHWNwzQ1/

Daily Mail: Bizarre conspiracy theory suggests celebrities including the Pope and even ROYALS who have been snapped with black left eyes are in the secret ILLUMINATI society (and puts the bruises down to an 'initiation ritual'):

- https://www.dailymail.co.uk/femail/article-5971319/Conspiracy-theory-suggests-celebrities-snapped-black-left-eyes-ILLUMINATI.html

Dean Martin's odd "gland" humour on the Johnny Carson 'Tonight' show, 1975:

- https://youtu.be/G9ozER2J-Q8

Los Angeles' Cannibal Club:

- http://www.cannibalclub.org/

Dark Outpost; Horrific Blood Files Surface:

- https://darkoutpost.com/satanism/horrific-blood-files-surface/

- Satanic Empire: Child trafficking, torture and murder by the Elite—with Adrenochrome, blackmail and cannibalism: https://pedoempire.org/tag/hampstead/

Adrenochrome Extraction From Children, Including Dates Taken, Blood Types, Disposal Dates, etc. Part 1:

- https://www.bitchute.com/video/JpUm9CGFgfIQ/

Adrenochrome Extraction From Children, Including Dates Taken, Blood Types, Disposal Dates, etc. Part 1:

- https://www.bitchute.com/video/AAaXsgVmJEdc/

'The Adrenochrome Witch' by Sean "P Diddy' Combs on Barnes & Noble:

- https://nook.barnesandnoble.com/products/2940162633464/sample?sourceEan=2940162633464

Are Red Shoes A Pedophile Signal? (Pizzagate—Pope connection?):

- http://pizzagateblog.blogspot.com/2016/12/are-red-shoes-pedophile-signal.html

Adrenochrome referenced in British TV show 'Lewis' in 2007:

- https://en.wikipedia.org/wiki/List_of_Lewis_episodes#ep2

Data Dump: Adrenochrome Paper Trail:

- https://www.bitchute.com/video/Q1MLBb5j4mz1/

Manic Street Preachers: 'Little Baby Nothing':

- https://www.youtube.com/watch?v=wM3N54avEQc

Paul McCartney's Heartfelt Tribute To Late Rolling Stones Drummer Charlie Watts:

- https://www.youtube.com/watch?v=MVoQMJiMnpk

Jeanette Archer; Satanic Rituals Exposed at London Hyde Park on June 26, 2021:

- https://www.brighteon.com/7d938fcf-0bdd-4ff4-bcc0-6212c3d1b633

Jade Bidwell's testimony regarding a childhood under Satanic Ritual Abuse:

- https://www.youtube.com/watch?v=EEX0gcTBlu4

Interview with Jessie Czebotar, Satanic Ritual Abuse Survivor:

- https://www.youtube.com/watch?v=hvJH-KsJoNA

CHAPTER 9

SOUND BITES, PART 4

"It took me so long to find out.
And I found out."
    The Beatles: 'Day Tripper.'

"The entertainment industry is a toxic cesspool of Satanic psycho-
paths. Am I exaggerating, here? No."
    Vigilant Citizen, 2021

As previously mentioned, a ridiculous amount of synchronistic correlations between the **Beatles** and the Roman Polanski-directed 1968
movie *'Rosemary's Baby'* exist. (The film, though based on a novel by
Ira Levin and ostensibly "fiction," actually tells us a lot about the true
nature of Satanic cults and the power that they wield in society. Guy,
Rosemary's husband, is a struggling actor looking for a break. After
unwittingly falling in with the group of Satanists based in the building where he lives, he gets taken into the fold and afforded the success
he craves when a fellow actor suddenly becomes blind, allowing Guy
to take his role. The inference is that the Satanists had caused this to
happen through the casting of spells. Guy is now beholden to the group
and owes them big-time. The price he pays is to give over his unwitting
wife to the cult to be impregnated by "the Devil" in a ritual, so she can
give birth to his spawn. Many household-name artists in the TV, film
and music fields will have had their fame and fortune facilitated by dark
occultists, and will have had to pay a similarly heavy price in exchange
for it — see *'Musical Truth Volume 1'*'s accounts of blood sacrifices for
more on this.)
    It's difficult to know where to start, but a good place might be to
note that *'Rosemary's Baby'* was set largely in a building called The Bram-
ford, which was in fact the Dakota building on the West side of New
York City's Central Park. This is where **John Lennon** and **Yoko Ono**

had an apartment for the last several years of Lennon's life. (Yoko has described herself as a witch with an interest in the dark occult.) Across from the building in Central Park is the "Strawberry Fields" memorial to John.

Early on in the film a young woman falls to her death from an upstairs window in the Bramford/ Dakota. Next to where her body is found is parked a white VW Beetle (Beatle?) car which is splattered with blood. This location is very close to the very spot where John Lennon was murdered in December 1980.

Mia Farrow, who portrayed Rosemary, accompanied the Beatles on their visit to the Maharishi Mahesh Yogi's spiritual retreat in India in February 1968, a few weeks before the release of the film. Also on the trip was Farrow's sister, Prudence, whose apparent reluctance to leave her accommodation and join the rest of the group in meditation practices inspired the song 'Dear Prudence' on 'The White Album' released later that year.

Although 'Rosemary's Baby' was released in 1968, the story is set in 1965 and '66. A 1966 calendar is seen on the wall during a New Year's Eve party as the Sidney Blackmer character, one of the lead Satanists, declares it to be "year one." The Church of Satan was founded in San Francisco by its High Priest Anton La Vey, (who is rumoured to have portrayed the Devil in the movie,) on the Pagan festival of Beltane on 30th April of that year. La Vey had decreed that 1966 should be "*anno Satanas*," the first year of the new reign of Satan. 1966 is persistently given as the year in which the original Paul McCartney (take a swig) died and was replaced, according the popular "conspiracy theory" known as P.I.D., or Paul Is Dead.

Another key movie released in 1968 was Stanley Kubrick's enigmatic '2001: A Space Odyssey.' The film's narrative was projecting 33 (a key Masonic number) years into the future, as if prophesying an epoch-shattering event at that time. As it turned out we got just that with the events of 9/11. In the same year as '2001's release, construction began on the first of the World Trade Centre towers in New York, (thought by many to be symbolic representations of Jachin and Boaz, the twin pillars of Freemasonry,) which would come crashing down 33 years later. On that date, 11th September 2011, Paul McCartney (swig) claimed that he was on a plane waiting to take off from New York's JFK Airport when the disaster struck.

Roman Polanski's wife in the late 1960s was Sharon Tate who—according to the official story at least—became one of the seven victims in the so-called Tate/ La Bianca murders of 8th and 9th August 1969. (One of the other victims was Jay Sebring, a hair stylist to Hollywood stars including Frank Sinatra, who at the time of *'Rosemary's Baby'* was the husband of Mia Farrow.) These killings were said to have been carried out by the so-called Manson Family, under the direction of their charismatic leader Charles Manson. In Manson's subsequent trial, in which he was found guilty of murder despite not having killed anyone himself, the L.A. District Attorney alleged that Manson was obsessed with the Beatles' recently-released *'White Album,'* and in particular the Paul McCartney-penned song (swig) *'Helter Skelter.'*

Manson was said to have adopted the phrase "Helter Skelter" for the apocalyptic race war he had hoped to spark. He reportedly claimed to have interpreted hidden meanings within certain Beatles songs. When police finally raided the Spahn Ranch hideout of Manson and his gang in November of '69, they reportedly removed a fridge door which was covered in haphazard scrawlings. Included among these was the phrase "1, 2, 3, 4, 5, 6, 7, all good children go to Heaven." Although from a children's nursery rhyme, this line was also included on the song *'The Long One'* from the Beatles *'Abbey Road'* album. *If* the lyric was a reference to the Beatles song, it would mean Manson and co. would have had to have had advance access to the album since it was not released until late September, and the gang had already vacated the ranch in the wake of the murders in August and moved to a new base in Death Valley.

Another track included on *'The White Album'* was *'Sexy Sadie.'* This had been the nickname given by Charles Manson to Susan Atkins, one of his "family" devotees, (and most likely the subject of mind-control programming, possibly at the hands of the C.I.A.)

Polanski and Tate were known to at least two of the Beatles. The pair had attended an exhibition of Yoko Ono's art at the Indica Gallery in London on 9th November (9/11) 1966. According to lore, this is the event where John Lennon first met his future wife, (and, according to many, mind-control handler—that's a whole different story!) The Indica was curated by Barry Miles, John Dunbar, Paul McCartney (swig) and **Peter Asher**, the brother of Jane Asher, Paul McCartney's girlfriend of the time. **Ringo Starr** was later pictured socialising with Roman and Sharon at the Cannes Film Festival in 1968. Polanski had a brief cameo in the 1969 movie *'The Magic Christian,'* in which Ringo had the main role. At that movie's premiere, Polanski attended along-side John Lennon and Yoko.

The word "pigs" is said to have been daubed in one of the victims' blood on to the wall at 10050 Cielo Drive, site of the Tate murders. Pig imagery is seen frequently in *'The Magic Christian,'* and *'Piggies'* is the title of a George Harrison-penned song featured on *'The White Album.'* Manson is said to have interpreted this reference to "piggies" as mean-ing anyone who belonged to the Establishment.

Sharon Tate's last movie, released some weeks after her apparent death, was originally titled *'12+1,'* later renamed *'The Thirteen Chairs.'* It is set in the Suffolk village of Lavenham, which reportedly has a long association with witchcraft, and had only the year before provided the setting for the Vincent Price-starring movie *'Witchfinder General.'* In December 1969, John Lennon and Yoko Ono turned up in Lavenham village square to film scenes for a short movie titled *'Apotheosis.'*

A few hours before the Tate murders are said to have taken place, on 8th August 1969, (one week before the epoch-marking Woodstock rock concert,) the iconic sleeve photo for the Beatles' upcoming *'Abbey Road'* album was being taken as the four members walked across the famous zebra crossing outside London's EMI Studios. This sleeve became one of the main sources of "clues" interpreted by adherents to the Paul Is Dead theory. Also in the photo was a white VW Beetle of the type seen earlier in *'Rosemary's Baby.'*

The Tate murders, (if they were real—some researchers claim they were a staged hoax with the willing complicity of the "victims" to help tarnish the image of hippie culture among the American public,) took place a stone's throw from the fabled Laurel Canyon district of L.A.'s Hollywood Hills. The late author and researcher David McGowan in his book *'Weird Scenes Inside The Canyon',* comprehensively detailed the military-intelligence family backgrounds of many of the prominent musicians that emerged out of this neighbourhood to birth the hippie/ Counter-Culture scene in the mid to late 1960s. There are a handful of Beatles connections to Laurel Canyon too. George Harrison is said to have written the song *'Blue Jay Way,'* included on the *'Magical Mystery Tour'* EP and album, after arriving at a rented house in the street of the song's name in 1967. Harrison was waiting for Derek Taylor, the Beatles' publicist, to arrive, and was struggling to stay awake following the flight from London to Los Angeles.

Taylor served as the Beatles' press officer early in their career, before relocating for a time to Los Angeles where he began working with many of the Laurel Canyon musicians. including **The Beach Boys** (who connect back to Manson through his friendship and musical collaborations with the group's **Dennis Wilson**,) **The Byrds** and **The Mamas & The Papas**. The latter group's key member was **John Phillips**, with whom Taylor worked on curating the Monterey Pop Festival in San Francisco in June 1967, a key Flower Power event in that year's fabled Summer of Love. Also on the advisory panel for the concert, even though the Beatles never performed at it, was Paul McCartney, (take a swig) who reportedly recommended that **The Who** and the **Jimi Hendrix Experience** be booked to play.

Alongside "Papa" John Phillips in the Mamas & The Papas was **"Mama" Cass Elliott**, and both were associates of Charles Manson who would frequently drop in at Elliott's L.A. home due to her "open door" policy as part of the 60s "free love" ethos. Actor Michael Caine has mentioned that he recalls meeting Manson at a party hosted by Mama Cass. (Caine starred in the movie *'Alfie'* alongside Jane Asher, who at the time was the girlfriend of Paul McCartney—take a swig.)

Elliott turned up dead on 29th July 1974, aged 32. Despite an urban myth claiming that she had choked to death on a ham sandwich, her autopsy concluded that the cause of death had been heart failure. She had died in a flat in Mayfair, London, owned by the singer/ songwriter **Harry Nilsson**. Four years later, on 7th September 1978, **Keith Moon**, the drummer with The Who, was discovered dead in the very same flat having overdosed on pharmaceutical pills. Like Elliott, he was 32. Earlier that evening, Moon had been socialising in London with . . . Paul and Linda McCartney. Take a swig. Are you still upright?

Nilsson, who spent his formative years in Los Angeles, connects back into the Beatles through his friendship with John Lennon. He became known unofficially as "the American Beatle." During Lennon's fabled "Lost Weekend" period of 1973/ 74 where he had temporarily moved in and begun a relationship with his and Yoko Ono's secretary May Pang, Lennon frequently went on drink and drug binges around L.A. with Nilsson, sometimes joined by Ringo Starr.

And, circling right back around to *Rosemary's Baby,*' the poster image for the movie features Mia Farrow in profile, lying back as if in a mind-controlled trance, with the pram containing the spawn of "the Devil" in front of her. A very similar image was employed for the sleeve design of Lennon's *Mind Games* album five years later. This image features Yoko Ono in profile, lying back as if in a mind-controlled trance, and made to look as if a rocky backdrop to a desert landscape, with the sun and moon both visible in the sky. Walking in the foreground is the figure of Lennon. Mind games indeed.

This album was released around the time of Lennon's "Lost Weekend," and here we get another reference to Polanski. May Pang has recalled that following one of his drug and alcohol sessions, Lennon had become so ensconced in a rage that he'd had to be tied to a bed to restrain him. As he'd tried to break himself loose, he'd reportedly screamed, for no reason that anyone could make out, "It's Roman Polanski's fault! Roman Polanski is to blame for everything."

More on Ringo, as identified by the razor-sharp researcher Matt Sergiou in a fascinating article on his *Occult Beatles* blog site: In 1981, Ringo released an album titled *Stop And Smell The Roses* with a cover image, appropriately enough, of him holding a bunch of red roses. This appears to mimic a scene from *Rosemary's Baby* where Mia Farrow's character arrives back in her apartment to find a vase of fresh red roses has been left on the table, and she walks over to smell them. Was Ringo, for whatever symbolic reason—possibly in another link into Freemasonry given that the rose is one of the symbols frequently employed within that fraternity—paying homage to this scene? Earlier, in 1973, Paul McCartney (swig) had appeared with a red rose protruding from his mouth on the sleeve to the Wings album *Red Rose Speedway.*'

Finally—for now—one last connection between The Beatles, the Dakota, Manson and Laurel Canyon. According to '*Hollywood Babylon,*' the book by dark occultist and Satanic film-maker Kenneth Anger, (real name Kenneth Anglemeyer,) Mark Chapman, who is acknowledged to have been John Lennon's assassin, (though many accounts claim he was merely the patsy programmed to take the rap for it!) once turned up at a screening of one of Anger's films in Hawaii and handed him two .38 calibre bullets, stating, "these are for John Lennon."

For a time, Anger was in a homosexual relationship with musician **Bobby Beausoleil**, who was part of the late 1960s Laurel Canyon set, and who composed the first music score for Anger's film '*Lucifer Rising.*' (The second was composed by **Led Zeppelin**'s **Jimmy Page**—like Anger, a devotee of Aleister Crowley.) Beausoleil's more unsettling claim to fame, however, was his murder of the music teacher Gary Hinman, allegedly upon the orders of Charles Manson, to whose "family" Beausoleil was connected. Anger, in turn, was a close associate of the **Rolling Stones**, the Beatles main "rivals," with **Mick Jagger** scoring the soundtrack for Anger's film '*Invocation of my Demon Brother.*'

The synchro-mystic connections between arguably the most famous pop group in the world and this most unsettling, yet revealing of movies, seem never-ending, and there are probably many more than those listed here. So much so that it seems beyond the realms of any human planning, and instead to be occurring at the hands of some unknown paranormal force of Creation.

*

To my thinking there are now very few sub-genres which remain untouched by the Hidden Hand of the industry's controllers, or which aren't being used as vehicles to push societal agendas. I had to turn my back on the mainstream rap and R&B output that I previously played as a DJ when these styles had become so debased and degraded that I could no longer, in all good conscience, assist in the peddling of them.

If there is one exception to this general rule, it would have to be the soulful, uplifting House genre. While most, if not all other expressions of club and dance music have long since been steered off in

Establishment-serving directions, this purest form of House music, its vocals often drawing on gospel influences and its lyrical themes steeped in love and high vibrations, has barely changed in its values in the 30-plus years it's been around.

It's there, tragically, that the exceptions to the rule end. I would love to have been able to proclaim that Reggae music could have been listed alongside Soulful House as being devoid of the usual Control System calling cards, but it's my unfortunate duty to state that this is not the case—at least within certain factions of this admittedly broad and all-encompassing musical category.

It's little wonder that the Reggae field has been singled out as rife for manipulation given that it goes beyond the music to incorporate an entire culture, lifestyle and ethos—rather like Hip-Hop. Reggae's origins can be traced back to the rhythmic drumming style known as "Mento" music coming out of West Africa, before this got exported to Jamaica. (**Harry Belafonte**'s '*Day-O (The Banana Boat Song)*' is often cited as an example of the Mento style.) This sound is acknowledged as having birthed the Ska and Rocksteady genres, which in turn mutated into what came to be known as Reggae in the late 1960s. Credit for the name of the genre falls to the group **Toots and the Maytals**, whose 1968 song '*Do The Reggay*' was the first to employ the term.

In the last book, I referenced comments made by The Black Dot and **Public Enemy**'s **Professor Griff** on how the explosion of Hip-Hop culture out of New York in the 1970s represented a re-awakening of ancestral instincts among descendants of Africans, and how cultural aspects such as turntablism, graffiti and breakdancing represented contemporary interpretations of tribal traditions in rhythm, art and dance. The same dynamic is at play with Reggae. The genre is intrinsically linked with the religious tradition of Rastafarianism, key aspects of which involve the deification of the long-time Emperor of Ethiopia Haile Selassie, and the ceremonial smoking of marijuana.

Reggae also has a complicated interplay with Judaism, Christianity and certain symbolism employed by Freemasonry. Its lyrics frequently talk of "Zion" as the promised land and of "Babylon" as representative of the New World Order control system, of which its adherents appear to have much knowledge. Selassie is symbolised as a "conquering lion."

Given its potential to spiritually enrich, culturally inspire, and unify large numbers of people, therefore, it's not hard to see why the "elite" social-engineers would wish to steer this art form off in their own desired directions, rather than let it flourish organically. The subject of Reggae's infiltration on this basis formed the theme of an episode of my '*Good Vibrations*' podcast with the New York-based author, lecturer and black cultural studies scholar R.A Ptahsen, more commonly known as Rodney Shabazz.

By far Reggae's most famous exponent was **Bob Marley**, and here we have a real paradox. Given the trends revealed by the research involved in these books, Marley's parentage gives some cause for concern. While his mother was a black Jamaican singer, his white father, Norval Sinclair Marley, was of Syrian-Jewish descent, and served as an officer in the British Navy, as well as being an overseer on a slave plantation. (Bob's son **Ziggy**, was perhaps honouring his grandfather's Jewish ancestry when he relocated to Israel, married an Israeli of Iranian-Jewish descent, and gave each of their four children Hebrew names. He has resisted calls to boycott performances in Israel over its political genociding of the people of Palestine.)

With Norval having died in 1955 when Bob was just ten, an argument might be made for Bob—similar to **Jim Morrison** with his Navy Admiral dad—having sought to distance himself from his father's values and to tread his own path. He certainly *appeared* to be a genuine and sincere artist, and became a thorn in the side of the Establishment through the political activism which led to the 1976 attempt on his life. '*Musical Truth 2*' detailed at great length the circumstances in which Bob finally succumbed to a highly suspicious variant of cancer in 1981 aged just 36, and the evidence that strongly suggests this occurred at the hands of the CIA.

Though musicians genuinely motivated by personal ideals rather than conforming to their owners' dictates may now be virtually non-existent, this certainly seems to have been a factor that would have been of concern to the industry overlords in decades past, and music lore is littered with accounts of artists who have fallen foul of those that first gave them their fame, and who paid the ultimate price as a result.

And so it has been in Reggae, Dr. Shabazz suggests. Alongside Bob Marley, there was **Jacob Miller**, lead singer with the group **Inner Circle**, (and a cousin of British Reggae singer **Maxi Priest**.) A practicing Rastafarian, Miller was similarly concerned with social and political issues. He had performed at the One Love Peace Concert at the Kingston National Stadium in 1978 alongside Marley, **Peter Tosh, Dennis Brown** and others. Miller and Marley were friends, and in early 1980, both had accompanied Chris Blackwell, the proprietor of the Island Records label, to Brazil, where plans were being drawn for new Island offices and a South American reggae tour. Shortly after returning home, Miller and one of his young sons was killed in a car accident as he left the home near Kingston which Marley had purchased from Blackwell. Like so many other prominent musicians who have died untimely deaths, Miler was 27.

Within a year Marley would also be dead, and six years later, the pair were joined by Peter Tosh, the remainder of what many consider to have been a "holy trinity" of conscious Reggae musicians. Just the previous year Tosh had complained at a press conference in New York about his album 'Captured Live' not being made available for sale in the US by EMI, the major label he was signed to, and of its video being systematically suppressed, (ironically comparing his situation to that of **Prince**, who was still riding high with his label Warner Brothers at the time, but would come to be embroiled in the same kind of corporate wranglings as Tosh.)

Incidentally, a fascinating anecdote came from Doug Wendt, who ran a Reggae radio show called 'Midnight Dread' for several years in the 1970s and 80s. In August 1983 Wendt got to interview Peter Tosh, (real name Winston Hubert McIntosh) in San Francisco. Tosh recorded the conversation on to a cassette recorder. He told Wendt he wanted the executives at EMI to hear him speak about how poorly the label was promoting his material and Reggae music in general. Wendt took the cassette home intending to prepare the interview for his next radio show, but when he scanned through the tape he was horrified to hear that after a few minutes Tosh's voice got lower and lower until it faded away into nothing. There was no usable material for airing. Disgusted, Wendt threw the tape into a box in his attic and forgot all about it.

Four years later, on the auspicious date of 11th September of 1987, Wendt received a call to say that Peter Tosh had been murdered. A gang led by a known criminal, Dennis "Leppo" Lobban had raided his home. Lobban and Tosh were former friends. Tosh had tried to find work for Lobban when he was released from jail. After reportedly demanding money from him, the gang shot Tosh in the head. Herbalist Wilton "Doc" Brown and DJ Jeff 'Free I' Dixon were also killed, and several other acquaintances who were at Tosh's residence were injured.

Instinct drove Wendt to retrieve the old interview cassette from his attic, and when he played it again, miraculously all the audio was intact, and he was able to air the interview in tribute to Tosh's memory. As Wendt wrote in 2002 on his *'Midnight Dread'* blog:

> *"Suddenly, it was all there. The magnetic particles had somehow, someway undergone spontaneous regeneration in the wake of Peter's passing. Some force beyond comprehension had decided that now was the time when Tosh's word sound power from August 17th, 1983 could be dispersed most freely and effectively. The hair on the back of my neck stood up."*

I had the same experience when first reading this story, as it reminded me of the one I related in *'Musical Truth 1'* about the backmasked Satanic message in Madonna's *'Justify My Love'* inexplicably being wiped from a reel of tape in a radio station when I tried to play it to another DJ, (named 'Priestley' appropriately enough.)

And so, back to my podcast conversation with Dr. Shabazz. In it, he turned his attention back to the aforementioned Chris Blackwell, head of the most prominent and influential Reggae music label of all. On the face of it Blackwell seemed an odd contender for the role given his background. He was born into an aristocratic family which was behind the Cross & Blackwell food brand. His mother was a Costa Rica-born Jamaican heiress, (originally of Sephardic Jewish heritage) and Chris spent his early childhood in Jamaica where, in yet another military connection, his father served as a Major in the Jamaica Regiment. After a spell at Harrow Public School back in England, Blackwell returned to Jamaica to take up the role of assistant to the island's Governor, Sir Hugh Foot.

Chris is later said to have developed an interest in the Jamaican music scene through his managing of jukeboxes around the island, going on to form his record label at the age of 22. He is also said to have been recruited as a location scout by the producers of the first James Bond movie, 'Dr. No,' in 1962. The reason for his choice may well have been down to his mother, Blanche, having been an illicit lover of James Bond creator Ian Fleming during his latter years living as part of Jamaica's British ex-pat community. Blanche was said to have been the inspiration for some of Fleming's more memorable literary characters, such as Honeychile Rider and Pussy Galore.

Blackwell resigned from Island Records in 1997, and the label was later sold to the PolyGram group. Over the years he has worked with artists as diverse as **U2, Cat Stevens, Roxy Music, Nirvana, Grace Jones, Steve Winwood, Nick Drake, Free, Melissa Etheridge, Tom Waits, The Cranberries, Richard Thompson** and **PJ Harvey**. He was always best known for his work within the Reggae field, though—producing many key albums as well as managing the musicians. His Establishment background has led to the inevitable suggestion that he fulfilled the role of a Gatekeeper to the fledgling Reggae scene and that, rather than allow that genre to develop naturally under the leadership of a black-owned label, the industry's controllers found it preferable to have one of "their own" at the helm.

Blackwell's name is not the only one put forward in this regard. For several decades the most prominent and influential Reggae DJ in Britain is acknowledged to have been **David Rodigan**. Indeed, Rodigan shares a characteristic with Blackwell; his father was also in the military. Rodigan himself was born on a military base in Hanover, Germany before settling back in England. There, after studying economics he trained as an actor, landing roles in such TV shows as the BBC's 'Dr. Who.' Rodigan's love for Jamaican music is said to have been sparked by his hearing Millie's 'My Boy Lollipop' in 1964, and he subsequently pursued his path as a DJ, ultimately landing a radio show on BBC 1Xtra. Rodigan has certainly put the work in over the decades, endearing himself to the Reggae community at home and abroad, and having competed in DJ soundclashes at hardcore events in Jamaica which are not for the faint-hearted or weak-willed.

Nevertheless, he has drawn suspicion from some quarters as to the true nature of his interest in the genre—a sentiment added to by his having been awarded an MBE—a Member of the British Empire gong. Again, a music genre and culture created by black people gets key aspects of it falling under the control of a white, middle-class candidate, rather than a member of the communities the culture claims to represent. Exactly the same dynamic has been seen in the British Hip-Hop scene, which for decades has seen **Tim Westwood** as the most prominent and influential DJ at its helm. Just like Rodigan, Westwood is white, middle-class and public school-educated. In his case, his father was an Anglican bishop. Westwood has presided over his allotted genre during its regression into the debasement and degradation in which it now wallows, and all the social-engineering agenda pushing it has done along the way.

Both of Rodigan's sons are now active in music: Jamie is a DJ and producer, and Oliver is better known as the artist **Cadenza**.

Another aspect discussed in my '*Good Vibrations*' episode was the emergence of the Reggae sub-genre known as Dancehall, and referred to for a period in the 1990s as "Ragga"—a shortening of the word "raggamuffin," defined as a "roughneck" or a "streetwise tough guy." In stark contrast to the "roots" and "conscious" aspects of the genre, which emphasised Reggae's links with spiritual and cultural pursuits, Dancehall concerned itself with the glorification of guns, criminal lifestyles, and promiscuous sex—"slackness" in Jamaican parlance.

One of the best-known exponents of recent years has been **Vybz Kartel** whose real-life exploits have echoed those in his lyrics; he was charged with murder, conspiracy and illegal possession of a firearm in 2012.

*

I covered in '*Musical Truth Volume 2*' some of the more intriguing aspects of Gary Webb under his alter-ego **Gary Numan**—particularly the obvious early nods to Transhumanism that his stage name (Numan = new man,) suggests. It turns out, however, that far from being limited to his late 1970s heyday, every stage of his durable career offers some eyebrow-raisers for those by now familiar with the machinations of the controlled music industry and the agendas it likes to push. (Big thanks to New Anger for his help with some of this information.)

After Gary had shown an interest in writing songs at the age of 13, his parents are reported to have bought him a Gibson "Gold Top'" Les Paul guitar when he was 15, which would have been a very expensive gift for a regular, working-class family to afford. Gary quit his job as a forklift operator at Heathrow Airport on the day that Tubeway Army's first single was released following their signing to the independent label Beggars Banquet. Gary has consistently told the story that the "Numan" name came from his playing around with the German-sounding Neumann that he had seen in an edition of the *'Yellow Pages'*, though he has recalled the business in question as having been, variously, a plumber, an electrician and an electrical wholesaler.

Gary Numan—pre-selected for fame?
https://commons.wikimedia.org/wiki/File:Gary_Numan_2011.jpg
Source: Flickr: Gary Numan
Author: Man Alive!

Although Numan remains best known for his soulless android-like persona, clearly influenced by German 1970s synth pioneers Kraftwerk, (and with his diehard fans referred to as "Numanoids,") when he first started out with his band Tubeway Army their sound was clearly rooted in the popular Punk and New Wave styles of the day. Numan's fascination with Dystopian science-fiction is said to have caused his orientation towards synthesisers—boosted by the oft-recited anecdote of him having stumbled upon a Mini-Moog synth that had been fortuitously left behind by the previous band when he went for his first professional recording session at Spaceward Studios in Cambridge. This musical signature in place, his success came very quickly, scoring him two British number one singles within the space of a few weeks, and all by the age of 21.

Within 24 hours upon the release of '*Are Friends Electric*,' Gary got to perform on the two most celebrated BBC TV music shows of the time—'*The Old Grey Whistle Test*,' which normally shunned new acts and electronic styles in favour of well-established bands, and '*Top of the Pops*,' despite the song not yet having entered the Top 40, exposing him to a new audience of many millions. It was also seen to that 20,000 picture discs of the single were released which was an extremely rare occurrence in 1979, especially in the case of a new artist. Numan embarked on a sell-out UK tour off the back of the two singles, only 13 months after his group had played their very first gig in a pub in West London. He was certainly on the fast-track route to mega-stardom.

An interesting lyric occurs in '*Listen To The Sirens*,' the opening track of the self-titled Tubeway Army album. Listeners hear the phrase, "Mr Webb, there is no way out." Could this have been an in-plain-sight reference to the fact that Gary had just signed up to become yet another controlled asset of the corporate industry, to be deployed in whatever way his new owners might see fit? And was Gary earmarked from his very early years as a future star? In an interview given in 2001 for a Channel 4 TV show called '*Top Ten: Electropop*,' Numan's uncle, Jess Lidyard, recalled that Gary had said from the age of 14 that one day he was going to have a hit with a song called '*Cars*,' but he didn't know what it was going to sound like. The video to '*Cars*,' when the song appeared seven years later, ran the full gamut of by-now familiar symbolism—Masonic duality, pyramids, multiple personalities, mirror images, etc.

Numan's fall from mass-market fame occurred almost as quickly as his ascent. Already by the time of his second album '*Telekon*,' (inspired by the psychic phenomenon of telekinesis) in 1980, some dark lyrical themes had crept in, with Gary talking of fame being over-rated and of his just wanting to be on his own. His career seemed to be all spent by the following year when he performed a series of "farewell" concerts at Wembley Arena. After some time spent living in the US and in Jersey, however (apparently for tax-avoidance purposes) he was back for another 40-date UK tour in 1983, and for this one appeared with freshly cropped and dyed peroxide-blonde hair. As previously documented, this is one of the visual indicators of the presence of trauma-based mind-control programming, and when an artist appears with this look after a period out of the spotlight, it often symbolises their having been back to the lab to have their programming "topped up."

By 1984, Gary had left Beggars Banquet and had set up his own label, Numa Records. After three flop albums, he then allied himself with Miles Copeland Jr., the son of the career military intelligence officer who was behind the success of The Police and so many other New Wave bands.

In 1997, Numan released the album '*Exile,*' whose lyrical themes examined the distinctly Satanic ideology that God and The Devil were interchangeable and with song titles like '*Dominion Day, 'Dead Heaven,*' '*Innocence Bleeding*' and '*The Angel Wars.*' He was back in dark, Dystopian territory with 2017's '*Savage (Songs from a Broken World,)*' described as "a concept album centred around the blending of Western and Eastern cultures in a post-apocalyptic world that has become desertified as a result of global warming." Interestingly, the cover depicts him standing against a desert backdrop wearing . . . a face mask. It could certainly be said that he was ahead of his time. '*Savage*' hit number two on the British album charts, almost 40 years on from Numan's first appearance—the latest in a number of highly improbable career resurgences. "Global" Warming was the name of the game with his 2021 album '*Intruder,*' too, and in more recent interviews Numan has, in all apparent seriousness, claimed that his Aspergers' condition has been caused by "Climate Change."

Gary's wife Gemma O'Neil warrants some further study, too. The murky spectre of the reviled Jimmy Savile crops up here, as it turns out that Gemma wrote to Savile's TV show '*Jim'll Fix It*' when aged 10, telling Savile she wanted to marry Gary Numan, and that she wanted to become friends with **Toyah Willcox**. She got both her wishes, it turns out, marrying Gary in 1997. The couple moved to Los Angeles some years later where they raised their three children. Gemma has since undergone extensive appearance-modifying surgery, particularly on her lips, looking like a cross between Pete Burns and Danniella Westbrook as a result, as well as undergoing an entire "body lift." Gemma is credited with having spring-boarded one of Numan's career revivals. Gary has talked of Gemma "rescuing" him.

Many Numan fans have complained about the controlling influence that Gemma seems to have had over him, (where have we come across that scenario before?) and chat threads have suggested that it was due to her coercion that he announced that he suffers from Asperger's Syndrome, a condition at the high-functioning end of the Autism spectrum. Many fans contend that he has never had this condition, but that he brings it up frequently in interviews as a marketing tool, or to garner public sympathy.

By way of an alternative narrative, however, could the Aspergers claim be used to explain away behavioural traits that may be the result of mind-control programming of the type that—as we know only too well—has been present with A-list music stars since the very inception of the industry? Gary is said to have suffered from depression during his teenage years, resulting in a visit to a child psychologist at London's St. Thomas' Hospital when he was 15.

The idea that there may be much more to know about Gary Numan's true nature was reinforced by Ade Orange, a former keyboard player in Gary's band. In 2020 he recorded an interview documenting some of his experiences in the group, and revealing that he was planning to publish a book to be titled '*Gary Numan—Are You Real?*' ('*Are You Real*' had been the title of a track on the first Tubeway Army album. Numan himself has published two auto-biographies—'*Praying To The Aliens*' in 1997, and '*(R)evolution: The Autobiography*' in 2020.

In the early 90s, by which point Numan's career was at an all-time low and he was virtually forgotten about in America, a fan there named Jim Napier started a North American fanzine, igniting interest in the singer from legions of new fans. Some animosity brewed after Napier became close to Gary and Gemma, however, and he has since been reportedly working on a film, to be titled '*Whispers of Truths,*' telling of his interaction with the pair.

For those always looking for military links, Numan's résumé doesn't disappoint. While his father is listed as having been a bus driver based at Heathrow Airport, Gary himself spent a period during his teens in The Air Training Corps, a youth volunteer organisation sponsored by the Ministry of Defence and the Royal Air Force. He went on to obtain a pilot's licence and an enthusiasm for flying light aircraft.

Perhaps most intriguingly of all, however—and possibly holding the key to his rapid rise to public prominence—the week in which Gary was born, in March 1958, was in the midst of what had been dubbed the National Child Development Study. Initially sponsored by the National Birthday Trust Fund and spearheaded by paediatrician Neville Butler, the idea was to monitor and chart the development of 17,415 children born in England, Scotland and Wales between 3rd to 9th March of that year. It might have been a rather boring study had none of the children surveyed gone on to obtain any kind of "celebrity" status. No cause for concern there, though; other famous names born that very week include comedy actors Rik Mayall and Miranda Richardson, and the Bee Gee that never was, Andy Gibb.

As such things are never openly admitted to, we're left to hazard an educated guess. But many trends and patterns that we've experienced multiple times before in these methods of research are present in Gary Numan's story.

Have we been witnessing, through Gary's long career, a '*Truman Show*'-style monitoring of every aspect of a man's life, many aspects of it engineered by those who specialise in being able to make such things happen, viewed through the microscopes of Tavistock-style social scientists, and with mind-control programming and agenda-pushing social-engineering never far from the surface? Was it always written that Gary Webb would become Gary Numan, and was there ever any way of him avoiding this fate?

*

The music industry's mind-control slaves often put in a lifetime of service to their overlords. Even after several years of dormancy, like a "sleeper" assassin of the type portrayed in CIA movies, they can be called back into service any time an agenda arises for which their input is required.

This would certainly appear to have been the case with **Sinéad O'Connor.** From her earliest days in the industry she portrayed all the signs of having been a trauma-based mind-control subject, the shaven-headed look for which she was famous serving as a tell-tale indicator, (see *'Musical Truth Volume 1.'*) O'Connor has commented that she "doesn't feel herself" with hair.

Although at times appearing to be on the side of Truth and the People, appearing alongside Ian Brown to decry Tony Blair's murderous incursions into Iraq and Afghanistan on *'Illegal Attacks,'* for instance, and calling out institutionalised paedophilia in the Catholic Church, Sinéad's messages have been mixed and confused to say the least, indicating that she is at the whim of unseen handlers, and her thoughts and will are truly not her own.

According to Fritz Springmeier, author of *'Bloodlines of the Illuminati'* and *'The Illuminati Formula Used to Create an Undetectable Total Mind-Controlled Slave,'* O'Connor was probably programmed by singer/actor **Kris Kristoffersen**, whose name has come up often in discussions of this nature. He is said to be a "Re-programmer" or "Booster Programmer" of slaves in euphemistic "rehab" centres. Springmeier has said that Kristofferson is a hugely important Rhodes Scholar and a member of the Council on Foreign Relations for world government.

Springmeier notes that the "Illuminati" often, but not always, choose their slaves from among blue-blood names, hence Sinéad O'Connor probably had some "blue blood" connection. She was sent to a "Magdalene asylum," an archaic institution for fallen women, at the age of 15 after a spate of shoplifting and truancy.

Little is known of her mother Marie, who died in a car accident on her way to Mass when Sinéad was 19, a year before she debuted on the music scene with her album *'The Lion and The Cobra.'* In her auto-biography *'Rememberings,'* (an interesting title given the claim that mind-control subjects can break their programming as time progresses and regain deeply-buried memories,) released in 2021, Sinéad revealed that her mother was "so evil" that she regularly stripped her naked as a child and kicked her in the genitals in an attempt to prevent her from breeding. (It failed; she has four children.) Talking of a time when her mother locked her and her siblings in a garden shed, she made the potentially revealing comment that: "That is when I officially lost my mind and became afraid of the size of the sky."

So many clues as to generational Satanic Ritual Abuse are in place here. Of her mother, Sinéad writes:

"I think she was an evil person. When I look at photos of the woman she was before she got married, she was a joyful, gleaming, happy young woman, and I feel something possessed her. It was the devil in her."

A further admission towards her own mental health issues, (and incarceration in a mind-control programming facility?) comes from her statement:

"I've spent most of the time in the nuthouse. I've been practically living there for six years. We alone get to call it the nuthouse—the patients."

At a performance at a **Bob Dylan** 30th anniversary tribute at New York City's Madison Square Garden in October 1992, O'Connor was booed by the crowd as she walked on-stage. She seemed to get diverted onto an anti-racism rant that had nothing to do with the live situation and may have been a damage-control routine induced as part of her programming. Kristofferson, who had introduced her as a woman of "courage" and "integrity," stepped in to hug her and lead her off-stage, while whispering something inaudible in her ear—quite possibly a mind-control trigger phrase indicating a handler/ subject relationship.

Many years later O'Connor ostensibly converted to the Islamic faith, changing her name to Shuhada' Sadaqat. She subsequently referred to non-Muslims as "disgusting" and wrote at one point: "What I'm about to say is something so racist I never thought my soul could ever feel it. But truly I never wanna spend time with white people again (if that's what non-muslims are called). Not for one moment, for any reason. They are disgusting."

She has exhibited similarly mixed, and disturbed sentiments towards **Prince**, who had penned what remains her most prominent hit song in 'Nothing Compares 2 U.' In 'Rememberings' she writes of an encounter with Prince at his mansion:

> "I believe he was involved in Devil business because an old girl-friend of his told me he had the power to make shit move around the room ... He got me up there to see, could this bitch be one of mine? I guess he didn't bank on the Irish in me telling him to go fuck himself."

Ironically, O'Connor shares a factor in common with Prince, in that both have asked to be known by different identities for a period. In O'Connor's case, she changed her name to Magda Davitt in 2017, before adopting the Shuhada' Sadaqat moniker the following year. Could these alter-egos be expressions of multiple personalities brought on by a lifetime of trauma-based programming?

Just as a common cliché in Hollywood movies sees 'former" intelligence service assets being called out of "retirement" for "one more job," so it seems Sinéad had been given a new mission in the post-Co(n)vid world of 2021 when she laid into journalists Gemma O'Doherty and John Waters, accusing them of being "right-wing racists" and calling for their arrest. O'Connor's actions resulted from comments made by O'Doherty and Waters questioning politician Leo Varadkar's right to serve on the basis of him not being Irish. The pair had previously campaigned for the restoration of Common Law in Ireland, and themselves called for the arrest of treasonous Irish politicians in light of the country's tyrannical Co(n)vid regulations, but it had been the sound of crickets from O'Connor concerning this issue.

It turns out O'Connor knows Waters pretty well. She had a daughter with him, Roisin, born in 1996.

*

I've waxed nostalgically in quite a few of my podcast interviews over the years, about how virtually the entirety of the 1990s was a personal golden period for me. Being in my 20s I had a ball for the whole decade—particularly as at that time I still had a long way to go before waking up to the cold, harsh truths of this world, a process which, I've found, isn't entirely compatible with carefree fun and enjoyment. Perhaps readers have noticed the same??

No such burdens were there to trouble me back then, and so I was entirely susceptible to all the leisure and entertainment trappings that era had to offer. I recall everything as outstanding, from the movies, to the fashions, and of course, the music. Dance had emerged out of the Acid House/ Rave scene to usher in the period of the superclubs, with ground-breaking new innovations in electronic music to match. Britpop and Indie music was at an all-time high. Most importantly for me, though—and many a fellow Hip-Hop head will be with me here—the period from roughly 1988 to 1994 marked an all time quality high for American Rap output—particularly material from New York. Every aspect of those times remains fondly etched into my memory, and though I'll be eternally grateful for having undergone such wonderful experiences and such great music, I now find it painful to bring them to mind, because I know they are gone for good and nothing of their like will ever be coming along again.

Which brings me to the point of this piece. Humour me for a moment here, but given the understandings about how all aspects of entertainment and popular culture are controlled by the Hidden Hand that we now have—is it possible that such high periods and golden ages are created with the *specific purpose* of being completely destroyed and obliterated further down the line as a masterful way of cruelly dashing the memories and the morale of those who lived joyfully through them, plunging them instead into melancholic despair? To make the point, any reader needs only compare the so-called "Hip-Hop" output of the period 2008-2014 with that of 20 years' previous, and nothing further will need to be said. And as a chapter of this very book has noted, in 2020, the Hidden Hand seemed happy to trash pretty much the entire entertainment industry it had spent decades building up as super-weapons in mind-control and societal conditioning, as if they had succeeded by that point in getting the consciousness of the masses exactly where they wanted it and—the job now done—it could therefore be discarded with complete indifference.

I know many will take issue with my deeming the 1990s a cultural high period, and that many readers older than myself will cite previous decades in such a way according to their own personal memories and experiences. But this factor adds further credibility to my suggestion. With every trend, scene or era that has ever died a death, it has claimed with it its own body count of nostalgic casualties.

It wouldn't just be in popular culture that forces have been built up to greatness only to be deliberately trashed later, either. Nations and civilisations throughout history may have succumbed in similarly calculated conditions. By way of a good example there is so much evidence to suggest that the Twin Towers of the World Trade Centre were constructed in 1968 in the full knowledge that (a nice Masonic) 33 years later, they would be deliberately destroyed, plunging the United States and the wider world into extreme trauma, fear and chaos.

If all of these aspects of popular culture really have been killed off, rather than their demises having been organic processes, any forces behind these deliberate destructions would, by necessity, have to be Satanic, evil, and *deeply* sick in nature.

Just another day in the office of the controllers of Organised Society then.

*

It seems a new revelation about prominent entertainers doubling as military-intelligence assets now emerges with every passing year. This is of course down to the opportunities for research and information-sharing now offered by the internet, but even so, in some cases the evidence is so compelling that we can wonder how these links were ever *not* known about.

Many claims have been made about **Leonard Cohen** by his former girlfriend Ann Diamond, (who has spoken of being a childhood victim of trauma-based mind-control at the hands of the CIA in her native Canada, (and not to be confused by the English TV presenter of the same name.) These include the allegations that Cohen's role involved much more than pushing the usual Satanic cultural subversion promoted by music stars, and that he was in fact a valued military-intelligence agent with connections to the Tavistock Institute. This notion is alluded to by Cohen himself in his own song, *'Field Commander Cohen.'*

> *"Field Commander Cohen,*
>
> *He was our most important spy.*
>
> *Wounded in the line of duty,*
>
> *Parachuting acid into diplomatic cocktail parties."*

Coming with connections to McGill and Columbia Universities in Canada and the US, Diamond wrote in a 2015 article for the Henry Makow website that in 1959, Cohen—born on the Spring Equinox of 1934—met Jacob Rothschild in London. Jacob, (now Baron Rothscihld) is the son of Victor, who is said to have secretly run MI5, MI6 and the KGB during the staged "Cold War" and also founded the Tavistock Institute, the birthplace of MK-Ultra mind-control and social-engineering. Tavistock brought the Cultural Marxism of The Frankfurt School to the world.

It will surely come as no surprise that Cohen's sleeve artwork and promotional imagery through the years has drawn strongly on Freemasonic, Kabbalistic, Babylonian, Egyptian, and other esoteric/ mystery school themes.

Diamond wrote that Cohen has always had a habit of arriving in distant locations just ahead of historic coups. He was in Greece before the Colonels, in Montreal on the eve of the War Measures Act, in Israel days before the Yom Kippur War broke out, and in Asmara, Ethiopia for the CIA and Mossad-backed overthrow of Haile Selassie. He also showed up in London shortly before the murder of **Jimi Hendrix** (as ordered by his military-intelligence handler/ manager Michael Jeffery,) and in New York shortly before the CIA-sponsored murder of **John Lennon.**

In an interview for Episode 58 of *'Conflict Radio',* Ann Diamond made further comments about Cohen's potential knowledge of the assassinations of various rock stars who had been deemed troublesome to the Establishment.

Among them were her assertion that "I think Leonard did know how Hendrix, **Joplin** and **Lennon** died," but that, "I never heard Leonard talk about how **Jim Morrison** died."

She said, perplexingly, that:

> *"Leonard was on Lennon's assassination team, but I am not fully convinced that they killed Lennon . . . Leonard was a right-wing Zionist, but Lennon was in the left-wing faction, often making Anti-Zionist statements . . . Leonard was in NYC when Lennon was shot, he was a mile away across the park and was there the whole week."*

She added that Cohen had left a Greek island on 5th December 1980 to be in New York, and had returned there on 14th December, some days after Lennon was reportedly killed. On his return he reportedly commented simply that, "I never liked the Beatles."

Cohen did not begin a music career until 1967, by which point he was 33 (!) years old. Although quickly becoming a celebrated figure on the Counter-Culture scene—and dating folk icon **Joni Mitchell** for a time—he admitted that he was never a fan of the times nor the values that they espoused, and by the late 1980s his songs had begun mocking the demise of that generation's ideals and charting, with apparent admiration, a world fast going to rack and ruin. From his 1992 album *'The Future,'* co-produced by *'The Hand That Rocks The Cradle'* actress Rebecca De Mornay, Cohen sang the title track from the perspective of "the Devil," suggesting advanced inside knowledge of coming agendas, including as it did lyrics like:

> *"Get ready for the future, it is murder."*

And:

> *"Things are going to slide, slide in all directions.*
> *Won't be nothing,*
> *Nothing you can measure any more.*
> *The blizzard, the blizzard of the world,*
> *Has crossed the threshold,*
> *And it's overturned,*

The order of the soul."

Diamond recalled that in 1990 Cohen had urged her to convert to Judaism because, he said, (echoing his Zionist poet friend Israel Lazarovitch,) "a holocaust for gentiles is coming in the near future." He seemed to score fairly accurately on the "prediction" front with his song *'First We Take Manhattan,'* initially recorded by Jennifer Warnes in 1987. Wikipedia remarks that: "The song's oblique lyric is suggestive of religious and end-time themes with references to prayer, meaningful birthmarks and signs in the sky." It has elsewhere been described as a threatening vision of social collapse and terrorism.

Anything happen vaguely related to terrorism, social collapse and "signs in the sky" and involving Manhattan in the intervening years, can anyone remember??

*

The controllers of Organised Society love their dialectics—just witness the two-party political system present in most "Democratic" countries to give voters the illusion of "choice" when, no matter who gets voted in, the agenda stays the same.

And so—observing the maxim that you should never let a good strategy go to waste—the same concept has been deployed in the music industry through the decades, with two apparently "rival" acts frequently pitted against each-other, though with both ultimately puppeteered by the same forces. In the 1960s it was the **Beatles** "versus" the **Rolling Stones**, the reality being that both were the tools of social engineers and were all good friends. The 1970s saw **Marc Bolan** positioned "against" **David Bowie**, even though both were pushing androgyny and even shared the same producer in Tony Visconti.

Prince was pitted against **Michael Jackson** in the 80s, the irony being that both ultimately shared the same fate when going up against their record labels. The '90s saw **Blur** "against" **Oasis** in the "Britpop" era—even though both were used to promote the concept of "Cool Britannia," in large part designed to make psychopath Tony Blair appear "cool" and palatable to younger voters to ensure that he was firmly installed as Prime Minister ready for his warmongering orgy of the following decade. The Irish got in on the act with **Boyzone** vs. **Westlife**. And somewhere in the middle, as the New Romantic phase got underway, teenage girls throughout the UK were being urged to pick their preferred pin-up idols as **Duran Duran** got pitched against **Spandau Ballet.**

While nefarious influences are less easy to spot with Spandau, with Duran, they're were never far from the surface—at least by the time they'd reached mega-stardom in 1983 with their album *'Seven and the Ragged Tiger.'* By this point occult symbolism had crept into their artwork and videos, most of which were being directed by Australian Russell Mulcahy. I covered in the last book the video to *'Union of the Snake,'* the very title alluding to knowledge of secret-society networks, and whose storyline depicts the existence of DUMBs (Deep Underground Military Bases,) where children are kept captive in cages. If this had remained a one-off, it might have been plausibly written off as random and meaningless. This, however, turns out to be far from the case.

The *'Arena'* concert film which Mulcahy also directed has AI and reptilian-like entities interrupting the songs for no apparent reason. The sleeve to *'Seven and the Ragged Tiger'* is laden with occult and esoteric symbols, some of which have been employed by the Church of Satan. From this point on the band, named after a character in the 1968 futuristic fantasy movie *'Barbarella,'* adopted a sigil consisting of single eye with pyramids above and below as its official logo.

The Wikipedia entries for the Duran members are woefully lacking in background detail for their parents, particularly in the case of **Simon Le Bon**, though his does note that his last name is "of Huguenot origin." We also learn that Le Bon "worked on a kibbutz—an Israeli collective community—in the Negev desert in Israel in 1978." Here, he wrote the song *'Tel Aviv'* which ended up on Duran's first album, before returning to England in 1980 to study in Birmingham, then joining the band which **Nick Rhodes** and **John Taylor** had founded two years before. Le Bon had grown up around Middlesex, attending the same school in Pinner that **Elton John** had a few years earlier, and trained as an actor before getting into music. Like so many other celebrities he had started out as a child star. While rock star wife **Patsy Kensit** had appeared in a Birds Eye peas ad and *'Tube'* presenter Leslie Ash was in a Fairy Liquid commercial, in Le Bon's case he featured in a TV ad for Persil washing powder.

Like Bowie, **Marc Bolan**, **Bryan Ferry** and so many before them, Duran, and especially Nick Rhodes, pushed androgyny and "gender neutralism"—yet another society-altering agenda straight out of Tavistock. Rhodes wore a pink suit and full make-up with frosted pink lipstick to his wedding in 1984.

In guitarist **Andy Taylor**'s auto-biography *'Wild Boy: My Life in Duran Duran,'* he talks of being introduced to **Led Zeppelin**'s **Jimmy Page** by **Michael Des Barres**, with whom he worked in the Duran spin-off outfit **The Power Station**. Of Page he writes: "What a sweet man. You'd never guess he was so fascinated by Aleister Crowley." (Des Barres is the ex-husband of notorious rock groupie Pamela Des Barres. Page was among the many, many rock stars she claims to have bedded. She is said to have been jealous when Page dumped her to start an affair with rival groupie 'Lightning' Lori Maddox who was 13 at the time. Maddox claimed to have previously lost her virginity to **David Bowie**, aided by Bowie's wife Angie! Despite this, I'm not aware of either Page or Bowie receiving a knock on the door from the police. Strange, that.)

In the same book, Andy Taylor reveals that one of Nick Rhodes' favourite authors is...Aleister Crowley. (Steps back in amazement.) Andy—one of three Taylors in the group, none of whom are related—has now been ostracised by his former bandmates, ostensibly due to "artistic differences."

The maxim "you can judge a man by the company he keeps" is oft-repeated. If this is the case, what are we to make of some of the associations that the Duran members have made? Famously, Princess Diana named the band as her favourite pop group, and they have been pictured hanging out with Princes William and Harry. Their appeal within "elite" circles seems to go further, however, since the group have become quite the socialites, Le Bon and Rhodes having been photographed hobnobbing with Nat Rothschild of *that* family, (son of Jacob,) and with Simon and Yasmin having attended the wedding of Jessica de Rothschild.

Also in Rhodes' social circle has been Andy Warhol, who has spoken of harbouring sexual desires towards two of the group. Warhol once confessed to masturbating while watching Rhodes in Duran videos. Rhodes' girlfriend Nefer Suvio could pass as a student of performance-artist witch Marina Abramovich if the dark artwork displayed on her Instagram page is anything to go by. In 2018 she posted a picture of herself and Rhodes accompanied by the caption: "Hell is empty and all the devils are here—The Tempest. Happy 2018!" Later in the year she posted a compendium of dark/ Satanic imagery, including a skull and a vampire, with the caption "My birthday party mood."

More ominously, meanwhile, Simon Le Bon and his wife Yasmin's names reportedly appear in the "black book" of Jeffrey Epstein, while Nick Rhodes was pictured out in 2013 with the aforementioned Nat Rothschild and Epstein's former mistress (and more) Ghislaine Maxwell. Rhodes seems to have had a string of socialite girlfriends since splitting from his wife Julie Anne Friedman in 1992, including the now-deceased Tara Palmer-Tomkinson. Another was Lady Victoria Hervey, who is also an ex of Prince Andrew, now disgraced owing to his close friendship with Jeffrey Epstein and the sexual misconduct charges against him. Hervey defended Andrew when the claims first emerged. She has also been a close friend of Ghislaine Maxwell. It's a small world, it would seem, when you move in "upper class" circles.

Perhaps as a reflection of the company with which he hung out, in 2017, an accusation of sexual molestation was made against Simon Le Bon by an American woman named Shereen Hariri. She claimed that Le Bon had groped her 23 years earlier in a record store in which she'd worked, and that she had only felt confident enough to come forward following the emergence of the "Me Too" movement.

The group released the Simon Le Bon-penned song *'Michael You've Got A Lot To Answer For'* as part of their album *'Medazzaland'* on 14th October 1997. It references Le Bon's friendship with **Michael Hutchence** of **INXS** who, a little over a month later, would turn up dead in a Sydney hotel room, reportedly having "committed suicide." (See *'Musical Truth 1'* for more on this. Incidentally, Michael's brother, Brett, has been well awake to the Co(n)vid scam and associated vaccine holocaust, as evidenced by a glance at his Facebook profile.)

The album also contained a track titled *'So Long Suicide'* which the group cut from their US tour itinerary upon the news of Hutchence's death. The album itself was named after Midazolam, an intravenous sedative Le Bon said he enjoyed being given by his dentist. Many years later Midazolam hit the headlines when it was revealed that Health Secretary Matt Hancock had sanctioned the drug's use in UK care homes during Co(n)vid, resulting in the premature deaths of many hundreds of residents.

In 1985, Duran split off into their side projects, The Power Station and **Arcadia**. The latter, consisting of Rhodes, Le Bon and Duran drummer **Roger Taylor,** (the namesake of the drummer from Queen,) with contributions from **Dave Gilmour** and **Sting,** demonstrated an interest in occult themes, with song titles including *'Rose Arcana'* (a possible Tarot reference) and *'El Diablo,'* (the Devil.) Could a clue to the key to Duran's success—like so many bands both before and after them—have been included in the lyric that goes:

> *"One life with the Devil do I play."*
> *"Oh, el Diablo, el Diablo, won't you sell me back my soul?"*

The words to *'The Flame,'* meanwhile, bring more than a slight evocation of the ritual scenes from *'Eyes*

> *Wide Shut':*
> *"Inside of smoky halls,*
> *A circle drawn and voices call,*
> *To raise some magic wind in my world."*

Could these have been written with some kind of inside knowledge or personal experience involved?

Later, Nick Rhodes formed another side band, **The Devils**, (!) with Duran founding member **Stephen 'Tin Tin' Duffy**. Their ambiguous song *'Dark Circles'* begins:

> *"You're moving in dark circles.*
> *Dark circles, show me your eyes.*
> *It's black magic with no perfume.*

You're all TV and white lies."

Perhaps most worryingly of all, we have the true meaning that was being conveyed by the Duran song *'Skin Trade'* to consider. Whilst on the surface the ambiguous lyrics could be written off as just another example of the self-important pretentiousness with which 80s synth-pop bands carried themselves, when the characters with whom the group are known to hobnob are thrown into the picture, along with some of the horrific activities in which their breed are known to partake, some of its lyrics could really curdle the blood:

> *"So . . . she smiles, but that's cruel,*
> *If you knew what she'd think, if you knew what she was after . . .*
> *"Doctors of the revolution gave us, the medicine we desired.*
> *Besides being absolutely painless it's a question of compromise . . .*
> *"Would someone please explain,*
> *The reason for this strange behaviour.*
> *In exploitation's name,*
> *We must be working for the skin trade."*

How many "coincidences" and "just one of those things" can get written off before patterns emerge, and a grown-up higher mind has to accept what is staring it in the face, and simply deal with it?

*

A handful of music concerts have resulted in the deaths of crowd members over the decades, the most infamous being the **Rolling Stones** at Altamont in 1969, **The Who** in Cincinnati almost a decade to the day later, **Pearl Jam** at Roskilde in 2000, and **Ariana Grande** in Manchester in 2017.

Another event joined their dubious number on 5th November 2021, when it was reported that eight young people had died with many more injured during a crowd surge at **Travis Scott**'s performance at the Astroworld Festival in Houston, Texas. The waters became muddied early on, however, when reports began emerging of crowd members being unwittingly injected with drugs, a narrative acknowledged by Houston police. According to officer Larry Satterwhite: "Suddenly we had several people down on the ground, experiencing some type of cardiac arrest or some type of medical episode."

Is it possible that what could really have been happening here was young people who had been coerced into taking the Covid vaccine suffering adverse effects and dying, with the drug injection narrative concocted as some kind of cover story? Or could the truth about the real nature of this event be even darker?

There are now so many vigilant researchers into such matters that it's never long before an event of this nature gets analysed down to the finest forensic detail. And the general consensus among many was that it constituted another energy-harvesting mass occult ritual of the type the controllers of the satanic music industry like to stage from time to time. Several factors were cited as evidence.

With the drama and horror already unfolding, Scott stood on a podium and chanted the word "dead," as if in a possessed trance, into a microphone, his audio drenched in the demonic Autotune effect to make him sound like a transhumanised robot. Elsewhere in the performance Scott and guest artist **Drake**, (real name Aubrey Graham, a former actor,) talked of "snatching souls."

The caption "see ya on the other side," which could be taken to have several different meanings, was in evidence throughout the performance. The stage decor involved huge concentric circles known to be triggers for putting viewers in a hypnotic trance. The same designs are used in news bulletins internationally with the intention of having the lies in the mainstream headlines more readily accepted by the viewing public.

Another key emblem in the stage decor was a huge model figure, seemingly portraying Scott, its mouth wide open. This has been linked to a 15th-century painting named *'Christ in Limbo,'* depicting the concept of purgatory—the middle ground between this life and Heaven or Hell. How charming.

On the same day as the multiple deaths, Travis Scott had released two songs, *'Escape Plan',* (something those in the audience could have done with,) and *'Mafia,'* both featuring the same image of a bat/ human hybrid creature, mid-scream, accompanied by the caption "The true dystopia is here."

Days after the concert came the news that Scott and Live Nation, the event promoters, were being hit with a lawsuit by one of the concert attendees who claimed the tragedy was the direct result of "a motivation for profit at the expense of concertgoers' health and safety" and involved the "encouragement of violence."

There was more unsettling strangeness from the news, announced the same weekend, that **Astro**, (real name Terence Wilson,) one of the original members of veteran Birmingham reggae band **UB40**, had died suddenly of "a short illness" aged 64. His passing joined those of many other sports stars and celebrities who were said to have succumbed to a "short illness." What could possibly have been causing these?

Astro's passing brought to light a social media post from former UB40 member **Matt Hoy**, made some weeks before, announcing that he had reluctantly left the band after he had refused to take the Covid vaccine. This strongly implies that he had been put under pressure to take the jab, and therefore that all other members of the group had taken it, or they would have been forced out as he was. This would have included Astro. (Interesting that his name is close to that of one of the main Covid vaccine manufacturers, AstraZeneca.) Could his "short illness" be code for death by vaccine damage? Or could his exit be down to more troubling factors?

What—honestly—are the odds of a musician named Astro *just happening* to die the same weekend as several others apparently did at a festival named Astroworld *if* these events weren't, in some way, connected and made to happen in tandem with each other? Can this really be written off simply as "coincidence"?

Either way, the Houston event bears all the hallmarks of a pre-organised satanic ritual, with death, evil and darkness woven into its very fabric.

Nothing to worry about though, folks. It's all just harmless "fun" and "entertainment,' right?

Resources:

The Occult Beatles: Here's Some Clues for You All? . . . Manson, Tate, Polanski, The Beatle.:

- https://theoccultbeatles.wordpress.com/2019/09/10/ heres-some-clues-for-you-all-manson-tate-polanski-the-beatles/

Good Vibrations podcast, episode 142: Rodney Shabazz — Babylon Infiltration of Reggae Culture:

- https://www.spreaker.com/user/markdevlin/ good-vibrations-podcast-vol-142-rodney-s

Doug Wendt's Peter Tosh 1983 interview:

- http://www.midnightdread.com/peter.html

Peter Tosh criticises EMI in 1986 New York interview:

- https://www.youtube.com/watch?v=eQPGKaqfBY8

Gary Numan's 'Barbie girl' wife who wanted to marry him since she was 10 shocks Loose Women viewers:

- https://www.mirror.co.uk/tv/tv-news/ gary-numans-barbie-girl-wife-11178576

Gary Numan & wife: Is this pop music's quirkiest couple ever?:

- https://www.dailymail.co.uk/news/article-8824779/Gary-Numans-superfan-wife-entire-body-lift-exploding-breasts.html

Paste magazine: Gary Numan Is Right at Home in Dystopia:

- https://www.pastemagazine.com/music/gary-numan/ gary-numan-intruder-interview/

Sinéad O'Connor booed by the crowd at Madison Square Gardens:

- https://www.youtube.com/watch?v=GzxTDHMQza8

Kris Kristofferson on his special relationship with Sinéad O'Connor:

- https://www.youtube.com/watch?v=o8B_J-Bd0iE

Sinéad O'Connor reveals her 'evil' mother stripped and kicked her as a child:

- https://www.sundayworld.com/showbiz/sinead-ocon-nor-reveals-her-evil-mother-stripped-and-kicked-her-as-a-child-40482622.html

Sinead O'Connor lets loose on Irish right-wing racists:

- https://www.irishcentral.com/news/ sinead-oconnor-petition-gemma-odoherty-john-waters

Ann Diamond for Henry Makow: Leonard Cohen- Illuminati Jewish Secret Agent?:

- https://www.henrymakow.com/2015/01/Leonard-Cohen-Illu-minati-Jewish-agent.html

Ann Diamond's book about her relationship with Leonard Cohen. 'The Man Next Door':

- http://www.lulu.com/shop/ann-diamond/the-man-next-door/ paperback/product-21758892.html

Conflict Radio, Episode 58: Project MK-Ultra—A Survivor's Story, With Ann Diamond:

- https://www.bitchute.com/video/rqeSJaYFnMYI/

Jeffrey Epstein's Black Book: All Names:

- https://epsteinsblackbook.com/all-names

The Tube: Simon Le Bon featured in Persil TV ad, 1963:

- https://www.youtube.com/watch?v=pbxo5XmyGcU

Simon Le Bon's Accuser In Sex Assault Claim Speaks Out:

- https://eu.freep.com/story/news/2018/07/12/simon-le-bons-ac-cuser-sex-assault-claim-speaks-out-awful/777106002/

Teenagers among eight dead in Houston Astroworld festival concert crush:

- https://www.theguardian.com/us-news/2021/nov/06/astroworld-festival-concert-crush-leaves-at-least-eight-dead?fbclid=IwAR0ezJHjfV464ZBhbqoFcupPKicyAnsL-aTnwRt0Nl-5j5USPtKIyJGPZZhk

- https://metro.co.uk/2021/11/06/ub40s-astro-dies-aged-62-after-very-short-illness-15557524/?fbclid=IwAR06JFlZM-wkExN1sOqav5gwUqGLHqlCPlZdHpjgUxmCEm-MwBeCv-Pgsw1BU

Billboard: Travis Scott & Live Nation Sued Over 'Predictable' Astroworld Tragedy:

- https://www.billboard.com/articles/columns/hip-hop/9656473/travis-scott-astroworld-live-nation-lawsuit-victim-lawsuit/?utm_source=twitter&utm_medium=social

CHAPTER 10

MORE McCARTNEY MUSINGS (SWIG)

Thought you had the whole "Paul Is Dead" enigma all neatly tied up with a bow? Give some consideration to the following and see if you still feel the same!

"You can fool some people sometimes,
But you can't fool all the people all the time."
    Bob Marley & The Wailers: 'Get Up, Stand Up.'

"How we did it no one knows,
I guess we must have had what it took."
    Paul McCartney: 'Spies Like Us.'

"The healthiest exercise is swimming against the stream"
    Unknown.

A pattern seems to be emerging—you may have noticed—that with each new volume in this book series I revise my position on the **Paul McCartney** enigma somewhat since the previous outing. I hope readers will appreciate that, rather than constituting any unreliable flip-flopping, this in fact represents me as a researcher being prepared to let previously-held beliefs go upon the emergence of new evidence. Personally, I've always been suspicious of researchers who maintain the same concrete-minded position on a subject decade in decade out, particularly when new data comes along which appears to challenge their deeply-held beliefs.

At least reassurance can be drawn from one factor which has remained consistent throughout; there has been more than one individual playing the public role of "Paul McCartney" through the decades. Of that much, at least, I can still be sure!

Paul McCartney. Which one? You decide! (And take another swig.)

https://commons.wikimedia.org/wiki/File:Paul_McCartney_ACL18051018-169_(44619444435).jpg

Source: ACL18051018-169

Author: Raph_PH

To recap, *'Musical Truth Volume 1'*'s largest chapter was the 15,000 words in which I documented the "Paul Is Dead" concept, the most enduring "conspiracy theory" in the genre of popular music. Here, I recounted the many symbolic clues—both in pictorial form in record sleeves and photographs, and in audio form, both forward and backwards—which reinforce the notion that the original Paul McCartney died in 1966 and was replaced by an impostor who has been playing the public role ever since. The candidate most commonly suggested for the replacement is an individual by the name of **William/ Billy Shepherd**, (nicknamed **Billy Shears**,) or in some variations, William Campbell. This idea has been very much fuelled by the two volumes of the book *'The Memoirs of Billy Shears'* by the American author/ encoder Thomas E. Uharriett, along with the *'Billy's Back'* side-projects, which purport to be the confessions of the McCartney replacement himself, spilling the beans on many of the occult and esoteric elements built into the story.

The audiobook version of *'Memoirs'* was voiced, incidentally, by Gregory Paul Martin, the eldest son of legendary Beatles producer **George Martin**. He also penned the foreword to 2018's *'The Nine After*

9-09' update of '*Memoirs*'. While Martin Sr. had shown himself to be a system player of the first order, it seems his firstborn has become something of a rebel and a loose cannon, having Tweeted consistently during the Co(n)vid Scamdemic about how the whole sorry Shit Show was really designed to push New World Order agendas and the vaccine holocaust. It seems Gregory is either a thorough researcher or comes from such a family background as to be privy to some inside knowledge of the gameplan. (He's also revealed himself to be no fan of **Mick Jagger!**)

Neither has Gregory shied away from controversy when it comes to Beatles-related material. Though he has stopped short of weighing in directly on the McCartney replacement theory—assuming he would claim plausible deniability for his participation in the "fictional" '*Memoirs*' project—he teased the release of his own 2020 auto-biography '*Isn't It A Pity*' with some contentious apparent revelations on his Facebook page:

> *"Time and again my father swore he was done, that he would never work with Paul again, time and again going back on his word—because they were friends and lovers—the last time driving down to Macca's Sussex farm for a fascinating confrontation. If you want to know what transpired between them that day, buy my memoir."*

And:

> *"The seven deadly sins, also called the seven capital sins or seven cardinal sins in Roman Catholic theology, are the seven vices that spur other sins and further immoral behaviour. The first is Superbia, vainglory, or pride, and that is the force that has our world in a vice-like grip, no one more guilty of it than Sir James Paul McCartney. I love Paul. The world would be a much darker place without his incredible music. But a little humility from him would not come amiss."*

And of **John** and **Yoko**:

"One of the many reasons God put me on the earth was to speak the truth and set the record straight for those who cannot do it for themselves. John Lennon died a very unhappy man, for the latter part of his life stuck in a relationship that was a hollow sham, unable to free himself from its clutches. To those of you who refuse to believe this I say you can't handle the truth."

No-one died in '66?

The Billy Shears replacing the original McCartney account seemed altogether plausible to me as a result of my many hours of painstakingly documenting the many clues that appear to have been placed in Beatles output over the decades.

It wasn't until I had begun work on *'MT2'*, however, that I had been alerted to the fact that, from the photographic and video evidence available, it did appear as if there had been two "McCartneys" both before *and* after 1966. There are notable differences in appearance, specifically in the ears, jawline, teeth, eye colour and height running all the way up to present day. This clearly throws a spanner in the works of the Died and Replaced in '66 theory. So in *'Volume 2'*, I explored the hypothesis put forward by the American painter-turned-researcher Miles Mathis, who had proclaimed that Paul was in fact one of fraternal twins who had been stepping in and out of the role, and that his "brother" **Mike McCartney** (known professionally as Mike McGear,) was in fact a hired actor designed to throw the public off the scent. I also examined the theory that the original Paul—for whatever reason—had bowed out of the spotlight in '66 to be replaced by...whomever, but that he then made a public return for the 1970-released movie *'Let It Be.'* (And possibly beyond.)

Of these, the latter hypothesis certainly held the most weight, given that there is no verifiable evidence for there having been McCartney twins. Mathis presents childhood photos of what is proclaimed to be the pair, but these still don't stand as indisputable proof in their own right. The footage for the *'Let It Be'* movie was recorded in January 1969, by which time "Paul" had grown a full bushy beard. Only four months previously, however, "he" was completely clean-shaven in the promo video for *'Hey Jude,'* and I have long surmised that it is impossible to grow a beard that full in such short time. So the September '68 and January '69 "Pauls" can be deduced to be different people, at least.

And so, here we are at the advent of *'Volume 3.'* By this point, you might think that, given the hours of my life that I will never get back which have been spent in pursuit of this accursed enigma, by now everything would be crystal-clear. In fact, the opposite turns out to be the case, and I suspect many others who have dared to skirt around the edges of the "Paul Is Dead" rabbit hole would join me in asserting that this subject like no other in music, succeeds in confusing and confounding a well-meaning researcher almost to the point of insanity. At this point in the game, therefore, allow me to throw some further reflections and revelations into the melting pot. After all, it's only fair that readers become as thoroughly perplexed as I am.

Occam's Razor?

Sometimes in life, it turns out that the simplest, and seemingly most trivial answer to a dilemma, really is the most valid. After tying yourself up in knots for days, weeks, months or years trying to get your head around all the apparent intricacies, having exhausted all options, you can find yourself coming back to Occam's Razor. I spent months obsessing over what could be causing my teenage daughter's violent, disruptive and volatile behaviour, considering all kinds of options, from mental health defects to demonic possession . . . until an older friend offered the advice that "it sounds to me like an extreme case of regular teenage behaviour." Sometimes that voice of reason that we need in a situation also turns out to be that voice of simplicity.

Conventional "Paul Is Dead" lore has it that the real James Paul McCartney died in 1966; opinion differs over whether this constituted a tragic unforeseen accident or a planned-for occult ritual, and the given date tends to fluctuate between 11th September and 9th November—both expressions of 9/11. It has been widely assumed that any sightings after this time are of the replacement, and the striking differences in appearance between the pre- and post-'66 Pauls are offered as evidence for this.

The theory explored in '*Volume 2*' suggests that the real Paul may have disappeared from the scene in '66 but didn't die, and indeed made occasional re-appearances after that date, before the impostor continued playing the role into modern times.

One particular photograph makes me wonder whether both these postulates may be flawed and that the truth may lie in a combination of the two. It is one of the set of pictures taken by the young German photographer Astrid Kirchherr in 1960. Astrid, (who died on my birthday in 2020 while this book was being written) was an associate of the early, pre-fame Beatles, and became engaged to the group's original bassist **Stuart Sutcliffe**. Her famous picture of McCartney from that session appears to show a very young version of the latter-day individual identifying as "Paul McCartney." His face is markedly thinner than that of what appears to be the "other" McCartney from the 1960s, and notably, he sports the very distinctive arched right eyebrow that Paul's father Jim did—an apparent family trait.

I've discussed this matter with my good friend Mike Williams, a.k.a Sage of Quay, who is of the view that this photo has been digitally manipulated—along with many other pictures and video clips on the internet—to make early Paul look more like latter-day Billy. In a world so full of duplicity of course anything remains possible. Incidentally, Mike's epic four-hour video presentation demonstrating how it is not logistically possible that Lennon and McCartney can have written all the Beatles songs with which they've been credited is an absolute must-watch. It's a meticulously researched masterpiece that stands as damning evidence that there was so much more going on with that group than the simple-minded official accounts of their ascent to success—constantly reinforced by new propaganda movies—would have us believe. It can be watched at the link detailed in the Resources section at the end.

Now, as previously surmised there have clearly been at least two "McCartneys," (possibly more, but we'll worry about the rest on another occasion!) on public display through the decades. If this 1960 Paul is indeed the present-day one, therefore, could this mean that, for whatever reason, one or more "doubles" was used consistently through the '60s and possibly beyond, therefore accounting for the differences in appearance that so many researchers have noted? And could this mean that the shorter, chubbier-faced character who most have assumed to have been the real "Paul" was in fact the "impostor," and the one mostly seen after 1966 and assumed to be the impostor...was in fact the genuine article? Wouldn't that be the ultimate mindfuck, a Satanic inversion? And aren't such ruses the delight of a priest class which loves to morbidly mock the ignorance and profanity of the masses? We can speculate on what the reasons for such a hoax may have been for days; possibly these were the subjects of a mind-control experiments; possibly it wasn't just Paul who was replaced but the other Beatles too and Paul just happened to be the one to be singled out; and possibly the experiment was on us, the public, to see whether the forces which controlled the Beatles could get away with such an audacious stunt right there in plain sight

Paul is John? (Pay attention – there'll be questions later)

If the above hypothesis is indeed true, it leaves us with the not unimportant question of who the candidate for the prime Paul replacement may have been. And a suggestion in this area came from a friend during some on-line correspondence during the course of this book being written.

The official notes for the recording session of *'Dear Prudence'* from *'The White Album,'* taking place at Trident Studios in Soho's Wardour Street, list backing vocals and handclaps as having been provided by one **John McCartney**, (with Paul listed separately as having been on the same recording.)

John turns out to be a little-documented American-based cousin of Paul's. Given that we have evidence of his appearing on at least one Beatles recording, could there have been others? And could his role have extended beyond this to having been Paul's stand-in for an extended period? This would certainly explain the physical resemblance with no need for the Radical Appearance Modification postulated by many P.I.D. adherents.

"John McCartney," meanwhile, is the fictional name of Paul's grandfather played by actor (and paedophile!) Wilfred Brambell in the movie 'A Hard Day's Night.'

It's a family affair

Ancestry and genealogy permeate the McCartney story, whether going down the route of the *'Memoirs'* narrative and the others which postulate a William Shepherd/ Billy Shears or William Campbell as having been the replacement, the assertion that Shepherd/ Shears is the illegitimate offspring of Aleister Crowley, or accepting that the current McCartney is and always has been the real one.

At the very least, some delving into biological Paul's ancestry brings a direct link to Freemasonry. This comes from Jacobus McCartney Jr., sometimes spelled as Jacobi in the records, who was the great-grandfather of Paul's dad Jim. He was born in Belfast in 1825 and died in Liverpool in 1857 aged only 32. The family name prior to Jacobus' time was evidently McCarthy before becoming amended. There was a lot of crossover between Ireland and Scotland in centuries past, with migration going on in both directions, so family names from the two nations are often interchangeable.

As membership of Freemasonry often passes down through new generations of the same family, it becomes entirely plausible that both Jim and Paul were inducted into the order as a birth right.

While the official record has it that Paul's ancestors hail from Ireland on his mother Mary's side, connections to Scotland persist within the P.I.D. narrative—particularly the *'Memoirs'* version of it. Scotland is, of course, the home of the 33rd-degree Freemasonry which permeates the entertainment industry. Paul seems to have love for both Ireland and Scotland. One of his earliest post-Beatles hits, and one of very few songs in which he has ever ventured into political or controversial territory, was *'Give Ireland Back To The Irish'* in which he criticised the subjugation of that nation at the hands of the British at the time that "the Troubles" were really heating up. He seemed to reinforce his Irish ancestry in that song with the line "meanwhile back in Ireland there's a man who looks like me."

Paul did of course own a farm in the wilds of Western Scotland, however, and composed *'Mull of Kintyre'* as an ode to the place he apparently so loved. **Linda** also had a tartan officially registered for the family in 1997, the year before her death. (Linda's maiden name was Eastman, yet this had been Anglicised by her father to sound less Russian-Jewish and more all-American when he emigrated the family. His original name was Leopold Vail Epstein. Incredibly, it does seem to be down to pure coincidence that the Beatles' original manager happened to be named **Brian Epstein**, as I'm not aware of any family connections between the two. Nor indeed to disgraced paedophile, child sex trafficker and blackmailer to the stars, Jeffrey Epstein (who didn't kill himself.)

That's a lot of Scottish love from the family of an ostensible Englishman and his American-Jewish wife.

While we're on the subject of bloodlines, there's just one more potential scenario to consider. There is no evidence to connect this historical figure with present-day Paul, so this remains within the bounds of speculation.

There was a very well-known British statesman, colonial ambassador and diplomat by the name of Lord MacCartney, (slightly different spelling to the one we're used to, but these can mutate over the generations.) George MacCartney, known as 1st Earl MacCartney, was born in Ulster in 1737, though again there is crossover between Scotland and Ireland as he descended from an old Scottish family, the MacCartneys of Auchenleck. MacCartney strongly endeared himself to the political and royal Establishment of the time, gaining key diplomatic postings all over Britain's overseas empire. His most dubious claim to fame was helping cultivate the opium wars in China on behalf of the king.

It would be wryly amusing if it ever turned out that Paul were descended in some way from Lord George, particularly considering the enthusiasm with which Paul pushed mind-altering drugs to his fans during the Beatles' counter-culture phase of the 1960s, just as George pushed opium on to the unsuspecting Chinese, each wreaking societal havoc in the process. Paul has also ingratiated himself to the Monarchy in the same way his potential ancestor did. He wrote the song *'Her Majesty,'* can barely contain his glee when meeting the Queen at public events, and was only too happy to accept his knighthoods and MBE as he entered the ranks of the billionaire class.

If Paul is related to Lord MacCartney that would mean his family had fallen from the Aristocracy by the time he was living in subsidised housing in Liverpool. As we've seen, however, he's had no problem with working his way up the social ladder.

Darker and weirder

And so we're back around to the idea that biological Paul did indeed die in '66. During the 2020 lockdown, what would have been considered impossible by many occurred; a "new" clue was revealed on the Beatles' *'Sgt. Peppers'* album sleeve which had remained undiscovered for over 50 years, by an Irish researcher and musician known as Mumble Bee. In the video which appeared on YouTube titled *'Sgt. Pepper—Hold My Beer,'* Mumble Bee demonstrated how Peter Blake's iconic sleeve design had cleverly concealed the word "Pleasington," and that this turns out to be the name of a cemetery in Blackburn, Lancashire. This, Mumble Bee surmised, is the burial place of the original Paul and adds new relevance to the Lennon lyric 'four thousand holes in Blackburn, Lancashire on *'A Day In The Life.'* Furthermore, he adds, what is taken to be the word "Beatles" in the flower bed actually reads "Bert Les" and this goes on to reveal the name under which Paul is buried. It's an utterly fascinating hypothesis that's well worth a watch on the link in the Resources section at the end.

One of the foremost researchers into the world of the occult, and its application within popular culture, is Richard Balducci. During a podcast interview with Australia's JC Kay in 2020, Balducci offered some mindblowing observations regarding McCartney and the ever-present dark occultist's favourite number, 666. Prefacing his findings, Balducci offered his take on why the controllers of every aspect of Organised Society have historically felt compelled to reveal their handiwork in cryptic, encoded form, for recognition only by those with the eyes to see:

"They're not revealing their hand to the general public. They're revealing their hand to the other Satanists, their buddies. You know, 'look what we did over here! We did 9/11. We did the JFK assassination. Oh, we killed

John Lennon. We killed James Paul McCartney. We did the Great Fire of London in 1666."

There were exactly 666 full lunar cycles of 29.5 days, from the first Jack the Ripper murder in London, (actually a Masonic ritual,) on 31st August 1888, to the birth of Paul McCartney on 18th June 1942. (31st August was the reported date of death of Princess Diana, often associated with the "Moon Goddess" archetype.)

Furthermore, there were also 666 full lunar cycles from the date often given for the supposed death of the original Paul McCartney, on 11th September 1966, to the date McCartney was due to perform on the (Masonic) Pyramid stage at the Glastonbury Festival shortly after the Summer Solstice in June 2020. (As it turned out, this entire event was cancelled, and I'm pretty sure readers by now will know the reason why!)

In the first volume of *'The Memoirs of Billy Shears'* meanwhile, in which Thomas E Uharriet makes the claim that the character currently playing the public role of "Paul McCartney" is named William Wallace Shepherd and is descended from William Wallace, the Scottish warrior portrayed by Mel Gibson in the movie *'Braveheart,'* we learn that there were 666 years from 1296, the year that King Edward I of England invaded Scotland sparking the revolution, and the release of the Beatles' first single, *'Love Me Do,'* in 1962.

Furthermore, of that single's release, Balducci added:

"In 'Memoirs'... Uharriet, through false Paul, mentions that the Illuminati declared war on Christianity on September 11th 1962. If you count from that day, as day one, to December 9th 1980, the day that the cremation ritual of John Lennon took place, out of sight out of mind, this spans a period of exactly 6,666 days. The Illuminati declares war on Christianity and then the guy that said the Beatles were bigger than Jesus gets dead 6,666 days later and cremated at that time.

"That's called planning."

Resources:

Gregory Paul Martin's Twitter feed:

- https://twitter.com/watchitcomedown

The Daily Beatle: Book from George Martin's eldest son:

- http://webgrafikk.com/blog/news/
  book-from-george-martins-oldest-son/

The Dark Occult: JC Kay Interviews Richard Balducci:

- https://www.bitchute.com/video/ceBtYfR1eq8T/

Beatles Facts: Paul McCartney's cousin, John McCartney, provided backing vocals for The Beatles' "Dear Prudence.":

- https://twitter.com/fabfourfacts/
  status/1700015907064717312?lang=en

Famechain: Paul McCartney's Family Tree:

- https://www.famechain.com/family-tree/11244/
  sir-paul-mccartney

Sage of Quay—Mike Williams—Did The Beatles Write All Their Own Music? (Apr 2020):

- https://youtu.be/ccEhmQ0M4FY

James Paul McCartney's ancestors at ancestry.com:

- https://www.ancestry.com/family-tree/tree/177597643/
  family?cfpid=132309881944

- https://www.ancestry.com/family-tree/person/tree/177597643/
  person/132309883907/facts

- https://www.ancestry.com/imageviewer/collections/60904/
  images/43991_3082375_0011-00125?usePUB=true&_phsrc=z-
  Js8&usePUBJs=true&pId=93190

House of Names: McCartney History, Family Crest & Coats of Arms:

- https://www.houseofnames.com/mccartney-family-crest

Sgt. Pepper: Hold My Beer:

- https://www.youtube.com/watch?v=Bhx1UqJ2qgA

Linda McCartney's Scottish tartan design:

- https://www.tartanregister.gov.uk/tartanDetails?ref=2876

The Beatles Book: Notes on John McCartney's inclusion in the 'Dear Prudence' recording session:

- http://www.beatlesebooks.com/dear-prudence?fbclid=IwAR-2r1xCowiNpL-vC0yZ_BVzOVYJliJSdCAWUsh07NQcgfB_X9UzFzuda5Dw

The Beatles Bible listing John McCartney contributing handclaps on 'Dear Prudence':

- https://www.beatlesbible.com/songs/dear-prudence/?f-bclid=IwAR2XcppuB6t-NxXnziIh8OdzVFNPM2Ypd-jWn208aj4eS8Tps8QvSApGGFnw

Lord MacCartney;

- http://afe.easia.columbia.edu/special/china_1750_macart-ney.htm

McCartney family crest:

- https://www.houseofnames.com/mccartney-family-crest

CHAPTER 11

THE BEST IS YET TO COME,
(NO – <u>REALLY!</u>)

And now the good news ... and Lord knows we could use some given the places our story has taken us. There is every reason to feel encouraged and uplifted ultimately. This Truth has been staring us right in the face in the form of some of our favourite rock songs all along. Who knew?

> *"All is Love. Fear is Illusion. All beings are Free. Truth can never be destroyed."*
>
> *Mark Passio*

> *"The earthly part of the universe would seem rude and savage without sweet melodies.*
> *This is why Atum sent down the choir of muses,*
> *to live amongst humankind,*
> *and inspire music."*
> *'Secret Teachings' from 'The Hermetica.'*
> *"So do not fear for I am with you, do not be dismayed for I am your God. I will strengthen you and help you; I will uphold you with my righteous <u>right</u> hand."*
>
> *Isaiah 41:10*

We've been to some dark and devastating places over the previous chapters and in the two books that preceded this one. But this is where our journey comes to an end. And I think any reader will agree that it was worth the wait, as stories don't end any more profoundly than this one. Again, we will get to the music-related content in due course, but some more scene-setting is essential to put everything into its full context first, so bear with me one last time.

In the club

For millennia, religious orders, mystery-schools and secret-societies have sequestered esoteric knowledge that has only been deemed worthy of their own initiates, and have systematically hidden it from the masses who, in most cases, have been deemed undeserving of being privy to such teachings. This has either been on the grounds that they have been considered too ignorant and profane to be apply it responsibly, or, in the case of the more malevolent organisations, to allow them to gain a tactical advantage over the masses through hoarding empowering knowledge to create a strategic power differential.

Those not "in the club," as the late, great George Carlin would have said, have been left wondering for centuries just what it is that these arcane institutions teach. It is only since the advent of the internet that aspects of this knowledge have been shared around the world among we "unworthy" ones. The cat has been let out of the bag regarding the doctrines of many disparate organisations—Freemasons have their distinct set of rituals, symbols and sacred texts, for instance, whereas the Rosicrucians, Jesuits or Opus Dei would have customs of their own—yet the full picture only emerges when the various puzzle pieces are put together.

What if the answer to the question of what kind of knowledge could have been considered so empowering all this time that countless souls have died to discover and to protect it, is actually very simple? What if, at the core of their teachings, once the individual twists and takes on it all have been stripped away, the knowledge jealously guarded by all these orders is actually the same?

While I've never been privy to any secret-society teachings myself, (and don't adhere to any orthodox religions,) it seems to me, after many years of reflecting and musing on this dynamic, that this is indeed the case. What all these groups concern themselves with is the true, infinite nature of we spirit-souls, our connectedness to Source, and the codes and actions by which we can live our lives to reconnect to what many would refer to as "God," "the Creator," "the Most High," or the various other names which have been attributed to this Divine power. This is knowledge which, if fully understood, absorbed and applied, can ensure that a human lifetime is *not* lived in spiritual darkness and ignorance, but is used to its full potential in order for the soul to grow and evolve, and take the knowledge it has accumulated back to Source when it passes on.

It would seem, from a sober study of the historical record, that many of the mystery-schools and secret-societies which concern themselves with dark occult practices such as Satanism and Luciferianism are clued-in on this knowledge, yet have sought to use it to dominate and enslave the rest of humanity. We have seen from their use of phenomena such as Predictive Programming and Revelation of the Method, that they recognise the dynamics of Natural Law. That human activity is governed by laws and conditions which have been set into place by the creative force behind the Universe, and that consequences occur in response to choices made and actions taken under the dynamic of free will.

These dark occultists have sought to cheat their way around the karmic consequences that they know get applied in response to action which causes harm to others, by tricking we "profane ones" into giving our tacit approval or unspoken consent to a situation. It's testament to the extreme hubris, arrogance and psychopathy by which these abominations operate, that they feel they can find sneaky loopholes around the governing dynamics behind human behaviour which have been in place for infinity. A key tenet of ideological Satanism is the initiates' belief that they themselves are their own "Gods." In their unfathomable arrogance, they grudgingly accept that Natural Law principles are in place in this reality, yet they hate that this is the case. They lack any true creative ability in themselves, leaving them capable only of taking something which is inherent to Creation, and twisting and contorting into a bastardised version of how it started out, often shaping it, through the harnessing of the natural dynamic of Duality, into the polar opposite of what it originally was.

This warped mindset explains so much about why Organised Society has been systematically structured over vast periods of time to be the way it currently is. Why the lifestyles lived by the majority of people in the world are unhealthy, unnatural and spiritually counter-productive. And therefore, why the mentally-ill maniacs who have worked their way into all truly powerful and influential positions in society, seem hell-bent on destroying Creation itself in terms of how it plays out in this (apparently) physical reality.

This is where factors such as Transhumanism, Artificial Intelligence, the Smart Grid, the Internet of Things, 5G technology, Social Credit Systems, and the raping and pillaging of the Earth's natural resources by demonic organisations such as Monsanto and so many others come in. All these activities represent the psychopaths attempting to destroy all that is natural and divinely-created, and replace it with artificial monstrosities which are Satanic, (meaning *anti*-God and *anti*-nature.) The much-lauded quote by the late author Michael Ellner bears some repeating here. As he famously wrote:

> *"Just look at us. Everything is backwards, everything is upside down. Doctors destroy health, lawyers destroy justice, psychiatrists destroy minds, scientists destroy truth, major media destroys information, religions destroy spirituality and governments destroy freedom."*

Of course, this book's special interest, the corporate music industry, plays *its* part as we've seen through these three volumes. Its key players, assets, Chosen Ones and Lifetime Actors have been used to, having first gained the trust and admiration of a fanbase through carefully-crafted public images, then push and promote various agendas which benefit the "Globalist" and "Elite" New World Order agendas but which—no great surprise here—*don't* have the spiritual advancement and uplift-ment of all of humanity in mind. I've presented a tsunami of evidence of this inconvenient truth through the past several years of my work, and no more is needed.

Shortly, it will become clear how the rest of this all connects back into the world of rock music. But first, we need to delve deeper into the spiritual component which, I believe, lies at the roots of all these ancient and sacred teachings.

Is there oil in your lamp?

Going within is the key, and the Truth that the controllers of Organised Society will do anything to keep you away from.

https://www.pxfuel.com/en/free-photo-omodl

In 2017, I recorded a show with the Canada-born, Mexico-based researcher and spiritual scholar who goes by the name of Charlie Freak, (named after the titular, fateful character of a **Steely Dan** song.) In it, he walked me through what I've since come to refer to as the "Internal Alchemical Process." It's alternatively known as "the raising of the Chrism oil" and it's something they just seem to have forgotten to teach us at school, college, University, medical school, church, and via the mainstream media. It is, however, fairly important. I guess that'll be why. (Other great work on this subject and all the allegory and metaphor it has entailed, has come from Bill Donahue at his website https://www.hiddenmeanings.com/, and Eric Dubay at https://ericdubay.wordpress.com/)

From around the age of 12, twelve times during a year, (just like lunar cycles or female menstruation periods,) a process takes place in the human body lasting around three days whereby a fluid is secreted in the brain. It consequently travels down the spinal column all the way to the sacrum, then back up again into the skull where all the magic happens. This is why the brain is housed between your two "temples," a temple being a holy place. More double-meaning word magic.

During this period, in order to truly benefit from the phenomenon and establish that re-connectedness with Source or "God," it's essential to live virtuously and to abstain from vices. I know more than anyone how difficult this can be, but this dynamic determines which of us get to "meet God face to face" and truly make the most of the experiences available to us in this "physical" life, and which of us don't.

The Chrism oil, (known as the "Christos" in Greek—this is "Christ Consciousness" and is the real meaning of "Christ," rather than some historical figure who walked the earth some 2,000 years ago,) begins from a place at the very back of our skull in between the horizontal divide between the left and right portions of our brains. At the back there is an opening on top of an indentation known as the Mercy Seat. It's possible to work out the days in each month where this process has the potential to occur based on our birthdates; effectively it's when the full moon enters our sun sign. At this time, the Claustrum—another section of the brain at the back of the skull—releases the sacred fluid and sends it down an opening shaped like a chimney. This runs from the Claustrum into the third ventricle in the very centre of the brain. (The place where the Bible claims Jesus was crucified was named Golgotha, which translates as "place of the skull"—more allegory telling the reader that inside the skull is where "salvation" and ascension lies.)

Once it reaches the Thalamus the oil is split, one half going to the pituitary gland, where it becomes a milky-like substance which easily spoils, (as does anything left out in the magnetic, feminine moonlight,) the other half to the pineal gland, becoming a honey-like substance which is preserved. (Did **John Lennon** and **Yoko Ono** know about this when they named John's posthumous album *Milk and Honey*? Yoko claimed the title was inspired by their living in the United States, "the land of milk and honey," but added: "But also in the Scripture the land of milk and honey is where you go after you die, as a promised land . . . So it's very strange that I thought of that title. Almost scary—like someone up there told me to call the next album *Milk and Honey*.")

The Biblical symbolism here is that the pineal, being masculine, represents Joseph, the father, whereas the pituitary, being feminine, represents Mary, the mother, and the Chrism oil itself symbolises the figure of "Jesus," or Christ Consciousness. When the Bible speaks of the only way to salvation being through Jesus Christ, it is this process to which it is metaphorically referring.

Here we get a reminder of the polarities that exist within God's Creation. Everything has a dualistic opposite. The pituitary gland represents magnetic energy (like the moon) and is feminine in nature; its balancing polar opposite is the pineal gland, representing electrical energy, (like the sun) and is masculine in nature. These polarities tie into the free will with which we are all gifted. The scale between one polarity and another gives an infinite number of choices that we can make along the way allowing for our unique, individual life experiences, with no two ever being the same.

Having completed its magic in the brain, the fluid then travels all the way down the spinal column to the solar plexus. During this time a "seed" is released and heads towards a small indentation in the sacral region. In more Biblical symbolism this seed is said to represent "Jesus" and it awaits the Milk of Mother Mary and the Honey of Father Joseph to arrive to fertilise it. Once done, the "Jesus" seed comes alive and is ready to begin its journey up the spinal vertebrae all the way to the skull. This time it's as cerebral spinal fluid. (This process is interchangeable with what is referred to as a Kundalini energy experience.)

After passing 32 of the vertebrae it reaches the 33rd, an exceptionally strong bone known as Atlas. In mythology Atlas was said to be carrying the world upon his shoulders. The Atlas bone is holding up the skull, where all the magic happens. In order for the fluid/ seed to pass this barrier it needs to increase 1000-fold, and this is the true meaning of the phrase "crucifixion" which has nothing to do with being nailed to a wooden cross.

This aspect of the Bible is more allegory for this wonderful story of our physiology, rather than being about torture and death. The seed goes on to ascend to the fourth ventricle of the brain via a very straight and narrow inlet. This is the origin of the phrase "on the straight and narrow," referring to somebody who is living as they should and doing the right thing.

When the seed crosses the Vagus Nerve at the Medulla Oblongata it is "crucified." The seed enters the very centre of the brain at the Thalamus and symbolically causes it to illuminate and fill the whole body with light. For this reason it has been known as the "Light of the World" (possibly inspiring the British jazz-funk band of the same name, or the 1974 **Kool & The Gang** album *Light of Worlds*?)

Readers may have noticed some direct symbolic connections between the Internal Alchemical Process and the event we refer to as Christmas, and this festival was indeed inspired in part by these events, and named after the Chrism/ Christos. Santa (sainted) Claus is representative of the Claustrum, from which the sacred gift of God is delivered. The oil being secreted down the chimney-like opening symbolises Santa bringing his gifts into the home through that opening. "Christmas" occurs when it does because, from the Winter Solstice of 21st December, the sun (masculine, representing the figure of Jesus) appears to "die" as it remains at its lowest point in the sky for three days, (three days just like the Chrism oil process,) as perceived from what we refer to as the Northern Hemisphere.

Then, on 25th December, it is perceived to start rising as it begins its journey towards its "rebirth" at the Spring Equinox around 21st March, (the solar year always used to begin in Aries before the Gregorian Calendar was introduced by the Catholic church to deliberately throw humans off-track from their natural connectedness to the rest of Creation,) all the way to its highest point at the Summer Solstice of 21st June.

There's all kinds of other symbolism tied in to the occasion of Christmas, or what the Romans celebrated as Saturnalia or Pagans as Yule, including a distinctive form of psilocybin mushroom which is red-and-white spotted, thus inspiring the red and white coat of Santa Claus, whose psychedelic effects are said to give the user the sensation of "flying"—just like Santa and his reindeer. "Christmas" is a real melting pot of different influences and symbolism, but the journey of the Chrism oil remains rooted at the centre of it all. In terms of its modern-day values, the controllers of Organised Society have taken the greatest story ever told and turned it into one of materialism and gluttony. But should we really be surprised?

381

When writing the above, a strange feeling swept over me. The subject matter seemed familiar even though I was apparently learning it and communicating it for the first time. It didn't feel as if I was learning it, though; it felt like I was *remembering* it. As if it's something we all inherently know but have been programmed to forget.

As above so below

These understandings were so important to the Ancients that whatever civilisation built the pyramids of Giza in Egypt, felt moved to encode brain chemistry into their construction. Egyptologists have puzzled and argued over the purpose of the Great Pyramid for generations, (though in reality many will have been shills on the Establishment payroll (Freemasons?) charged with deliberately concealing the truth.) Taking a cross-section of the Great Pyramid reveals the King's and Queen's Chambers, the Grand Gallery and the so-called Hidden Chamber. Taking the pyramid to be a representation of the human skull, the King's and Queen's Chambers appear relative to where the Pineal and Pituitary Glands are located, hence the ascribing of male and female qualities to them respectively. Furthermore, the so-called "Eye of Ra" which appears in many Egyptian hieroglyphics, highly resembles the human Pineal Gland, (commonly referred to as "the Third Eye") surrounded by the Corpus Callosum, Medulla Oblongata, Hypothalamus and Thalamus, suggesting that this is the true meaning for its wide symbolic prevalence within that culture.

The full empowering effects of the Internal Alchemical Process can be enhanced through the practice of meditation — of "going within." A skilled and experienced meditator is able to shut out the chitter-chatter of the "monkey mind," which is the left brain ego's dominance of an individual's consciousness, and instead to go a still and silent place devoid of the distractions and temptations of this material world. (I have a *long* way to go in that regard and am very much a work in progress!

On that note, it has been suggested that the King's Chamber was designed as a sensory deprivation centre, where initiates would go to experience total stillness, darkness and quiet in order to enter a meditative state. Having been inside the smaller of the three pyramids, I can attest to just how shut off from the outside world it causes a visitor to feel.

The "going within" involves going to "inner space." This is where we rediscover our Divine nature. All the answers are within us and not "out there." This is why the dark occult priest class have invested so much in the concept of "outer space" — of convincing us that we are tiny, unimportant specks in a vast, never-ending universe with untold numbers of planets and galaxies, that we're the result of a random, meaningless, Godless process called the Big Bang, and that we could be wiped out and annihilated any moment just like the dinosaurs were, so we might as well just make the best of the short time we have here before we perish and go into oblivion.

These are all atheistic, Satanic lies, with the fingerprints of the sick ones all over them. The Big Bang, dinosaurs, and the concept of limitless "outer space" are all wicked deceptions devised to keep us away from the truth that this Earth is the centre of all things and that the Sun, Moon and stars revolve around *us*, not the other way around, and that it is still and silent — just as we ourselves become during meditation. So many TV shows and movies have pushed the idea of "outer space" aided by the lying frauds at N.A.S.A. and implanted shills like Stephen Hawking and "Professor" Brian Cox (whose credentials for the role involve having been the keyboardist in the group **D:Ream**. I'll leave readers to research for themselves the slang meaning of "reaming.")

There is no "outer space." It all happens within.

The meditative process is a human's way of reconnecting with his or her divine essence and higher spiritual self. Little wonder then, that daily life in Organised Society is deliberately kept busy and chaotic so that most find it difficult, if not impossible, to switch off and go within — or even spare the time for it in the first place. Our demonic would-be controllers understand the powerful effects of meditation only too well, and the last thing they want is for all of us to re-discover our true, God-like nature and the infinite power to create our own experienced reality simply by applying our consciousness and Will. To quote George Carlin again, 'they're not interested in that at all."

As if the correlations of the Great Pyramid weren't mindblowing enough, we also have the amazing spectacle of what's referred to as "The

Holy Land" of Israel/ Palestine, an ariel view of which appears to encode the route of the Internal Alchemical process! The Sea of Galilee acts as the human skull where the magic begins, the winding River Jordan (in which I was baptised in 1993 when identifying as a Christian) playing the part of the spine along which runs the Kundalini energy, and the Dead Sea at the bottom representing the Sacrum, from which the process begins all over again. It's called the "Dead" Sea because it represents the part of our physiology associated with the lower three chakras. If we live our entire lives out of these without ever ascending to the higher chakras, we will never ascend spiritually and will remain rooted in base consciousness and doomed to go round and round the Samsara reincarnated into life after life, as is Bill Murray symbolically in the movie 'Groundhog Day,' until we can get things right.

There are also correlations between the Pyramids of Giza and the three stars of Orion's Belt in the night sky, all of which serves as a reminder of the concept of "as above so below," the Hermetic Principle of Correspondence, and how we, and the place in which we live these lives—Earth—are inherently connected to the Heavenly realms above. Ultimately, all is as one. This is the *real* singularity, not the maniacal vision of the demented Transhumanist Ray Kurzweil who is fond of using the term.

Get on the Good Book

Though orthodox Christians will hate to hear it and doubtless brand me a heretic, the stories in the Bible have been misrepresented as real historical events. In reality they are all allegories referring to human physiology and the human brain. The book is the story of each and every one of us. The stories are not to be taken literally. Jonah did not get swallowed by a whale, stay there for three days, then get spat out again. This parable refers to the "going within" to a still and silent place that is achieved through meditation, and the three days refers to the period during which the Chrism oil process takes place. Similarly, Jesus did not die, get placed in a tomb for three days, then resurrect. This story refers to the same process. The story of Jacob's Ladder in Genesis first depicts Jacob crossing a river to the right, leaving behind his family and all earthly belongings, and wrestling with a manifestation for an entire day. This is his own ego of the left-brain as he seeks to defeat its domination and live instead out of the higher-mindedness of his right brain. The story later implies that he has had an experience with God who has told him that he is to be named "Israel" from that point forward.

Elsewhere in Genesis in his "dream" Jacob undergoes a Chrism oil experience, ascending "the ladder" and "meeting God face to face" as the process completes and the oil re-reaches his pineal gland and illuminates his seventh, out-of-body chakra. "Meeting God" simply means re-establishing the inherent connectedness we all have with Spirit Source—our true nature as spiritual beings undergoing human experiences, *not* human beings undergoing spiritual experiences. The passage speaks of Jacob's "seed," "oil" and his naming of the place "Bethel," (the site of the famous Woodstock rock concert was Bethel Woods,) all pertaining to Chrism oil-related aspects.

Jacob named the place that he visited in his dream "Peniel" (pineal,) stating "I have seen God face to face, yet my life has been spared." Clue much?! Our task during these temporary lives of ours is to establish the balance between our physicality and our spirituality. *This* is the Truth that has been systematically occulted from the bulk of humanity and jealously guarded by the secret-societies, so that only a few in each generation get to achieve this procedure. As this information becomes more freely communicated, however, and as the control system's stranglehold over humanity hopefully begins to wane, this process of re-connecting with "God" should become experienced by so many more.

The temple that Solomon built was the temple in his own mind as he "went within." The ark that Noah built amidst all the chaos and violence of the Flood, was an ark in his mind, the two of each animal symbolising the preservation of life until such times as the volatility has died down, (the internal battle with his left-brain ego.)

Left, right, left, right

Living out of the right hemisphere of the brain is the key to the whole process that has been so intricately encoded in so many places through the ages. The left brain is associated with carnal desires and lower-minded, base consciousness, whereas the right side is all about "Godliness," spirituality, higher-mindedness and connectedness to Source. The right side also allows for the activation of the sixth sense of intuition and the seventh sense of telepathy, whereas most people live only through the five physical senses and have no idea this potential even exists inside of them. If the Chrism oil process is not harnessed and wilfully engaged with through meditation and other virtuous pursuits, the oil will die within the first 24 hours. It cannot exist within an acidic body; only one that has been alkalised, (more polarities) can fully embrace the Alchemical wizardry.

The clue is right there in the language. it's no coincidence that "right" has a double meaning. As well as being the opposite to left, it also means "correct." The language is telling you that the right is the "right" way to live, because to the right is where the Pineal Gland, or "Third Eye" is located. This explains why so many owned celebrities have been pictured covering their right eye and leaving their left exposed. It's communicating that they have chosen (or been instructed to take) the Left Hand Path of base consciousness. It's also why **Beyonce** began her song 'Irreplaceable' with the catchy hook "to the left, to the left." Though the song implies she's telling her ex to move "everything you own in the box to the left," the song managed to get millions mindlessly singing the line "to the left, to the left" and subconsciously implanting the idea of living out of the left side of the brain into their own minds.

When thinking about these lyrics it reminded me of something else I'd heard which I couldn't quite bring to mind. Later it came to me. In Oliver Stone's 'JFK' movie Kevin Costner's character is describing the process of President John. F. Kennedy getting shot by snipers, (not by a lone nutter named Lee Harvey Oswald!) and mentions that the bullets came from the front and to the right, causing the President to fall "back and to the left," which he repeats three times. If Kennedy really was the well-meaning and Godly man that he has been consistently portrayed as in the alternative media, the symbolism of him falling back and to the left would appear to stand as Satanic mockery of a much-loved hero to millions, as it is the polar opposite of heading "to the right" or embracing righteous living.

Incidentally, here would appear to be a good point to address another favoured symbol of owned celebrities, which is their flashing up of the so-called "666 sign" using the forefinger and the thumb. There is nothing inherently "evil" about the number 666, just as is the case with any of the "Illuminati" signs and symbols such as pyramids. As with all things, it comes down to the will and the intent of the practitioner in terms of what that symbol becomes adopted to represent.

When it comes to 666, therefore, the book of Revelation states: "Here is wisdom. Let him that hath understanding count the number of the beast: for it is the number of a man; and his number is 666." Therefore it is the number of a beast *or* of a man. It is a choice. The number can represent good or it can represent evil depending on the consciousness which is applied to it. We're back to free will, the greatest gift with which we have been endowed by the Creator. To superstitiously denounce this number as "evil" is to miss the wondrous point that human life is carbon-based. Carbon is made up of 6 protons, 6 neutrons and 6 electrons. Hence in our material form we represent 666. The evildoers have hijacked this number for their own nefarious means and tried to negate its positive connotations such as this.

To take this idea further our bodies have 33 vertebrae, (Jesus being said to have been 33 years of age when he was crucified is more symbolism for this. It also explains why 33 is such an important number within the degrees of Freemasonry as it refers to the ascension of Kundalini energy up the 33 vertebrae of the spine to where spiritual enlightenment can be achieved. There's more fun with language to be had here, too. "Light" refers both to a lack of density and to brightness, as in a negation of darkness—all ideas associated with spiritual ascension and the idea that our souls' natural home resides up in the Heavens rather than down here in the solid density of Earth. (The bastardisation of the English language reveals so much when decoded; God is simply the word "good" with an "o" removed, and is the reversal of the word "dog"—someone's idea of a sick joke? Devil, on the other hand, is "evil" with a "d" added. Both words are telling you what they really represent. The English language is full of not-so-hidden revelations such as this and is replete with word magic(k.) Little wonder that words are said to be "spelled."

Right is right

The opposite instruction to "to the left, to the left" comes again from the Bible, where the figure of Jesus tells his followers to "cast thy net to the right" if they wish to catch fish. Again, this is allegory, and he is not talking literally about going fishing. The fish are symbolic of the constellation of Pisces which represents wisdom, and the followers are being told that if they wish to reap wisdom they should live out of the right hemisphere of their brains.

It's interesting also that, on a compass, east lies to the right, and this is where the life-giving Sun rises, or is "re-born" each morning, before symbolically "dying" in the West, to the left, each evening. This seems like further confirmation that right and left are associated with life and death respectively.

So many cultures through the ages have taught that learning to live virtuously and to let go of over over-attachment to physical things, is the key to escaping the cycle of death and rebirth and to finally ascend to higher consciousness and return to our true spiritual home. The Hindu and Buddhist philosophies teach of the Samsara, the cycle of birth, death and rebirth. But there's an escape route referred to as the Moksha, in Sanskrit literally meaning "escape from Samsara." Hinduism, Buddhism, and Jainism teach the same concept. Wikipedia describes this process as:

> "...freedom from "dukkha" and "samsāra," the cycle of death and rebirth by knowledge of the true self (Atman-jnana,) the lack of a permanent essence, and the release from craving and clinging to passions and the mundane mind."

This experience involves illuminating the out-of-body crown chakra, and is achieved through going, again, to the right side of the brain. This is why in all classical images of Jesus, Mithra, Krishna and Buddha, they are depicted with glowing halos above their crowns, because they have illuminated the seventh chakra and are showing the way we should all be living.

These are complicated metaphysical concepts and I'm aware that many readers will be champing at the bit to get back to music. And we will shortly as we start to examine some songs. But this is all important prefacing that needs to be covered in order to get the most of what all the lyrics that we will examine would appear to have been communicating.

Although it's responsible for our processing of facts, figures and logic, the left side of the brain, though a similar size to the right, accounts for only ten per cent of our brain's capacity. The right accounts for the remaining 90 per cent, yet so few ever tap into all of that potential. This is where the concept of tithing within the Church comes from. The giving of ten per cent of all you have is subliminally reinforcing the idea of living out of the limited ten per cent of the left brain, rather than fulfilling the true, holistic potential of embracing the right.

Back to school

Our experienced reality in this realm acts as a kind of schoolhouse where our souls come to learn the lessons and undergo the experiences they need to grow and evolve into advanced states of consciousness. I watch zero TV any more, but a show which had a very profound effect on me some years ago was 'Ashes to Ashes,' screened on BBC1, incredibly enough. This was part police-procedural drama, part early 1980s nostalgia vehicle—at least according to its surface narrative. Like all good allegories, however, its true meaning was hidden some layers beneath the surface. It's a process I tried my best to incorporate into my allegorical novel 'The Cause & The Cure' in 2019, (the "Before Times!")

In the final episode, the audience comes to discover that the cast of cop characters are all actually dead having been killed in the line of duty, and have found themselves in a kind of purgatory limbo land where they must come to terms with aspects of themselves and accept them before they can move to the next stage of their spiritual journey, (symbolised by a noisy pub!) One of the characters asks, "what is this place?" to which another replies, "it's somewhere we come to sort ourselves out." Rarely has a more telling metaphor for our shared human experience been presented through a popular culture vehicle—especially on the BBC.

It's not just in the Bible that these profound spiritual truths have been intricately encoded. The speciality of spiritual scholar Santos

Bonacci, known as "Mr. Astrotheology," is what he refers to as "Syncretism" — taking the ancient teachings of many cultures and traditions from all ages and all different parts of the world, and examining the commonality between them. Invariably, they all end up demonstrating widespread knowledge of the same basic truths. Some years ago Santos stunned the audience at a Truth Juice event in Birmingham by showing how the Internal Alchemical Process had been encoded into a great many children's nursery rhymes. These metaphysical understandings seem to be deeply woven into the collective human psyche and are subconsciously evoked when conveyed through vehicles such as movies, TV shows, songs, novels or poems. Santos revealed that for the decoding process, he was drawing on the writings of none other than the dark occultist so beloved of the demonic controllers, Aleister Crowley.

The interpretations he was drawing upon are from Crowley's *The Equinox, Book Four, Part 2, Chapter VII ("An Interlude")'* The link to a blog article containing the full range of decodes is in the Resources section at the end. As noted by the article's writer:

> *"Every nursery rhyme contains profound magical secrets which are open to everyone who has made a study of the correspondences of the Holy Qabalah. To puzzle out an imaginary meaning for this "nonsense" sets one thinking of the Mysteries; one enters into deep contemplation of holy things, and God Himself leads the soul to a real illumination. Hence also the necessity of Incarnation; the soul must descend into all Falsity in order to attain All-Truth."*

For the purposes of this chapter, we'll focus on the two most potent of Crowley's observations, indicating that he clearly comprehended the life-affirming miracle of the Internal Alchemical Process. This only makes the personal choice he clearly made, to stray from this righteous path to instead pursue one of wickedness and deviation that he must have known would lead to his soul's demise, all the more perplexing. We might also ponder what it is that has made many a rock star follow this same path when they must have been privy to the same revelations.

Either way, here's what The Great Beast had to say about *Hickory Dickory Dock.'* (Crowley was writing in the verbiage of his time, the post-Victorian era, but his writings re-affirm what is being attested to by so many of the songwriters examined later in this chapter.)

> *"Hickory, dickory, dock!*
>
> *The mouse ran up the clock.*
>
> *The clock struck one,*
>
> *And the mouse ran down,*
>
> *Hickory, dickory, dock!*
>
> *Here we are on higher ground at once. The clock symbolises the spinal column, or, if you prefer it, Time, chosen as one of the conditions of normal consciousness. The mouse is the Ego; "Mus," a mouse, being only Sum, "I am," spelt Qabalistically backwards.*
>
> *This Ego, or Prana or Kundalini force being driven up the spine, the clock strikes one, that is, the duality of consciousness is abolished. And the force again subsides to its original level."*

And of the eternal schoolyard favourite *'Humpty Dumpty,'* Crowley wrote:

> *"Humpty Dumpty sat on a wall.*
>
> *Humpty Dumpty got a great fall.*
>
> *All the king's horses,*
>
> *And all the king's men,*
>
> *Couldn't set up Humpty Dumpty again.*
>
> *This is so simple as hardly to require explanation. Humpty Dumpty is of course the Egg of Spirit, and the wall is the Abyss. His "fall" is therefore the descent of spirit into matter; and it is only too painfully familiar to us that all the king's horses and all his men cannot restore us to the height.*
>
> *Only The King Himself can do that!"*

(The King refers to the sovereign man or woman concerned, who remain the true master of their own destiny.)

And so, after such an epic journey into esoteric realms we finally get back into the territory of popular music, as we discover that the very same spiritual teachings have also been sitting right there in plain sight for decades in hordes of favourite and beloved rock songs. All have been cleverly dressed up to appear as something else so their true meanings only become revealed to the initiated and the consciously-awakened. But they are there nevertheless and will remain so timelessly.

Roll the Rock

Appearing on the *'Great Awakening'* show with Joanne-Divine Life Yogini in 2021, Charlie Freak stated:

> *"And so what meditation is, is everything, because it's the gateway to the other world, to the other realm, which traditionally we know as the Blue Shift, or the Right Hand Path, or the Heaven versus the Hell. This is Ascension meditation ... because what meditation does is it activates your pineal gland. And believe me, one of the things that I do is I decode an enormous amount of things, especially rock 'n' roll music, which, by the way, is "roll the rock." They spun it the wrong way.*

> *"So really rock 'n' roll is roll the rock, and roll the rock is moving the fornix which is in the third ventricle of your brain. And the fornix is like the stone ... And so the oil must raise up to the third ventricle. It rests for two and a half days upon the slab, which is your hypothalamus. And then it trans-mutates and activates the pineal gland. And then an electronic signal is sent to this little fold and it connects to the roof of your third ventricle. And when we activate our pineal gland, it "rolls the rock." That's rock 'n' roll!*

> *"When you decode the lyrics to virtually 90 per cent of these beautiful bands, they were all speaking about God, God's creation, and this meditative process of going within—that the Kingdom of Heaven is within you."*

The songs which encode much of what has been mentioned above are primarily from the 1960s and 70s, with a few spilling into the 1980s. Charlie Freak is of the view that by 1982, the music industry's controllers had got wind of the secrets that these musicians had been covertly revealing in their recordings, and which had so far flown under the radar of the corporate bosses, and so moved to put the brakes on any further esoteric content, forcing their artists to release only "approved" material. A small handful of songs still appear to have slipped through the net beyond this point, but by and large, meaningful mainstream music was dead by this point. And that's a *long* time ago.

These music-makers were young men and women, for the most part only in their 20s. A big question instantly emerges, therefore. How were they so clued-up on such empowering information at such a young age? They certainly understood the power of it and the dangers involved with coming right out and saying it, hence why they had to cloak it so cleverly in allegory and metaphor.

The possibilities are, firstly, that they felt personally compelled to research this material. In the decades before the internet, this would have involved going to specialist libraries or bookshops and digging for arcane literature. It seems unlikely that so many young people, surrounded by all the potential for fun that being in one's 20s brings, would choose to spend this important decade of their life in such a way, and that all those in question, widely scattered as they were, would all make such a decision at the same time.

A more likely option as far as my suspicious mind is concerned, is that they emanated from family backgrounds where such knowledge was taught as a matter of course, or that they were initiated into some kind of mystery school teachings. Certainly, many of the artists involved in putting out the most profoundly powerful songs were part of the much-documented Laurel Canyon crowd, with all the military family connections involved there.

The only remaining possibility that some readers may entertain is that, as creative types, they were somehow channelling this information from the Muses or some similar source, and that the lyrics were flowing through them. This does stand as a credible option for me since, in many of my public talks, it's felt as if channelled information is flowing through me. I can watch back a recording of one of my presentations and think, "Wow. I said that? Where did *that* come from?"

All that said, let's get into a handful of the songs in question. A respectful nod goes to Charlie Freak as most of these decodes are his. His Rumble channel at https://rumble.com/user/CharlieFreak contains a whole host of videos breaking down these tracks individually, and there's more in his 150-part mini-book series on the most important rock albums in history which can be accessed here—https://www.lulu.com/spotlight/charliefreak1

Pink Floyd: 'Dark Side of the Moon' (album)

We start with not a singular song, but an entire album which appears to encode great truths. It's not for nothing that it remains lauded as one of the greatest albums of all time, as well as one of the best-selling, and the one to have spent more weeks on the official album charts than any other. It's open to question as to how many of its listeners have picked up on what the album appears to be communicating, rather than simply accepting it on its surface value.

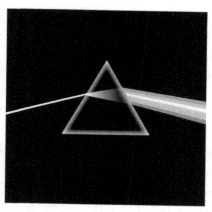

The album chronicles the human journey through life in present-day, (things weren't so different in 1973 than they are now) within Organ-ised Society. Appropriately enough, the first thing the listener hears is a steady heartbeat as the introduction to the track *'Breathe,'* indicating the first moments of a new life. The song charts all the hope and potential that a new birth brings.

"Long you live and high you fly,
And smiles you'll give and tears you'll cry,
And all you touch and all you see,
Is all your life will ever be."

It's never long before the controllers of Organised Society get a hold on a new slave to the system, however:

"Run, rabbit run.
Dig that hole, forget the sun.
And when at last the work is done,
Don't sit down, it's time to dig another one.
For long you live and high you fly,
But only if you ride the tide,
And balanced on the biggest wave
You race towards an early grave."

The constructs of Organised Society ensure that most human lives are not lived to their full, holistic potential, and that they don't last as long as they are designed by the Creator to last. Ever noticed how the so-called "elite" class often live beyond 100, whereas few within regular society make it beyond their 80s?

'Dark Side' was constructed as a concept album, and to be listened to in one continuous session. Dipping in and out of the tracks individually will not bring the album's message to bear. Each track, therefore, morphs into the next. As 'Breathe' becomes 'On The Run,' the message of how life on Earth has been structured to exploit regular members of society and to keep them away from spiritual pursuits is continued:

"Ticking away the moments that make up a dull day,
You fritter and waste the hours in an offhand way.
Kicking around on a piece of ground in your home town.
Waiting for someone or something to show you the way.
"Every year is getting shorter, never seem to find the time.

Plans that either come to naught, or half a page of scribbled lines.
Hanging on in quiet desperation is the English way.
The time is gone, the song is over.
Thought I'd something more to say."

(I like the line about what constitutes "the English way." It was the case in 1973, and it's still the case now, which goes some way to explaining how the Co(n)vid Scamdemic was able to be got away with for so long!)

'The Great Gig in the Sky' makes for, in my book, 'Dark Side's most fascinating track. Over the top of a Richard Wright-composed instrumental, the listener gets almost four minutes of heartfelt wailing from session singer Claire Torry. Her vocals build in intensity from the first strains, becoming overwhelmingly impassioned, before gradually becoming calmer and settling down into clam, melodic tones. 'Great Gig' could be interpreted as a reaction to the life experience—dealing with the tests and challenges of everyday existence in this constructed realm, before slowly coming to terms with an accepting of one's lot in life. It has alternatively been interpreted as an observation of ailing mental health, with the singer descending into sheer madness, before being calmed.

The most pertinent observation, though, is that it deals with the mortality of human life and an accepting of the physical death, (which doesn't really mark death at all, of course, merely the passing from one state of consciousness to another.) A tell-tale sign of this comes from the only words spoken among the wailing. As Torry's state begins to change from intense to settled, she utters the words "oh, God," as if she has had an epiphany and has experienced a connection with the Creator. Following this moment her wailings begin to calm, suggesting an acceptance of the physical "death" and a readiness to embark on what lies beyond.

Reinforcing this idea is the voiceover of an Irish studio-hand who was present at the time of recording, and whose utterances, legend has it, the band decided to record and use. He is heard on top of the instrumental saying:

"And I am not frightened of dying. Any time will do. I don't mind.
Why should I be frightened of dying?
There's no reason for it. You've got to go sometime."

With this, side one is done, and side two charges straight off into *'Money,'* on any level a damning indictment of life in a capitalist society, and the way the acquisition of material wealth has become an over-riding factor in how most people live their lives—all by design to keep us away from the pursuit of what *really* matters in these lives, of course.

"Money, get away.
Get a good job with good pay and you're okay.
Money, it's a gas.
Grab that cash with both hands and make a stash.
New car, caviar, four-star daydream,
Think I'll buy me a football team.
Money, it's a crime.
Share it fairly but don't take a slice of my pie.
Money, so they say,
Is the root of all evil today.
But if you ask for a raise it's no surprise that they're giving none away."

The (systematic) polarity between the world's wealthy "elites" and everybody else—with a focus on the industry of war—is explored in *'Us And Them,'* and it rather begs the question of what inside knowledge writers Roger Waters and Richard Wright really had of the secret-society classes, and how they work to manipulate every aspect of daily life for the "useless eaters" given Richard's own Aristocratic upbringing and Roger's attendance at public school:

"Us, and them.
And after all we're only ordinary men.
Me, and you.
God only knows it's not what we would choose to do.

"Forward he cried from the rear,
And the front rank died.
And the general sat and the lines on the map,
Moved from side to side."

There is a harking back to the album's much-celebrated sleeve image, (devised by the agency Hipgnosis, as detailed in this book's first volume,) on the second instrumental track *'Any Colour You Like.'* Rather than referencing a quote by the American car manufacturer Henry Ford, this evokes the prism of the LP cover, refracting white light and dispensing it in seven different colours.

This is a metaphor for the human chakra system, with each spinning vortex of light carrying its own signature frequency and colour. (The corresponding seven colours in a rainbow remind us of the connectedness between our human physiology and the natural world.) The song's title is cryptically reminding the listener that it is always a matter of choice as to which of the chakras an individual chooses to live their life through—whether through the limitations of the base chakra associated with fear and lower, carnal desires, through the higher-minded consciousness and attached-ness to spirit associated with the crown chakra, or through any point between.

'Brain Damage' is said to be an ode to Pink Floyd founder Syd Barrett, who is reported to have descended into irreversible mental illness as a result of ingesting too much L.S.D. during the counter-culture years of the 1960s, but who almost certainly was the victim of trauma-based mind-control programming. See *'Volume 1'* for more on this. Certainly, the opening lines hint at nostalgic memories of a young life which was cut short and ruined in its prime:

"The lunatic is on the grass.
The lunatic is on the grass.
Remembering games and daisy chains and laughs.
Got to keep the loonies on the path."

The fourth verse hints at the performance of a lobotomy, to completely cut off an individual's Godliness and to render them nothing more than a barely functioning flesh robot. This may have been Syd's fate, but symbolically, it represents how so many are conditioned into this state of degraded consciousness through all the assaults on our higher-mindedness presented through everyday life in our "developed" nations. (It's another factor that explains so much about how the Convid scam wasn't challenged by higher-minded critical thinking and basic common sense on a massive scale.)

> *"The lunatic is in my head.*
> *The lunatic is in my head.*
> *You raise the blade, you make the change.*
> *You re-arrange me 'til I'm sane.*
> *You lock the door and throw away the key,*
> *There's someone in my head but it's not me."*

Some further relevance to Syd's plight, (more of which came later with 1976's *'Shine On You Crazy Diamond'*) comes from the lines which appear to address the change in the sound of Floyd from the psychedelic rock of his era to the high-brow Progressive sound which *'Dark Side'* represents:

> *"And if the band you're in starts playing different tunes,*
> *I'll see you on the Dark Side of the Moon."*

'Brain Damage' segues skilfully into the album's closing track, *'Eclipse.'* This re-assesses all the experiences that most humans undergo in this life with lines such as:

> *"All that you touch,*
> *All that you see,*
> *All that you taste,*
> *All you feel.*
> *All that you love,*
> *All that you hate,*
> *All you distrust*

All you save."

It ends on a jarring note by indicating that everything in God's creation in this realm was designed to holistically co-exist with everything else, divinely synchronised into a symphony of beauty and wonder—"and everything under the sun is in tune."

But... there's a problem, as the song's final lyric surmises—"but the sun is eclipsed by the moon." It's a devastating realisation that what we experience here in this expression of existence has been distorted and inverted by an opposing, parasitic force.

With most of *'Dark Side's* lyrics having been penned by Roger Waters it indicates some inside clueing-in to these dynamics—particularly considering the band members were still only in their 20s at this point, yet had somehow accumulated lessons in life that most only achieve by the time they are at least twice that age—if they ever do at all.

This album clearly demonstrates esoteric knowledge which is being openly communicated to any listener with the ability to discern what is being conveyed. Yet somehow we have to reconcile this factor with the more recent mixed messages being put out by Roger, (see the earlier chapter, *'All Assets Deployed,'*) and his obedient towing of official lines just like the rest of his controlled peers. Roger himself, Floyd as a band, and *'Dark Side'* as an enduringly omnipresent album, therefore, all remain as fascinatingly enigmatic as they ever were.

We're left wondering, also, what Floyd knew of the true nature of the moon, which cannot possibly be a chunk of rock that a rocket can be landed on, but displays all the evidence for being simply a disc of light, or a "luminary."

The old Irish fella has the album's last say in one of his applied voice-overs:

"There is no dark side of the moon really. Matter of fact it's all dark."

Simon & Garfunkel: 'The Sound of Silence'

This perennial favourite is very easy to decode. It refers to the process of meditation—of "going within" to that still and silent place. As Paul Simon's opening line has it:

> *"Hello darkness, my old friend,*
> *It's good to see your face again."*

He is speaking of the bliss of entering into a meditative state. He goes on to reference his eyes being "stabbed by the flash of a neon light," evoking the process of illuminating the pineal gland and the crown chakra as addressed earlier.

> *"And in the naked light I saw,*
> *Ten thousand people, maybe more.*
> *People talking without speaking,*
> *People hearing without listening."*

Here, Simon appears to be documenting the telepathic process, the inherent "knowing" that we can tap into where words become unnecessary and great knowledge is channelled. The next lines are very revealing considering the earlier assertion that these songwriters felt the need to covertly communicate their truths, knowing they could not come right out and say them.

> *"People writing songs that voices never share.*
> *No one dared,*
> *Disturb the sound of silence."*

Roberta Flack: 'Killing Me Softly'

Though a 1973 hit for Roberta Flack and revived for a new generation by The Fugees in the 1990s, this song was written by Lori Lieberman, reportedly as the result of her attending a gig by Don McLean at L.A.'s fabled Troubador club.

The powerful messages and truths in McLean's songs had a profound effect on Lieberman, and caused her to begin questioning the false image of herself associated with her "pain body." It felt as if McLean's music was "killing" her left-brain ego and causing her to access the higher consciousness associated with the right brain. Thus the genius lyrics: 'Strumming my pain with his fingers, singing my life with his words, killing me softly with his song" make direct reference to this process.

Procul Harum: 'A Salty Dog'

The meaning of Procul Harum's big hit 'A Whiter Shade of Pale' has confounded and puzzled music scholars for decades. This song, however, written as all of the band's were by Keith Reid and Gary Brooker, is easier to decipher armed with the knowledge we have explored in this chapter.

It uses seafaring symbolism to describe the Chrism oil process, the crucifixion of the left-brain ego, and the attaining of higher-minded Christ consciousness. The song's ship apparently faces doom as it gets lost at sea—a metaphor for we humans becoming trapped in base consciousness and separation from our Higher Selves. But on the "seventh sea-sick day," (a nod to the body's seven chakras perhaps?) the ship finds land:

> "Upon the seventh sea-sick day,
> We made our port of call.
> A sand so white, and sea so blue,
> No mortal place at all.
> We fired the guns, and burned the mast,
> And rowed from ship to shore.
> The captain cried, we sailors wept,
> Our tears were tears of joy!"

After much hardship the sailors—us—have activated the Kundalini experience and escaped the trappings of the egoic self, and are experiencing all the bliss that this re-connection with "God" brings.

The Eagles: 'Hotel California'

One of the most analysed songs in rock history, the meaning that most seem to have put on *Hotel California* is that it is a metaphor for the music industry itself, the soul-selling that it involves, and the absolute ownership of its key musicians given away by the line "you can check out any time you like, but you can never leave." Writing credits for the song, released in February 1977 as the title track from the album of the same name, go to Don Henley and Glenn Frey for lyrics, and Don Felder for the music.

There are alternative interpretations, however. The early line "this could be Heaven or this could be Hell" reminds us that everything in this life is a free will choice. The chorus is the voice of the left-brain ego and all the temptations that exist in the carnal, physical, 3D world to keep us away from exploring higher consciousness:

> *"Welcome to the Hotel California,*
> *Such a lovely place,*
> *Such a lovely face.*
> *Plenty of room at the Hotel California.*
> *Any time of year,*
> *You can find it here."*

Making that left-brained choice brings its eventual regrets:
> *"And she said 'We are all just prisoners here, of our own device.'*

And killing the beast of the left-brain ego is a difficult task that few manage to achieve, as the song's narrator reminds us:

> *"And in the master's chambers,*
> *They gathered for the feast.*
> *They stab it with their steely knives,*
> *But they just can't kill the beast."*

In the last verse, the narrator says that the last thing he remembers is running for the door. He has forgotten everything else. Just as, if we fail at getting it right in this lifetime, we find ourselves back on the samsara, the cycle of birth, death and rebirth, and come into a new life with our memories wiped clean—a necessary factor if we are to learn, grow and evolve.

Don Henley once commented that the song was about "a journey from innocence to experience...that's all."

Was that all??

Led Zeppelin: 'Stairway To Heaven'

If the aforementioned is the most analysed song in rock history, then this must rate a close second. We'll leave aside the presence of Satanic backmasked messages (covered in '*Volume 1*') for the purposes of this and focus solely on what appears to be the song's benevolent message. Its apparent ambiguity fades when you realise it documents a woman who is trying to achieve her way to Heaven, or spiritual enlightenment. We meet her in the opening lines:

> "*There's a lady who's sure all that glitters is gold,*
> *And she's buying a stairway to Heaven.*
> *When she gets there she knows, if the stores are all closed,*
> *With a word she can get what she came for.*"

As Oscar Wilde would have said, she knows the price of everything and the value of nothing. This woman, (possibly inspired by Somerset Belenoff as detailed in one of the earlier '*Sound Bites,*') sees the attainment of Heaven as a necessary evil and thinks that she can buy her way there, rather than do the internal work necessary.

We get another reminder that everything in this life is a choice, and that it's never too late to change paths and make better choices, with the lines:

> "*Yes, there are two paths you can go by, but in the long run,*
> *There's still time to change the road you're on.*"

By the end of the song we've been re-acquainted with the lady from earlier, but by now, she appears to have learned the value of doing the internal work and is radiating light as a result of undergoing that alchemical process:

> *"And as we wind on down the road,*
> *Our shadows taller than our soul,*
> *There walks a lady we all know,*
> *Who shines white light and wants to show,*
> *How everything still turns to gold."*

The "turning to gold" evokes once again the "honey" of the pineal gland, that portal to enlightenment.

Steely Dan: 'King of the World'

This song charts "the hero's journey" — the successful killing of the dominance of the ego, the embracing of the Chrism/ Kundalini experience, the illumination of the crown chakra, and the coming "face to face with God." Where the narrator of *'Hotel California'* failed in this excursion because he couldn't let go of the chattering voices in his head and enter a meditative state, the writer of *'King of the World'* has succeeded.

The entire song, its lyrics deeply ambiguous, has been interpreted as a conversation between the narrator, who is doing the work to ascend to Heaven, and 'God."

> *"So all I can say is I'm alive and feeling fine."*

This is, I've survived the chaos of the left brain and now I'm ascending.

Some very crafty wordplay from writers Donald Fagen and Walter Becker who were geniuses in their game, then occurs in the chorus:

> *"No marigolds in the promised land.*
> *There's a hole in the ground,*
> *Where they used to grow."*

"Marigolds" can be split to give us Mary, the archetypal Mother and expression of the sacred feminine, and gold. As previously discussed, in the Internal Alchemical Process, the chrism oil splits with half going to the masculine pineal gland, the "honey," and half going to the feminine pituitary gland—the "milk." But there's no milk and honey in the "Promised Land," which is living in the world "out there," the fake, illusory world "promised" by the controllers of Organised Society. There's just a hole in the ground.

Then:

> *"Any man left on the Rio Grande,*
> *Is the king of the world,*
> *As far as I know."*

The Rio Grande is the great divide between the left and right hemispheres of the brain. Any man who has "left" the left side and crossed over to the right has become the king of the world.

When the narrator goes on to say:

> *"I'm reading last year's papers,*
> *Although I don't know why.*
> *Assassins, cons and rapers.*
> *Might as well die."*

He is reflecting—accurately—on the nature of life in the 3D physical reality of Organised Society, which is sick, diseased, violent and only getting worse. All the more reason for the left-brained ego to "die" and for us to ascend to higher consciousness, as it's not as if there's anything worthwhile being left behind.

> *"If I stay inside*
> *I might live 'til Saturday."*

The writer is evoking meditation, the "going within" and mentions staying until Saturday because that was the original Sabbath/ holy day before Sunday got adopted for that role in Western traditions.

America: 'A Horse With No Name'

A song written by Bunnell Dewey that speaks to the process of meditation. The narrator tells of heading into the desert to go on a journey of discovery, which is to go inward in our minds—perhaps breaking away from the noise and busy-ness of Organised Society for the first time to try and discover who we really are at the core of our being.

The character states that the first things he experienced were plants and birds and rocks and things, sand, and hills and rings. These are all the things we notice with our five physical senses. This indicates that the narrator is approaching things from this physical perspective only, through the left-brained carnal realm.

Shortly afterwards, however, the character has embarked upon meditation and gone to that still and silent place, as evidenced by the lines:

> *"It felt good to be out of the rain.*
> *In the desert you can remember your name,*
> *'Cause there ain't no-one for to give you no pain."*

This has always been a popular song, often on radio rotation, and part of the reason may have been that the lyrics are awakening deep-rooted archetypes within our consciousness of which we're not overtly aware. The narrator's journey is the potential journey of each of us.

The Band: 'The Weight'

Written by the Canadian half-Jewish/ half Native American Robbie Robertson, right from the off the lyrical clues are there. "I pulled into Nazareth" tells us this is a song about "Jesus" but with him symbolising us. Like so many of these other songs, it's about human physiology and relatedness to divinity.

> *"Take a load off Fanny.*
> *Take a load for free.*
> *Take a load off Fanny,*
> *And (and) (and) you put the load right on me.*

(You put the load right on me.)"

The chorus line is as spoken by "God" who is inviting us to leave behind the heavy loads and burdens of this material life, (euphemisms aside, "Fanny" is a representation of the sacred feminine/ Mother Mary) and the machinations of the controllers of Organised Society who seek to keep us encumbered by it all and enter right-brained higher consciousness. "God" is offering to carry these heavy loads for us if only we would make the free will choice to go the higher-minded spiritual route.

Much cryptic anecdotal storytelling occurs in the rest of the song, including the verse:

> *"Crazy Chester followed me and he caught me in the fog.*
> *He said, 'I will fix your rack if you'll take Jack, my dog.'*
> *I said, 'wait a minute, Chester, you know I'm a peaceful man"*
> *He said, 'That's okay, boy, won't you feed him when you can'."*

This is a conversation between the storyteller and "God." "God" is saying, just do the best you can in this life. Do what you know to be right and strive towards being virtuous the best you can."

What better advice could there be?

The Allman Brothers: 'Melissa'

The song was written by Gregg Allman for his older brother Duane, less than a year before Duane was tragically killed in October 1971 when his motorcycle collided with a flatbed truck. Duane was reportedly a deeply spiritual man who practiced meditation, and seemingly went into meditative states when playing his extended guitar solos, as many other famed musicians appear to. They go "somewhere else." This was not a lucky band. Bassist Berry Oakley was also killed in a motorcycle accident just over a year after Duane, and Gregg and Duane's father Willis, an army officer, was murdered when they were young children.

Despite these tragedies, Gregg crafted the deeply meaningful *'Melissa.'* Although on the surface appearing to be a song about a girl, "Melissa" is derived from an original Sanskrit word, birthing a word used later in Greek. "Malita" means "honey sweet" and "mulatos" is honey. So the name Melissa is a reference to sweetness from honey and this, as we discovered earlier, ties into the Chrism oil process, being the sacred masculine associated with the pineal gland. Gregg's talk of running back to Melissa doesn't mean he's running off to some girl the minute he gets the chance. It means he takes the opportunity to practice meditation in order to illuminate the pineal gland and make that connection back to Divine Source.

Matthews Southern Comfort: 'Woodstock'

Although best-known in its Matthews Southern Comfort form, which became a UK number one single in 1970, this song was originally written and performed by Joni Mitchell. Ostensibly about the infamous Woodstock concert at Bethel Woods in August 1969, which, although celebrated as the ultimate Hippie gathering, actually occurred as that movement was entering its death throes, not helped by the so-called "Manson murders" having happened in L.A. only a week earlier and being used to tarnish the reputation of "hippies" in the eyes of the mainstream media-consuming public.

Nevertheless, this song is also a beautiful ode to the relationship we spiritual beings having a temporary human experience retain with "Heaven" or "God."

> *"We are stardust, we are golden.*
> *And we've got to get ourselves back to the garden."*

The chorus refers to the Garden of Eden, a biblical Utopia before the sin and chaos of the left-brain ego had set in and led humanity astray.

More of the same with:

> *"Well, maybe it's the time of year,*
> *Or maybe it's the time of Man.*
> *And I don't know who I am,*
> *But life's for learning."*

This song must have had a profound effect on listeners when it first appeared, as—contrived and infiltrated as it may ultimately have been—the counter-culture/ hippie scene must have felt very special and very spiritual to those who got caught up in in it—'something in the air" in the words of Thunderclap Newman—and very much "the time of Man" with all the talk of the incoming Age of Aquarius that was around at the time, (and which is still being talked about as imminent all these decades later!)

The song's final verse ends:

> *"And I dreamed I saw the bombers,*
> *Riding shotgun in the sky,*
> *Turning into butterflies,*
> *Above our nation."*

We might imagine the same for these times, only with chemtrail planes instead.

Prince & The Revolution: 'The Ladder'

As this book's predecessor surmised, although Prince is best remembered for his lewd and lascivious mainstream output, tucked away on all of his albums are some deeply spiritual and contemplative outings. This gem from 1985's *Around The World In A Day* album demonstrates advanced metaphysical knowledge, suggesting Prince was clued-in on such liberating teachings, possibly through mystery-school initiation. Perhaps tellingly, Prince's father, the jazz musician John L. Nelson, is credited as a co-writer of the song.

It's pretty clear that Prince is referring to the Chrism oil/ Kundalini energy process, and the fact that very few ever achieve this experience, in the song's chorus:

> *"Everybody's looking 4 the ladder,*
> *Everybody wants salvation of the soul.*
> *The steps U take are no easy road.*
> *But the reward is great,*
> *4 those who want 2 go."*

410

And later:

> *"What's the use in half a story, half a dream?*
> *U have 2 climb all of the steps in between."*

Howard Jones: 'Hide & Seek'

I did cover this song's meaning in the previous book's section on 1980s video symbolism, but here is certainly the rightful place to give it another airing. This record is quite incredible considering the deep message it put across, all under the guise of a mainstream synth-pop hit with a catchy chorus. It addresses the creative force behind the Universe, the Most High, and this force—in Singularity—wishing to create a playground—this Earthly realm—into which it can split itself into individuated units of consciousness, lose itself, and enjoy the experience of re-discovering its true nature—a cosmic game of Hide & Seek.

> *"There was a time when there was nothing at all,*
> *Nothing at all, just a distant hum.*
> *There was a being and he lived on his own.*
> *He had no one to talk to, and nothing to do,*
> *He drew up the plans,*
> *Learnt to work with his hands,*
> *A million years passed by and his work was done."*

Forgetting itself is vital to this process, just as we ourselves forget our true nature when we incarnate into human form. If we remembered who and what we really are, we would not gain the benefits that our life experiences bring to us. The song's message is that the tools are there for us to rediscover our true, divine nature if we wilfully set out to do so.

The next verse is very revealing:

> *"So she had built her elaborate home,*
> *With its ups and its downs,*
> *Its rains and its sun.*

411

She decided that her work was done.

Time to have fun.

And she found a game to play.

Then as part of the game,

She completely forgot where she'd hidden herself,

And she spent the rest of her time,

Trying to find the parts."

Note that the "he" of the previous verse has now become a "she." In the Godly realm, masculine and feminine are interchangeable because there is no duality, only "the one."

Michael McDonald: 'Sweet Freedom'

And to finish, an unexpected offering from this former Steely Dan and Doobie Brothers member, and from outside of the familiar timeframe, as late as 1986. Although taken from the soundtrack to the highly forgettable movie *'Running Scared'* this song, with writing credits going to long-time Michael Jackson collaborator Rod Temperton of the British group Heatwave, is all about attaining "sweet freedom" from the entrapment of the left brain by "going within."

"No more runnin' down the wrong road,

Dancin' to a different drum,

Can't you see what's goin' on,

Deep inside your heart?"

The opening lines seem fairly clear in this regard, reinforcing how the way in which we live our lives remains a free will choice.

"Always searchin' for the real thing,

Livin' like it's far away.

Just leave all the madness in yesterday.

You're holdin' the key,

When you believe it."

We're reminded that the secret to rewarding living lies within all of us if we can entrain ourselves to leave the noise and madness of everyday life behind. It's never far away when you learn the skills.

*

We've been on quite a journey across these three books, and I've learned just as much as I've conveyed along the way. I won't lie—it's been a depressing process at times to discover that no-one in the world of music that I once loved is who I thought they were, and that seemingly fun and innocent forms of entertainment so often had malevolent agendas running underneath. Nostalgic memories have been tarnished, and music just hasn't meant what it used to.

The contents of this final chapter, however, have reminded me that eternal Truth can never be destroyed, that we do have an innate connectedness back to our Creator, or Higher Selves, and that it's always a matter of personal free will choice as to whether we utilise that connection or not. We need be under no illusion; the self-work called for is hard and not for the lazy or easily-distracted. But the potential rewards are out of all proportion to the effort. And it's truly mindblowing to consider that these young musicians appear to have known all about this and felt moved to make it the subject of their songs.

The concept of Placing the Truth in Plain Sight has cropped up a lot in the context of these volumes, and it's usually in a malevolent context. But the songs analysed above, and so many others like them, remind us that the Truth staring us right in the face, if only we could know how to decode it, can sometimes be offering us our greatest gift—knowledge of how to escape the Hellhole that is this physical reality full of pain and strife and hardship, and take ourselves somewhere so much better—both within these lives and in what lies beyond

I can think of few more positive and inspiring notes on which to leave this story.

It's been a privilege for me to have fulfilled the role of communicating this information, and it's both gratifying and humbling to know that my words will live on way beyond me and will hopefully continue to inspire new generations long after I've gone. 20 years ago, running from party to party as a DJ and living only for the next gig and the next hot tune, I could never have imagined I would be doing this now with my life. But fate has a habit of leading you off down unexpected routes once you bite the bullet and dare to take a walk on the wild side.

As the researcher and broadcaster Crrow 777 is fond of saying—"I would like to wish you all a happy, healthy and higher-minded new era."

Resources:

Children's Nursery Rhyme Meanings Explained By Aleister Crowley, From "The Equinox":

- https://www.ashtarcommandcrew.net/forum/topics/children-s-nursery-rhyme-meanings-explained-by-aleister-crowley

The Moksha in Indian religion:

- https://www.britannica.com/topic/moksha-Indian-religion#:~:text=moksha%2C%20also%20spelled%20mok%E1%B9%A3a%2C%20also,literally%20means%20freedom%20from%20samsara.

Waking Times: Pineal Gland—Portal of Higher Dimensions:

- http://www.wakingtimes.com/pineal-gland-portal-higher-dimensions/

Meditation: Spiritual Awakening: This Video Can Awaken You (And the WORLD)

- https://www.youtube.com/watch?v=EyVyipGTa1g

One of the websites that anyone can use to calculate their own days of the chrism experience during the month is here:

- http://moontracks.com/lunar_ingress.html
- https://sacredlighthealing.blogspot.com/2018/12/the-story-of-santa-claustrum-its-not.html

Good Vibrations podcast: Charlie Freak—The Greatest Story Never Told:

- https://www.spreaker.com/user/markdevlin/good-vibrations-podcast-vol-134-charlie-

Charlie Freak's Rumble channel:

- https://rumble.com/user/CharlieFreak

Charlie Freak's 150-book series on the most important rock albums in history:

- https://www.lulu.com/spotlight/charliefreak1

Santos Bonacci: The Secret Christ Within (The Sacred Oil, Jacob's Ladder):

- https://www.youtube.com/watch?v=7TJx8BaTP5c

Santos Bonacci: Secret Esoteric Knowledge of the Christ Within—El Secreto Sagrado del Cristo en el Interior:

- https://www.youtube.com/watch?v=bcaM3rGWaBE

Santos Bonacci: Universal Truth School: Raising The Chrism:

- https://universaltruthschool.com/syncretism/raising-the-chrism/

Bill Donahue's website:

- https://www.hiddenmeanings.com/

Eric Dubay's website:

- https://ericdubay.wordpress.com/

For many videos on meditation/ kundalini energy and other spiritual processes:

- https://www.youtube.com/c/TheSpiritScience

APPENDIX 1

DJs EXPOSED: PAUL VAN DYK

In 2018, I had intended to begin a new series of articles—separate from any book—focusing on big-name DJs and producers, and drawing attention to their questionable affiliations and family backgrounds, and the agendas which they have been used to promote. This was to have been in the same vein as the Lifetime Actors chapter in the last book, applying similar scrutiny to that which has now been applied to many rock musicians and pop stars. After all, DJs are the heroes and role models of their scene, and are held in just as high regard as the likes of **David Bowie**, **Mick Jagger**, **Bruce Springsteen** or **Prince** are in their own respective fields. More importantly, given the phenomenal stronghold on youth culture that the dance music scene has managed to achieve over the past three decades, they possess the potential to hold influence over extremely large groups of people the world over.

It was clear that nobody else was ever going to take on this job—largely because it requires an interest in and a knowledge of the worldwide Electronic Dance Music and Club scenes, which seems to be palatable to very few other conspiracy researchers. I therefore resolved myself to taking on the task.

My intentions were good. Regrettably, however, it soon became clear that I had been rather too optimistic in expecting to get the time to continue the series. (The same is true of my reading schedule; my bedside table is usually laden with so many books waiting to be absorbed that if the pile ever fell on me while I slept it would surely kill me.) As usual, work and home commitments took their toll, and the "series" remained at one solitary article.

If I *had* carried the series on, it *would* have included names such as **Tiesto**, **Paul Oakenfold**, **Pete Tong**, **Fatboy Slim**, **Skrillex** and **Carl Cox**. But to be honest, the finer details aside, these articles would only have continued to emphasise the same points about how the leaders and flag-bearers for *any* popular scene never get there off the back of sheer hard work and good luck alone, but are chosen and placed there for the services they can perform for those who covertly control these genres. My readers will, by now, be *more than* familiar with this concept!

As in rock and pop music, sometimes it's family connections and ancestry that leads to superstar DJs being selected, and sometimes it's down to them showing some skill and talent early on in their career, then being approached and elevated to lofty heights. Either way, it's just another day at the office in the worlds of cultural manipulation and mass mind-control.

Doubtless, many in his legions of diehard fans would accuse me of "picking on" **Paul van Dyk**. A random glance at any of the threads on his Facebook page provides instant confirmation of the religious fervour displayed by so many of his followers, with phrases like "you are my God," and "I would die for you, Paul" on frequent display. His sway over his fans borders on being a mind-control cult. The music genre he represents wasn't named "Trance" by accident.

Far from me "picking" on him, however, his story ticks so many boxes that there can be few, if any, better examples of a manufactured hero with a gifted career.

That being said, let's examine the fascinating and revelatory story of this hero to millions.

One day in the East

The "Paul" part of Paul van Dyk actually comes from his last name. He was born Matthias Paul on 16th December 1971 in the town of Eisenhuttenstadt. At the time, in the midst of the Cold War, this was in what was still referred to as East Germany, close to its border with Poland. All biographies state that he was born into a single-parent household, and no details have been made available on the identity or profession of his father. Van Dyk has never adequately explained why he chose this name as his artist moniker.

When asked in a 2020 interview by *'Billboard'* magazine about his parents and what they did for a living, van Dyk responded by only talking about his mother, an interior designer. He would appear to have been an only child. Through comments made in various interviews, van Dyk has painted his childhood as being one of hardship, the harsh reality of daily life in oppressive East Germany being very much in contrast to the relative freedom enjoyed by those West of the political border. An anecdote relayed many times involves him having tuned in, through boredom and curiosity, to radio stations from the West—technically banned in the East—where he got to hear music from the likes of **New Order** and **The Smiths**. In addition, he has told the story of his grandmother smuggling back an **Orchestral Manoeuvres In The Dark** vinyl album for him from over the border. This is said to have sparked his lifelong obsession with electronic music, and to have fired up the first sparks of creativity in the young Matthias.

At the end of 1989, at which point he was about to turn 18, the Berlin Wall came down, symbolic of the apparent collapse of the Soviet Communist regime and in turn, marking the end of the Cold War. The young van Dyk had reportedly moved with his mother to live in Hamburg two weeks before the historical event. Shortly afterwards, he was seduced, magnet-like, to the German capital. That year—1989—saw the very first Love Parade in Berlin, an event which grew to colossal proportions in subsequent years and became a significant showcase for Trance and other forms of Electronic Dance Music

As the former East Germany began to catch up with the culture and freedoms of the Western side of the country, Electronic Dance Music began to take a hold—particularly in Berlin, historically a hotbed of artistic creativity and counter-culture. Van Dyk's official biographies have him developing a fascination for the early House and Techno sounds that were beginning to be cooked up by imaginative producers in the city and wanting to be a part of the movement. With a day job as a carpenter, he began buying records and establishing himself as a DJ, securing fortuitous early slots at nightclubs such as Tresor, Turbine, Dubmission and Brain, all highly celebrated venues in early 90s Berlin club folklore.

Soon after his debut as a DJ, van Dyk had already moved over to record production, creating electronic dance tracks in the studio. An invitation to visit London to attend a performance by **Depeche Mode** evidently made a big impression, as he recalled in a later interview.

"At the beginning of the '90s, Mute Records founder Daniel Miller phoned me up, looking to sign me to the label. I was totally over the moon. He said, 'Why don't you come to London? There's a concert of Depeche Mode and we can talk about the artist contract?' I went, and of course it was phenomenal. To top it all off though, they started the show with 'A Question Of Time.' That meant so much to me. When I was in East Germany, I could never buy any records. I could never go to any concerts, and there I was, two years after the wall came down, at Wembley, watching them perform 'A Question Of Time'."

Van Dyk went on to release his first single, *'Perfect Day'* under the name **Visions of Shiva** in 1992. The following year, he cemented his reputation as a remixer by re-working *'Love Stimulation'* by **Humate**, regarded thereafter as an evergreen classic in the genre of electronic music that would come to be known as Trance. In 1994, he produced what came to be recognised as his crowning moment of glory with a track which has retained its "classic" status ever since, with *'For An Angel.'* This appeared on his first artist album, *'45 RPM,'* released on MFS (Masterminded For Success.) By this time, his international touring as a DJ had begun, with a fortuitous start in the clubs of New York City. As he explained in a 2017 interview with the *'DJ Times'* publication:

"I was really lucky. That's when the (long-defunct conference) New Music Seminar was going on in New York, and they had what was billed as a German night. They were bringing all these famous German DJs over, but one of them couldn't do it—and I was the substitute. I made the best of my chance, and I really connected with the audience that night. Howard Schaffer, who used to run the Happy Colors DJ agency—which I think was the first DJ agency in the world—saw me, and said, "I think you are really talented. We should do something together. Come by the office on Monday." And after that I was playing in Limelight every month, and then started doing tours."

In the UK, the era of the "superclubs" had begun, as the early raves, warehouse parties and dance festivals had moved over to licensed and more easily-controlled indoor venues, and van Dyk quickly carved a reputation for himself on this scene, playing at clubs such as Ministry of Sound, Cream, Renaissance, and becoming a regular visitor to the highly influential Trance music haven Gatecrasher in Sheffield.

With his dedicated fanbase growing exponentially with every passing year, a new ambassador for the international Trance music clubbing scene had been created.

Creating a Pied Piper

German DJ/ producer Paul Van Dyk, international ambassador for "Trance" music—what's in a name?

https://commons.wikimedia.org/wiki/File:Paul_van_Dyk_NO_ (cropped).JPG

No real explanation has been given as to why Matthias Paul chose Paul van Dyk as his professional pseudonym. Fans have asked him if his last name should be spelt 'van Dyk' or 'van Dyke,' and he has replied that "either is fine." On other occasions he has quipped about his last name, stating "there's no e in Paul van Dyk," seemingly suggesting that he abstains from Ecstasy, or MDMA, the recreational drug of choice long connected to the scene for which he has been such a flag-bearer.

By the early 2000s van Dyk's touring schedule had reached the point where he was playing gigs in multiple countries across all continents, all year, every year, a factor determined by the growing popularity of Trance itself as a major force in youth culture all around the world. (Though in later years, van Dyk attempted to distance himself from the genre in which he had made his name, applauding fellow DJ **Gareth Emery** in a 2006 interview for branding 95 per cent of Trance music "unplayable derivative shite.")

He went on to occupy a spot in the Top 20 of '*DJ Magazine*'s Top 100 DJs poll—considered the industry's ultimate arbiter of success—for 15 years straight, taking the top spot in 2005 and 2006. He was nominated for a Grammy in 2005 and won one in 2008 for his remix contributions to '*The Dark Knight*' film soundtrack. '*Forbes*' magazine named him one of the world's greatest DJs in 2012.

As dance and club music continued to grow in popularity and the festivals and large-scale clubbing events grew in size and stature as a result—so a disturbing element began to creep in, acknowledged by only a tiny handful of researchers who have commented on it in recent years, and with the vast overwhelming majority of fans remaining seemingly oblivious. Symbolism, aimed straight at the subliminal mind where it remains below the threshold of conscious recognition, was becoming routinely employed in the visual displays and backdrop decor of many major events.

Consistent themes involved imagery of a spiritual, metaphysical, other-worldly or religious nature. In more recent times, this has largely shifted to embrace ideas pertaining to Transhumanism, Artificial Intelligence, and a "virtual" future world controlled by technology. As I wrote in Chapter 2 of '*Musical Truth Volume 2,*' this shift has been reflected in the very names of some of the largest events on the scene, and van Dyk has been personally involved as an artist at most of them:

"The titles of the dance events and festivals at which van Dyk has been a headliner in recent years are interesting in themselves. The likes of Dreamstate in California, Trance Nation and Luminosity in the Netherlands, Velvet Hypnotized in Bali, Atlantis in Australia, Spring Awakening in Chicago, Awake in Dresden, Awakening Fridays in

LA, Dream Beach in Spain and Delirium Eternity in Argentina, all have spiritual and esoteric overtones. Electronic Family, Digital Society and Toronto's Digital Dreams all hint at electronic ways of doing things being the new norm for humanity, while Tomorrow World in Atlanta, Tomorrowland in Belgium, Future Music Festival in Australia and New Horizons in Jakarta all evoke the Futurist society which is known to be in the plans of the United Nations Agenda 2030 architects. The wording of the events Global Dance and Global Clubbing Nation speak for themselves.

"Let's not forget Miami's Ultra Festival (as in MK?) And could van Dyk's own event brand, We Are One, be taken as a subliminal reference to a one-world government? In 2017, van Dyk began dropping references to ETs and aliens into his Tweets, a picture from one of his events featuring an inflatable Roswell-style "grey" among the gathered throng. Additionally, phrases such as "welcome to the future" and "this is the future" began appearing in the promotional blurb for his upcoming gigs."

The social-engineers and manipulators of culture would never pass up such a massive opportunity to subconsciously sow themes and ideas into large groups of young malleable minds as is offered by the world-wide dance music scene. And those attending such events are wide open to a cocktail of influences to potentially affect them on many different levels—through the mind-altering drugs in wide supply; through the sound frequencies involved in the music, all of which is now digitally-produced allowing for all kinds of undetected sonic manipulation; through the images flashed, often split-second, into the subconscious mind; and through the collective consciousness of the crowd, creating what's been referred to as a "hive mentality." All on someone else's terms rather than according to the conscious will of those involved.

Prior to their sudden demise in 2020, Electronic Dance Music festivals had become vital vehicles for pushing the above-mentioned themes under the guise of "fun" and "entertainment." And every scene needs its Pied Pipers, entrusted with ensuring it goes off in pre-approved directions, and with the fans in close pursuit. Again, from *'Musical Truth Volume 2'*:

> *"DJs had gone from straight record-spinners to quasi-religious leaders, controlling the spiritual and conscious state of the assembled throng from their vantage point of DJ booth-turned altar."*

Van Dyk had clearly become one of the most prominent of all names to lead dance music's charge into these new thematic territories. By the time of his 2020 *'Guiding Light'* album the imagery had become so blatant as to no longer be ambiguous, featuring a human hand reaching out to touch a robotic one, suggesting humanity fulfilling its destiny to fully merge with technology to become "God-like."

Just as blatant has been the strange sigil which has adorned his art-work and live stage shows for many years. It appears as an inverted tri-angle, apex pointing downwards, with additional triangles built into the upper corners. No explanation has been given as to what this symbol represents, though it's notable that, if the triangle is turned back so that the apex is pointing upwards, it becomes very similar to the logo that was used for MI5—British Military Intelligence—from the 1950s to the 1970s, right down to the cut-out corners.

As if recognising that by this point the use of symbolism had become so blatant—even though most fans still seemed completely oblivi-ous—Team van Dyk pulled an outrageously audacious stunt in 2018, when his upcoming album release was said to be titled *'Symbols,'* and its artwork featured his eye contained within an "Illuminati" pyramid, evoking the "Eye of Providence" as it appears on the back of the US dollar bill, set against a kind of zodiacal wheel adorned with hiero-glyphs. After a few weeks of promotion, all references to *'Symbols'* were rapidly dropped and the album was renamed *'Music Rescues Me,'* with new accompanying artwork. The episode appears to have amounted to satirical mockery on the part of van Dyk's camp, in recognition of how obvious his association with "Illuminati" symbolism had by that point become—and the fact that, even in spite of it, he still was not getting called out by the vast, overwhelming majority of his diehard followers.

A question which remains hard to answer is, at what point was he co-opted into the agenda? Did he achieve a certain amount of success off his own back early on, and was he invited into the inner circle as a result? Or was he always earmarked for such a role from his pre-career days? A clue may be offered by an answer he gave in his 2020 interview with *'Billboard'* magazine to the question 'What was the first track you made?'

> *"It was a remix for a project called Effective Force called "Illuminate the Planet" in 1993. The remix was called "New World Order Mix," because I was a fan of New Order and because it was two years after The Wall went down and everything was different. My first own track is called "My World" in 1994."*

Was the "New World Order" title just innocent wordplay? Or did it hint early on at the "elite" masterplan of population reduction and the subjugation of the masses by the few? It's telling that a promotional picture from this period in the 90s has him making a hand gesture in front of his closed left eye — the type of image often displayed by owned assets in the rock and pop fields, and by Hollywood actors. At gigs, he has frequently been pictured throwing up the "devil horns" hand sign, similarly favoured as a calling card by many a rock star.

Pizza: other food types are available

In *'Musical Truth Volume 2'* I drew attention to the suspicion among researchers into trauma-based mind-control and how it plays out in the entertainment industry, that artists appearing with newly-dyed blonde hair is indicative of their having been subjected to re-programming. The website www.vigilantcitizen.com has many articles on this subject. Artists cited as fitting the bill in recent years have included **Katy Perry**, **Miley Cyrus**, **Justin Bieber** and **Kanye West**, all of whom have also displayed bizarre behaviour at one point or another, consistent with them having had their minds tampered with. The peroxide blonde look has been a staple part of **Eminem**'s image since his emergence, and Mia Farrow's character in the Satanism-exposing movie *'Rosemary's Baby'* undergoes a similar makeover at a key point in the story.

Some years ago, van Dyk began rocking newly-dyed blonde hair with no explanation for the change. Given that the leading lights in so many other expressions of entertainment display signs of being assets whose behaviours are determined by mind-control programming, it becomes only reasonable for a researcher into van Dyk's runaway success to ponder whether that element may be present in this story. In June 2012, a spate of PvD gigs was suddenly cancelled just as he was to begin his Summer residency at Cream in Ibiza. The reason given was that he had to undergo emergency dental surgery. While there's no way of any outsider knowing if this was actually the case or not, it should be noted that "emergency surgery" has been used as a euphemism for a subject needing to have their programming topped up.

Some imagery of—potentially—yet more concern has also presented itself, however. The latter part of 2016 saw what has come to be known as "Pizzagate" make mainstream headlines out of the US This pertained to what was alleged to be a paedophilic child trafficking network centred around the political establishment of Washington D.C., and with many of its well-known names reportedly involved, as well as several household-name celebrities. The "pizza" part came from an F.B.I. document detailing the codewords that paedophiles were said to be using in e-mail communications to each-other when referring to the children passed around to undergo sexual abuse. "Hot dog" and "pasta" were terms used to refer to little boys, "cheese" and "pizza" to little girls. The mainstream media worked to quickly "debunk" the "Pizzagate" scandal, particularly as names like Hillary Clinton, Barack Obama and John Podesta were frequently being suggested as connected.

While the story went away from the headlines, what didn't go away was pizza-related imagery in the output of many celebrities. In 2013, for example, Katy Perry put out the song *'This Is How We Do.'* Its accompanying video, directed by New Zealand film-maker Joel Kefali, included items of food dancing around in animated scenes, including slices of pizza. It may or may not be significant that one of the video's brief settings is a ping-pong table, "ping pong" having been identified by the F.B.I. as a code-phrase for the passing around of a child for sexual abuse. (The D.C. pizzeria around which the original Pizzagate allegations were based was named Comet Ping Pong Pizza. Intriguingly, in the opening scenes of Stanley Kubrick's *'Lolita'* movie, depicting two paedophiles doing battle over a 14-year-old girl, the character played by Peter Sellers is seen playing Roman Ping Pong.)

Perry has also declared some of her live shows to be "pizza parties," inviting children from the audience to join her on stage. Miley Cyrus and Justin Bieber appeared in a promotional picture eating slices of pizza. **Lady Gaga** has a song simply entitled *'Pizza,'* proclaiming "all we want is hot pizza," and Gaga has shown a further propensity towards the Italian favourite, having bought it for fans after cancelling a show in Montreal, and having helped deliver it to victims of the 2018 California (engineered—what else?) wildfires. In 2020, *'The Blast'* website declared in a headline, *"Lady Gaga's 'Obsession With Pizza Is Unreal"* after picturing her stepping out for a pizza takeaway. In Prince Andrew's disastrous TV interview of 2019 where he attempted to justify his friendship with convicted child sex trafficker Jeffrey Epstein, (who didn't kill himself) he made a point of stating that he remembered being at a Pizza Express restaurant in Woking on the date he was alleged by his accuser, Virginia Roberts, of having sex with her after she was trafficked by Epstein. Quite a remarkable recall.

Which brings us to pizza as it relates to PvD. In 2018, the DJ Tweeted a picture of himself tucking into a plate of the stuff with the caption "More pizzaaaa!!" Of course, this could be construed as innocent enough taken in isolation. But a few months later it was followed up by a picture of him riding a giant slice of pizza through space, as if in a dream, accompanied by the caption, "yesterday I really wanted pizza. Now I'm eating pizza."

To be clear, of course none of this stands as evidence of any wrongdoing on the part of PvD. But there's no way, given the high-profile coverage that Pizzagate and its food-related terms received in entertainment circles, that PvD—or whoever runs his Twitter account—cannot have been aware of the connotations of the term, and as such, these seem like pretty ill-judged posts to have put out.

Fall from grace?

An incident which would be life-changing by anyone's standards occurred to Paul van Dyk in early 2016. On the night of 27th February, he was DJing at the State of Trance Festival at a venue named Jaarbeurs in Utrecht, Netherlands. In the midst of his performance, he walked to an area of the large stage which he had assumed to be a solid surface, but in fact concealed a sheer drop of several feet, concealed only by a thin sheet of material. He is said to have plunged through the gap, falling to the level below and undergoing instant concussion.

Once the confused promoters and crowd had realised what had happened, the show was brought to an abrupt halt and van Dyk rushed to the nearest hospital. Upon regaining consciousness, he was reported to have cracked his spine and to have succumbed to a severe head injury. He remained in the Netherlands hospital for several days before being deemed fit enough to be moved to one in Germany. He was finally allowed to return home in late May. His entire gig schedule for three months was cancelled.

Recalling the incident in an interview with Billboard magazine in June of 2016, Van Dyk had the following to say. (I find it interesting, in the context of this book's studies into mind-control techniques, that he displayed a knowledge of how trauma is processed by the human brain.)

"I don't remember the fall itself any more. That's what luckily enough the brain does—it protects you from those traumatic memories.

"...I had many talks with the doctors: I had a traumatic brain injury, I broke my spine twice, I had a lot of bruising, and an open wound at the back of my head. The brain injury was and continues to be the biggest struggle of it. If you imagine that you break your spine and that's the easy thing, then you can imagine what the last three months have been like. And what the future months to full recovery will be like.

"... The first four or five weeks I was actually still in the wheelchair. Because of the brain injury, I had to learn to walk again. I'm still a bit slurry with speaking. I had to learn how to speak; I had to learn how to eat. I can do a lot of things that I was able to do before, but it's still a long way until I'm at the point where I want to be—and the point that I came from."

While the incident *appears* to have been a devastating accident that nobody could have foreseen, given van Dyk's history of dabbling with occult and esoteric symbolism, and armed with some knowledge of how the upper levels of the music business are controlled, another possibility has to be considered. Could the event have been, in some way, ritualistic, symbolising some kind of fall—from grace, or in consciousness? The industry's occult practitioners have a history of employing ritual aspects to many large-scale stage shows, several of which were detailed in *'Musical Truth Volume 1.'* If this was the true nature of this incident, it raises the further question of whether van Dyk was in on it, or whether it was lined up for him, whatever the intention may have been. If it was the latter, there was the very strong possibility that the accident could have killed him. In the event, it certainly kept him away from playing his extremely profitable stage shows for over three months, resulting in much lost income for his management and the event promoters concerned.

The only other possibility is that the incident was some kind of hoax, designed with who knows what deceptive purpose in mind. In the photographs eventually released which purported to show van Dyk in his hospital bed, he appeared remarkably well-groomed and full of colour, and not like someone who had spent several weeks in a coma. Though his P.R. statements claimed he would have to slow down his schedule considerably upon his return to touring, there was little evidence of this, as he made well over 50 international trips in the remainder of the year from June, seemingly making a remarkably thorough recovery to full operating capacity in a short period of time. Van Dyk was said to have recovered sufficiently just in time for his Summer season for Cream at Amnesia in Ibiza and played his first gig there on 23rd June. On 2nd January 2017, he married his second wife, a Colombian, at the Hotel Charleston Santa Teresa in Cartagena. Despite his two marriages, he evidently doesn't have any children.

Conclusion

Given that PvD's meteoric rise to stardom echoes that of so many singers and musicians in every genre of the rock and pop fields, we can reasonably conclude that the Electronic Dance Music genre is, in its very upper levels, controlled, directed and steered in exactly the same way as all other expressions of entertainment are. It is also reasonable to deduce that, as one of its utmost "elite" players, PvD is an owned asset, deployed in exactly the same way as his peers in other genres can be seen to be. Naturally, for instance, he was on board with pushing the "stay home, stay safe" nonsense during the Co(n)vid scamdemic, along with the rest of his peers.

The placing of occult symbolism, the embracing of social-engineering agendas such as the push towards A.I. and Transhumanism, and even some highly questionable pizza symbolism are all there. In van Dyk's case, because any information on his father is lacking, we cannot be sure that the reason for his exposure is that he hailed from an important bloodline family. On the surface at least, his story appears to be one of his starting out from humble roots and achieving—through a combination of personal skills and drive and some good fortune—a reasonable amount of success under his own steam. This potential may well have been noted by those who closely observe such industries, at which point he may have been made an offer of extended fame and fortune that would have been very difficult to have turned down.

As we have learned by now, however, such gifts always come with a heavy price, and it can *never* be worth the price paid. My old Dad always taught me two maxims—that if something appears too good to be true, it is, and that there's no such thing as a free lunch.

In the music business, it seems the same applies to glittering careers.

Resources:

Subliminal and open brainwashing through visuals at trance events:

https://www.youtube.com/
watch?time_continue=2586&v=w3n6Kfns_nY&feature=emb_title

APPENDIX 2

DJs EXPOSED: TIM WESTWOOD

His own on-line biography sums it all up: "Westwood is the most recognised urban DJ of the decade. He is regarded as the most influential figure in Hip-Hop in Europe and as a pioneer of the UK scene."

For more than three decades, he has held a weekly radio show on some of the UK's most listened-to stations, headlined at festivals and club events all over the UK and overseas, and has been the go-to man on the British Hip-Hop scene for any visiting American artists. At the peak of his 19-year tenure at BBC Radio 1, an appearance on his show could mean the difference between a new artist breaking through to the UK market, or not.

So how *does* one individual gain such a prominent and influential position in a market as competitive and turbulent as the Rap music genre? Is it really possible to achieve these lofty heights randomly, through hard work and good luck? Particularly when one's family background and early years are about as far removed, culturally, from the lifestyle they represent as it's possible to get?

I'll get my disclaimer out of the way early on, before anyone brings it up themselves. **Tim Westwood** used to be a personal hero of mine, and was a hugely inspirational figure in the early years of my becoming a radio and club DJ myself. My love of early to mid-90s Hip-Hop was almost entirely down to hearing him play it on his *Capital Rap Show*, and his profile within this genre was what spurred me on to adopt this music and play it myself. I saw a middle-class white man having apparently made a success of himself in a music genre and culture primarily dominated by black people, and I naïvely figured if he could achieve such a feat off his own back, then so could I. Over the years, as well as attending many of his events, I came to associate with Westwood at club gigs where I was the support DJ on the same bill. All of this was in the days when I knew no better; when, hopelessly naïve, I was still under societal mind-control. I was starstruck in a way, it seems, almost everyone is by someone at some point in their lives.

It's painful for anyone to have to grudgingly accept that someone they had previously regarded as a hero is not, in reality, who they thought they were, and it's a difficult task to have to reluctantly expose their true nature. So it is for me here. I would not be doing so if I didn't feel driven to it by the ongoing wrong action and harm being put into the world by this individual and his activities, and if I wasn't absolutely certain of the validity of the information here presented. (All of which, incidentally, is backed up by primary citations and references, all of which reside in the public domain, and all of which can be independently verified by anyone who cares to. I have included a list of resources at the end of the chapter.)

Now into his 60s, and at an age by which you might think a man would have matured and started behaving in a manner more befitting a person of their years, Westwood shows no signs of abating in his harmful activities, and as such, his true motives become more transparently obvious with every passing year.

A Lifetime Actor is Born

Timothy William Westwood was born on 3rd October 1957 in Lowestoft, Suffolk, England. Although he has spent his entire adult life residing in London, (and has lied publicly on occasion about having been born there,) his formative years were spent growing up in East Anglia, a fact betrayed by the strong Suffolk twang to his accent which he has never been able to lose, making his voice distinctive and instantly recognisable. He was born the son of the Reverend Bill Westwood of Gloucestershire, but whose positions as a Deacon, a Curate, an Honorary Canon, a Rector, a Vicar, and latterly an Archbishop within the Anglican church, saw him posted to various regions of England. He was best known as the 38th Bishop of Peterborough, a position he held from 1984 to his retirement in 1995. Bill was a rector in Lowestoft at the time of Tim's birth. Bill and his wife, Shirley, also had a daughter.

On the surface of it, this seems a most unlikely upbringing for someone who would go on to head up a music genre perceived to be edgy, dangerous, and never without controversy. Westwood's defenders would doubtless argue that his chosen profession was as a direct result of the restrictions his family history brought and was an act of direct rebellion against it. I used to believe this too. Certainly, we're entrained to accept this notion as valid when it comes to celebrities whose personas fly in the face of their upbringings. Doors frontman Jim Morrison springs to mind, as does Bob Marley's half-Jewish father. The Dad of **Jerry Dammers** of **The Specials** was, like Westwood's old man, a religious leader, in his case an Anglican Dean. The father of **Joe Strummer** of **The Clash**, was a Foreign Office Diplomat.

The young Tim attended public school in Norwich, (Norwich School, known formerly as King Edward VI Grammar School,) within the grounds of Norwich Cathedral. This is said to be one of the oldest schools in the UK, its history traceable back to 1096. The school counts among its former pupils the likes of the naval admiral Lord Nelson, the philosopher Samuel Clarke, former Deputy Chairman of the Conservative Party Michael Ashcroft, and the 20th-century Post-Impressionist painter, Edward Seago. Tim reportedly moved from there to a local mixed comprehensive. According to a 2013 'Daily Mail' article, fellow students have said that they remember him as "an unremarkable and rather strait-laced student with short, spiky hair and thick-rimmed National Health glasses." Westwood has stated in interviews that he suffered dyslexia at school, making him a poor student. He has said that there were no subjects in which he excelled, and that he left school at the age of 16 having flunked all his exams.

In an interview with www.shortlist.com in 2016 he stated: "I left Norwich when I was 17." Reverend Bill is reported to have received his consecration as Bishop of Edmonton, in North West London, in June 1975. Assuming Tim was still living with his parents at that time, this posting is, presumably, what facilitated his move from East Anglia into London.

It is at this point that there are several missing years in Tim Westwood's biography. His name first started to appear on flyers for London club events from early 1982.

In the very early days, he played Soul, Funk, Boogie, plus some Reggae and Electro styles of Hip-Hop—broadly, all the black dance

music styes of the day. Countless Westwood biographies, plus comments
in his own interviews, have it that he started out as a glass collector at
Gossips nightclub in Soho. He quickly graduated, so the story goes, to
warm-up DJ, opening for larger-than-life soul spinner **Steve Walsh**,
and reggae supremo **David Rodigan**. (Walsh remained a high-profile
club and radio DJ on the South East's soul circuit until his untimely
death at the age of 29 in 1988. Rodigan's background bears some sim-
ilarities to Westwood's. Also white and middle class, he trained as an
actor, appearing in episodes of the BBC's *Dr. Who*, and was the son of
a career army officer who was born on a military base in Hanover, Germany. He is now an MBE.

Crafting the Construct

By early 1984, Westwood had landed himself a show on the pirate station L.W.R., (London Weekend Radio,) which appears to have been
his first stint on the airwaves. L.W.R. 92.5FM, initially broadcasting
from a Peckham tower block, was one of a raft of "illegal" black music
pirates operating in London in the early to mid-80s, alongside the likes
of Solar, Horizon, Invicta Radio and, from 1985, the earliest incarna-
tion of Kiss FM. These were the days before the Radio Authority had
granted "legal" licences to any black music stations, the pirates offering
Londoners their only opportunity to hear these styles on the airwaves.
National Radio 1 was still a long way from adopting such sounds, their
only black music programmes being Robbie Vincent's soul show and
the Ranking Miss P's reggae show, both on Sunday nights.

Many tapes of Westwood's L.W.R. shows have been circulated
on-line and reveal him to have sounded awkward and nervous in his
early years, his accent and vocabulary very much giving away his public
school background. His first stint was on Wednesday nights from 10pm
to 1am, where he became one of the few London pirate DJs to play electro Hip-Hop styles. He went on to host afternoons on L.W.R. six days
a week. According to the website mikeallencapitalradio.com, (mainly
concerning the activities of the DJ Mike Allen, Westwood's forerunner
on Capital Radio,) "Westwood had a strong bias towards New York

Hip-Hop and was adept at obtaining pre-releases, imports, exclusive acetates and recordings of live jams and MC/ DJ battles."

All of this then, begs the question of what the young Westwood was doing between 1975, when he claims he left Norwich, and the early 1980s when he first cropped up on the London nightlife scene, since there are no accounts of him having attended any college or university. The timeline gets rather murky here as the result of some inconsistencies in Westwood's own accounts of his activities, and offers our first examples of his tendency towards, at best mis-remembering the past, and at worst, blatantly lying, since examples of his giving false information in interviews are, provably, manifold.

For a period in the late 1990s, when he was into his 40s, he consistently told journalists that he was 29. He has frequently claimed to not drink or do drugs. He told the UK's 'Daily Mail' in 2010 "I do not condone the use of drugs and I do not drink or take drugs myself," yet in several of his videos he appears inebriated when interviewing artists, (such as when with the rapper known as Young Thug here—https://noisey.vice.com/en_uk/article/6wqzzn/young-thug-tim-westwood-interview,) and in 2018, posted a video of himself celebrating '4/20' day by sparking up a cannabis joint and drinking a measure of Hennessy. (The video can be viewed on this link: https://www.YouTube.com/watch?v=E1wK35dXQYg)

During his performance at 2010's Bang Festival, he addressed the crowd of young people by shouting: "Damn, how many people are taking some fucking drugs this weekend? If you're taking some motherfucking drugs this weekend, make some noise! Damn, how many people are getting drunk this afternoon? How many people are going to have sex tonight? Make some noise!" At a 2013 gig for teenage students of Leicester University, when 56 years of age, he was reportedly heard saying over the microphone, "Girl in the front row with the black dress on, I will be fucking you later." Westwood has spoken in interview of the strong "moral code" that his father's influence instilled in him, yet in the 90s, regularly started his microphone links at gigs with the blasphemous phrase "Jesus H. Christ!," which would, presumably, fly in the face of his dad's beliefs, and be far from what he would have considered "moral."

It would seem that Westwood takes care of his own personal health, (and would have to in order to maintain the number of late-night gigs a man of his advanced years is able to handle without consistently falling ill,) having posted Instagram pictures of himself at the gym and having spoken of consuming 'Tim's green stuff'—freshly juiced vegetables. Yet he doesn't seem to have any qualms about promoting unhealthy lifestyles to his fans, frequently talking favourably of late-night, post-club fast food. He has also promoted soft porn in many of his YouTube videos.

In reference to the Bishop, a 2004 article on Westwood in '*The Guardian*' newspaper states: "Westwood shielded him from the details of his first forays into the London scene when he was 16." (Despite Westwood stating himself that he didn't leave Norwich until he was 17.) In a 2016 interview with '*XXL Magazine*,' Westwood said of this period:

> *"As a young kid, I was just working in clubs, so I started really early in the game. And I was also hanging around sound systems as well, like reggae sound systems and 16, 17, I was always in clubs, man. I used to just live my life at night. From that, I had a love of the music 'cause I was working in, like, reggae clubs and R&B clubs, like, black-owned spots in the West End. And then from that, I got the opportunity to get on the set 'cause I was just checking records, loving the music."*

Precisely what drew Westwood to this world and sparked his enthusiasm for black styles of music specifically, in light of such a conservative background, has never been adequately explained in any public interviews.

The '*Guardian*' article continues:

> *"He was a glass collector at Gossips in Soho, and would earn 30-minute warm-up slots on the record decks by bringing in 50 people from Hammersmith and Ladbroke Grove. He was paid £15, and his earnings increased when a regular DJ quit. Initially he played jazz-funk, but occasionally a new Rap record arrived from New York: Rappers Delight by the Sugarhill Gang, The Message by Grandmaster Flash & The Furious Five, The Show by Doug E Fresh."*

'*Rappers' Delight*' appeared in late 1979, by which point Westwood would have just turned 22. This turns out to be a very revealing period in his past as he seems to have made a cameo appearance in the official music video to The Police's hit single '*Message In A Bottle*,' which was filmed in London and released on 21st September, (the Autumn Equinox) 1979. Eight seconds into the video stands a character very much resembling a young Westwood, doled up in a navy blue blazer, with a bowtie. In his early years, he rocked a moustache in a look reminiscent of Freddie Mercury, Tom Selleck or Burt Reynolds. Although there's nothing on any public record to confirm that this character is actually Westwood, the appearance and the height certainly tally, and match photographs of him from this period. In the video, as in the early pictures, alongside the moustache he is still rocking the spiky dark hair and thick-rimmed National Health glasses that he is said to have worn in his schooldays.

If it is him, a very pertinent question becomes: how does a complete unknown, (as he was then,) get to feature in the final cut of a video by one of the most famous (C.I.A.-controlled) bands in the world?

In *XXL Mag's* 2016 article, Westwood stated:

> "*I used to make a lot of trips to the States and had some good connects in those early days over in the States. So I used to go over and go to places like Latin Quarter, Union Square and clubs like that, and I'd roll with people like Harry Fox (former security guard at Union Square,) rest in peace, like some early dudes in the game, and they'd look out for me. And I just got to see Hip-Hop in its essence in the States. So I'd go to things like Run-DMC at Madison Square Garden. I was just there for those early days. So that was like the beginning of my journey.*"

Again, at this point, Westwood was still a small-time player in the London scene, by his own admission, taking the night bus to and from gigs with his crates of records, and starting out on a nightly fee of just £15. How were regular flights to New York being funded on such little income, and how was a young unknown able to make such key contacts in New York so easily?

Questionable Alliances

1984 was a key year in Westwood's burgeoning career. As well as his L.W.R. show starting, he began writing a column for *'Blues & Soul'* magazine in London, named *'Zulu Nation.'* The title—and much of the content of the articles—was inspired by the Universal Zulu Nation, the collective headed by **Afrika Bambaataa**, consistently credited as the founding father of Hip-Hop culture, and one of three characters whose influence in sparking the genre has long since passed into legend, the others being **Kool Herc** and **Grandmaster Flash.**

Bambaataa's heroic public image was intact until Spring 2016, but in March of that year took a devastating blow when two former members of the Zulu Nation, (which had evolved out of street gangs The Black Spades and the Bronx River Organisation in the Bronx borough of New York,) accused Bambaataa of having sexually molested them over a prolonged period when they were minors. This prompted other names from within the organisation to step forward and back up the claims, stating that Bambaataa's predilection for sex with underage boys was an open secret within the organisation.

Bambaataa himself escaped any legal action as the result of a Statute of Limitation being in place in New York City, which bars child sex abuse victims from pursuing criminal charges after their 23rd birthday. Ronald Savage and Hassan Campbell, Bambaataa's two main accusers, did not come forward until decades after their alleged molestation through, they stated, intimidation and fear of retribution.

This affair has called into question the true nature of the Universal Zulu Nation, which has devoted members all over the world, and which appears to have been run as a quasi-religious organisation since its inception, bearing many of the hallmarks of a cult. Bambaataa's own public image, and that of his performance group, the Soul Sonic Force, are steeped in occult symbolism, much of it depicting solar worship, and some of it similar to that which is found in Freemasonry. Through the decades, Bambaataa has made constant references to U.F.O.s, off-world entities, "a Galactic Federation," and has referenced doctrines put forward by the Nation of Gods and Earths, otherwise known as the 5 Per Cent Nation, an occult mystery-school established in 1964 as an offshoot of the Nation of Islam. He has appeared regaled in robes similar to those found in degrees of Freemasonry and has regularly flashed up the hand signal commonly referred to as "the horned hand", taken by many researchers to be an evocation of the entity known in occult circles as Baphomet, at his live shows. (I cover far more on all of this in 'Musical Truth Volume 2.')

Also in 1984, Westwood helped organise a Hip-Hop festival alongside the Greater London Council at the South Bank Arts Centre, which drew in excess of 30,000 people. The same year, Afrika Bambaataa came to the UK on tour and used L.W.R. to popularise his Zulu Nation movement, and to recruit British members. In a photograph dating from around these times, Westwood is seen flashing up the same "devil horns" hand sign favoured by Bambaataa, which seems to have been something of a greeting for Universal Zulu Nation members and affiliates. It is also a sign used within Freemasonry.

From roughly the same period again, came an intriguing picture of a young Westwood, (which he posted himself on his Instagram page in 2018,) with his right arm tucked inside his jacket. This is another gesture used within the fraternities of Freemasonry, signifying the "Hidden Hand" that this network constitutes within society, and as a way of one member of the Brotherhood identifying himself to another.

Westwood has been completely silent on the subject of Bambaataa's alleged paedophilia since the accusations emerged. Indeed, there seems to have been something of a blanket silence throughout the mainstream media regarding the story. It could be put down to the media's general dis-interest in the art-form of Hip-Hop, which many non-fans prefer to just completely ignore. But even radio stations such as BBC 1Xtra, Capital Xtra and Kiss FM, which pride themselves on being in touch with youth and "urban" culture, have sidelined the story. This seems very strange considering Bambaataa's reputation as one of the founders of the genre. It's akin to somebody like **Jimmy Page**, as an acknowledged Godfather of blues guitar, or **Kurt Cobain**, a pioneer of Grunge, having been subject to the same accusations, and the media completely neglecting to give it a mention.

At the very end of this 2012 sequence recorded for Westwood's Radio 1 show, Bambaataa ends his monologue with the questions:

"Do you trust Westwood? Do you trust me?," before his entourage begin laughing at the apparent in-joke: https://www.YouTube.com/watch?v=eYe2xGLBNHo

It's a good question.

If one of its founding fathers has been declared a predatory paedophile by several members of the organisation he reportedly founded, but with so few in the industry and the mainstream media keen to address the subject—what other awkward questions must a truly open-minded and conscientious researcher now ask themselves about the very origin of this culture, and of those key figures who helped get it established in both the US and the UK? Certainly, names of prominent players such as Grandmaster Flash, **Grandmaster Melle Mel** and **Grand Wizard Theodore** must raise some curiosity in light of their obvious Freemasonic overtones. In a 2015 video available on YouTube, pioneering rapper **KRS One** responds to a question about Freemasonry within Hip-Hop by stating:

> *"I'm not a Mason. I've studied Freemasonry, though. I've studied for coming up on 20 years now . . . I've known Freemasons all my life. They trust me with their secrets, they trust me with their symbols, they trust me with their knowledge. I'm considered a 33rd degree Master Mason, but I'm not a Mason. I'm sort of what you call an 'honorary member', because I understand the truth."*

I'm not entirely sure how you can be "considered" a 33rd Degree Master Mason—which is the highest level that can be attained within the Scottish Rite—without actually being one. It's a bit like putting "O.B.E." after your name, when you haven't actually been awarded one. Also, Freemasonry—as with all secret societies—is founded on oaths of secrecy, whereby members swear not to divulge the inner workings of the group to anyone who is not a member. KRS One was one of a handful of familiar names who weighed in on the Bambaataa scandal when it first broke in early 2016. For his part, KRS initially stated: "For me, if you keep it Hip-Hop, nothing can be taken away from Afrika Bambaataa. Nothing. Just keep it Hip-Hop. But if you want to dig into dude's personal life and accusations that's being made and so on . . . personally—me personally—I don't give a fuck. Personally."

Connections for days

As the 1980s wore on, Westwood's clubland profile increased, with residencies and guest spots at many happening nights across the city, continuing to popularise Hip-Hop's changing sounds, styles and acts to the capital's clubgoers. (Among his appearances were gigs at Covent Garden's Africa Centre, a spot that hosted the legendary Soul II Soul parties fronted by **Jazzie B** (now an O.B.E.,) in the late 80s, and which had earlier figured in the London counter-culture scene of the LSD-laden 1960s, when it had been the setting for various "avant-garde" art events.)

He remained at L.W.R. until late 1986, at which point he was recruited by DJ Derek Boland, (better known as British rapper **Derek B**,) as one of the DJs on his new W.B.L.S. pirate radio operation, inspired by the New York station of the same name. 'B.L.S. was short-lived, on air for only three weeks before a raid by the Department of Trade and Industry shut it down for good. (Derek B died of a heart attack in 2009, aged 44.) Immediately upon W.B.L.S.'s closure, Westwood moved across to Kiss FM, at that point also an "illegal" pirate. He is reported to have become a part-owner of the station in the few months he was there, departing in September 1987 to join London's Capital Radio, the UK's original independent commercial radio operation, and his first forays into "legal" radio. Beginning first with an hour late on a Friday night, by the following year he was presenting his '*Capital Rap Show*' on both late-night Fridays, and from 8 to 10pm Saturdays, a timeslot he held until 1994. He has been on the radio on Saturday nights consistently for over 30 years.

It was through his Capital tenure that Westwood really made a name for himself. His shows inspired legions of loyal followers who would pack out his club nights, and the strong production values, careful track selection, and unique style of presentation on the radio shows, earned the praise of both Rap enthusiasts and his radio industry peers. He picked up the Best Specialist Music Programme gong at the Sony Radio Awards, (the Oscars of the British radio industry,) in 1990 and 1991.

Besides big club nights, many of which he staged and promoted himself through his company Justice Entertainment, (which had a record label offshoot through which he released tracks by the likes of General Levy and London Posse,) it was during this period that he became a mainstay at London's Notting Hill Carnival, the huge street festival staged annually over the August Bank Holiday. By 1994, he had secured a commanding position for his sound system under the arches of the Westway flyover, at which tens of thousands gathered. A few years later, Westwood lamented that he had been banned from further appearances by the Carnival committee, due to the violence and disorder that routinely broke out around his stage.

His Carnival set-up allowed him to bring over and present many of the prominent names from the US Hip-Hop scene of the time. He frequently DJed at many of these artists' London shows also, and regularly travelled to New York to present radio shows with pioneering DJs **Marley Marl** and **Funkmaster Flex**. The most notorious club event of this time was Sunday nights at The Tunnel in Manhattan, hosted by Flex. The Tunnel attracted many key players from Hip-Hop's royalty; big-name rappers would frequently go there to party. Violence and robberies broke out often, and eventually caused the night's demise.

By this point, the awkwardness of Westwood's early radio style had gone, masked by a well-rehearsed and over-exaggerated persona, heavy on street lingo and all the latest Hip-Hop slang being dropped by his New York counterparts. His apparent attempts to disguise his East Anglia accent resulted in a bizarre, and truly unique vocal style which has been mocked and mimicked and was reportedly the inspiration for the Ali G character created by comedian Sacha Baron-Cohen, popular in the early 2000s. Baron-Cohen has said: "Once I found out he was actually the son of a bishop, it became even more absurd. He was so keen to be presented as a gangsta." (Ali G is presented as a middle-class youth from a privileged upbringing within the well-to-do stockbroker belt of London, presenting himself as a tough street gangster, complete with rehearsed and over-exaggerated mannerisms and street talk.)

Hip-Hop output itself had changed beyond all recognition from Tim's early days in the game, too, when he played the now very dated electro styles. Westwood had been at the helm of the UK scene for the entire transition and would remain there for many more.

His big breakthrough to household-name exposure came when he was poached from Capital Radio to join the ranks of BBC Radio 1 in late 1994, earning a peak-time, three-hour Saturday night show, and opening up the music, and himself, to a nationwide audience for the first time, (which became a potentially worldwide audience a few years later when Radio 1 began streaming live in the early days of the internet.) He was reportedly hired upon the recommendation of fellow DJ **Pete Tong**, (now an MBE) who was tasked by BBC bosses with modernising Radio 1's image.

It turns out, however, that his Radio 1 tenure was far from Westwood's first forays into BBC broadcasts.

Tim's father, earning himself the nickname "Bishop Bill," had been a regular contributor to the religious '*Thought For The Day*' show on BBC Radio 4. This may have stood the young Tim in good stead to be called upon by the BBC's World Service to guest on a show called '*Meridian*,' talking about emerging Hip-Hop culture, way back on 23rd March 1985. The following year he was given a two-hour Saturday slot on BBC Radio 1 to present highlights of the World DJ Mixing Championships that had occurred as part of that Summer's New Music Seminar event in New York. Then, in August 1987, he got his first shot at TV when his self-produced documentary on London Hip-Hop culture, titled '*Bad Meaning Good*,' was screened on BBC2. Many of his latter years at Radio 1 were also spent presenting shows on its sister station, 1Xtra, dedicated to black music styles. For a few years he presented the daily 4-7pm drivetime show. (His other forays into TV were for non-BBC stations—a period presenting late-night Rap videos on ITV's *Night Network* in the late 80s, followed by a stint as presenter of the UK version of *Pimp My Ride* on MTV in the 2000s.)

Emergence of an Agenda

Hip-Hop output began to change noticeably from the time of Westwood's instalment within Radio 1. Many commentators concur that the murders of **Tupac Shakur** and **Notorious B.I.G.** were symbolic of the "death" of the meaningful days of the art form. As the 90s moved into the early 2000s, mainstream output lost all hint of any political or anti-establishment sentiment. By the end of the decade, productions built around samples of old soul and funk tracks, which had been a staple part of Rap output in the 80s and 90s, had all but disappeared. Beats were now being produced digitally and electronically, in line with other changes in society. The period also saw the emergence of Auto-Tune, a production technique which renders a human voice to sounding akin to that of a robot. So-called "Hip-Hop'" "R&B" and "Reggae" records were suddenly awash with this treatment.

By this point a pattern had emerged with regard to the lyrical content, too. It was no longer possible to hear any song from within these genres played on the radio, that dealt with anything other than the promotion of partying, drug-taking, excessive alcohol consumption, spending money on material brands, toting guns, or promiscuous sex. Within a few years, American "Hip-Hop" output had moved on to become a vehicle for the promotion of Artificial intelligence/ Transhumanism, and the Transgender/ LGBTQ agenda—all tactics to gradually shape and mould societal attitudes, almost exclusively among young people, in which organisations like Tavistock, the Frankfurt School, and military Intelligence agencies like MI6 have specialised for decades, all sneaked in below the radar under the guise of "entertainment."

One might reasonably assume that a man advancing in years—by this point well into his 50s—who had lived through many previous eras in the music and culture, might have grown disillusioned and jaded by what it had now become. Particularly someone who, by virtue of his reputation, would have had many career opportunities available to him other than playing toxic digital "music" every single weekend to young people of an appropriate age to be his grandchildren, and who was already reported to be a millionaire. I personally know many DJs from the same era who, by this point, decided enough was enough, and that they could no longer stand to be around this degenerate and morally repugnant scene. Many left DJing and took on other jobs instead. I did so myself.

In 2009, to mark the 30th anniversary of **The Sugarhill Gang**'s landmark '*Rappers' Delight*', I recall Westwood being asked by an interviewer what his favourite era in all of that time had been, presumably expecting him to get nostalgic about his early days. His generic and non-committal response that, "I love them all, man. I think every era has been tremendous," speaks to his enthusiasm to remain relevant to the younger generation, and the lack of emotional connection he seems to feel towards his roots. Westwood has always been reticent to dwell on too many details of his past in interviews, (and when he does they are frequently embellished with provable lies,) always preferring to talk only about the present.

Making Wars of Occupation 'Cool'

An extra-curricular role for Westwood became apparent when in 2011, he made two visits to British military bases in occupied Afghanistan, flying out on aircraft from R.A.F. Brize Norton. The first, in February of that year, was seemingly in a personal capacity, during which he pledged to return with BBC 1Xtra later in the year. In late May he did just that, with the station broadcasting his show live for a week from Camp Bastion. During the broadcasts, he mingled with military personnel, and jokes were made around his catchphrase "drop the bomb." These visits were blatant public relations exercises to encourage public support for "our boys." The BBC, being a propaganda arm of the British government, has a track record of unquestioningly supporting colonialism and military action.

The cynical nature of this exercise did not go un-noticed by the conscious rapper known as **Lowkey**. He had earlier turned down an invitation to appear on Westwood's YouTube channel, and went on to pen an open letter explaining how Westwood's stance on Afghanistan had swayed his decision.

Lowkey wrote:

> "This naturally prompts a question: what does 'black music' have to do with the occupation of Afghanistan? And why should BBC Radio 1Xtra listeners be subjected to this propaganda? Indeed, even setting aside the broader fact that as a citizen of this country my taxes were being spent to station an army, supposedly representing my interests, in over twenty countries, I found this entire press release very alarming.

"... The Ministry of Defence are precisely the people who send our young men and women to kill and die in our name. As such, this was clearly a concerted effort to target the very demographic they look to recruit. After all, who do the Ministry of Defence rely on to leave their homes in Britain and sacrifice their humanity thousands of miles away? It is, as Rhys Hughes put it, the 19-year-olds that are 'perfect for our audience.'"

Lowkey went on to highlight the trivial way in which Westwood's catchphrase "drop the bomb" had been adopted by the British soldiers, asking:

"Have the people underneath those bombs ceased to be human? ... Can Tim Westwood imagine for one minute how it feels to have your country violently invaded, occupied against your will, and then see those foreign troops literally treat the corpses of your countrymen as a toilet? No he can't. Can he imagine his country being occupied four times by the same foreign power in less than two centuries? Why do the British keep going back to the Afghans' land? A land almost everyone knows to be the 'graveyard of empires'?"

It was already clear by this point that Lowkey was no fan of Westwood. During a 2012 show at London's Brixton Academy, he berated him for not supporting "real" Hip-Hop by underground artists like himself and Immortal Technique. It didn't take much reading between the lines to understand what he was hinting at when he added immediately afterwards: "And all I will say right now is, Jimmy Savile isn't the only one who's been up to that type of shenanigans." (Earlier that month, former BBC radio DJ Savile had been revealed, posthumously, to have been a serial child sex abuser over the course of decades, many of his offences having allegedly taken place on BBC premises.)

Lowkey's comment joins one from UK rapper **Plan B** in 2007, who told the Gigwise.com website:

"The thing is, man, that all Tim Westwood gives a fuck about is money and hoes and rims and fucking crystal, man. That's why he sucks up to these Americans, so that he can get backstage at parties and fuck little girls ... little 16-year-old, 17-year-old girls."

The Promotion of child molestors

It's not just pornography, gang violence and drug-taking that the bishop's son has enthusiastically pushed during his recent years. He has also used his radio show to promote artists who have either suspected, or provable links to child sexual abuse. Afrika Bambaataa has already been discussed. The R&B singer and producer **R Kelly** has been the subject of several investigations into allegations of paedophilia over the years; he was illegally married to the late singer Aaliyah when she was just 15 years of age.

Westwood maintained a close relationship with Kelly during the early 2000s. In May 2003, Kelly invited Westwood on a trip to his hometown of Chicago for a radio interview series. Earlier that year, Kelly had been arrested on charges of possessing child pornography, allegedly appearing in sexually explicit photos of a female minor. The previous year, a video tape had been leaked, allegedly showing Kelly having sex with, and urinating on, an underage girl. These charges were later dropped yet were far from Kelly's only forays into such salacious territory. By 2017, Kelly had been accused by three sets of parents of running a communal sex cult, in which their daughters—along with several other children—had been sexually molested by him. A former partner of Kelly's stated the following year that he had knowingly infected her with a sexually transmitted disease

In Westwood's defence, many would argue that at the time of his Chicago jolly no charges had been brought against Kelly, and the later offences had yet to come to public light. Yet all such excuses were absent when, in 2018, Westwood flew out to Amsterdam to attend a performance by the rapper known as **Tekashi69**, or **6ix9ine**, (real name Daniel Hernandez,) later recording an interview feature with him for his radio show and YouTube channel. Having grown up as a drug dealer and street gang member, with jail time served as a minor on assault and heroin distribution charges, in 2015, Hernandez pled guilty to having used a 13-year-old girl in a sexual performance. In July 2018, only weeks after his Amsterdam show, he was arrested for an outstanding warrant related to his alleged choking of a 16-year-old girl in a separate event. Many other incidents followed linking Hernandez to violent gang activity, racketeering and other crimes. By November 2018, he had been jailed.

61-year-old Westwood's response to this was to post a photo on his Instagram page of himself and Hernandez, with the caption, "Keep your head up. Stay strong my G."

There are multiple Hip-Hop artists promoting positive, uplifting and meaningful messages through their output. These are never the ones championed by the large and powerful record companies or TV and radio stations. Nevertheless, this output *can* be found by anyone who searches hard enough for it. Rather than ever seeking to feature artists or recordings of this ilk, Westwood instead uses his influential position, (and strong "moral code," allegedly,) to push the likes of 6ix9ine.

'Drill': Where "Art" and Violent Crime Meet

His friendship with 6ix9ine is far from the only occasion on which Westwood has courted controversy by associating himself with violent gang culture. As the form of music known as "Grime" began to flourish in the early 2000s, Westwood was right at the helm of the scene, for a time hosting a two-hour Sunday night showcase on BBC 1Xtra. This led to the creation of his regular 'Crib Sessions,' filmed for his YouTube channel, where he invited both established and upcoming Grime MCs to his home to perform exclusive freestyle sessions.

On 4th August 2018, '*The Sun*' newspaper published an article titled "How bishop's son Tim Westwood 'profits from warring Drill Rap videos' fuelling gangland warfare in London—and inspired Ali G." The piece highlighted Westwood's promotion of "Drill" videos, where members of criminal street gangs taunt each other with violent threats. The article highlighted how **Moscow 17** crew member Siddique Kamara, known as **Incognito**, had been stabbed to death on a South London street by a member of one of the opposing gangs promoted by Westwood's YouTube channel. Kamara himself had been cleared of murdering an associate of the **Zone 2 Drill** mob months earlier. Another of Westwood's videos had featured crew member Rhyhiem Ainsworth Barton, who was shot dead in a gang feud, aged 17.

'*The Sun*' posted a photo of a 60-year-old Westwood posing with a toy machine gun fashioned out of a Moet champagne bottle, subsequent to the fatality. It went on to claim that Westwood was worth an estimated £9 million, and that the YouTube channel which hosted the Drill videos, with 724,000 subscribers, had become a significant source of income to him.

Anti-knife crime campaigners publicly blasted Westwood's promotion of criminal gangs. Jen Lock from the Lives Not Knives Ealing group complained about his influence on youngsters, stating afterwards: "He knows exactly what effect it's having. I asked his team how he can justify getting gangs on to promote, glorify and encourage them. They said it's an expression of art. It makes my blood boil that he tries to play innocent. He's making blood money off the hits it's generating on YouTube. He has blood on his hands."

This did little to harm his career, however. His bosses at Capital Xtra seemed unperturbed, and Westwood turned the situation into a PR opportunity later in the year by delivering a talk at a performance of the "You Choose" knife crime prevention project at the BRIT School, posting on his Instagram page afterwards: "Just seen The Brit School Knife Crime Project. The cast did an amazin (sic) & emotional play. Awareness is so important. Big up."

This was not Westwood's only brush with controversy over the alleged promotion of violence through the music he promotes. Back in 2006, British Prime Minister David Cameron had accused BBC Radio 1 of promoting knife and gun crime, singling out Westwood's Saturday night show in particular. Cameron had stated: "I would say to Radio 1, do you realise that some of the stuff you play on Saturday nights encourages people to carry guns and knives?"

One day in July

A key event in Westwood's life in which he himself succumbed to extreme violence, was his reported shooting in South London in July 1999. The story goes that, shortly after performing at an open-air event in Brixton's Brockwell Park, his jeep was fired at by an unknown assailant on a motorbike while it was stopped at traffic lights.

A bullet apparently passed through Westwood's right arm. Six people in the car are said to have been injured, including a personal assistant said to have had his kneecap shattered. Westwood himself is said to have been taken to St. Thomas' Hospital in Lambeth, where he was given a police guard throughout his stay. Speaking to reporters at the time, he stated: "I thank God I'm alive and that everyone has survived. Everybody at the hospital has been great. I feel fine."

When asked about the shooting in subsequent interviews, he has frequently repeated the remark, "what doesn't kill you only makes you stronger," (a line later used in the hook of Kanye West's record '*Power.*') He boasted in later years of having kept one of the bullets which had lodged itself into his car's bodywork as "a souvenir," and told one interviewer: "Before the shooting, the only people who knew me were the Hip-Hop crowd. But the truth is that was real gangster shit. It made me big. I wish I had an album out at that time."

As with Tupac Shakur, the Notorious B.I.G. and many other Rap stars who have succumbed to shootings, the police failed to catch anyone for the incident. Speculation was rife as to the motive, with rumours of Westwood having fallen foul of territorial gangland feuds, having been warned to stay away from South London. Much media fanfare was made of the event to highlight the increasing lawlessness on London streets, with blame being placed on "Yardie" criminal gangs from Jamaica. The incident certainly increased Westwood's own "street cred" among many of the American rappers with whom he associated. In his 2016 interview with shortlist.com, he stated: "Looking back on it now, not trying to be flippant or anything, it put me on the front page of the newspapers. So I think it was definitely a shot in the arm for my PR. I would probably pay to have it done again."

A few weeks after the incident, Tim's Dad, Bishop Bill, passed away aged 73, following a reported stroke. Tim commented in later years that the stress of dealing with his son's shooting had contributed to his death.

Revelation of the Method?

In several interviews over the years, and in comments he has made on his radio shows, Westwood has spoken of his own activities using the word "we," rather than "I" Could he be subconsciously acknowledging his part in a wider agenda controlled by others with such talk? Another possibility is that he is knowingly giving listeners the opportunity to understand that he's part of a larger community. Within Freemasonry there is a tenet known as "Masterful Speech." As subjects move up through the different degrees, they become permitted to divulge certain elements of the Brotherhood's activities—but only within closely controlled parameters. The idea is to reveal just enough—often in cryptic, coded form that only those well-versed in these areas would be able to understand, and to allow for plausible deniability when needed—but to still keep the important secrets well-hidden. The idea of Westwood being a Mason and employing the Masterful Speech tactic is one which cannot be discounted by anyone seeking to get to the true nature of his persona.

A Speculative Conclusion

Given that the whole point of Lifetime Actors and the agendas which they uphold is to keep their true motives concealed, while giving onlookers just enough cryptic information that the claim cannot be made that they weren't, in some way, given the opportunity to know, I can only speculate by way of a conclusion. But I would suggest that this is a reasonable summary for anyone to arrive at, taking into account all of the information presented above.

Tim Westwood's father, the Bishop, may well have been a high-ranking Freemason, as many Establishment figures of his ilk are. Some researchers into the workings of secret-society fraternities would maintain that a career as prolific as his is not possible without being well-connected at the upper levels of society. Membership is often retained within families, so Tim may well have been inducted into the ranks early on. The type of "elite" public school education he received is not available to regular members of the public, and it seems unlikely that anyone having undergone one, when faced with the chance of taking on a well-paid "respectable" profession within society, would instead opt to drop out, turn their back on the family wealth, and work themselves up from the bottom as a glass collector, box boy and warm-up DJ in sleazy nightclubs. However, Westwood himself has admitted that he was a poor student, and he seems to struggle with literacy, so the plan may have been for him to be groomed, with Masonic brotherhood influence, for some other career path, but that the plan was altered at some stage, and the decision was made for him to become a future influencer of culture instead.

The social engineers who manipulate the entertainment industry plan their moves decades in advance, so it's feasible that even back in the 1970s and 80s, it was already known how black music and culture was to be steered and directed in the decades to come, and the controllers would have wanted "their" personnel to already be in established positions to guide it and act as controlling gatekeepers. Westwood's role involved spending several years *appearing* to struggle to get a foothold on the ladder of DJing success and making all the right moves in order to cement his credibility and acceptance in the game—but with it never being an option that he would fail. His years of "keeping it real" and *appearing* to be an authentic champion of Hip-Hop culture in its golden years, were a necessary component.

As the years progressed, and the culture-changing agendas behind Rap music became clearer, so Westwood's sphere of influence increased, ensuring that he was in place on BBC Radio 1, where he would become a household name, during the crucial years of the 1990s and beyond.

The multitude of ways in which "Hip-Hop" music and urban culture have been systematically debased and degraded—in line with many other engineered changes to society—speak for themselves, and Westwood has maintained his position as the most recognisable figurehead and "go-to" man for these "styles" throughout. Even though his Radio 1 tenure came to an abrupt end in 2013, it did little to dent his reputation or recognition. He has been faced with many opportunities to step aside from peddling toxic influences to children. Yet he has continued on with pushing degenerate behaviour to young people, year after year.

Westwood never married or had children and is therefore ideal for his role with no danger of being distracted from it by such commitments. It's easier for someone lacking in morality to push agendas which do harm to other people's children when they have none of their own to worry about.

Is it *really* conceivable that a man into his 60s can find any kind of genuine personal satisfaction immersing himself in all that Westwood still does—emulating the behaviours of people young enough to be his grandchildren, with fake, exaggerated mannerisms more befitting an immature adolescent than a man approaching his pension? Would some dignity and maturity not have kicked in decades ago as part of the natural process of a normal adult's evolution through life? Can someone of his heritage and track record really be naïve enough not to understand the true forces that run the corporate music industry, and the malevolent agendas that they employ to control the thoughts and behaviours of young people? Is the only reasonable conclusion to reach, therefore, that he is a knowing and willing player in what he is a part of, and has no troubling qualms or conscience about what he's doing, possibly out of some oath of allegiance to a secret society brotherhood?

False heroes and role models always let you down in the end. The only solution is to let them *all* go.

Resources:

- https://en.wikipedia.org/wiki/Bill_Westwood

- https://www.dailymail.co.uk/news/article-389880/The-phoney-cynical-world-Ali-Gs-role-model-.html

- https://en.wikipedia.org/wiki/Steve_Walsh_(DJ)

- http://www.mikeallencapitalradio.com/home/the-competition/the-pirates/lwr

- https://www.theguardian.com/music/2004/oct/03/popandrock

- https://www.YouTube.com/watch?v=MbXWrmQW-OE

- http://www.xxlmag.com/news/2016/08/tim-westwood-interview/

- https://vigilantcitizen.com/vigilantreport/the-hidden-hand-that-changed-history/

KRS One—Explains the Illuminati, Freemasons, and if he's a member:

- https://www.YouTube.com/watch?v=IZqghCSEj94

- http://www.ibiza-voice.com/news/news.php?id=581

- https://www.thestar.co.uk/lifestyle/features/i-inspired-bruno-not-ali-g-jokes-radio-1xtra-tim-westwood-video-1-305478

- https://en.wikipedia.org/wiki/Gargoyle_Club

- http://www.urban75.org/london/gossips-club-london.html

- https://shapersofthe80s.com/clubbing/69-dean-street-and-the-making-of-uk-club-culture/

- https://www.dailymail.co.uk/tvshowbiz/article-1269929/BBC-Radio-1-DJ-Tim-Westwood-YouTube-video-urging-festival-drug-taking.html

- https://www.shortlist.com/news/
  tim-westwood-id-probably-pay-to-be-shot-again/56003

- https://variety.com/2017/music/news/parents-accusing-r-
  kelly-of-holding-daughters-in-cult-to-hold-press-confer-
  ence-1202497833/

- https://www.thesun.co.uk/news/6938673/
  tim-westwood-Drill-Rap-profiteering-ali-g/

- http://news.bbc.co.uk/1/hi/uk_politics/5055724.stm

- https://www.thesun.co.uk/news/uknews/6921180/
  camberwell-stabbing-Rapper-killed-Drill-tim-westwood-latest/

- https://www.YouTube.com/watch?v=JYsDmebykLs

- https://www.gigwise.com/news/27593/

INDEX

N

Q

R

T

Z

Made in the USA
Middletown, DE
17 March 2024